The Dream Rescuer

Michael Frickstad

Published by MOCH Arts
Parker, Colorado 80134

Dedication

To the two most loving and encouraging women I know:

My sister Amy Rea, not only for editing the story and stretching my writing vision, but for picking up the pieces of family crises.

My wife Diane DiCarlo, who called me a writer before I did and who teaches me daily to see God and story ideas in everything and everybody.

Love you both.

PART ONE

IMPLORING HANDS

1

What You Do Is What You Are

Mount Komu ("The Entry")
British Columbia, Canada

The woods leading up the back side of Mount Komu trembled with promise as the tall, bearded man lifted the front brim of his hat and sniffed the air. "Enough searching," he urged himself. "Time to find."

As if preparing for a hunt, he adjusted the lasso hanging on his lean hips, then tested the edge of his curved knife with his thumb. The blade sank into his flesh until a drop of blood bubbled to the surface. Insensitive to pain, he sneered at the cut and licked away the blood greedily until a thin, harsh odor jolted his sinuses. In the breeze above him, the leaves trembled and rattled. He wrinkled his nose and hacked as he searched the sky.

"*Smoke*," he thought.

But it was more than smoke, he knew. It was the reason he came to these mountains. Somewhere nearby was a presence. A soul. An animal. Human and not human.

The man crouched and peered through the brush around him. Light gray wisps hovered, drifting through the undergrowth on the breath of nightfall. His eyes followed them upwind to a small opening in the shadows.

His face brightened.

A lone figure crouched beside a fire pit, stoking a burning pile of twigs and leaves. Carefully, the creature—whatever it was—bent forward and blew into the smoldering pile of branches and wood scraps until they ignited. Soon, flames billowed from the pit.

Sitting back on its haunches, the figure admired its work, then rearranged the larger limbs to accommodate a cast iron skillet placed over the coals. Satisfied the branches could hold, he reached for a clear plastic packet, meticulously peeling off slices of bacon and laying them onto the hot pan.

The air burst into a discordant symphony of sounds and aromas: the percussive crackle and sizzle of exploding fat; the seductive, harmonious odors of charred wood and blackening meat; the trilling rustle of leaves above the fire.

The secret observer lifted the rope hanging from his belt and laughed to himself. This was almost too easy. Quietly, the man slipped his knife from under his poncho and eased his way toward the fire. As he approached, he had no interest in the animal's species, its gender, nor even its size. All that enticed him was the fat—the snapping, sputtering, tantalizing fat.

Oddly, the creature barely moved. With its back brazenly defying the advancing danger, the thing—whatever it was—calmly poked a stick at the frying bacon.

With every unanswered step, the man checked his progress—each one slower, more erratic, more uncertain—until his faltering legs refused to move. The indifference of the creature's back revealed the man's undeniable dread.

He doubted.

He had never doubted. Not his appetites. Not his power. Not himself.

But this being calmly ignored him. It had to know he was there, the man thought. It had to. And its animal sense should warn of his viciousness. Yet it calmly poked at the bacon.

The man's eyes narrowed as he pulled back his poncho and raised his curved knife. He *would* intimidate. He *would* terrify.

He cleared his throat.

Oblivious to the sound, the figure ignored him.

With his free hand, the lean man raised his hat to reveal his ravenous green eyes, then called. "Hey, stranger! What are you cooking?"

Without turning or even flinching, the figure replied in a detached monotone, "Bacon."

The lean man again tested the knife's sharpness against his thumb.

"Supper?" the man asked.

"Nope," the figure replied, its face still intent on the sizzling bacon before it. "Bait."

"Bait?" the lean man said, looking up from his knife. "For what?"

The creature turned its voracious grin on the lean man. Beneath a splitting upper lip, skin stretched back from its jaws, revealing ever-sharpening teeth. A scar ran from the creature's left ear to the corner of its mouth. "You," it said.

The lean man shrank back, his small finger quivering on the skin-wrapped knife handle. "Me?"

The figure nodded. "You can put the blade away. You won't need it and it wouldn't help you anyway."

The lean man paused and gauged the figure's size and strength. "*I can do this*," he thought, struggling to convince himself.

Summoning all his strength, he sniffed, snorted, and growled. Then, recklessly raising his knife, the man lunged forward. Before the gap between them closed, the nimble creature whirled away and stood haughtily, fists on its hips while its body stretched higher and wider, a creaking mass of elastic flesh and bones.

The lean man dove to the ground as the creature burst through its shredding clothes, but before he could wriggle to safety, a giant claw-like hoof smashed into his back, jamming his face into the ground.

The man thrashed to free his arms as he sank into the ground, gagging on the dirt and leaves clogging his mouth and nostrils. Above him, the beast swelled taller and wider, heavier and stronger with a sharp knee crushed into the man's back. Flippant, bony fingers snatched the man's hat and flicked it into the brush before yanking back his head. Before the man could even wheeze, the creature drooled yellow slime into his face while its face receded from its sharp, clattering teeth.

"I've been waiting for you," it growled. "I know who you are. I know what you've done. I know what you still want to do."

The man writhed, his tortured wail echoing across the cold, indifferent mountains.

"Oh, don't worry," the figure said. "I'm not going to kill you. You have nothing I want. I just want you to know I'm not afraid of you. Understand?"

The figure rolled the man onto his back. "Do you understand?" it repeated, leaning into his face.

The man shrank as the creature's eyes sunk deeper into its skull. "What do you want with me?" his voice quavered.

The skeletal demon with dripping teeth straightened in order to regain its human form. When it had melted back to mortal proportions, it hulked over its enfeebled quarry, the scar above its mouth reddening and throbbing. The beast explained, "Ah! I'm a recruiter. I want you to meet somebody. Follow me."

The creature stepped back. Insensitive to heat, it lifted the skillet from the coals and let the bacon fall into the fire. Then, playfully, it tossed the cast iron into the bushes. Loose leaves smoldered as the figure strode triumphantly away.

"Wait!" the man called. "The brush is burning!"

The creature chuckled, then turning to the smoking bushes, it shrieked until the sound crumbled the bushes, the skillet, and even the rocks beneath them to powder.

The embryonic brushfire miscarried. The campfire stove vanished. Once again, the cold mountain air blew through the opening in the brush.

The man gaped at the creature.

Calmly, it nodded at him. "Bring your hat, your knife, your rope. You'll need them later." Then it turned and walked through the trees up the mountain.

The man scrambled to recover his tools. "Hey, what's your name?" he shouted.

The creature stopped and sneered. "You can call me Frank."

In the Land of Great Silence, above and beyond, Counselor sighed. "And so it begins once more."

"Yes," the Word answered.

"These allied with the Earth Man?"

"And the rest of the matchi-auwishuk, as it ever was."

"Despite all the battles lost, they continue?"

"Yes."

"Why?"

"It's a challenge. They believe they know how."

"Do they this time?"

"They have decided to destroy hope and dreams instead of destroying flesh. So yes, they know."

Counselor stared into the darkness. "That's why you called me."

"Yes. Throughout the ages and across the universe, you have played herald to unwitting generals and unwilling messiahs countless times."

"In the new and changed battle, am I finally a warrior?" he asked.

"I know that is your wish, but you are needed as you are. Over time and space, you have discovered that only an aroused spirit understands Truth; only such a spirit can teach; and you have become that spirit. That is why you are chosen. Your incarnation will change, but your essence remains the same."

"Where am I to go?"

"A world you know."

Counselor concentrated and saw floating in a creation far away the planet he often inhabited. As often as he had been there, he had not seen the part revealing itself to him. Here, dawn rose on a still, mountain lake. Trees on the margin danced and swayed in adulation. Above, the mountains themselves, like a congregation of penitents, raised their desperate, imploring hands to the heavens for direction and deliverance.

"You know what you must do," the Word said.

In disappointment, Counselor said, "Return, reveal, and rescue."

"Returns and reveal, yes, but rescuing is somebody else's job. You are to teach and lead. The task will be no simpler than before. Despite his defeats, the Earth Man now exists with more powerful allies to unleash devastation on people you know. They are the reason it is you who must go."

"Who am I to teach?"

"The new Trinity of the Original Thought, the Sacrifice, and the Dream Rescuer."

"Do I know them? Where will I find them?"

"Among broken dreamers—the children and the dead. When misery overwhelms, train them to seek as you have sought. In their grief, be their comfort. In their joy, praise. In their fear, inspire. When the lies of the

Earth Man confuse and corrupt, lead them to the Source, the Origin of all that is, that was, and will ever be. "

"I never did that as herald."

"This journey you will be more than herald, more than human. You will be what you must.

In the quiet dark, Counselor shook off all doubt and protest, embracing destiny. "Show me where to begin," he said.

2

The Glory and the Dream

Fort Repentance, British Columbia
Canada

Jeannie Jones hunched over and grabbed her knees, tension shaking her shoulders. Yes, she loved soccer, but this—

"I want to play. I want to play," she repeated to herself.

The Game of the Year. The Langley Lynx and the Fort Repentance Rockers. Both teams with records of 5-0.

Already owning more 12-and-under records than anybody in Fort Repentance history, Jeannie had hoped for elevation to the traveling varsity team, but now that she was there, the bright lights blinded her. Her cheeks puffed. Her chin shuddered. Her sour throat closed.

"Jones! Jones, you okay?"

Jeannie uncoiled, trying to wave off the Rockers' head coach Andre Demoya striding toward her. "I'm okay, Coach. Honest."

Demoya raised his cap. His muscular chest stretched against his Rocker polo shirt. His clean-shaven, square jaw frightened, intimidated, and captivated her.

"Really. I'm fine," she said, her voice breaking.

She swayed under his scrutiny. *"Stop it, Jeannie!"* she scolded herself. *"He's out of college and you're only in junior high. Besides, you've only known him a week during practice."*

As he scanned her from head to toe, her body trembled and her shoulders shook.

"Still—Maybe—" she thought, examining her socks and shoelaces.

Demoya's face tightened. "Yeah. Okay. Walk with me a little."

Jeannie tried to shed her girlhood. She wanted to look at the coach, to be close to him, to run with him to the parking lot and escape the world that kept them apart. Instead, she walked with her head down and tortured her fingers. Neither said a word. They walked toward the end line, Demoya with his arms crossed watching the ground in front of him, Jeannie checking the crowd and teams behind her.

"Big night, Jones. You up to this? We don't need you barfing on the field."

Demoya nudged her with his shoulder. Jeannie coughed and forced a laugh.

"Hey, it's your birthday, right?" he asked.

Jeannie felt a lightness in her stomach as she glanced up at his stone-cut face.

"What is that symbol on his necklace?" she wondered. *"It's not a peace symbol. I've never—"*

"Isn't it your birthday?"

Jeannie averted her eyes and sucked in her cheeks. "Yeah."

"Thirteen, right?"

She nodded, proudly.

"Thirteen years old. A spot on Fort Repentance's traveling team. Pretty big time stuff."

"Big time," she repeated.

"Come on. Tell him what you feel. Tell him."

"Play big, Jones," he said. "Make 'em forget you're the youngest Rocker ever."

Jeannie dipped her chin and examined the chalkline. *"I'm not that young. You're not that old."*

She forced a smile and flexed her knees. "Right. Play big. I'm ready."

His strong hand on her shoulder halted her confidence. "I need you to know something. Okay?"

Demoya looked around them, then leaned his head close to Jeannie's ear. "I lobbied hard to bring you up here, 'cause I know you can help us, but let's face it. You're the new kid and these other girls have won all these games without you. They're watching every move you make. They're looking for any sign of favoritism, anything that can be taken as a snub. I'm not saying they're out to get you, but—"

"They're out to get me," Jeannie murmured.

"Right. Sorry. That means I gotta ease you into your on-field role in order to keep peace as much as I can. You okay with that?"

Jeannie gulped down the disappointment, biting her lower lip. She looked down at Demoya's shoes and nodded. Steadily, the coach lifted her chin. She couldn't look away. She didn't want to.

"But know this: I didn't bring you up here to sit on the bench, okay? You're too good for that. You *are* going to play."

She clasped her hands behind her back. "Okay, Coach," she mumbled.

Demoya patted her on the back.

"Oh. One more thing. No barfing."

Jeannie forced a smile, waved shyly, and trotted to the Rockers' bench. As she bent to re-tie her shoes, two seniors—Barbara and Angie Something— stood in front of her, stretching their backs and thighs. "By the way," Barbara said, "he likes blow jobs."

Neither said another word. Neither acknowledged she was even there. They simply ran onto the field, leading the fans in the cheer "Go Rockers!"

"Blow what? Were they talking to me? What does that mean?"

In a bouncing, howling cluster, the team raised their fists. "Go Rockers! Go Rockers!"

Jeannie shook off her bewilderment and dashed to join the chant.

In the first two minutes of play, the Lynx pounded the ball past Rocker goalie and team captain Barbara Bowes three times. The Rockers, on the other hand, never got out of their own end.

Jeannie slumped on the bench counting blades of grass, her hands shielding her eyes. Occasionally, she spread her fingers, noting Demoya's every movement, every shout, every scowl, his shirt, his pants. Everything.

"*What's a blow job?*" she wondered.

She glanced down the bench to make sure nobody heard her thoughts. Nobody paid any attention to her at all. Despite what Coach had told her, she wanted to barf.

When the first half ended mercifully, the bedraggled Rockers, their sundrop yellow uniforms streaked with mud, grass, and sweat, slouched toward their bench, avoiding each other's eyes, especially their goalie's.

Barbara shoved her wide shoulders past the other girls, slamming her gloves on the team bench. Savagely, she kicked at the ground and dropped herself next to Jeannie. "Jesus Christ!" she barked at the sky.

"You got a problem, Bowes?" Demoya turned his cap backward and strode menacingly toward his goalie. His thin lips, his fierce eyes terrified and tempted as Jeannie tipped her head away from the confrontation.

Barbara grabbed a yellow team towel and wiped her flushed face. Furiously, she leaned over her long, muscular legs. "Three goals. Three fucking goals. Did you see that?"

"Yeah. I saw. You're having a pretty rough night."

"*I'm* having a rough night? I'm doing everything I can out there! It'd be nice if I could get some God-damned help," she shouted down the bench.

Demoya raised his eyes. He scowled, then pulled back his shoulders, measuring his words. "Help? You want help? You tired?"

"Hell, yes, I'm tired! Every time I think I can breathe, here comes that fucking ball. I'm throwing myself all over the goal mouth, but it doesn't matter. These pussies just wave *Olé* at the Langley bitches and *BAM!* Here comes the ball at my head."

"I tried—" Marjorie Pitts interrupted.

"Oh, shut up, Pit-face. You're the worst of all. You smile, curtsy, apologize for getting in Langley's way, then make a dash for Alberta. Shit, Coach. I can't do it all myself."

Demoya tightened his crossed arms and scrunched his mouth. "It's 3-0 and we've got another half to play," he said, narrowing his eyes and daring her to speak.

"Great! So we'll lose 6-0. Fuck!" Barbara said, wiping her thick forearm across her muddy forehead.

Demoya scowled and bit his lip. Slowly, he walked the length of the bench, his eyes darting from one player to the next. Nobody looked up at him.

"You got quite a mouth, Bowes, but you're right. You can't do it all. In fact, you can't seem to do anything. Good thing Pitts can play goal 'cause you're done."

"Wait! No!" Marjorie panicked.

"What?" Barbara jumped to her feet, flinging her towel to the ground. Demoya confronted her, his face pinched and dark. As his jaw muscles pulsed, he inched closer, towering over her. Although her tight lips expressed defiance, her body betrayed her, cowering and lowering itself back to the bench.

"We have a game to win," Demoya said quietly, although everybody could hear, "And we're going to do it without you."

He rose and walked back down the bench. "Pitts, you're in goal. Bowes, you can go home. We don't need you."

The Rockers hid their faces as Barbara gaped. She stomped the ground and shouted, "You can't do that, Demoya. You know it. You owe me. Remember? You owe me."

The coach glared at her. "I owe you nothing. Go."

The girl's nostrils flared and her head jerked from side to side. Demoya, his jaw set, maintained his steady gaze. When Barbara snorted and bared her clenched teeth, the coach didn't move.

With a loud groan, she flung her gloves into her bag, flipped off Demoya, and dipped under the restraining rope to find her parents. The crowd parted as she stumbled through them, tears flooding her mud-spattered face.

Demoya ignored the silence and called together his team. "All right, Rockers. We're going to do this. Warm up."

The team leapt to life, stretching and jogging.

"Jones!" Demoya shouted.

Lost and confused, Jeannie raised a hand to her throat.

Leaning forward, his hands on his knees, Demoya examined the girl's face. "Pitts is going in goal. You're the new forward."

Jeannie gasped. "Me? No. Other girls—I—I don't think—"

"I don't want you to think. I want you to play. That's why you're here.

She adjusted her headband and gulped. "I'll do my best."

Demoya slapped his hands together. "Okay, team. Here's the deal. Pitts is in goal. Jones takes her place. Got it?"

"Yes," came the tentative answer.

"What?"

"Yes, Coach."

"I can't hear you!"

"YES, COACH!"

Slowly, he chanted. "Rock-ers! Rock-ers! Rock-ers!"

Deliberately, the team circled their coach him, clapping and shaking their fists at the sky. The chant swelled to a shout with the throng yellow mob bouncing and syncopating the claps. "Rock-ers! Rock-ers! Rock-ers!

When the Fort Repentance faithful joined in, the Lynx scoffed and pointed at the scoreboard. However, within the opening seconds of play, Jeannie's speed and Marjorie's steel-curtain defense erased the Langley swagger.

Futilely, the midnight blue Amazons stumbled and bumbled after the spritely Jeannie as she rang up three goals in five minutes. Meanwhile, Marjorie pounded away every shot near her goal. In total disarray, the Lynx littered the field, wandering aimlessly after the ball and into each other.

Before Langley could recover, the ball bounced loose once more, Jeannie gaining control. Without giving the Lynx a chance to blink, she slammed it past the goalie, vaulting the Rockers ahead 4-3.

The Fort Repentance crowd erupted. Fathers pounded each other; mothers squealed. Coach Demoya leaned back and bellowed, "I love you, Jeannie Jones!"

The Rocker sideline roared.

In that shout, the fans and team heard encouragement. Jeannie Jones heard, "I love you."

Her distracted moment of joy ended with a jolt when a careless Langley pass bounced off her shin. Instantly back in the game, she punched the ball toward the Lynx goal once more.

She never saw the Langley striker coming.

The two collided at midfield and splayed across the center line. Jeannie lay on her back, blinking at the blue and yellow flashes streaming above her while the ground thundered beneath her.

"*That's weird,*" she thought. "*I can feel the earth rotating.*"

"Jones! Jones! Get up," Demoya shouted somewhere.

Immediately, both girls scrambled to join the mob sweeping across the field. Desperately, they struggled against each other, pushing and jostling. Before they could free themselves, their scuffling legs tangled, hurling both girls back to the ground. A loud *pop* and *thud* extinguished the light.

Jeannie couldn't see. She couldn't breathe.

"Jones! Jones! Are you okay?"

"Help me, Coach. Help me," she gasped.

She blinked her eyes—once—three times.

Peering through the field lights, she recognized the Big Dipper. "*Ursa Major,*" she thought, recalling its Latin name. "*The Great Bear.*"

The first constellation she ever learned. The Guide to the Guide, her father called it.

Like her father taught her when she was eight, she used the Pointer Stars at the front of dipper's bowl to find the North Star. "*Five times,*" she remembered, twisting her head to follow the path. "*Count the distance five times.*"

"*And there's Polaris. The North Star. Forever north. I knew I liked bears.*"

A cough wracked her lungs as a rumble of feet rushed toward her. She turned her head as the Langley striker rose and walked away. Jeannie reached for her, but pain wrenched her knee and swept up her thigh.

Her scream stunned the crowd.

Before she could breathe again, a strong hand encircled hers while another pressed her head to the ground.

"It's okay, Jones. It's okay. Hang on."

Jeannie looked up into Coach Demoya's face. Beneath his head hung his necklace. "*What does that symbol mean?*" she wondered.

"Coach. I—I—" The pain severed her words. She broke off screaming and writhing.

"What is it? Your head?"

Jeannie clenched her mouth. "No," she groaned.

"Your leg?"

She nodded.

"Okay. Let me—"

She flinched at his hand on her thigh.

"Holy shit!"

Another body squeezed next to Demoya. "Jeannie! Jeannie! Are you— Oh, my god, baby."

The coach jumped to his feet, wildly beckoning the sideline. "Ambulance! Bring the ambulance!"

Jeannie's father Beecher gagged, then knelt woozily at her side, averting his eyes.

Her step-mother Amanda squeezed next to him and stroked Jeannie's forehead. "They're coming. Just hang on."

Suddenly, pain shot up the girl's leg to the back of her eyes. She howled and flopped her head from side to side.

"Coach!" she cried. "Coach!"

Demoya pushed himself in beside her and took her hand. "Yeah, Jones?"

Jeannie gazed at him. She had wanted to say something, but she couldn't remember what.

"I like—I like bears."

Demoya laughed. "What?"

"I mean—I—I just wanted to say—I'm sorry."

"For getting hurt?"

Jeannie bit her lip. "*No*," she thought, "*but—*"

She nodded her head.

Demoya smiled. "You and your folks go to the hospital and fix this. Okay? I'll see you when you get out."

She squeezed his hand.

"Okay," she whispered.

Jeannie's eyes flickered at the recovery room light. Amanda sat next to her, smiling. "Oh, good. You're awake."

Jeannie wiped her mouth. "Yeah. Where's Daddy?"

"Down the hall. He just went out to get a candy bar or something."

She never looked at Jeannie's face.

"Am—Am I crippled?"

"No. No, the doctor says you'll be fine." She held Jeannie's arm and looked at the floor.

"You're not telling me something. What is it?"

Amanda stepped to the end of the bed and rubbed her finger along the bed rail. "Well, it's two things."

She hesitated.

"Should Daddy be here?"

"Probably, but he's not really comfortable talking about this, so he left me to do it. It's a guy thing."

"What?"

"Okay. When the nurses were cleaning you up—uh—Well—As I was saying, it's a guy thing to be uncomfortable talking about a girl thing."

"I don't get—"

Amanda cleared her throat and brushed back her hair. "We talked about this before. Remember?"

Jeannie rested her hand on her thigh. "Oh, wait. You mean—?"

Amanda nodded and twisted the corner of Jeannie's blanket. "Do you need to ask me—?"

"No. I—I probably will later, but—I—I don't know."

Amanda smiled.

Jeannie laid her head back on the pillow. *"So it's not really a girl thing. It's a woman thing—Coach—"*

She looked up at her stepmother. "You said there were two things Daddy didn't want to tell me."

"Yeah." Amanda sighed and looked away. "I don't want to tell you this either—"

"What?"

"When you were in surgery, we got a phone call from one of the Rocker moms and—"

Amanda looked away.

"You're not going to be playing for the team anymore."

Jeannie swallowed. "We lost, didn't we?"

Amanda shook her head. "No. Actually you, Jeannie Jones, you beat Langley all by yourself with your four goals. No. This has nothing to do with anything on field at all. This has noth—It—There are no more

Rockers. The board fired Coach Demoya tonight and disbanded the team."

"Fired Coach? Why?"

Amanda sat on the edge of the bed and laid her hand on Jeannie's. "Coach Demoya—Did he ever—you know—try anything with you?"

"Like what?"

When Amanda looked directly into Jeannie's eyes, she knew the answer. Her stomach twisted and she couldn't breathe. She smoothed her gown.

"*He likes blow jobs,*" she remembered.

Jeannie covered her mouth. "Who?"

"Barbara Bowes, Marjorie Pitts, Angie Whitfield."

A tear slid from Jeannie's eye and her lip quivered. She rubbed her face dry with a fist. Frustrated, she leaned back and chewed the inside of her cheeks. She sniffed and tugged at the blanket.

Amanda gently took Jeannie's hand and smiled. "It's okay. I understand. That jaw is gorgeous."

As her stepmother kissed her hands, Jeannie—the girl—felt safe, warm; Jeannie—the new woman—felt lost, alone.

Her shoulder-shaking turned to body-wracking sobs. She buried her head into her stepmother's shoulder until the weeping faded to sniffs. Looking up at Amanda, she gave a half-cry/half-laugh. "When I scored the fourth goal, he said he loved me."

Amanda smiled.

Tears flowed freely down Jeannie's cheeks. "I only met him a week—I just—I didn't want to feel this way. I still don't."

"Of course, you don't. And nobody's blaming you. Andre Demoya is a beautiful young man."

Jeannie sucked her lips into her mouth.

"But for your sake and all the Rockers, he had to go."

The door opened. Beecher stood awkwardly glancing from his wife to his daughter. "Jeannie, you're awake," he said.

Amanda stood and kissed her husband. "Ah. Right on time."

"On time? Wha—?"

Jeannie laughed and wiped her face with a tissue. "It's okay, Daddy. We talked about everything we needed to talk about."

Everything?" Beecher asked his wife.

"Everything. She knows it all."

The nervous man relaxed his shoulders. "You all right, baby?"

His daughter nodded. "Evidently, I'm not a baby any more. Remember?"

"I meant about the Rockers and Coach Demoya?"

Her lower lip quivered. "It hurts."

"As bad as the leg?"

"Pretty close."

"Stupid soccer," he joked.

"Stupid soccer?!" Jeannie exclaimed.

"Dumbest game ever invented. I told you to play something safe, like rugby or hockey."

The tissue box whizzed past Beecher's head.

Jeannie's eyes narrowed. "It's a good thing I like you," she said, raising her arms toward her father.

3

Arguing with Reality

Winthrop, Michigan
USA

A car door slammed outside, jolting Brandon Whistler awake. He stared at his bedroom ceiling and heard his mother Joanne rise from the living room couch, her soft footsteps swishing through the carpet.

"Finally," he thought.

He and his mom had waited for days for his father to come home from wherever and whomever.

"Bastard," Brandon thought, hugging his pillow to his stomach as he turned onto his side and listened intently.

The front door opened. Angry whispers.

The front door shut. More whispers.

Then silence.

The bathroom door. The medicine cabinet.

Brandon lifted his head. A thin strip of light glowed beneath his bedroom door, then disappeared.

More angry whispers.

The front door opened again. And closed.

Brandon's breath shivered.

Outside, the car door slammed again. The engine ground and clattered to life, then died.

Again, the car door slammed.

Then silence.

From down the hall, snoring seeped through the walls. His father, not his mother. Where'd she go?

Brandon scrunched his eyes and wished the images away. He curled around his pillow and hid his head under the blanket until sleep finally engulfed him.

The next dawn, gray light reached through Brandon's curtains, gently shaking him awake. He stretched and turned to his other side.

Morning birds chattered and screeched outside, the only sound in the yard. Down the hall, the night's gasps and rattles had softened to regular wheezing.

Brandon pushed back the covers, slowly lowering his feet to the carpet. Although the naked air sweat, the rug-clothed floor chilled.

Rummaging under his bed, he found his slippers, then shuffled warily down the hall toward the low rumble in the living room where his father lay awkwardly sprawled across the couch. Brandon winced at the stench of whiskey. He scowled at the rattling snorts.

"Fucking drunk," he muttered as he tightened the drawstring of his pajamas.

He slapped a hand over his mouth and tried to wring the curse from the wet air. His mom always told him not to swear. His father had made him good at it.

"Shit! Shit! Shit!" he chastised himself.

Rubbing his eyes, he shuffled back towards his parents' room. Outside the door, he hesitated. "Maybe she can keep me from killing the son of a bitch."

He steeled his determination and knocked. "Mom?"

Donald's snoring drowned out any answer. Brandon tapped and called again, "Mom."

Still nothing.

He blew on both his hands, then carefully pushed open the door. He saw only darkness.

Brandon let out three short breaths, wiped his sweaty hands on his pajamas, then snapped on the light. The empty, undisturbed bed mocked him.

"Mom," he called louder.

Brandon checked the sides of the bed, then knelt and searched underneath.

Nothing.

He wrapped his arms around his chest, pondering the perfectly made bed. Shaking his head, he returned to the hall.

The bathroom door stood ajar. Brandon crept to the doorway, placed a hand on both sides of the frame, and leaned in. Above the sink, the mirrored cabinet yawned open. Wet, rumpled towels lay scattered on the floor. Brandon's stomach leapt; his fingers numbed. He stepped around the door and slid the towels behind the toilet with his foot.

Further inside, the shower curtain stretched from wall to wall.

"Mom?"

He reached for the curtain, but jerked back his hand. What if—? He wiped his wet lips on his forearm. Cautiously, he reached again, caught the plastic, then yanked it aside.

Water dripped slowly from the shower head into the empty tub.

"What the hell?" Brandon thought as he scooped up the damp towels from the floor and stuffed them into the hamper. He let himself into the hallway, then trailed his hands along the wall to the kitchen.

The counters, the stove, the refrigerator, all sparkled in the light filtering through the glass door. A damp rag hung over the faucet.

"She's been here. Where did she go?"

The living room couch grunted.

Brandon moaned and grabbed the counter. "Dad," he yelled, "have you seen Mom?"

Donald snorted incoherently.

"Damn it!" Brandon stormed into the living room, snatching open the curtains. His father hacked at the light and threw an arm over his face.

"Dad. Dad! Where's Mom?" He shook his father's shoulders.

Swinging wildly, Donald flung Brandon off him with a roar. The boy landed on his back, but scrambled to return to his father. "Dad! I can't find her. Do you hear me? Where's Mom?"

His father squirmed into the couch cushions. "How the fuck should I know?" he grumbled.

Brandon jumped onto his father and bounced his shoulders. "Dad, I'm telling you! I can't find Mom."

"All right!" Donald bellowed, hurling off Brandon's hands. He spun over and pressed his palms into his eyes.

"Shit," he mumbled. Brandon cringed as his father took two deep breaths and struggled to sit up. After weaving to a reasonably vertical position, Donald laid back his throbbing head and hid his face under both arms.

"Dad?"

"Uhhh!" Donald caught his breath. "Did you check the bedroom?"

"Yeah. She's not there. Where is she?"

"Great fuckin' Christ, Brandon! I don't know! Shut up! God, let me think." He leaned forward, elbows on his knees. His hands cupped his face like a cantaloupe. "God, my head hurts!"

Brandon threw open the front door. "You're no help. You know that?"

"Well, yeah, I do. I've known that a long time. But you know what, kid? Right now, I don't give a shit about anything, least of all your mother."

"Well, I'm going to look for her."

Brandon thrust open the screen door and froze. Beneath the oak tree next to his grandfather's farmhouse, the family car sat awkwardly, ghostly and covered with mud.

"Dad?" Brandon wiped back his hair.

"What?" his father grunted.

"Did you park the car by Grandpa's house?"

"What? Fuck no. Why would I do that? I ain't been in that place since your grandfather died."

Brandon stared at the unmoving vehicle. His father fell off the couch, rose, and stumbled next to him.

"See?" Brandon pointed at the car.

Donald's face dropped. Brandon heard words and images clattering around his father's brain. Donald put a hand against the door frame. "Brandon, wait here until I get back."

"Why?"

"Just do what I say!" Pushing through the door, he lunged across the muddy yard in his stocking feet.

Brandon watched helplessly as his father staggered to the car and braced his knees against the door. Shielding his eyes, he peered through the side window. Fruitlessly, he squeezed his fingers into the crack below the window, struggling to open the door.

"Use the handle," Brandon yelled.

Donald pounded and pushed on the window to try to lower it.

"I said use the handle!"

Frustrated, Donald kicked the side of the car.

"Use the—"

A groping hand unlatched the handle and flung the door open. Donald swayed widely, hanging above the mud.

"My god," Brandon muttered as his father regained his footing.

Cautiously, Donald placed his hands on the seat and leaned in. A moment later, he teetered to a standing position and scanned the yard.

"Find anything?" Brandon called.

His father ignored him, then saw something at the farmhouse. He slammed the car door, stumbled up the steps, and disappeared inside.

"Dad!" Brandon jumped off the step, hopping and darting across the spongy yard.

Near the car, his feet slid from beneath him, tossing him into the mud, flailing and flopping. As he sloshed to his feet, a glimpse of the car's interior shook him.

Garbage everywhere. A brown paper bag. Drenched, rumpled tissues. A whiskey bottle. A prescription bottle.

He remembered the bathroom.

"*The medicine cabinet.*"

He could not connect the two images in his brain.

"Dad!" he bounded up the farmhouse's front steps, dripping and puzzled. Inside, his father bellowed. Brandon slung open the screen door and called again. "Dad?"

Donald burst from the kitchen, his face blanching at the sight of Brandon. He grasped at the back of the recliner, his arms shaking. His head twitched as he stared at his son.

"Dad, who were you yelling at?" Brandon asked, bracing himself against the doorjamb.

Donald leaned forward, hiding his face. His shoulders shuddered.

Brandon crept forward. "Dad?"

His father slowly shook his head.

"What?"

Deliberately, Donald raised his red, swollen face. With his eyes bulging, he summoned all his strength, hoisted the recliner and flung it against the wall. With the chair and all the pictures crashing to the floor, he charged his son and thrust the boy toward the door.

The boy thudded into the doorjamb and slid to the floor, stunned.

"Get out!" Donald shouted. "It's gonna get fuckin' nuts here and we don't need—"

"Dad, what—?"

Donald hauled up his son by both shoulders and wrenched the boy's face to his. "GET OUT OF HERE!"

Overcome by smell and spittle, Brandon fell wheezing and writhing to the floor.

"No! No, you don't. Get up. Get up!" Donald wailed, hoisting Brandon over his shoulder and lugging him through the kitchen. With a mighty heave, he sent the boy wheeling off the porch. Exhausted, he fell to his knees and slapped both hands against the wall, his voice rasping.

Struggling through the mud, Brandon gulped for air like a dying fish until he slithered behind the car. "Dad, come on!" he called. "What's going on?"

Donald's eyes groped the yard for something familiar—a tree, a tractor, anything—finally settling on the car. He blinked once. Twice. When Brandon peeked from behind the vehicle, the man gasped and staggered against the door frame. Unbidden, his feet slopped to his son's side. With his breath shaking, he braced himself against the car and lowered himself to his heels. He touched Brandon's shivering shoulder.

The boy flinched.

Donald dipped his head and lowered his hand. "I'm sorry, son. Stand up."

Brandon cringed, but struggled to his feet. When Donald reached for him, he ducked away from his father's touch and hugged himself against the cold. Protectively, he flexed his legs in case he had to flee.

Donald searched the sky, then sat in the mud against the car. "Brandon, your mother's gone."

"I know. I told you that." Brandon started toward the farmhouse.

"No!" Guttural noises rose in Donald's throat as he pulled Brandon back to the mud.

The boy stifled the bile rising in his throat. He would not be intimidated. Clenching his jaw, he glared his father into submission.

Donald lowered his head. His chin quivered. "She's not gone away. She's dead."

Brandon's legs buckled as his father rose next to him. "Dead?" he whispered.

Donald's suddenly steady shoulders spoke truth.

"How?"

His father dropped his hands. "It doesn't matter. Just get back to our house and wait for me there. I gotta get the cops and ambulance, and you need to—to not be here. Now go!"

Gently, he turned Brandon toward their house, nudged him toward it, and staggered back to the farmhouse.

Brandon stumbled to a stop in the driveway. He watched his hands as mud dripped through his fingers. The sky blackened and hung on his shoulders. His legs quaked under the weight and dragged him to his knees. With one wracking convulsion after another, his vomit flooded around his legs.

Empty of hope and food, he sat back on his feet, raised his head, and howled.

No one heard. No one cared.

Inside the farmhouse, doors slammed and his father wailed. Brandon wiped his face on his sleeve, then stumbled into the black, thawing field.

Brandon never asked for details of his mother's death and his father never gave any. The truth came in whispered fragments at the funeral.

"Donald came home…"

"…drunk…"

"…an argument…"

"…Donald passed out…"

"…Joanne…"

"…pills. Lots of pills."

"…her old bedroom at the farmhouse…"

"The police said…"

Word by phrase, Brandon cobbled the pieces together. Amidst the funeral flowers, the swirling voices, and the blankness that surrounded him and his father, he understood what his mother had done.

He also grasped why none of the voices had mentioned him. He was not the scandal.

Winthrop thrived on scandal. Although Brandon didn't know all the details, scandal had killed his grandfather and his mother. Scandal had destroyed his father.

"My time's coming," he thought.

Home from the service, he retreated to the solace of his closet to slice and gouge at his scarred legs; meanwhile, his father retreated to the bottle to obliterate his memory.

Neither spoke.

Neither moved.

Days became weeks. The spring mud dried around the house and the fine dust of summer coated the leaves. For three short weeks in June, Donald returned to his job, focused and sober. On Monday of the fourth week, Brandon found him passed out on the back porch, reeking in his own vomit. His working days were over.

Without employment, what little money Brandon and his father had, dwindled and evaporated. For a while, compassion tolerated the rising debt. "For Joanne," the town said. Furtively, the store clerks at O'Neill's grocery slipped extra potatoes and cold cuts into Don's weekly shopping bags. Packages of clothes and shoes appeared on the front steps for a growing Brandon.

However, patience with Don's drinking shriveled in the summer heat, as did the charity. Desperate for cash, Donald sold his father-in-law Harvey's farm equipment piece by piece in Winthrop's back alleys. Brandon turned to theft, first out of necessity, then out of habit, and finally out of greed. What he wanted, he took—food, shoes, jewelry. Donald sold what he owned; Brandon sold what he found. Between the two of them, they survived.

Through neglect and scavenging, the farm decayed beyond recognition, brush growing around the old farmhouse, the fields overrun with noxious weeds. Eventually, Joanne's employers at the town law firm convinced Donald to sell the remnants of the farmhouse and acreage to Buck Hornsdorfer. Donald and Brandon could keep the house Harvey had built them, but they needed to sell the rest and take what they could get.

It was hardly enough. Winthrop gossip said Donald took a third of what the farm was worth. As summer slipped away, the school year loomed and money fluttered away into the chilling air.

In the quiet of an early September morning, Brandon crept out of his room and down the hall to what had been his parents' room. He slowly opened the door and found the room empty—except for his mother's metal three-drawer jewelry box still on her dresser.

The rising sun shone through the window, illuminating the dresser like a shrine. The sacred gilded jewelry box glittered under a brightening halo, beckoning the reluctant Brandon.

Quickly scanning the hallway, he abandoned sentimentality, stepped into the room, and gently closed the door. A cloud passed outside, but still the box glistened, luring him forward. At the dresser, he held perfectly still, listening for his father outside.

He heard nothing. However, he smelled everything. Everything he had forgotten.

Traces of his mother's perfume wafted from her business suits and favorite baseball jerseys hanging in the closet. Her lavender shampoo lingered on her pillowcase, dominating his father's grimy stench on the pillow next to hers. Traces of her powdered neck and face tingled through Brandon's whole body.

Squeezing his eyes shut and setting his jaw, he conquered his emotion and opened the box.

His hand hovered over his mother's single gold wedding band. He had not seen it since the funeral when his father had the mortician remove it from her finger.

Brandon fumed. "It's not his. He didn't even buy it for her. She bought it for herself. Fuck that shit."

He slipped the ring onto his pinky.

Another cloud passed between the sun and window.

Brandon narrowed his eyes and cocked his head. He glanced behind himself, then emptied the drawer onto the dresser top.

He held each item up to the light. First, her club pendant and her golden watch. Then, the diamond-encrusted spider brooch. When his inexpert eyes finished examining all the jewelry, he held each item between his teeth and rubbed his tongue against the metal, tasting for authenticity.

The flavor of genuineness escaped him. Instead, when he tasted the ring, the watch, and the brooch, images of his mother flickered through his brain—her face, her voice, her laughter, her touch. When he tasted the pendant, he saw a faceless redhead—naked, wet. She was not like the Playboy pinup hidden under his mattress. She was real. He felt her breath, her lips. He gasped. In an instant, the glimpses of his mother and the woman disappeared, although their essence remained.

Brandon leaned back and rubbed his forehead. The halo around the box had disappeared. No longer a relic, it stood open and vulnerable.

Quickly, he hung the pendant over his neck, swept the rest of the contents into his hand, and dumped them into his pants pocket. The box's sanctity now removed, he closed it and restored it to its normal position on the dresser. Easing the door open, he checked the empty hallway.

Nobody.

He sniffed the air and pressed an ear against the wall, seeking any sign of his father.

Again, nobody.

He slunk to his room and slid through a tiny opening. After closing and locking the door, he hid his loot, including his mother's ring, at the bottom of his underwear drawer.

Convinced of the security of his stash, Brandon walked back down the hall to his father still passed out on the couch. He stood over the snoring, rattling body, flexed his fists, and bit his lips.

The light shifted once again, and an ominous new truth shivered around him. Tangible, yet undefined. Words both surrounded and avoided him.

He opened the front door and stared out the screen. Across the yard, his grandfather's empty, faded farmhouse glowered, daring him to speak.

Before Brandon could open his mouth, a bird flew out of the barn and landed on the ground beneath the rotting steps of the farmhouse. It established its stance, cocked its head, and regarded Brandon.

The boy didn't know what kind of bird it was, nor did he particularly care. He just wanted it gone.

Before Brandon could drive the bird away, a voice spoke within his brain. "What is the truth you feel? Your truth."

Startled, Brandon furtively locked the screen door, but he could not walk away.

"Yes, I talk. It's an important question. Answer me," the bird said.

"I—I don't know!"

"Search. Think. Realize."

"Search? Search what?"

"Look."

Brandon gazed at the bird for a moment, then glanced around himself.

"What's to search? It's empty. We sold everything."

The bird lowered its head and shook it from side to side, its luminous purple neck ruffling and stretching.

"Ask yourself what is empty."

Brandon evaded reality. "The house? Mom's bed? The jewelry box?"

"They are unimportant. What you have sold is unimportant. What else is empty?"

Brandon circled his hands, rubbing his arms, his hair. The pendant burned against his chest. The words stuck in his throat. Snuffling, he gathered as much air as he could. "EVERYTHING!"

On the couch, his father snorted. Brandon glared at him until the peaceful snoring resumed.

The pendant cooled. Brandon leaned his head against the screen door and wept. "Everything's empty."

He collapsed into a heaving, gasping lump.

The satisfied voice said nothing. The bird turned, spread its wings and flew over the farmhouse and across the field beyond.

Brandon coughed and stumbled to the kitchen table. His head swam. His throat tightened. With his elbows planted on the table, his head sank into his hands.

In the living room, his father coughed and dropped unconscious to the floor.

The air in the room froze. Paralyzed, Brandon listened for Donald's breath. At first, he heard nothing. Then a gurgle. A snuffle. A phlegm-filled hack followed by slow, relaxed breaths. Deep. Long. Loud. Rhythmic.

Convinced that his father still lived, Brandon retreated to his room and hid in his closet. There, hunched behind his hanging shirts and pants, perched atop boots and shoes, he pressed his hands against his head and cried.

"Everything *is not the right answer*," he thought.

Unbidden, the correct response arose from his toes through his knees into his elbows, finally seeping into his brain from his open fingers.

Images glowed and glimmered in the tears that filled his palms. From one hand, his grandfather watched, waited, and wondered. In the other, his mother tipped her head, smiled, and reached toward her son. However, as his tears dried, the two visions faded, softer, darker, until they vanished completely.

Through the hanging clothes, a faceless red-headed woman glowed on the back of the door. Brandon reached a trembling hand toward her, but stopped short. The woman disappeared, replaced by the bird, its glimmering head cocked, waiting for an answer. "What is empty? You know."

As if alive with the truth, a sleeve wrapped itself around Brandon's arm. Perturbed, Brandon pushed it aside, then noticed it was the shirt he had worn to his mother's funeral. His fingers rubbed the fabric.

"You know," the bird said.

Brandon absorbed the sleeve's reaction.

"What is empty? Life. I mean everyone is gone. My grandpa, my mother, my drunk-ass father, even the red-headed woman," he said.

"Which means—?"

"*I'm* empty."

"Yes, but only for now," the bird said. "*Now* is only made up of *where*, *what* and *who*. *Now* disappears."

"Everything and everybody. Just like the woman I just saw."

The bird shook its head. "Not her. She is more than *now*."

"How can anyone be more than *now*?" Brandon scoffed.

"By becoming *how* and *why*. Transforming to *forever*. *Forever* never disappears."

"Shit! I'm may not know much. I'm only thirteen, but it seems to me *now* is plenty."

"*Now* is settling."

Brandon raised a hand to his mouth and tasted the saltiness of his tears. "Then I guess I'll settle."

He reached for the door knob as the bird fluttered away. Blank again, the door opened to Brandon's empty room.

4

Unfolding Life

Peru, South America

Tuta lay in the dusty darkness of her hut, holding the newborn to her sweaty breast. Through the open window, the breeze off Lake Titicaca cooled; the lapping water calmed. Three shiny, black stones lay on the window sill awaiting Viracocha the Creator to arise in the East bringing light and life.

Alliyma, the village midwife, sat at the bedside, wiping Tuta's face with a cold cloth. Her stern expression and severe black hair spoke as harshly as her words. "The little girl ran far to find me."

"Thank you for coming," the exhausted Tuta answered. "He would not wait."

Alliyma nodded, unsmiling. "He is strong-willed, anxious. There is much to see. Much to learn."

The baby twisted in his sleep. Tuta gasped.

"Don't worry. He will rest," the midwife said. "Then he will begin."

The mother kissed the baby's dark hair and gently patted his back.

As she rinsed the cloth in cold water, Alliyma noticed Tuta's bare fingers. "He has a father?" she asked.

Tuta's face darkened. She bit her lip, avoiding the midwife's eyes. "The man is in Lima."

Alliyma's jaw jutted forward as she wiped the cool cloth across Tuta's forehead and down her cheeks. "He will be back soon?"

Tuta recognized the accusation. Instead of speaking her truth, she shook her head and snuffled. "He's—He's gone."

The baby twisted and whimpered. Tuta held him closer, protecting, comforting.

Alliyma rinsed the cloth again. "His name?"

Tuta hardened her face and gazed at the ceiling. "Umaq." *Traitor.*

The midwife shook her head. "I meant the baby. What will you call him?"

Tuta turned her head to the window. "Chaupi." *The middle of everything.*

Taking a worn towel from her bag, Alliyma covered the boy. In his sleep, the boy grasped her ring finger.

"No!" Tuta cried, her dark face blanching. "Stop him!"

Startled, Alliyma recoiled. Still, the baby clutched her finger. Then she remembered the legend of the village: "Gold poisons."

She set her jaw, nodded, and patiently peeled the infant's grip from her wedding band. Protectively, she wiped his hand on her dress and wrapped the towel tighter around him, binding his hands.

"Thank you," Tuta said. "He is precious. He must remain pure."

After organizing her instruments, the midwife began cleaning the room. "I will come back later in the week. It is a far walk, but I will come. Will somebody be with you?"

Tuta watched her helplessly. She bit her lip. "Huchuysisa. Chaupi's sister. I call her Sisa."

Alliyma began to speak, then stopped herself. She glared at the limp woman on the bed. "Huchuysisa. *Little Flower.* The girl is young."

Tuta sighed. "She is my daughter."

Sullenly, the midwife gathered her basket and walked to the door. Tuta reached out to stop her. "I hear your thoughts. *Another child in a town with no fathers, another mouth in a world with no food.* He is sent by Viracocha, the Creator. He is protected. He is more than we have ever known."

Alliyma looked to the floor, then raised her chin at Tuta. "I will send in the girl."

She closed the door behind her.

Tuta turned to her window. The top of the sun slipped above the lake, its red light sparkling off the stones on the sill. "Viracocha the Creator," she whispered.

The baby whimpered and twisted, searching for food.

The door reopened. A barefoot girl, skinny and ragged, twisted from side to side. Barely six years old, she dipped her head and scratched her belly, then hid her scabbed and dirty arms behind her.

"Mother?"

"It's all right, Sisa. Come and see."

The girl crept to the side of the bed, warily watching mother and baby. She gently pointed her tiny fingers. "What is that?"

"This is your brother. His name is Chaupi."

Sisa recoiled and rubbed at her itchy skin. "He looks like a bug."

"A bug?" Tuta laughed. "He's your brother. Come closer."

The girl leaned forward and tilted her head.

"You can touch him."

Reaching forward, Sisa touched the baby's face and shrank back.

"What is it?" her mother asked.

"He has no teeth. I don't like him. He's ugly."

"He's a baby. Babies have no teeth. They are young, not ugly."

Sisa shook her head. "He's not a baby. He's a—a—"

"What?"

"He's a beetle. I don't like beetles." Sisa climbed upon the bed and snuggled close to her mother.

Tuta kissed her daughter's forehead. "It's all right. I'll teach you how."

Outside, the sun rose above the water, its light turning to orange and yellow. Inside, Sisa watched it lift over the window sill.

"Mother?"

"Yes."

"What are the stones for?"

"It is said the stones of Lake Titicaca are pieces of the Creator and his two sons Imahmana and Tocapo. As the sun rises on them, Viracocha breathes his life, his spirit, into them."

"Then what?"

"We give those stones to the baby to guide him until he is complete, until he is prepared."

"Prepared for what?"

"Prepared for life with Viracocha Himself."

Sisa scowled. "But Teacher says Viracocha ran away, that he and his sons ran across the ocean."

Tuta nodded. "There are many stories about Him. Some say He had no sons, only daughters. Some say the sons went east over Lake Titicaca and the Father walked away to and over the ocean to the north. Yes, many stories. Some to be believed, others to be ignored."

The girl raised her eyes to her mother. "But the gods are gone. I don't see them. Why did they leave?"

The mother hesitated. "Maybe—Maybe they were not escaping, as Teacher told you. Maybe, as tradition says, they were leading."

"Leading who? To where?"

Tuta kissed her daughter's head and then the infant lying on her breast. "Leading all who will follow to where they belong."

The mother reached to the window and gathered the stones in her hand. "That is what I choose to believe."

"The stones will lead Chaupi?"

"Yes."

The girl twisted her face. Tutu held her close. "It's all right, Sisa. Viracocha created all. Chaupi will be fine."

"I still say he looks like a beetle," Sisa said.

Years later in Lima, Father Luíz and the boy waited at the roadside, watching the heat waves rise from the empty street outside the church. Blocks away, a red and blue bus turned the corner and rumbled its way toward them. The priest clapped the nearly grown young man on the shoulder and handed him a loosely packed suitcase.

"Many years inside this bag, my son. It is not much, but it is time. You must go."

The boy hid his arms behind his back. "But where? I am frightened. I have no family. No friends. Now not even the Church. What am I to eat?"

"You need not be frightened of your present or your future. The Creator will take care of you."

"Viracocha?"

Father Luíz winced. He could never erase the natives' loyalty to the old ways, the old deities. Not through words, threats, or promises. Not through punishment or reward. His pointless efforts had failed the boy and God Himself.

"*God by any other name*," he thought.

"Call Him what you will," the priest answered. "Yes."

The boy rubbed the stones sewn into his pockets. "I am still afraid," he said.

The priest calmly placed the suitcase in the boy's hands. "Of course, you are. It is a large responsibility to accept who you are and where you will be. Now you know why your mother named you Chaupi, the Middle of Everything."

The boy nodded reluctantly.

"The nuns also called me Beetle, a bug, a nothing."

"A silly, jealous name given by a sister long gone. One day, it will disappear, as will Chaupi. You will receive your true name. You must go now."

The bus sputtered to a stop in front of them. When the door opened, Father Luíz patted the boy's back.

"The bus will take you to Cusco, then on to Machu Picchu," he said. "In the dormitory, you will receive food, clothes, and shelter. You will learn your heritage, your culture."

"Without you, who will teach me?"

The priest breathed deeply, remembering all the lessons he had written, all the prayers he had prayed, all the frustrated arguments he had lost to a teenager. He knew the old ways needed no teacher.

"You do not need me. You need no school. The Creator will teach. You will learn," he said.

The boy climbed onto the bus and sat, staring straight ahead and clutching the suitcase in his arms. As the bus turned toward the mountains, the prayer-less priest repeated, "You will learn."

5

Trapped in Opposites

Mount Komu ("The Entry")
British Columbia, Canada

The naked woman lay on her back and turned her head. "Are you finished?" she asked the man, pushing her long black hair from her face.

The carnally exhausted Earth Man grunted, lifted his softening member from the disinterested vessel beneath him, and turned his rotund body to its side. "For now."

"Thank God," the woman said.

The Earth Man sat up and grabbed his pants from the floor.

"I wasn't going anywhere," she said. "Do I really need this chain?"

"Don't think of it as a chain," he said, pulling his pants up over his hips. Wobbling off-balanced, he reached for his shirt. "Think of it as decoration, a necklace. The gold came from this cave. I made it myself. Pretty, don't you think?"

Sarah, his captive, fingered the golden links about her throat. "Gorgeous," she mumbled. "Now what?"

The Earth Man stood, buttoned his pants, and pulled his shirt down over his head. "I told you this was forever. No going back. No more Beecher Jones. No daughter. None of it. But you didn't believe me."

"You hear my thoughts?"

"I always have. You know that. You were going to walk away, so now this."

He lifted the gold necklace from her chest. "Every time you get the urge to leave me or whenever I get the urge to fuck your brains out, this will remind you where you need to be."

"You can't kill me, you know," Sarah said. "I'm already—"

"Already dead. Yes, I know. But you're not indestructible. You still bleed. You still burn. This will remind you."

"In other words, a chain."

He reached forward and rubbed the gold between his fingers. "Isn't it beautiful?"

He licked the drool from his lips as he laid the necklace against her bare breast. The gold sizzled against her skin.

Sarah winced, then lifted her head defiantly. "Just fabulous."

"Hey, Boss—" The creature Frank burst into the room, jolted to a stop by the naked woman lying on the bed. "Sorry. I didn't— I just— I'm sorry."

Glowering at Frank, the Earth Man tossed a blanket over his queen's body. "What do you want?" he growled.

Sarah huffed and carelessly threw the blanket aside. Ignoring the men, she stood, stretched her arms to the ceiling, then shook out her hair. When she pulled her robe over her body, Frank wiped the drool from his lips.

"Frank! What do you want?" the Earth Man demanded.

"Oh, yeah. Look what I found." Frank opened the door. "You can come in," he called outside.

A lean man wearing a wide-brimmed hat entered the room.

The Earth Man's face brightened. "Ah," he said. "Pishtaco. Good to have you here."

Unperturbed by the men, Sarah stepped past them to check her appearance in the mirror.

His face reddening, the Earth Man rapidly rubbed his hands over the bed to flatten it. "Here. Here. Have a seat."

As if nobody else were in the room, Sarah adjusted the robe's collar to reveal a touch more cleavage, brushed back the raven hair from her shoulders, then adjusted her chain.

Wary of the others, the pishtaco eased himself onto the bed and removed his hat. After combing his fingers through his long hair and taming his beard, he flexed his fingers on the hat brim. "How do you know who I am?" he asked the Earth Man.

The Earth Man laughed and playfully backhanded Frank. "I sent out my weendigo and told him not to come back until he brought you with him. Plus, you fit the description: the boots, the hat, the knife and lasso, the green eyes, the hair and beard. If you're not the pishtaco, you really need a makeover."

With slow, sultry hands, Sarah smoothed the robe over her chest, her hips, her thighs. Satisfied with her look and the men's reaction, she turned and glided to the door. As she passed Frank, she trailed a finger across his shoulder and asked, "Having a good day?"

He glanced at the Earth Man and coughed as she left the room.

As a newcomer, the pishtaco observed the scene closely and immediately took sides. Brushing the dust off his hat, he narrowed his eyes and glared at Frank.

"Forget her," the Earth Man said. "It's just her way of teasing me. It happens all the time. No need to be mad at Frank. Besides, he brought you here for a reason."

"What's that?" the pishtaco asked.

"I have a proposal I think is going to be right up your alley. Wanna hear?"

The pishtaco sniffed the air and looked for a way to escape. Finally, he nodded.

"Good. Frank, give us a couple minutes, will ya?"

"What? I—"

"I said give us a couple minutes. When I need you, I'll call."

Frank glanced between the Earth Man he owed his existence and the pishtaco he had defeated so soundly in the mountain woods. Neither acknowledged his presence. The weendigo's loyalty to his boss wavered so when the door invited him to follow Sarah, he accepted the summons.

Alone with the Earth Man, the pishtaco said, "Frank doesn't like me."

"He doesn't like anybody. He's afraid you're going to replace him."

The pishtaco removed his knife and drew in the dirt before him. "He just beat the shit out of me. Why would he think that?"

"Because you're going to replace him."

The pishtaco's head snapped up. "Replace him as what?"

The Earth Man leaned back, folded his hands on his ample belly, and grinned. "Have you ever heard of the Trinity of the Word?"

"No."

"That's a good thing. I doubt they've heard of you either. The personnel keeps changing."

"Who are they?"

"The Word claims they're the ultimate force for Good."

"So?"

The Earth Man sneered. "I'm the ultimate force for Bad. I don't like anything good. From what I hear, you don't either."

"Good. Bad. I don't care."

"That's what I thought, but you have appetites, right?"

As the pishtaco wiped the knife on his boots, he examined the drawing he made in the dirt. A headless stick figure.

He licked his lips, then nodded.

"Hah!" the Earth Man exclaimed, clapping his hands. "That's what I thought. Vicious and vile, right? Me, too. You know what I really like? Victory, especially over the Word."

Resting his arms on his thighs, the pishtaco looked up at the Earth Man. "Had a lot of that?"

The Earth Man's face soured. "No. Oh, I've won a skirmish here and there, but His Trinity always wins the battle and I'm sick of it. That's where you come in."

"I'm not much of a fighter."

"I don't want you to fight."

"Then wha—"

"The Trinity is in transition. It needs new people. Oh, the Word has people in mind, but humans can be distracted. That's what I want you for. If he has no one to recruit, there's no Trinity. With no Trinity, everything is mine."

"Distract them? How would I do that?"

"Scare the shit out of them. Destroy their hopes and dreams. Remove all desire to fight."

"Why me? What's wrong with Frank?"

"He's a great starter, but he can never finish a job."

"Finish?"

"Like he loves terrorizing. However, he leaves survivors. I mean you're still here, right? I knew that's what would happen. He'd bait you into his woods, threaten you, do the whole weendigo 'grow-and-roar' thing, and, as you say, beat the shit out you, but he wouldn't kill you. You, on the other hand— I mean, killing is your thing. Right?"

"You want somebody killed? I thought you wanted me to scare."

"By killing one person, you can scare a thousand people." The Earth Man spread his arms and smiled.

"You could get a human to do that."

"Yes, but humans are really a nuisance. They always need reasons, justification. On the other hand, a monster—a pishtaco, for example— kills…" The Earth Man waved his hands urging the pishtaco to provide the right words.

"What?"

"For the hell of it."

The pishtaco pulled at his beard and thought. Between two fingers, he cleaned the curved blade of his knife, sheathed it, and replaced his hat. Kneeling in front of his recruit, the Earth Man dipped his head to see the green eyes beneath the brim. "Right?" he asked.

The creature's lips curled into a smirk. He nodded.

"Ready to start?"

The pishtaco stood, adjusted his lasso. Again, he nodded. When he opened the door, the Earth Man's queen was leaning against the jamb, fingering the chain around her throat. Each dared the other to speak. Neither did. The pishtaco craved. Sarah glowered.

Finally, the Earth Man interrupted, slapping the pishtaco's back. "Come on. Let's go make some plans. You got any friends?"

"There's this guy in Mexico."

"Good. Tell me about him." As the Earth Man pushed past his queen, he eyed the bare skin below her throat and chain. "Don't go away," he said. "I'll be back soon."

Sarah lifted her head, her frigid, gray eyes burning into his. "I can hardly wait," she muttered as she slipped past him and shut the door behind her.

6

Arrival

The Land of Great Silence

Counselor breathed to the Word. "Four visions to form a trinity?"

"Yes."

"Trinity is three."

"Yes."

"One will be eliminated?" Counselor asked.

"Trinity is three," came the answer.

Despite the numerical anomaly, no further explanation came. Counselor did not doubt. The Word could not be wrong.

"The people—Some I know."

"Jeannie Jones and her family, the Earth Man and his queen, Frank the weendigo. Yes. You knew them from when you were Art Benson. You are no longer him. They will not know you. They do not need to."

"Brandon Whistler, Chaupi, the pishtaco?"

"You will learn. There is much to know. All is new."

Counselor recalled battles past—different worlds, different weapons, different warriors.

"Your memory is correct, but—" the Word said.

"But?"

"This time the Earth Man has new monsters. As you have seen, the children are young, inexperienced, susceptible to corruption."

"How can I help them?"

"You will be more than human, what you need to be."

Over eons of existence and experience, Counselor had learned better than to question or protest the Word. He fortified himself. "I'm ready," he acceded, awaiting his new incarnation.

Mount Elder
British Columbia, Canada

Whenever Counselor had made the transition from spirit to flesh, sunlight blinded, gravity cramped, and his nerves rattled until his next identity revealed itself. This time, cool air tickled his nostrils.

Stretching his back along the solid ground, he flexed his new muscles, allowing strength to flow from the earth and energize his brain. Around him, he recognized the familiar—blue sky, trees, mountains, rocks. A familiar planet. Earth. He had been here before. He could adjust.

Clumsily, his hand thumped against his elongated nose and startled him. It should not have even though he usually came as lame, blind, or twisted humans. *"The Word said I would not be human,"* he thought. *"So I have a snout, I guess."*

Snuffing and snorting, he rolled to his side and bent his head to examine his new anatomy.

Paws, not hands. Claws, not fingers.

Flipping over onto his back, he stretched and examined his arm.

"I guess that would be a leg. Four legs."

He reached out his long tongue and drew it across one of the limbs. *"Fur, not flesh. White fur. So I'm an animal. What animals have muzzles instead of noses, paws instead of hoofs, and white fur?"*

The names eluded him.

"It's too warm for polar bears. The legs are too fat to be either a cat or wolf. At least I'm a mammal."

He turned onto his wide stomach and crawled out of the brush. Light streamed through the branches above. Snorting loudly, he planted his four feet on the ground, and pushed himself up. Awkwardly, his knees flexed as he stood and shook his round body. He sipped the cool air, rejuvenating his taste buds. A familiar sensation twisted his head, flopping his tongue against the sides of his snout.

"I think I'm thirsty," he decided. *"Is that the feeling?"*

A flapping sound above him, as well as a breeze rippling his hair, startled him.

"Thirsty and hungry." The familiar voice resounded in his brain.

Counselor searched the sky. *"I hear without sound,"* he thought.

"And speak the same way," a pigeon answered, landing in front of him.

Once a shapeless spirit, the bird folded its wings against its chest, the sun sparkling off its iridescent neck.

"The Word," Counselor thought.

The bird bobbed its head.

"Am I to speak?" the mammal asked.

"Yes."

Still tired and stiff, Counselor yawned and massaged his backside against a tree. Turning to the trunk, he used his front claws to pull himself to stand on his hind legs. He stretched all four limbs, then rubbed the top of his head against an overhanging branch. Down the mountain through the trees, he spied glacial green water sparkling in the sunlight.

"If I go to the water, I can see what I am," he told the bird.

"Go," the Word replied.

As the pigeon flew ahead, Counselor huffed and lumbered toward the lake, letting gravity lower him to the shore. At the water's edge, he leaned forward over the mirrored surface to examine his reflection. The bird landed at his side.

"I'm a bear," Counselor said.

"Yes, and you are Counselor."

"Why am I here as an animal?"

"It is right."

"A white bear, but not a polar bear. Am I an albino?"

"No. A white black bear."

"I've not seen this before."

"You will learn," the bird said, then flew into the woods.

The bear nodded and waded into the water. Still unsteady on his feet, he ate what he could easily reach, then lapped up enough water to satisfy his burgeoning thirst.

A sharp sound stung his ears, and a harsh buzzing tingled his nose. He jerked up his head.

Something, someone was out there across the water. Counselor narrowed his eyes and focused on the opening in the trees across the lake. In front of a cluster of cabins, a girl stood on a dock, watching him.

All five senses rushed messages to his brain. He knew her. Jeannie Jones. He rose to his hind legs, waving his front paws and roaring incomprehensibly.

"Careful," the pigeon told him. "She doesn't know or understand you yet."

Far away, the girl rushed off the dock and up the lakefront.

"Jeannie!" Counselor shouted. As he leaped to chase after her, his new muscles twisted and tangled against the defiant water. His massive body swayed once, twice, then splashed sideways into the lake. When he rolled to find footing, water surged through his nose and mouth in an enormous wave that clogged his ears and flooded the shoreline clear to the trees.

Spitting and spewing, the bear slapped at his face and shook his head sharply, falling again backward into the lake. Finally rising to all fours, he shook his head, spraying the air with glittering mist. When he could breathe again, he narrowed his furry brow and confronted the far shore where the girl rushed onto the dock, dragging a man and woman with her.

The bear lowered himself into the water, barely peeking his eyes above the surface. *"Beecher? Amanda? Am I here for them?"* he thought.

He raised his nose above the water and breathed, motionless. Across the lake, the girl pointed toward him, but the adults never saw him. The man kissed the top of the girl's head, then took the woman's hand, walking back into the trees. The girl scanned the lake once more, then disappeared after them.

Counselor sniffed the air, then rose and sloshed back to the shore. The Word stood, waiting.

"Beecher and Amanda Jones?" the bear asked.

The bird nodded.

"The Storyteller and the Flame?"

"At another time, yes."

"I was the Herald."

"The old Trinity. Yes."

"And their daughter Jeannie, older than in the vision."

"Time moves as needed. As I told you, part of the new. The battle to come is the same."

"She is so young."

"She will grow. She will learn."

"What am I to do?"

"Wait. Watch. Be there when she needs."

"And the others?"

"The same."

"That could be forever. What do I do until then?"

The bird fluttered up and landed on the bear's snout. "Time is not an issue. You are a spirit bear. You will eat. Much of the time, you will sleep. In that sleep, you will dream. In those visions, *you* will learn of the Trinity, of their fears, their hopes. When all are ready, you will teach and lead them where they need to be."

"And the battle?"

You will be there when it's over."

"But—"

Without another word, the bird lifted off and called into the woods. The shore behind them bustled with sound and energy. Animals peeked around the trees. Moose. Mountain goats. Deer. Squirrels. Beavers. Rabbits.

"You are here," an unspoken voice said to the bear.

"More speech with no voice," Counselor thought to himself.

"Yes. Yes, I am here," he answered.

"But here?" a deer asked, advancing slowly, one hoof at a time.

"Yes."

The other animals joined the deer and lowered their heads.

A courageous beaver waddled forward and twitched his nose at Counselor. "A spirit bear removed from the ocean or the Sacred Island? We have heard of this, but never seen."

"True, but I belong here," he said to the animals.

"You will eat us?" the rabbit asked.

"No," the bear said, looking up the mountain. "There are places I must go. You will show me."

The animals surrounded him. Testing the air and ground with their noses and feet, they felt his warmth, tasted his breath, knew his heart.

"We will show you," they said, turning to the woods and moving up the hill.

"And I will understand why?" Counselor asked the bird above him.

"You will understand."

Through trees and scattered rocks, Counselor lumbered back up the mountain behind the animals. Below, the squirrels scurried; ahead, the deer slipped through low-hanging limbs; above, the bird soared and flitted ever upward until they all reached the brush where the bear first appeared.

The bird lit on a branch and waited until Counselor arrived, his round body twisting and turning as he searched the woods below and the horizon beyond.

"This is where I awoke. Why are we back here?" he asked the bird.

"This place is for you. To learn, to contemplate, to dream."

"To sleep?"

"To hibernate, yes."

"I just got here."

"Yes, but you have been gone a long time. The world is bigger than it once was. You have changed. People you once knew have changed. People you never met need you to know them."

"The new Trinity."

"Yes. Your vision will reveal what you need to know."

The other animals nodded to the bear and urged him under the brush. Counselor took one last look down the mountain, nodded to the bird, and nosed his way inside to learn what he must.

Michael Frickstad

PART TWO

FOUNDATIONS AND SHIMMERINGS

7

The Life Beneath

Mount Komu ("The Entry")
British Columbia, Canada

Across the valley from Mount Elder, atop the rugged crest of Mount Komu, Sarah twisted her black flowing hair and pulled it tight against her chest, her regal bearing defying the wind that blew cool and strong across the snow-topped peaks and deep green valleys of the Purcell Range. Discounting hundreds of misshapen crags and vast naked slide zones, her steel-gray eyes scoured the landscape for the beauty of liberation.

A beauty that eluded her.

Thousands of years before, the violent earth had shifted and snapped the once strong and majestic Mount Komu in two, one half shattering into shapeless rubble, the other resembling a prone sentry surveilling the Purcells for possible invaders.

"Rage is not beauty," Sarah thought, releasing her hair to the wind. She lowered herself, draped her legs over the cliff, and braced her hands beside her. With her balance secured, she leaned forward over the edge.

Hundreds of feet below, piles of broken rock—the hellish corpses of the ancient avalanche—grappled with the torment of gravity and erosion.

Sarah's chest fluttered as the golden chain around her neck singed and dug into her flesh, the stench crushing her lungs. Gasping, she fell back from the edge, clutching at the hot metal.

With her eyes clenched to prevent the earth from dropping away, she lay on the ground powerless until finally a fresh mountain wind fanned and cooled her skin. Still, the chain tingled in her grip to remind her that although she may already be dead, she still existed. She knew seeking annihilation by jumping to the rocky ghouls below was no escape from the torture; they would not release her. Only the Earth Man could grant that. The chain burned once more and she gulped again for breath, clutching futilely at the ground beneath her.

A single finger brushed a rough stone resting by her thigh. Her reflexes strung tightly, the other fingers snatched the pebble into her fist and pressed it into her palm. Through the life and fate lines of her palm, panic gushed over the stone's curves and corners until, as unruffled as a purring kitten, it eased into her grip and massaged her resistant muscles. As it nestled into her hand's pressure point, her whole body unknotted.

Finally calm and able to breathe, Sarah sat up, raised the stone to her face, and scanned the gem-like years which wind and rain had etched into the surface. Serenely, reverently, the stone rested on her palm—spotless, natural, righteous. The woman weighed its purity in her hand.

Above her, the sky darkened shade by shade. Her eyes narrowed and her mouth stretched thin. As she rose to her feet and braced against the wind, contempt clutched her soul tighter.

Tighter.

Tighter.

In a deafening roar, her fury erupted and she heaved the stone over the cliff into the depths.

Down, it plunged, deeper and deeper into the thickening air, finally disappearing into the grappling rock corpses. The grayness around them flickered with each bounce—once, twice, three times—and then returned to its unwavering gloom.

Sarah waited. Finally, a pop, a click, and a rattle wafted on the breeze up to her. Then, too, the clatter passed into the oblivion of the spectral multitude.

Hanging her head, the woman pulled back from the cliff. Across the valley, Mount Elder and the other mountains rolled in layers across the horizon.

"*Some things never change,*" she thought.

Even though long ago her worldly husband and daughter scattered the ashes of her dead body over Lake Bemidji in northern Minnesota, her present faculties still responded to reality. The colors of sunrise dazzled; the sweetness of fruit, the dark thrill of meat tingled on her tongue; and heights still stunned and enticed her.

The chain tightened. Her thighs shivered. She shook off her contemplation.

"The Earth Man," she said. He had changed the least.

Over millennia as the monarch of evil, he had assaulted the desert and the deep, the mountain and the marsh, to frustrate Good and the all-knowing, all-powerful Word. He chased the vulnerable. He enlisted the hideous. He employed every physical and spiritual weapon at his disposal. Yet his reckless forays gained nothing. The omniverse still endured, unaltered and unruffled.

He and his queen Sarah owned no palace, ruled no land. Their subjects—the matchi-auwishuk (the Ojibwe word for all the evil spirits)—knew nothing of peace or luxury. United in futility, they all existed in the bowels of the earth, secluded amid maze-like caves, rocky crevices, and bottomless swamps, surviving on mayhem and destruction.

Unable to blame himself for his life, he retaliated against her.

The woman sat, scowling at the sky. Absently, she rubbed her faded purple robe between two fingers. She sighed.

One night in the long-ago world, she lay on her deathbed and the Earth Man pledged deliverance from a mutilated face, promising her eternal allure and authority in exchange for her loyalty. She accepted gladly. However, the blessing of his eternal promise turned to curse. The thrill of coronation withered faster than a blink, crumbled to dust, and vanished into the void.

To the Earth Man's credit, she remained beautiful, and for her part, she remained loyal, carrying on as his queen. However, to ensure her devotion, the Earth Man forged her necklace, the gold chain that enslaved her. With it fastened securely about her neck, she could not return to what she once possessed. She could not pursue Life and Truth. She could not envision Possibility.

The gold was effective. When its links of distraction scorched, she tolerated the Earth Man's tirades and infidelities. When the links of avarice strangled, she endured his exploits and failures. When the links of self-persecution gouged, she braved his defeats and revenge. Most destructively, the links of lechery and lust continued to titillate her physical sensibility whenever she smelled the dusky man who once promised her the Orgasm of the Soul.

The wind eased, and she leaned her head back, basking in the sunlight. As the cliff urged her forward, the chain warmed against her skin. She stopped short.

"*Relax, Sarah,*" she thought. "*It only lasts forever.*"

Forever. The word clicked through her mind like the bounding stone, unconnected, softening, haunting.

The necklace cooled. Beneath the hands that supported her, the woman sensed primitive drums and dancing pulsating deep within the mountain. She sighed and stood up. She must go back. She had nowhere else to go.

8

The Fear

Fort Repentance, British Columbia
Canada

Jeannie lay on the window seat of the tower dome high above her parents' house in Fort Repentance, British Columbia. Below her, the city lights began to blink on. Beyond the harbor and foothills, the last rays of sunlight bathed the mountains in a golden orange. Widening shadows crept up the slopes, directing Jeannie's eyes to the darkening sky above her.

Like the city street lights, stars popped to life. One. Five. Thirty. A thousand. A million.

With her throbbing leg bent, her breaths short and erratic, she closed her eyes and dreamt of flying through the vast emptiness from planet to planet, star to star, galaxy to galaxy. Traveling faster than light, faster than thought, farther and farther through the nebulae and void into forever.

That word.

Forever.

Right now she couldn't even stand and walk across the room.

Somewhere in forever.

She opened her eyes and gazed at the materializing constellations overhead.

When her family had moved to Canada, her father Beecher offered to make her room unique. Unlike anything in Fort Repentance. Unlike anything in Canada. Unlike anything back in the States.

He had expected her to ask for posters and special furniture, not a tower topped by a glass dome. "What eight-year-old girl wants a tower with a glass dome?" he asked.

"Me!"

When Beecher asked why, his wife Amanda hugged the girl's shoulders and explained, "To make the sky and forever home."

A smile spread across his daughter's freckled face and her red pigtails bobbed up and down. He recognized the truth of his wife's words.

So he built Jannie a tower and a dome. For good measure, he outfitted the room with a telescope he had as a child and taught her to love the stars. Particularly the North Star. Polaris. Patiently, he had shown her how to use Ursa Major and Ursa Minor—The Great and Little Bear—the Big and Little Dipper—to find the star because, as he explained, "Polaris is a guide. Think of it as God trying to help us find our way here on earth and in the future."

She loved her father. When she told him she wasn't sure she believed in the God of Superman and Santa Claus, he didn't scold or preach. Instead, he pointed the telescope at the moon and let her discover. Slowly, she panned the lens across the bright lunar surface. When the light plummeted into the emptiness of space, she gasped, her knees buckled, and her puny butt plopped to the floor.

"God *isn't* Superman or Santa Claus. I was right!" she exclaimed, dazed and groggy. "God is… God is *Forever!*"

When her father smiled and nodded, Jeannie realized another truth. "That's where Mom is," she said.

Although her mother had been dead for years, Beecher and Amanda let her believe.

That was long before her injury. Now, if they would just come help her stand up…

Pain jabbed at her knee. Jeannie grimaced and her jaw trembled. *"What did I do wrong?"* she thought. *"I didn't trip. I didn't twist anything. I just stood up and—"*

"It doesn't matter," she said, resting an arm across her face.

Slowly, the crippling, shrill stab eased to a tolerable, dull ache.

Outside, the sun dipped below the horizon and the harbor to the west, while stars twinkled to life in the blackening sky above the tower's dome.

"That stupid Langley bitch," she thought.

Despite assurances of doctors and therapists, the collision had ended Jeannie's soccer career. Since that night, abrupt, debilitating spasms wrenched her knee without warning, knotting every muscle between her thigh and toes.

Jeannie shuddered and wiped the sweat beaded on her forehead. She sank into the softness of the window seat.

The attacks usually lasted only minutes and disappeared as soon as the knee popped back into place, but they were excruciating. Over the year, she had endured and kept most of them secret, hoping they'd vanish all together. Tonight was the worst since the accident.

She groaned, struggling to straighten her leg. "God, that hurts."

On her back, she faced the darkening sky above her. Clouds swerved and swelled nervously across the pink, orange, and gray of evening. Jeannie's chest tightened.

"Breathe. Just breathe."

Clutching her hands over her stomach, she inhaled slowly, deeply until her heartbeat eased and her joints relaxed. Abruptly, the knee snapped and loosened, allowing Jeannie to slowly lower her whole leg to the window seat. "Thank you!" she said, closing her eyes and resting.

No matter how completely her torso relaxed, no matter how she calmed her muscles and bones, her brain still needled. She could not shut it off.

Frustrated, she sat up, leaned against the windowsill, and watched the final city lights flicker to life in the faded afterglow.

Cautiously, she massaged her leg, kneading the thigh and working her hands down to the knee. Although still tender, the tense muscles eased under her grip. Emboldened, she thought, *"Maybe just a step or two."*

Gingerly, she lowered her feet to the floor and turned to the lamp.

Before she could reach the switch, light burst through the room, obliterating the world. Jeannie dropped back to the seat, blinded and stunned. Desperately, she clenched her eyes, but the light punctured her consciousness, glaring into the cracks and crevices of her brain. Gasping and writhing, she watched helplessly as the light sucked the color from the world, gold to red, red to blue, then splintering into black nothingness.

In the silent dark, Jeannie held her breath, waiting. When nothing happened, she carefully grabbed her arm to assure herself she still existed.

Her grip convinced her.

She could feel. She could think. She just could not see.

When she finally chanced a breath, a new reality flared before her.

The stark, glass and steel skyscrapers of Fort Repentance vanished and a different city emerged. A city where low, multicolored adobe buildings— beige, tangerine, peacock, turquoise, black—lined a cracked and abandoned street. Wooly white clouds bashed and billowed into a cobalt sky. In the distance, a brown and white, twin-steepled cathedral loomed above a deserted plaza of flattened cacti and enrobed, faceless statues.

"What—? Where—?"

The unfamiliar world swirled around her, expanding, shrinking, twisting, turning, stretching, drawing her deeper into the city.

"It's too—too—too fantastic. Bizarre. Real. Too everything!"

Jeannie knew the town existed. However, she could not exist in it. She could only watch. She could not move, no matter what she saw. She saw more than she wanted.

A noonday heat stifled, emptying the street and shuttering the windows.

Outside El Loco Lobo, a decayed cantina, the thirsty Oaxaca sun lapped at the fading remnants of brown paint surrounding the heavy wooden door. Decorative iron grates over the boarded glass sagged and pulled at their rotting anchors in a vain attempt to escape the heat and light. The salt-pocked walls cracked and crumbled. Fine dirt clumps broke off and slid noiselessly to the sidewalk below. In the recessed entrance, a scruffy, old dog wheezed into the cool shadow and lay on the rotting floorboards, its nose burrowed into the darkness.

Inside, Guillermo, the dull owner/bartender/waiter, shuffled to the door and cracked the skylight, allowing a narrow shaft of light to angle across the dusty room and dimly lit bar area.

"¿Cuál es el punto?" he wondered. *What's the point?* It would be a slow day.

They were all slow days.

Once, he had cared. Back when El Loco Lobo promised success and security and he had believed. Back when words equaled truth. Back when ambition conquered failure. Before the dullness and heat sapped all the energy from the building. And him.

Guillermo looked around the vacant room. The empty tables confirmed what he already knew. What his father had always told him.

"Too far from the tourists," the cynical old man had warned him. "Too far off the Zócalo, too far from Santo Domingo or Monte Alban, too far from the money. El Lobo es muerto." *Dead.*

"You keep saying that," Guillermo said. "Why?"

"There is no future there."

"But, Father, the cantina has been in Oaxaca as long as I've been alive."

"And now it is dead. The songs, the dreams, the ghosts have gone."

Guillermo gazed across the dark room. He snorted and wandered back to the bar where, defiant of the cantina's financial state, he poured himself a beer. Even that was dusty. Disgusted, he wet a towel and wiped the bar for the third time since unlocking the doors only an hour before. Then, he drenched the towel again, this time with cold water, and wiped the sweat from his face.

The door latch clicked.

Before he could look up, chills bristled Guillermo's neck. His hands stopped and he raised his head.

Across the room, a tall, emaciated man dressed all in black slipped into the darkness of the decaying cantina. A wide-brimmed hat hid his face's features. Still, the sunken red eyes, the skeletal cheekbones, and the thin, translucent skin penetrated the shadow. Long strands of desiccated hair straggled out from the hat and across the man's shoulders. In one hand, the man lightly carried a shoulder-length walking stick more as decoration than support.

Guillermo's throat caught.

His father's tales of a mystic guide leading people through the spiritual world, the legends of his tribe's shaman, echoed and flickered through Guillermo's brain.

"*The Seer? It cannot be. Too young. Too real*—" he thought.

A deep cough wracked his lungs until his eyes watered. Shaken, he set down his towel, waited for the man to speak, and prayed that he would leave instead.

The man did neither. He said nothing. Not a muscle moved, not even to inspect his surroundings.

Guillermo waited, his heart pounding in his chest.

After a moment, the man simply pulled his hat lower, crossed the room, set his pole against the wall, and took a booth in a corner where he could watch the door.

Guillermo swallowed, then reluctantly grabbed a drink menu. Scratching at his bare arm, he edged toward the man, knees bent ready to flee. Before he could say a word, the man curtly ordered, "Una cerveza," and dismissed him.

Relieved and terrified at the same time, Guillermo escaped to the bar, poured a glass of beer, served it, and abandoned the man to the gloom. Back at the bar, he pretended to read a three-day-old periódico, occasionally glancing up at the man across the room. Guillermo's neck still crawled with chills.

Meanwhile, the man held his glass in both his pale hands, staring steadily at the door, willing and daring another customer to come in.

The old dog wheezed as the door opened. Guillermo set down his periódico and squinted at the form standing in the dusty light.

A mestizo. A mix of native and European.

More European, Guillermo guessed, given his height, luminous skin, and thick beard.

Unlike the cautious, unapproachable tall man sitting in the corner booth, the mestizo brazenly burst into the room. Dressed all in khaki, he exuded confidence. One hand on the coiled rope on his belt and the other wrapped around the hilt of a knife, he quickly surveyed the room. His face brightened as he spied the tall man's long legs protruding from the booth.

He closed the door, then strode to join the other man. Sliding behind the table, he pushed himself back against the wall. Haughtily, he threw an arm over the booth back, and, like his counterpart, raised his legs onto the seat. Like the other man's, his boots dangled over the end of the bench. Smugly, he pulled off his felt hat, blew away the dust, then hung it on the corner of the table. He wiped his face with his neckerchief before shaking out his thick hair and combing his long fingers through it.

Before the shivering Guillermo could even move, the mestizo glanced at the first man, smiled and called for a beer as well.

Reluctantly, Guillermo poured the drink and brought two lunch menus to the table. "Tienen hambre?" he mumbled at the two men, his eyes fixed on the floor. *Are you hungry?*

The mestizo stroked his long beard without turning from the thin man and smiled. "No lo creo." *I don't think so.*

The menus leapt from Guillermo's hands, landing and sliding across the floor. Hastily, Guillermo set the mestizo's drink on the table and grappled for the two menus, stammering, "Okay. Okay. Gracias. Muchas gracias."

The very atmosphere around the men hissed and growled at Guillermo until he scurried back to the safety of the bar.

With Guillermo gone, the mestizo dropped his feet to the floor and faced the skeletal man. He crossed his arms in front of himself, his green eyes peering beneath the other's hat. The cadaverous skull beneath smiled, then its emaciated body sat back and raised the brim. The skull gazed back with glowing red eyes.

The two exchanged no words. Only thoughts.

At the bar, Guillermo nervously wiped the glasses, furtively watching the silent men.

The dimness, protective of the cantina's owner, spoke to him of the mestizo's lasso and the tall man's walking stick. The chill of the thin man's small, silver blade and the mestizo's curved knife numbed Guillermo's arms. The anxious bartender reached under the bar and rubbed the baseball bat he had hidden for protection.

Occasionally, one of the men tilted his head as if questioning the other, then nodded in understanding. The other always smiled viciously. Neither spoke.

"Están tramando algo," Guillermo thought. *They're plotting something.* Just what or how, he didn't know. He didn't care. He just wanted them to leave.

Suddenly, a *thock* echoed from the table. The mestizo laughed loudly and shook the tall man's bony hand. He stood up and waved to Guillermo. "Él va a pagar." *He'll pay.*

Guillermo nodded darkly and returned to the periódico.

The mestizo swaggered out of the room and into the heat of the day. Relieved, Guillermo sighed and shook his head. The danger had left. He returned to wiping the bar glasses.

A crash, a whoosh, a shriek rattled the windows and walls.

A rotting smell engulfed Guillermo. Before he could scream, before he could think, he saw—the skeletal face, the straggling hair, the sunken red eyes, the clenched teeth, the walking stick swinging toward his head.

The glass in Guillermo's hand shattered to the floor as the unspoken words echoed in the dusty air: "It doesn't matter."

Two boys kicking a soccer ball heard the ancient dog barking from the open door of El Loco Lobo.

It was they who found Guillermo's butchered corpse. It was they who called la policía. It was they who spread the forbidden facts: the severed finger on the table, the owner's mutilation, his missing liver.

The monsters' names—pishtaco, baykok—went unspoken. The fear spread on its own.

In darkness, a voice—not her conscience, but a real voice—spoke to Jeannie. "There will be more."

She slid to the floor and grasped at the carpet. "What?" she whispered.

"What you saw, what you heard, what you felt. There will be more."

She desperately searched the room for the source of the words.

"More locked knees. More Shimmerings. More visions. More places. More people. Those you know. Those you must know. More."

The words did not originate outside her. They coursed through her until she felt and saw.

"Shimmering. Is that what that was?"

"Yes."

"I'm only fourteen. I don't want more."

Suddenly, images of Guillermo, the mestizo and the tall thin man flitted across the sky, expanding, swirling, flashing—brighter, faster, harsher—driving Jeannie back to the floor.

Replacing them were a mountain, a boy, a man, her mother, a bear, a bird, herself—exploding, crashing, torturing, tearing—and then they stopped.

Cautiously, Jeannie rose and sat on the window seat.

Outside, city lights twinkled yellow, green, and red, and streaked paths through scattering clouds to the stars above Jeannie's dome. She turned to the northern sky as the unmistakeable shape of the Great Bear peeked through the shadows. Automatically, she located the pointer stars and found Polaris.

She covered her mouth with a hand and pulled her lips together.

"There will be more," the voice said.

She exhaled shakily, then delicately rose, guarding her fragile knee. The Great Bear twinkled above her as she shuffled to the circular stairway and disappeared down the hole to her bedroom.

9

Diversions and Distractions

Winthrop, Michigan
USA

At the Winthrop-Elysium football game, Brandon sprawled across three seats in the corner of the bleachers above the band, self-exiled from the crowd. In his light tan jacket and a dark blue Milwaukee Brewers baseball cap, he defied the chilled air and dared anybody to approach him. Winthrop's social convention may say the field was the place to be on a Friday night, but Brandon's turned up collar and curled lip said, "School is worthless shit. Football? Pansy bait that lets guys play grab-ass."

"At least it has cheerleaders," he thought.

And cheerleaders had tits.

Especially Nancy Kirkman.

Senior.

Everybody in school loved Nancy Kirkman. Outside her space bubble, girls fawned on and copied her shoulder-length hair, her smile, the lilt in her walk. Boys gawked and whispered.

Brandon pulled at his tightening crotch. Since his mother died and his father boozed everything away, he didn't talk to anybody. He simply dreamed of Nancy Kirkman and tried to hide his perpetual hard-on.

While he watched Nancy on the sidelines pumping her fists to rouse the crowd, the club pendant he stole from his mother's jewelry chest warmed his chest.

Hiding his eyes under the brim of his cap and tugging his jacket over his lap, Brandon squirmed. He fantasized about her and jacked off whenever he could, but he had no delusions his hopes would ever be realized. He barely had eight whiskers on his cheeks and maybe twice that many on his balls. Plus, he was a freshman loner with no money, no family, no name. She was everything. He was nothing.

He still wanted her.

At halftime of a scoreless game while the band broke into the school song, Nancy and the other cheerleaders waved their pompoms and barked lyrics no one could hear. Brandon refused to stand. He simply raised his cap above his eyes and strained to see around the bundled bodies and clapping mittens. He had to watch Nancy. Despite the players, the band, and the other cheerleaders, there was no one and nothing else to see.

He didn't realize anyone was watching him.

After the song ended and the fans yelled *Gooooooo, Wolves*, Nancy rushed to the restraining rope and beckoned Brandon's classmate Toni Sharpe. Brandon faux-ignored the two as Nancy covered her mouth and spoke into the shocked clarinet player's ear. He simply closed his eyes and rested his head on the back fence, waiting for the kickoff. His chest jumped into his throat when Toni brazenly thumped up the steps and dropped next to him.

Brandon grabbed the railing next to him and pulled himself up. Toni turned away refusing to look at him. Instead, she twisted her mouth and huffed.

"I can't believe I'm doing this," she said, sniffing back the cold, thin snot dripping from her nose. She forced herself to turn and glare directly at Brandon. "What are you doing after the game?"

"I—uh—I guess I'm going home."

Toni shifted violently. "No, you're not. Listen. I think you're a loser. This is not for me."

Brandon sat up and examined the bundled mass next to him. "*I'm a loser?*" he challenged .

"Yes! Always by yourself, pissed off about something. Hell! Everything! I swear you're gonna blow up the school some day, but what I think doesn't matter to some people."

She shook her head, disgusted.

When she couldn't talk, Brandon snarled, "What?"

Toni wrapped her arms around her chest and said, "Okay. Here's the deal. You know how to get beneath the bleachers?"

Brandon shrugged. "I guess."

"After the game, go there. Somebody wants to talk to you. Somebody you want to talk to. Someone everybody wants to talk to."

A whistle blew on the field, and immediately the cheerleaders began a cheer. Brandon glanced at them.

Toni backhanded his chest. "Did you hear me? Somebody wants to talk to you. A girl!"

"Yeah? Why doesn't she just ask me?"

"'Cause she's got a reputation, dipshit. And so do you. People wouldn't understand. So meet her under the bleachers after the game."

"Meet who?"

Toni shook her head. "Nancy Kirkman."

Brandon's jaw dropped. "Nan—"

Toni backhanded him again. "Shut up! Nobody's supposed—Just— Just be there. Okay?"

"I—I don't know."

"You don't know?! All the boys would give their left nut just to have her say their name and you don't know? You're gonna be there or I'll cut your dick off. Got it?"

Her enraged eyes shook Brandon's cold shoulders. He nodded sheepishly.

"Okay," she said. "This has been a weird night. I'm going home."

Brandon shifted in his seat as Toni clomped down the bleachers. He glanced around, then settled back to endure the final half.

On-field, the game fell apart. With three minutes left to play, Elysium, winless in every sport for five years, led 64-0. Fans dwindled to a handful of frustrated parents, the gloating Elysium alumni, and the stalwart Winthrop cheerleaders.

And Brandon Whistler.

With one minute remaining, he slipped to the loose fence covering the end of the stands and edged underneath. Streaks of light filtered through the planks and beams, mutating the murkiness into a ghastly maze. Cloaked in shadow, Brandon huddled against a support and peered out the wooden slats at the cursing remnants of the Winthrop crowd.

When the final whistle blew, Nancy flung her pompoms at the first row and slumped onto the seat. She leaned forward, elbows on her thighs, and peered at the ground. She did not move. She did not speak.

Although the cold and the wooden bleachers separated them, the heat of her breath staggered him. Tentatively, he reached a shivering hand forward and touched the bench where she sat. Without looking, she reached back and covered his bare flesh with her wool mitten.

Neither saw the other. Neither moved.

The other cheerleaders and the last fans mumbled their goodbyes and slumped to their cars. Nancy still did not move. Far off, the field supervisor yelled, "I'm gonna turn off the lights, Nancy."

"Yeah, okay. There's a full moon. I'll be fine. Just a few more minutes."

The bright lights popped off and Nancy sat motionless, staring at the ground.

When the final cars drifted away, she stood and surveyed the empty field. Her silhouette in the moonlight simultaneously chilled and warmed. Then, she slipped around the bleachers and asked quietly, "Brandon?"

He hugged himself against the cold and shivered. "Yeah."

The chain link barrier rattled as she squeezed into the dark. Brandon weaved his way around the supports to her perfume.

"Here I am," he mumbled.

She followed his voice, bouncing and rubbing the leather arms of her letter jacket. When she found him, she wrapped an arm around his waist and rested her head on his shoulder.

"Football really sucks. You know that?"

Unsure what to do with his hands, Brandon searched the shadows for anybody else who had heard the blasphemy. His chest shuddered. "Yeah. I guess," he mumbled.

Nancy held him closer, then asked, "So. How're you doing?"

Brandon's head lightened as her body thawed his icy limbs. His penis strained against his jeans. His mother's pendant heated his chest. Timidly, he reached around her and held her loosely. "Fine. I guess."

She pulled him closer.

"A little confused?"

He looked down at the top of her head. He didn't remember being taller. "Um—Yeah. I guess."

"You gotta be someplace?"

"Well—uh—My dad's at an AA meeting. I'm supposed to meet him so he can drive me home."

Nancy touched his elbow. "Donnie Whistler, right?"

"Yeah."

In the darkness, her eyes searched his. Her right hand reached up and caressed his face. Brandon's jaw trembled.

"Follow me."

Outside, they ducked through a small opening in the brush and into the woods. A leafless path led around the outskirts of town to the alley behind Shorty's Bar. "I need to show you something," she said. "Stay out of the light so we don't attract attention."

She bent at the waist and led him, hunching and weaving through the parking lot until she found Donald Whistler's Ford.

Brandon straightened and glared in silence.

Nancy examined his puffed and glowering face. "You knew he wasn't at AA, didn't you?"

"Not for sure, but—How'd *you* know?"

Nancy took a deep breath. "Because the Toyota next to it is my mom's. They've been here a lot lately."

Brandon scrutinized her face.

"Mom's had—this problem for a long time. For months, she told us she was going to AA. She'd leave maybe three times a week, then get home late after my dad and I went to bed. Something didn't seem right. And then—"

She slid down the side of the Toyota and sat on the cold, hard ground. She wiped at her eyes.

"Some of the girls and I were driving around after practice one night, and Mom drove right past us. She was supposed to be at a meeting. She said she had a meeting."

Nancy bounced a fist off the ground at her side.

"So I followed her, and she ended up here. Parked next to this car, and—this guy gets out. They—They get real friendly-like and go into the bar."

Brandon leaned against his father's car, shivering. He wished he had a letter jacket like Nancy. The two examined the ground without speaking. Music thudded inside the building over the cackling laughter of unseen patrons.

"I asked if any of the girls knew who the guy was. Andrea told me it was your dad."

Brandon looked to the dark sky and saw his drunken father lying on the couch, snorting and slobbering, while in the farmhouse across the yard, his mother killed herself.

Gagging, he clenched his fists and sat next to Nancy. He slapped his baseball cap on the ground, wiped the back of a hand across his mouth and nose, then rested his arms on his knees. Blinking back the tears, he hid his face from Nancy

"No perfect families, right?" she said.

Brandon's chin quivered and his teeth chattered. "Did you tell your dad?"

Nancy laughed. "Hell, no. It was already bad enough."

She pressed her mouth against her knees. "Did you know there is no AA in Winthrop? The nearest chapter is in Grayson."

Brandon bit his lower lip, his breath erratic and strained.

Nancy held his arm. "It doesn't do any good to get mad or try to get back at them. They don't get it. They're sick."

Brandon gazed between the parked cars to the thumping bar. "He's done this before. The whole married woman thing."

"I kind of thought so."

He reached under his collar and pulled out his mother's necklace and held out the pendant. "Do you know what this symbol is? My mom used to wear it."

Nancy nodded. "Aphrodite or Venus. Goddess of Love. Beauty. Sex."

Brandon leaned his head back against the Toyota. "I guess that makes sense."

"The Aphrodite and Adonis Society," she said. "It's a club. They wear these medallions and—they share themselves. Your father has a medal something like hers, doesn't he?"

Brandon's breath drifted in a thin fog above them. He nodded. "Now what am I supposed to do?"

Nancy adjusted her Wolves headband. "Come on. I'll give you a ride home. I want to show you something."

Neither spoke on the walk back to school nor inside Nancy's Honda Civic. Not when they pulled out of the parking lot. Not when they left the city limits. Not even when Nancy turned off the road to Oakley's gravel pit.

In silence, the Civic wound down the truck path into the excavation. At the bottom, Nancy switched off the headlights, driving in the yellow glow of her parking lights through the piles of sand and rock. She pulled the car around the mound away from other darkened vehicles and switched off the engine. With both hands on the wheel, she breathed deeply, then pulled off her headband and combed her fingers through her blond hair. Sliding down, she laid her head on the seat back and with a lazy hand unsnapped the top two buttons of her letter jacket.

Bewildered, Brandon checked left, right, and behind the car.

Next to a second mound, a dark pickup bounced and rocked in the shadows.

"Are they—?"

Nancy patted his thigh gently. Brandon looked from his leg to her closed eyes. Softly, her hand fell to the seat and rested by her side. Her breathing became slow and steady.

Brandon glanced at the pickup. Reaching over, he gently touched her hand. "Nancy?"

"Hm?"

"What were you going to show me?"

She opened her eyes, then wrapped her hand around his. Brandon felt his face redden, and he turned to his side window.

"Look at me," she whispered.

Brandon inspected the sheer wall of dirt that led to the woods above.

"Look at me," she insisted.

Brandon reluctantly turned his head to her.

69

"I know all the shit you're going through," she said. "Your grandpa dying. Your mom. Now this with your dad. You're pissed."

Brandon inspected the floorboards beneath his feet. His mouth twisted. Nancy reached over and rubbed his back.

"You should be. The whole world is pissed," she said. "About a lot of things. But most of us find ways to deal with it."

Brandon shook his head. "Things like what?"

"What I brought you here for."

She unbuttoned the rest of her jacket and pulled it off.

Monday morning, Nancy found Brandon in the hall of Winthrop High before classes. She looked around them, then grabbed his arm. "Let's go in here," she said, pulling him into the biology lab.

"Is something wrong? I mean if I did something wrong Friday night—"

"Brandon, you were great. No. Nothing bad. In fact, that's what I wanted to talk to you about. Here. Sit."

The two settled onto their separate stools, facing each other. A lightness stirred Brandon's belly. Nancy quickly checked to make sure the room was empty, then leaned close to him. She reached out and laid a hand on his thigh. "Here's why. Remember when I told you a lot of us are pissed and had ways of dealing?"

"Uh—yeah."

"You know Carol Ellison?"

Brandon nodded and cocked his head, warily.

"Denise Rentz? Kristin Zolnowski? Them too?"

Again, he nodded.

"Rachel McDonald?"

"Um—"

"Maybe you don't know her. She's younger than you. She's an eighth grader."

"Oh, McDonald! Mr. McDonald's daughter."

"It doesn't matter who she's related to. The important thing is those girls are pissed just like us. I want to introduce you to them."

Brandon started to speak, but realized he had nothing to say. Nancy took his hand and squeezed it. "It's an opportunity," she said. "A great opportunity."

Brandon shook his head. "I already know who they are. 'cept for that Rachel girl. And isn't—Didn't Carol Ellison graduate?"

Nancy shook her head. "Yes. You know who they are. They know who you are, but I want them to know you as I do."

The words struck Brandon hard. Unexpected, but welcome. "Because after Friday, you and I are—like—? I mean, sure. If you want to be—Yeah. Great!"

Nancy held up a hand. "No. No. Wait. You think I want us to be boyfriend and girlfriend?"

"Isn't that what you—"

Nancy took both of Brandon's hands. "Brandon, I want them to—KNOW—you."

Bewildered, Brandon shook his head.

"I mean I want you to explore gravel pits together."

She held his gaze.

Stunned, Brandon leaned forward and rubbed the tabletop absently. "You don't want—me?"

"It's not that. It's—" Nancy leaned her head into her hands. "Brandon, Friday was your first time. We were just dealing. It was just sex."

Brandon pulled at his shirt and stretched his neck. "I really thought—"

Nancy patted his hand and shook her head. Brandon blinked and scratched his elbow. Darkly, he turned away and explored the floor.

Nancy raised his face. "You wanted a relationship. I get it. I've been there. My first time—the guy dumped me without even saying goodbye. Thought I'd die."

"What did you do?"

"I fucked somebody else."

"Did it help?

Nancy shrugged. "I got what I needed."

"What was that?"

"A distraction."

Brandon folded his hands on the table. "Did it help?"

"Not the way I wanted. I was stupid and thought fucking would make somebody love me, but it didn't. That's when I decided just to take what I could get. No expectation, no fantasies."

"And that's what those girls want?"

Nancy nodded. "A distraction. Right. Brandon, nobody *needs* a relationship. Oh, we're told we do, but nobody even wants one. Especially when life is fucked. I mean look at your parents with their Aphrodite and Adonis club. No expectations. No complications. Just sex."

Brandon grimaced. "Sharing."

Nancy patted his thigh. "Right."

Brandon bit his lip and sat motionless. "I really think I—" he started.

She reached out and stroked his cheek. "Love me? Brandon, we're not even real people yet. We don't know love from too much chili."

"So you're dumping me." He gazed at the floor beneath his legs.

Nancy held his arm. "No. I'm postponing you. In the meantime, there are these girls."

He held the his mother's medallion in his hand. The metal tingled. Glancing at Nancy, he stuffed it under his collar.

He wrung his hands and scanned the room. His eyes stopped on the stuffed bird above the storage cabinets. He flinched and rubbed his legs, remembering the bird in his yard.

"What is empty?"

"EVERYTHING! Everything's empty."

He pushed harder and harder against his thigh.

"What about the girls, Brandon? We only have a couple minutes."

"There is more to life than now. *Now is settling,"* the bird had said.

He heard the words and bit his lips.

"Well?"

Brandon looked to the ceiling, then to Nancy. "Introduce me."

10

A Vision of Death and Drunks

Fort Repentance, British Columbia
Canada

Jeannie scowled at her tray as she crossed the Harbor Mist High School cafeteria. Fish sticks. Mashed potatoes and melted butter. A peach half. Milk.

"A masterpiece in yellow and white. Disgusting!" Her freckled forehead crinkled.

"And a little brown," she added, pushing at the fish sticks with a finger. "Might as well eat sand."

Her high, tight red ponytail bounced and swished as she hunted for an empty table away from the cliques and clowns. She had long ago had enough of people who had enough of her. Squeezing through the chattering, chewing mass, she searched for the overlooked spot stashed in the far corner of the platform that led to the school auditorium.

Squinting through the crowd, she spied the table's blue vinyl top inviting her like an old friend, cool and comfortable. Jeannie relaxed her forehead and wormed her way through the maze.

Jeannie's pursuit of solitude did not come of weakness or reserve. In fact, the Shimmering vision of Mexico, as well as countless nightmares, had

73

inspired her to begin a covert strength-building regime to rehabilitate her trick knee. The daily excursion across the packed cafeteria and the steep steps boosted her balance and dexterity, while the table's remote location allowed her to perform covert isometric exercises to strengthen the muscle.

From the platform a powerful female voice barked at the whole cafeteria. "Boys! Food is for eating, not throwing. Don't even think about it."

The room erupted in laughter. The three boys sitting by the base of the stairs lowered their hands and hunched over their trays.

"Oh, I see you," the woman called. "You think you can hide from me? Uh-uh!"

"Morning, Mrs. Roche," Jeannie said as she passed between the boys and the woman on the platform.

Jeannie's art teacher and cafeteria monitor, Mrs. Roche was a tall black woman who wore a perpetually paint-spattered apron that barely covered her wide frame. She feebly disguised her bright personality with a pasted-on frown and gruff voice.

"Morning, Miss Jones. Wait a minute. What do you have there?"

Bracing her hands on her knees, she bent forward, lowered the glasses on her nose and peered over them. "Mmmm. Fish sticks. And potatoes. Looks positively—" The adjective eluded her.

"Beige," Jeannie said, climbing the three steps and setting her tray on the table.

Mrs. Roche leaned back and laughed. "Well, bon appetite," she said, smacking her wide, dark lips. "Mm-mm-mm."

"Thanks." Jeannie crossed behind the table and faced the lunchroom. She crawled over the bench, but before her foot even reached the floor, the table attacked her.

Her bad knee clanked off the support, and she collapsed onto the bench. The rebellious joint instantly locked, and Jeannie clutched the side of the table. "Oh, God!" she whimpered, swallowing the agony. Her jaw shook uncontrollably.

"It's not just the pain," she thought. It was the words she heard after that night in her tower: *"There will be more."* It was the images of Mexican monsters and a dead bartender. It was that first Shimmering.

"Not here," she whispered. "Please!"

Tears blurred her eyes as she looked across the cafeteria and waited. "Don't look at me. Don't look at me," she silently ordered the inattentive crowd.

Above the noise and clamor, the fluorescent lights flickered. The adolescent bodies vibrated and blurred.

"*Here it comes,*" Jeannie thought. The cafeteria faded as she crossed her arms on the table and buried her head in them. The vision engulfed her.

Inside a dark room of a decaying ranch house on a Michigan farm, the pushbutton lock popped open, the door jolted, then it silently swung open. A scowling, boy about Jeannie's own age, sneaked into the room and waited, expecting something or someone to move. Finally unable to hold his breath, he whispered, "Dad?"

When nobody answered, the boy closed the door behind him and turned on the lights. "It's all wrong," he said as he explored the contents. Obviously, nobody was there, but somebody had been.

"*The bed—it's too precisely made. The pillows are too fancy, too fluffy, too just right. Although nobody's slept here in months.*"

The boy haltingly opened the closest. It only held his mother's clothes hanging straight, precise. "*That's wrong, too,*" he thought. "*She was never that neat. She would never categorize by season. Sure as fuck not my dad. Probably Lacey before she and Sean moved away.*"

On the bedside table sat his mother's Brewers cap, its bill askew atop a baseball glove wrapped around three balls stuffed into its pocket. The glove was also his mother's.

"*Lacey knew she loved baseball.*"

Brandon detested it. No matter how hard his mother had tried to convert him when she was alive. He did like the cap, however. He even had one of his own. Even though he hated Milwaukee.

He hated lots of places. Lots of things. Lots of people.

Setting the cap backward on his head, he placed two of the balls between the fancy pillows while he gently tossed the third in one hand.

He put on the glove, but found it stiff, resistant to movement. "Did she even try to break in the pocket?" he asked aloud. "Shit."

His mother had taught him that a week of sleepless nights with a glove wrapped and stuffed under your mattress, then countless hours of slamming baseballs into the webbing would loosen the leather enough to play catch effortlessly.

"Evidently she had other things to do," he thought.

He sat on the bed and threw the baseball into his mother's glove.

Thwack! Leather slapped on leather. The sound, the impact felt good. He threw harder.

Thump! The sound snapped louder. His wrist twisted and sprained. Still, he threw again. "Harder!" he commanded himself. "Throw it harder!"

Whack! Again! Again! He couldn't stop. He didn't want to. Each throw intensified.

Thwack! Thump! Whack!

Faster and harder, he hurled the ball into the glove, his face twisting and twitching. His thumb and forefinger, the whole palm of his glove hand ached and stung until the glove was no longer leather. Each throw was a different face, and the boy rejoiced each time the ball slammed into the webbing.

First, into his father's head. Then, his grandfather's. His mother's. Flinging. Moaning. Loathing.

His furious face sweaty and grotesque, he jammed the ball into the glove one last time, shoving it deeper and deeper, leather upon leather, vengeance upon vengeance, rage upon rage.

Grimacing, he removed both glove and ball from his hand, then wedged them between the mattress and boxspring. With a lung-shattering roar, he jumped on the bed again and again, harder and higher, crushing every person he ever cared for.

"Brandon?" a shaky voice called from the mirror hanging on the back of the door. "Brandon, are you okay?"

"Mom?" The boy's head jerked up. In the glass he saw a yawning, waking woman wiping her forearm across her eyes, her mousy brown hair clinging to her face.

"You never even liked the game, did you?" his mother said.

The boy sheepishly rescued the glove and tossed it on the bed. He kneaded his hands together as he sat guiltily staring at the floor. "Sorry," he mumbled.

Although they had talked this way many times since her death, sitting silently, absorbing each other's presence, they had never done so in her room.

"Are you okay, honey?"

The boy said nothing. He loved the sound of his mother's voice.

"Missing Grandpa?" she asked.

Of course, he did, but he bit his lip and shook his head. Light from the mirror brightened the floor. He breathed in his mother's freshness, energy, and life.

"Me?"

Leaning forward over his knees, he sniffed and hid his face.

"It's all right to miss people when they're gone."

The boy's shoulders shook and he struggled for breath.

"Your father?"

Brandon paused, then looked up at the mirror and his mother's face. "He still sleeps on the couch. I don't miss him that much."

"Yes, you do. He's not what you wanted. Or needed. You're upset."

Brandon's face twisted and tensed. "I'm more than upset. I'm pissed."

"I don't like that word, but I understand. You're pissed because he's drunk and most of the time he's gone. You're pissed because you don't know what to do."

Sucking in his lower lip, Brandon blinked back tears.

"And you're pissed because you want to protect me even now. I know how you feel and you don't like that either."

"It's not that. It's—"

The boy turned away and clutched at something under his shirt.

"What?" the mother asked.

He crossed to the dresser and rested his chin on his hands. He avoided his mother behind him as he searched for words. His mother waited patiently, then uttered, "Me and your father."

Brandon thought a moment, then in a low voice asked, "Mom, why did we come here? To Winthrop? In the Middle of Jesus Christ Nowhere, Michigan? Why did we leave Madison?"

The woman examined her son's back. "Brandon, it had nothing to do with you."

He turned and pulled the pendant from his shirt. "Did it have to do with this?"

She closed her eyes, breathing deeply.

"A friend of mine says this is a symbol for a sex club or something. Was it for you and Dad?"

The woman gazed at the pendant with blank eyes.

"Was it?" Brandon insisted.

The woman raised her hand, then looked straight at him. "Yes. It was— is a—a club."

Her son twisted his face. Sarcasm dripped from his mouth. "Like Boy Scouts and Girl Scouts. Right?"

"Of sorts. Brandon, your dad and I did some very bad, very stupid things in Wisconsin. Things we never thought anybody would know about. I'm not going to give you details. I'll just say we hurt others, each other—"

"Me?"

The woman nodded again. "Yes, you. So we came here, hoping it would all go away."

Brandon scowled and lowered his head. "And it didn't."

His mother shook her head. "No."

"That's why you guys were gone every weekend. That's where Dad probably is now."

The woman sucked in her lower lip. "Probably. Yes," she whispered.

"Shit," Brandon muttered, gazing at the floor, working his lips in and out his mouth. His eyes narrowed on a piece of lint from his socks stuck in the carpet. The scabs on his calves itched. His feet quivered.

He escaped to the window. Outside, high in the tree next to the farm house, two crows cackled at each other.

He turned and sat back on the sill, flexing his fists.

"I'm not just pissed, Mom. I'm FUCKING pissed. At you and Dad and Grandpa and—and EVERYBODY!" He slammed both palms against the wall next to the window, cracking the sheetrock.

Joanne hugged herself and looked away. "You should be. Well, not with Grandpa, but—"

"Mom, he died! He died!" he wailed, tearing the curtains from the windows. Throwing both arms across the dresser, he swept it clean, scattering picture frames and the empty jewelry box. "He left me!" he screamed.

Yanking out dresser drawers, he scattered clothes across the room—sweaters, pants, t-shirts—and then smashed the empty drawers against the floor, walls, and bed. Exhausted, the boy fell to his knees, tears pooling on the carpet beneath him. Only his heavy breath broke the silence.

Lifting his arms, he spoke to his empty hands. "He left me."

Then, he raised his lost and ravaged face. "Just like the rest of you."

His mother's chin quavered. "Brandon, I didn't want to. I just—I just—I couldn't stay. There was no other way. I'm sorry."

Brandon looked back at the floor. After a moment, he rose and sat on the bed, glancing at his mother in the mirror. He pulled at the edge of the bedspread. He glimpsed at Joanne, then returned to the fraying cloth. "Everything's broken, you know?"

The woman agreed. "Yes. You really need to clean up this place."

"No. Not that. I mean everything's broken. Everything—everybody's just falling apart."

"That's a good way to put it, sweetie."

Tears again formed in Brandon's eyes. "I don't know how I'm going to get through this, Mom."

"You have a friend who tells you things?"

"I do, but—"

Outside the window, the crows were silent.

"And she has friends. Right?"

Brandon laughed and took off the necklace that had once been his mother's. The chain jangled as he bounced it in his hand. "Oh, yeah. Really good friends."

His mother smiled back at him from the mirror. "Friends like the redhead centerfold in your desk?"

Brandon gasped. "You know about—?"

His mother's image wavered as she shook her finger at him. "I'm God. I know everything."

Brandon's eyes widened. "Everything?"

"Centerfolds. Gouged legs in closets. Cheerleaders in gravel pits. Yep. Pretty much everything."

The boy paused, then said, "Really shit!"

"By the way, that centerfold?"

"Yeah?"

"Nice… eyes. Kinda freckly, but beautiful. Something to look forward to. Good luck with that. No, forget that. You don't need luck. You have good taste. You'll be fine," she said.

Her image faded from the mirror and she was gone.

Brandon smiled and shook his head as he eyed the mess he had made. The scattered clothes, the fragments of drawers, the dents in the walls.

"I'm screwed," he thought. What the hell was he thinking? How could he return this to normal?

"Start at the beginning," a voice told him.

So he did.

Methodically, he picked up the clothes, folding them neatly and stacking them in organized piles. With that finished, he gathered pictures and stacked them on top of the bed.

Proud of the headway he had made, he turned to the wood scraps scattered across the room. His shoulders dropped.

"How do I fix this?" he wondered.

"You don't," the voice told him. *"You just clean up and throw away the trash."*

"What do I tell my father?"

No answer came. Confused, Brandon surveyed the room. Atop the pile of photos lay his parents' wedding portrait. His mouth curled to a sneer.

"Of course!"

Furiously, he collected shards into a pile, then hauled them out to the garbage bin. He vacuumed. He dusted. He rearranged.

When finished, he stood at the door and inspected his work. "Good enough," he told himself. "When the son of a bitch asks what happened, I'll tell him he did it. He was just too drunk to remember."

He turned off the light and locked the door behind him.

The school cafeteria flickered back to life before Jeannie's bewildered eyes. The foreign and the familiar jumbled in her brain.

"Jeannie girl, you sure you're all right?" Mrs. Roche stood over her and gently massaged her shoulder.

"Um—yeah." Jeannie shook her head and bent to retrieve her fork. "I'm fine."

The kindly monitor lifted Jeannie's chin and examined her eyes. She laid the back of her hand on Jeannie's forehead. "You sure? You seemed out of it there for a second."

"I—uh—was just thinking about—" A lie would not form.

Mrs. Roche's deep brown eyes scoured Jeannie's.

"A—a boy."

"What the—Why did I say that?" Jeannie thought.

"A boy?" Mrs. Roche stood straight and cocked her head. "Do I know him?"

"Huh?"

"Do I know this boy?"

Jeannie closed her mouth. *"A boy in a bedroom? I can't tell her that,"* she thought.

She shook her head.

"You're rubbing your leg. Are you sure you're all right?"

"I bumped my knee on the table leg when I sat down. It will be fine."

"Fine?"

Jeannie nodded.

"Let's talk," Mrs. Roche crossed to the opposite side of the table.

"About what?"

"About this boy."

Jeannie forced a smile. "You just want to see if I'm okay."

"Humor me."

The whole table lurched when the teacher plopped onto the bench. "This boy. Does he go to school here? How old is he? Where'd you meet him?"

Rattled, Jeannie said, "I don't know him that well. I mean he's not that kind of boy."

"What do you mean 'that kind of boy'?"

"I mean he's not my type."

"Not your type. Uh-huh."

"I mean he's—uh—little. He's a boy boy."

"Oh. Like a kid."

"Right."

"You babysit him or something?"

"Uh—Yeah. Babysat him last summer in—uh—Wisconsin."

Jeannie's stomach dropped. *"Wisconsin? Why did I say Wisconsin?"*

"I thought you and your folks went to California."

Jeannie clutched the bench with both hands.

"Oh, yeah. We did go to California, but we stopped and saw some friends of my dad's in—Madison—yeah. We stopped in Madison on the way back."

Mrs. Roche whipped off her glasses. "Madison, Wisconsin, is not on the way from California to British Columbia. It's at least a thousand miles out of the way."

"That's what I told him, but we went anyway." She forced a laugh.

"Anyway," Mrs.Roche said, leaning forward on the table. "What about this boy?"

"I—uh—just found out he and his family moved."

Mrs. Roche waited, then asked, "His family moved. And—?"

Jeannie cleared her throat. "I'm worried about him. He's kind of—different. Horrible temper, and—I don't know. I worry about how he's going to react and stuff."

Mrs. Roche took one of Jeannie's hands. "There's nothing you can do about it here, missy."

"I know." Jeannie forced a worried expression.

Mrs. Roche encircled Jeannie's wrist with a powerful hand. "Tell you what. Take a couple of minutes. Get yourself together. Finish off what food you can, then get back to class."

"I'm going to be late."

"I'll take care of that, okay?"

Mrs. Roche struggled to her feet, clapped her hands and yelled to the whole room. "All right, kidlings. Just two more minutes. Return your trays and let's get ready to learn!"

The boys at the table below the stage groaned.

"Yeah, yeah, yeah. I know, but if you don't get a move on, I'll tell your parents about your obsession with super glue and sequins."

As the crowd grumbled toward the tray return, Mrs. Roche leaned back to Jeannie. "Just finish your food. I'll be back in a second. I'll take you to class and explain to your teacher, okay?"

"Um, ma'am? You're my teacher."

Mrs. Roche smiled. "Well, hurry up, you slacker."

The heavy woman hopped off the stage, landing remarkably lightly, then herded stragglers toward the door. She flicked the light switch. "Come on, people. Let's go."

Jeannie's knee twinged.

The original Shimmering voice had told her, "There will be more. You will know."

Jeannie scowled and poked at her potatoes with her fork.

"Keep eating, Miss Jones," Mrs. Roche yelled across the room.

Jeannie waved and looked down at the remains of the the tray.

"Nope." She dumped her fork onto her plate.

At the tray return, Mrs. Roche asked, "Are you done already?"

"Yep. I've had enough." Jeannie pounded her platter against the inside of the garbage can.

"No voice this time," she thought as she whacked her tray one last time. *"Good. I've had enough."*

11

Nancy's Graduation

Winthrop, Michigan
USA

Nancy Kirkman certainly had friends. Lots of friends. Friends who, like Brandon, had issues. Friends who, like Nancy, had ways of dealing. Older, younger, bolder, wiser friends eager to share and become Brandon's friends as well.

At first, Nancy had acted as Brandon's agent, lightening the distaste of his scowl and his pariah status. Eventually, as his personality and prowess improved, he no longer needed help or encouragement. He secured partners on his own.

Over time he also discarded his commitment fantasies, fully embracing Nancy's maxim *Screw it until you like it.*

After his gravel pit initiation, he developed refined critical skills, becoming independent, discriminating, and secure in his judgement. He escaped the sorrow over his lost mother and grandfather, as well as the contempt for his father.

Through the remainder of the year, Nancy remained his mentor. And friend.

In the reception line after her graduation ceremony, Nancy stopped him.

"Brandon! Good. You're here. I have something for you. Follow me."

Waving off the row of well-wishers, she grabbed his hand and guided him through the crowd into the darkened hallways to the biology room. After checking to make sure they were alone, she reached inside her gown and removed a key.

"What's that?" Brandon whispered.

"Master key," she said, smiling.

Brandon's jaw dropped. "Where did you get that?"

"You don't want to know. I hid something for you in here."

"For me?"

"Just a little something."

Once inside, she again checked the hall, then closed the door. Brazenly, she grabbed a stool off the lab tables and set it in front of the storage cabinets. Flinging aside her shoes, she climbed onto the stool and pulled down Peter Pigeon.

"Here. Hold Pete a second." Stretching high on her tiptoes, she reached far back to the wall and pulled down a tubular package. When she turned, she found Brandon staring up her gown.

"Hey! None of that!" she laughed, bonking him over the head with the present. "Give me a shoulder."

"Nice thighs," he said, turning away his head and snickering.

"Yeah, yeah, yeah. Just stop it, boy."

Nancy steadied herself with one hand on his shoulder and stepped down. "Here. This is for you."

"For me? What for?"

"Graduation day. Take it."

"But this is your celebration. I'm supposed to do this for you." He ran his hand over the long, thin package.

"I don't need anything. Believe it or not, you've given me a lot. Besides, since I'm not going to be around much anymore, I thought this was important."

He removed the wrapping paper and peered into one end of the tube. "What the—?"

He tuned over the cylinder and shook it. A rolled piece of white rubber extended beyond the end. "Really now. What is this?"

"It's a shower mat."

"So—" Brandon hesitated. He sniffed his armpits. "I stink and need a shower?"

"Oh, shut up. Just unroll it."

Brandon pulled the mat from the tube and held it up in front of him. It was a simple square with a black circle in the center. Inside the circle read the words "MY OWN."

"I still don't get it," Brandon said.

She snatched the mat from his hands and laid it on the floor. "Stand on the circle."

Unsure of himself, he obeyed.

"Now, every time you think you need me—for anything—friendship, advice,—"

"Sex?"

"ESPECIALLY sex—I want you to turn on the shower with cold water, stand on this, and say to yourself over and over, 'I can stand on MY OWN. In fact, I *am* on MY OWN.' Got it?"

Brandon grinned. "You are really sick."

Grabbing his shirt, she drew his face to hers. "GOT IT?"

She pecked his mouth.

Brandon laughed. "I got it."

"One more thing."

"What's that?"

Nancy reached behind her neck and unbuckled her necklace. "I want you to have this," she said, putting the strand into his hand and closing his fingers.

"What is—" Brandon opened his hand. "Your cross? Why?"

She patted his hand with both of hers. "Remember that first night in the gravel pit? I took off my shirt and you couldn't look at my tits for a long time. You kept gawking at my cross. Remember?"

Brandon blushed. "I was—nervous."

Nancy laughed. "Yeah, I guess that's one way to put it. You came in your pants before we even got started."

"I made up for it."

"You did, and very well. Anyway, I want you to remember where your head was at the time. And where it is now. You've come a long way, Brandon Whistler."

Brandon's lip trembled and pressure built behind his eyes. "What am I going to do with my mom's Aphrodite medal?"

Nancy smiled. "You take mine. I'll take yours. If you don't mind."

He pulled his necklace over his head and held his mother's pendant next to Nancy's cross. The cheek beneath his eye twitched. Sucking air between his teeth and lips, he handed the Aphrodite medallion to Nancy.

"Thanks," she said.

"What's up with the crosses?" he asked. "You and all those girls have the same kind. Are they—"

Nancy stroked his cheek with a single finger. "It doesn't matter. This one's yours. Theirs mean something totally different to them than this does to you. For now, it's best if you just keep it out of sight. At least for awhile."

As she bent to gather the loose wrapping paper, Brandon stopped her. "Nancy—uh—Thanks. For everything, you know?"

Nancy smiled. "Put the pigeon away, will you? I gotta go."

"Yeah. Sure," he said, climbing on top of the stool as she walked out the door.

"Oh, and Brandon?"

"Yeah?" He peeked back under his arm as he placed Pete back on top of the shelf.

With one hand, Nancy flashed her naked crotch. "See ya!"

She waved and rushed into the hall.

12

Wedded Forever

Fort Repentance, British Columbia
Canada

Pulling her robe around her, Jeannie shuffled into her bathroom. Her shoulder-length hair clung to her sluggish morning face.

She swore the soft red freckles across her forehead and cheekbones had multiplied during the night. With her dark eyebrows, they did liven her gray eyes, but any lively disposition lay dormant somewhere in yesterday.

"Ugh," she grunted, sticking out her tongue at her reflection and pulling her open fingers through the red tangles that still clung to her nose and chin. "Not even a shower is going to help this nest."

She ruthlessly slapped her face with cold water, then stepped back from the counter to regard her reflection.

"*Sixteen is so much older than fifteen,*" she thought.

Jeannie flexed her left knee easily, then carefully tested the right one. A slight tinge cautioned her to lower her leg.

"*That could still take a while,*" she thought, "*but the rest is coming along nicely.*"

She would not fear.

Since her soccer injury, she had worked tirelessly to rehabilitate her knee. Since her Oaxaca and Michigan Shimmerings, she worked even harder to build and sculpt the rest of her body.

Stretching her arms high above her, Jeannie turned to the side and studied the curve of her chest. She traced a finger across the speckles covering her sturdy shoulders, her rounded biceps, her flat stomach and her taut thighs.

"*Isometrics does wonders,*" she thought. "*Strong, yet feminine.*"

Lowering her hands to the counter, she closed her eyes, but she could not turn off her mind.

The Shimmerings.

Oaxaca: The mestizo with his knife. The killer with his walking stick.

Michigan: The dead woman in the mirror. The furious boy craving redheads.

She opened her eyes and found herself staring down the cleavage between her two breasts. "I bet he'd really like these," she said.

Her cheeks flushed as she tipped back her head and lightly pinched her nipples. She gasped and closed her eyes while her hands explored her skin.

Jeannie's eyes popped open.

Unable to breathe, she caught herself against the counter. "No," she wheezed. "That's just—just— He's really not my type. That's just sick."

"*No, not sick,*" she thought. "*It's normal, but—*"

Jeannie dropped her arms and shook out the tension. The thought was not the Shimmering voice. It did not stand apart and observe. It did not command. It did not judge. It was the same conscience she had argued with since her girlish crush on Andre Demoya, her soccer coach.

Lowering her head, she let it roll around her neck. "Dumb, Jeannie! Dumb. You're better than this," she fumed.

She loved the idea of being an adult, but she hated the whole process of getting there. When she raised her eyes once more to the mirror, traces of the rough-edged, freckle-faced girl still remained, but softly focused in the misty surface smiled a powerful, naked woman.

She had become herself. "I *am* better," she said.

Leaning over, she shook out her hair, grabbed the shampoo bottle from the counter and hopped into the warm shower. The spraying water and swirling mist energized her skin and lungs. As she sang an unrecognizable tune, she scoured her legs and torso.

"Can't scrub away the freckles," she giggled, then bent for the shampoo. A little too quickly. A little too carelessly.

The soapy shower floor slid beneath her, and her legs splayed across the stall. She caught herself against the wall, but it was too late. Her knee locked.

The Shimmering voice spoke clearly. "There will be more."

It wasn't fear. It wasn't hallucination. The words were real.

"Oh, God! Not you! Here it comes," she moaned, bracing herself against the slippery enclosure. "Calm. Gotta keep calm."

Her hands grappled to turn off the water. On one good leg, she breathlessly opened the door, wrapped a towel around her shivering body, and lowered herself to the floor.

"Just relax and watch. Relax and watch."

Then she leaned her head back to the wall and waited for the revelation.

The moon cleared the mountaintops around Mount Elder, bathing the opening in soft white. Just off the hiking trail, newlyweds Georgia and Victor Radcliffe lay wrapped in their two-person sleeping bag, their backpacks at their heads. Only their breathing and the breeze from the valley broke the silence.

Farther down the path, just inside the woods, a lanky figure dressed in khaki-colored pants and shirt leaned against a tree cleaning his fingernails with the tip of his curved knife. His black fedora hid his green eyes in shadow. A thick beard covered his strong face and solid jaw. Occasionally, he glanced across the clearing to the formless lump just off the trail.

Since early morning, he had trailed these two, silently and invisibly, as whiffs of their sweat led him up the switchbacks. When they stopped to rest, he held back, relishing their fatigue and frustration. That afternoon, he savored their lovemaking and resulting brawl. He accepted their reconciliation.

Now it was time.

He drew the sharp blade across his thumb and sucked his own blood as an appetizer. He closed his eyes and beamed. Blood trickled out his mouth.

Out in the clearing, the sleeping bag wriggled again, at first tentatively, then insistently, rolling in tandem, the fabric stretching and rising over and over, until it collapsed, again drained of passion and lust.

The man in the trees shook out his thick black hair, swept it back, and replaced his hat. He wiped the knife blade on his shirttail and sheathed it. Satisfied it was secured yet readily accessible, he picked up the coiled rope and hung it over his shoulder.

"Here we go."

His high boots glided silently over the rocky path until he reached the inert bag. He grinned and scooped up dirt from the trailside. Carefully, he plucked out strands of grass, then trailed his index finger through the soil. The dirt dissolved into glimmering dust that sparkled in the moonlight. He knelt next to the sleeping bag, blew on his hand, then leered as the sparkles settled over the couple.

He crouched and roughly shook the bag. "It's time," he sang.

The lump jerked alive.

"What the—?"

Victor's head popped out of the bag as the man leaned over him and winked viciously.

"Georgia! Georgia! Wake up!"

"Wha—?"

Georgia screamed at the menace looming over them. More specter than human, the man rose to his full height. His skin gleamed beneath his flowing hair. His knife hung from his belt, its snake-head hilt poised to strike.

"What—What do you want?" Victor stammered.

The man smirked at the pair's ample cheeks and plump shoulders. He smirked, then wrinkled his nose. "Entertainment."

Paralyzed by the bag and the magic dust, the couple cowered under the man's sunken eyes.

"What do you mean *entertainment*?" Georgia whimpered, desperately clinging to her husband.

The man laughed and knelt next to them. He raised his left hand in front of their faces.

"Watch."

One by one, he flicked at the long, skinny fingers. Each made a *thock* as it popped off, rattled and flew onto the couple's faces.

Victor's cries vanished amidst Georgia's screams. The detached limbs writhed into slimy, ravenous worms that wriggled across the couple's faces, down their shoulders and across their naked bodies.

"Keep screaming," he cackled. "I love it!"

He unsheathed his knife.

The next morning, the Wandering Old Farts, a senior hiking club from Calgary, discovered the blood-soaked sleeping bag at the bottom of the mountain where the trail began. Pinned to an odd piece of rope that sealed the zipped bag, a crudely-lettered note said, "Leave no trace."

The letters, written in blood, cracked and flaked as the investigators untied the rope. Inside the bag, park police found human remains—two fleshless skulls; four bloody legs, arms, and hands; knots of hair; and strips of flesh. Also amidst the grisly contents, investigators found IDs, scraps of clothes, dismantled backpacks, and waste bags. At police headquarters, examiners determined the composition of the sealing rope—human skin.

Tracking dried blood and scuff marks up switchbacks to the clearing, Mounties discovered the murder site. Just five skinless fingers lying on the trail next to a vial of human fat with a note written in the victims's blood attached. "The rest is mine," it said.

Officials agreed to withhold the nature of the deaths from the public, closing the park while they searched for evidence leading to the killer. Evidence they never found.

Months later, after the first heavy snowfall, they abandoned their hunt. In the spring the park reopened, but only after workers had erased all remnants of the fatal trail while local and provincial offices shredded the crime's sordid details.

While physical testimony disappeared, the truth survived, prolonged by rumor and fear circulated by hikers, authorities, and the Radcliffes' colleagues at Categorical Chaos Advertising Agency in Vancouver.

Jeannie awoke on the floor, exhausted and alone. Droplets of shower and sweat chilled her naked body. Retrieving her towel, she wiped her face and neck, then kneaded the muscles around her knee with her empty hands.

She struggled to forget what she had just seen and heard.

"It will be fine," she told herself. "It will all be fine."

Her body did not believe. Her dripping nose and quivering chin told her it would not be fine. The Oaxaca killing. The Michigan boy and his dead mother. Now this.

"*I've been to Mount Elder. I love Mount Elder,*" she thought. "*That was our first trip to the mountains. I thought my knee was all better. AJ and I beat Daddy to the summit. That's when I knew I loved mountains. All mountains. I forgot all about the Shimmerings.*"

Jeannie wiped her face with the towel.

A light flashed and an image of Mount Elder snapped onto the shower room wall while pain twisted and jabbed Jeannie's knee. Place and time splintered the image into a jigsawed mirror of fantasy and reality, legend and rumor, words spoken and revealed.

"Wait! What's—"

A sharp thrust dislodged the pieces, smashing them to even smaller bits, then dashing her memories across the floor, glaring in a blinding, yellow light. Glints and glimmers of people and places, of deeds and neglect, swirled stronger and deeper, faster and brighter, then into blackness.

Jeannie gasped. "Wha—?"

The Shimmering voice spoke. "Like maturity, dreams are normal and real even when you don't want them to be."

"Are those people—Victor and Georgia—real? I don't understand."

"They are part of the whole, part of forever. To understand, you must see, you must hear, you must remember."

"Remember what?"

"The Shimmerings. All of them. The people. The places."

Jeannie thought for a moment. A hole opened in the darkness.

"The killer on the mountain just now. He's real. He was at the cantina in Mexico. He was the mestizo," she said.

"Yes."

"The boy and his dead mother in the mirror?"

"They are real."

"I don't remember."

"Hold onto them. When the time comes, remember them. Remember all."

"All what?"

"All you have seen. All that is to come."

"I told you. I don't want more!"

Jeannie turned to her side and curled into a ball.

Quietly, the voice said, "What you will see is not what you want. It is what you need. There will be more."

The bathroom light rose around her. Jeannie's knee relaxed. Slowly, she sat up, wiping the tears and sweat from her face.

She flung the towel to the floor, dragged herself to her feet, and slammed the shower control to hot. With sweltering fog filling the room, she stepped into the enclosure to steam the voice away.

Above the sink, the mirror disappeared.

13

Agitating the Coals

Mount Komu ("The Entry")
British Columbia, Canada

Deep under Mount Komu, the pishtaco scowled across the royal fire of the Earth Man at the only creature who did not fear him. Frank Thorstad. The weendigo. The man-become-spirit who stood between the royal couple, haughtily scanning the nightly gathering.

As the wood before pishtaco crackled and popped in the flickering flame, he strained the smoky air through his teeth. He spat on the cave floor and ground the spittle into the dirt with his boot.

The weendigo noticed and pointed a long finger. With his eyes fixed on the pishtaco, he leaned to the Earth Man's ear while furtively rubbing his hand across the queen's back, exploring, caressing, lingering.

The queen's skin reddened beneath the gold chain around her neck. She patted her chest and glanced sidelong at the weendigo.

A growl rattled the pishtaco's throat. He spat again, this time into the fire. He knew the story of Frank and Queen Sarah in their human life. The matchi-auwishuk whispered it among themselves every day. He hated it.

Before death, Frank and Sarah lived in the same small town, stripped of all inhibition, quenching their fiery lust in the Minnesota snow. Their attachment was temporary. When he later rejected her, she slammed his unsuspecting body into a tree with her car, nearly erasing herself from existence. However, inspired by their lechery, the Earth Man rescued them both from oblivion, enlisting them in his mission of corruption.

In pursuit of evil perfection, the regal monster restored Sarah's physical beauty to make her his queen. Seeing Frank as instrumental to destroying humanity and the Word, he transformed the mortal into a weendigo.

There they sat across the room. Two men. One woman. The woman the pishtaco wanted for himself if he were human. He lowered his hat brim to hide his eyes.

The story disgusted him. He hated Frank and the Earth Man. He hated himself.

Glancing across the flames, the pishtaco picked up the stick next to him and jabbed at the fire.

"Like Sarah, he has nothing to fear. He's already dead."

The pishtaco gritted its teeth. *"He defeated me once. Once. Never again."*

The burning wood popped, sending sparks into the air. The pishtaco jabbed at the fire again and felt the Earth Man watching him. He churned the coals once more.

"The Earth Man needs me to kill. But he says Frank doesn't kill. Why's he needed then?"

The flames grew higher. Across them, Sarah leaned back in her throne and nibbled quietly at her pointless meal. Already dead, she no longer required food. Still, she ate. Her breast rose as she inhaled deeply. The pishtaco licked his lips.

When the Earth Man leaned closer to his queen, the pishtaco dropped his eyes to the flame, absently wiping at his mouth with his sleeve. He had no fear of humanity, spirits, or the Word, not even when the Earth Man whispered into Frank's ear. They were all just obstacles.

Ignoring the sovereign and servant, the pishtaco concentrated instead on Sarah. Stretching his neck, he peeked under his hat at the animated dead woman. Her hands. Her chest. The gold chain that enslaved her to the Earth Man. Her hair.

Abruptly, her silver eyes glanced up and drilled into his skull. Just as suddenly, the weendigo broke her spell.

"Dreaming of bacon?" Frank taunted, punching at the pishtaco's knee and squatting next to him. "Or is that more of a nightmare now?"

The pishtaco shifted, turning his back to the weendigo.

"Hey, I know. I'm just teasing. I saw you looking at Sarah. Something, ain't she? Don't worry. I won't say anything. The boss likes you. He was just telling me. He especially likes that killing and fat-draining shtick. Funny. I never saw that in you when I was beating the shit out of you."

The pishtaco shrugged, unsheathed his knife, and drew with it in the dirt before him. He concentrated on the fire, struggling to ignore Frank.

"Quiet, ain't you? Was it something I said?"

The pishtaco shook his head. "I've been busy."

"Oh, yeah. That's right. Killing fat fuckers wrapped up like hot dogs in a sleeping bag. That musta been back-breaking for you."

The pishtaco curled his lips and continued drawing in the dirt with his knife.

"By the way, how does it feel to suck the fat out of somebody? I mean, is it like 'Mmmm. Tasty'? Or more like 'Could use more salt'? Come on. Tell me."

The pishtaco grinned at Frank. "Humans call it orgasmic."

Frank sat down roughly and punched the pishtaco's side. "Woo! Orgasmic. I like that. That good, huh? Give me details."

The pishtaco closed his eyes, reliving the first taste of Georgia Radcliffe. "It's not a flavor or a texture. It's victory and surrender all at once, consuming you from the inside out. It persists. Since you're a weendigo now, maybe you don't remember orgasms."

Frank glared. "I remember."

The pishtaco sniffed and scowled. "With Queen Sarah?"

Frank sneered. "Yeah. Doing it in the snow is pretty damn hot. Something you'll never know."

"True. As a pishtaco, I don't need sex; I just need somebody to kill. It's a hundred times better," the pishtaco said, glaring at the weendigo.

"You know what makes it better?" he continued. "I don't have to share the experience. I don't think I could watch like—" He stopped, then nodded toward Sarah and the Earth Man. "Well, you know."

He tested his blade against his thumb. "But it's okay. If you like watching, this is the place for you, isn't it?"

Frank looked across the fire as the Earth Man sat on his throne stroking Sarah's thigh, his chubby fingers inching closer to her crotch. The weendigo flexed his fist and turned to the pishtaco. "I should have finished you off the day you came here."

The pishtaco glared into the weendigo's eyes. "Maybe you should have. Things have happened since."

Frank towered over the pishtaco, his mouth opened wide, revealing his sharpened teeth. "Careful, fat sucker."

The pishtaco shook his head at the knife in his hand and called across the room. "Earth Man!"

The Earth Man, Sarah, and their matchi-auwishuk glanced up disinterestedly.

The pishtaco shouted, "I just want you to know this has nothing to do with you, all right?"

The firelight flickered in the silent room.

The Earth Man glanced at Sarah, then back at the pishtaco. "What has nothing to do with me?"

"This!" The pishtaco lunged forward, thrusting his knife into Frank's groin and slitting up to his chin. Yellow slime erupted from the weendigo's throat, covering the pishtaco's face and arms.

Before the Earth Man could react, the pishtaco slashed across Frank's neck, cracked his spine, and ripped off his head. Lifting the skull, the monster opened the mouth and let the yellow ooze dribble onto his tongue.

Sarah screamed. "No! No! Frank!"

The pishtaco, his green eyes glowing and glaring, wrapped the head in both hands and marched to her. Brandishing it to her face, he growled, "Right. No Frank."

Then he turned to the Earth Man. "No Frank."

Carelessly, he tossed the head into the flame, then strode around the pit for the torso. With bloody hands, he hoisted the carcass over his head and heaved the lifeless mass into the fire. The blaze exploded, engulfing and vaporizing all trace of the weendigo. The blast flung the pishtaco, Sarah, and the Earth Man against the stone walls. Stunned, the three sank to the floor amidst the shivering matchi-auwishuk.

The pishtaco moved first. Slowly, he rose to his knees and crawled to the dazed Earth Man and Sarah. He rose to his feet, pulled back his shoulders, and glared down at the man and woman.

"There is no more Frank Thorstad. No weendigo. Just me." He snapped his fingers loose and tossed them at the royal couple.

As the bony digits turned to wriggling, slithering worms, the Earth Man batted them to the floor, gathered them together, and blew his cold breath upon them. Instantly, they turned to icy dust.

Convinced of the worms' destruction, the Earth Man, dumped the dust into the fire pit, then strode threateningly to the murderer. Defiantly, the pishtaco raised his hat brim and flared his nose.

The Earth Man's glower softened to a grin. He patted the pishtaco's face. "Nice job. I knew I liked you."

Wrapping an arm around the pishtaco, he said, "Remember the big thing I had for you? I think you're ready. Come on. I'll explain."

Turning to her side, Sarah clutched her chain as the Earth Man and pishtaco disappeared through the curtain to the royal bedroom. A matchi-auwish stepped forward and offered her a hand.

"No. I'll be fine," she said, her eyes intent on the curtain. The skin beneath her chain burned.

Sarah stood. "I'll be fine." She disappeared up the tunnel to the outside.

14

By Any Other Name

Fort Repentance, British Columbia
Canada

While she climbed the hill toward her house, Jeannie curled her backpack like a dumbbell, separately with each hand. After three years, the practice had built her arms and upper body stronger than either the hockey players or the swimmers at school. Avoiding the bus and walking the hill strengthened her legs and increased her lung capacity.

The work paid off. She felt good and she looked good. And she knew it.

Lifting the backpack over her shoulder, she leapt up the porch. She burst through the door and yelled toward her parents' office, "I'm home! I'm going to take a quick nap. Okay?"

Amanda emerged from the office as Jeannie bounded up the stairs. "Let me know when you wake up so I can start dinner," she called.

"Yeah, okay." Jeannie waved, vanishing down the second-story hall. She disappeared behind the door and trudged up the stairs to her attic room. After slinging off her backpack, she plumped up her pillows and retrieved her worn copy of Dante's *Inferno* from the bag.

"Nothing better to induce sleep than Dante, although I probably shouldn't tell Mr. Bridges that," she muttered as she riffled the book's pages to locate her dog-eared bookmark.

Opening the notebook, Jeannie squinted at her handwritten scrawls for the day's assignment. "Okay. Too much decoration. I really have to stop that. From now on, just letters and words. No curlicues. No serifs. No illustrations."

She tilted the bookmark and pulled it close to her nose, "Ah! Canto V. Right after Canto IV. Duh."

Pulling the packet of summary notes from the back of her notebook, Jeannie found the section's outline. "Let's see. 'The Second Circle: Minos: The Carnal Sinners.' Oh, good. Family reading. Light, fluffy, morally instructive. That should put me out in about five minutes."

She climbed onto the bed, leaning against her pillows and bending her legs into a makeshift easel.

"All right. Let's see who's in this section," Jeannie said, referring to her character list.

"'Minos—Judge of the infernal regions. Sentences sinners to hell.'" Jeannie scrunched up her mouth. "Hmm. The amiable type.

"'Dido—kills herself for love.' Oh, good. A romantic suicide.

"Oh, these two look fun. Paolo and Francesca—adulterers. Well, of course. Nothing says Fourteenth Century literature like fornication and infidelity. So intriguing. So inspiring. So downright dirty."

Jeannie replaced the notes in her backpack. "It *is* advanced English, I guess. And it beats the heck out of vampires and prom queens."

That's why she liked Mr. Bridges. Even though he was the youngest teacher on staff, he avoided all the crappy literature her friends wanted to read. Adamant that teenagers deserved better than dancing bloodsuckers, he taught them classics. And he smiled. If she hadn't sworn off authority figures after Coach Demoya, she could—

"Get over it, Jones," she scolded herself. "Take your nap."

She laid her notes on the floor, stuffed *Inferno* under the pillows, then lowered herself.

Before she could adjust her face on the cool linen, she heard a click. "*What was that?*" she thought. She swept her hands across the bedspread beside her, but found nothing. Leaning over the side of the bed, she searched the floor.

Still nothing.

"What the heck?" She returned to her back.

When she tried to straighten her leg, she knew. Her right knee had locked. But this was wrong. Every previous incident had wrenched and paralyzed.

"This doesn't hurt at all," she marveled. *"What's the Shimmering for this going to be like?"*

The revelation was inevitable, she knew. She could never prevent the afflicting dreams before and doubted this time would be different. However, she had learned the faster she could reset her knee, the quicker the vision occurred. The sooner it started, the sooner it was over.

Carefully, she rose and placed her foot on the floor, gently applying pressure. Painlessly, her stiffened right leg popped and the kneecap returned to its natural position.

"Phew! That wasn't so bad. Maybe—"

Before she could finish her sentence, trembling sunlight glowered down the circular stairway from her tower.

Frustrated, Jeannie bounced herself back on the bed. "Really? That's all it takes now?"

The unmistakeable sign—the quivering light—convinced her. She summoned her calm, wrapped her arms around her pillows, and quietly anticipated the vision to come.

By day, Beetle, the teenaged Quechuan once named Chaupi, wore a red poncho and wide-brimmed hat, working for food and clothes as an "expert native guide" to the ruins of Machu Picchu. As a teacher, he exceeded the authenticity of his costume and limitations of his age as he spoke of the supernatural achievements of the Inca civilization. Not only did he lead tourists through the grounds, he protected the vulnerable sites and sacred altars from vandalism and sacrilege.

By night, the ancient remains became his teacher and schoolhouse. He needed no books, no laboratories, no mentors. Instead, free of misinterpretation, he absorbed the pure instruction of the grass, stone, and sky. While lifetimes swirled through the ancient city, he inhaled the air of his ancestors and listened to the shifting shadows of mountains, the clouds, and his three smooth birth stones from Lake Titicaca

He saw all.

Women. Men. Children. Farmers. Weavers. Artisans.

Animals. Plants. Trees. Stones.

Worshipers. Priests. Gods.

He marveled as ever-shifting winds carried the ghosts and fog from the Urbamba River up through the jungle and cliffs to the ancient avenues and temples. Legends and tales danced on the terraces and platforms, a ritualistic performance in hushed homage to Viracocha, Creator of All Things, the Eternal Substance, God of Sea and Storm.

If the weather were warm and clear, he lay on the vast plaza, staring at the sky. Lulled by silence and the rocking movement of the cosmos, he heard the ancient tales unfold. Voices spoke to him through the stones in his hands, the grass that cushioned him, and the very air he breathed.

He learned all the stories. The fabled and the genuine. The virtuous and the wicked. The exhilarating and the paralyzing.

Paralyzing. Like this night.

Huddled in a doorway in Machu Picchu's lower town, Beetle rested against the stone frame, sweating in the frigid night air, too sick to care about learning anything. He should have returned to the dormitory below with the other workers. Desperately, he leaned his face into his poncho to escape the cold.

Without warning, the ground lurched, tossing his fevered body to the floor. The elastic foundation rose and fell in wave after wave, propelling Beetle across the room into a solid wall. His senses jumbled and his breath flew into the darkness.

The room vanished.

Later—he didn't know how much later—a cleansing breeze soothed his moist face and eased him awake.

No human touch. No Sisa. No midwife. No priest. Those healers were gone.

"Earthquake," he thought.

Slowly, he stirred from beneath his poncho and hat, touching each of the Three Stones of Viracocha in his pocket. He was weakened, but safe.

Exhausted, he dragged himself to the doorway. Outside, the shadowy ruins stood solidly intact.

Leaning on the entryway with one hand, Beetle laid the back of the other hand against his forehead and understood.

He relaxed. *"A broken fever. The lesson will be strong. I must go to the plaza."*

As he felt his way down the narrow grass-covered street, his strength and apprehension grew until below him, the Great Plaza extended toward the mountain's edge. Slowly, he lowered himself down the steps and eased his way through the grayness to the center, searching the sky for an illuminating dream.

This time the lesson was not a vision. Instead, the world sang a hymn, an unrecognizable dissonance that strove toward a harmonious declaration. Alert to the voices of nature, Beetle flattened himself to the ground, prone and stationary, awaiting the upcoming revelation.

Suddenly, the music stopped. Beneath the mountain, the jungle throbbed in a cacophony of silence. He flipped onto his back. Above him, a curtain of fog hid the moon and stars.

His bones spoke to him: "Truth is the rock of existence, not the emptiness of endless space. It is not shaken. It does not fly on the wind. Do you understand?"

"Yes," Beetle said.

"Good," his bones replied. "The final lesson has begun."

"Jeannie! You okay?"

Jeannie jolted upright. Her father's voice mixed with the Shimmering vision. She shook her head.

His question rang off the stairway walls.

"Oh. Yeah. I'm fine. I was just sleeping."

"Okay. Want something to eat?"

"Yeah. I'll be right there."

Again, she shook her head, then tried to rub away the ruins, the boy, and the dark. *"What was the lesson?"* she wondered. *"What did he see?"*

Jeannie swung her legs over the side of the bed. The voice had warned her of more pain, more visions. This was nothing. Her knee barely twitched. In this Shimmering, there were no monsters. No killing. No violence at all. Just a boy and and the ruins of Machu Picchu. What was she supposed to remember?

"What was his name?" she asked herself. She looked to the blank ceiling, awaiting the voice she had heard the other times. Instead, she remembered.

"Ha! Beetle! That's it. He really needs another name. I could help him with that."

A pigeon landed on the windowsill at the end of the room, scrutinizing her. Jeannie grinned and asked, "Any suggestions?"

The bird cocked its head and turned away.

Jeannie laughed.

Stretching her arms high toward the tower opening, she rolled her head over her shoulders, then rubbed her neck. She felt no heat in the air, yet her neck sweat.

"Hey, Dad!" she yelled down the stairs. "Do we have any ice cream?"

"Yeah. Lots. Want some?"

"If there's chocolate."

"We have that."

"Great! Be right down."

She pulled on her slippers. "Who needs boys and dreams?" she said, clambering down the steps.

The bird hopped across the floor to the picture on Jeannie's bedside table. In front of Cinderella Castle at Disney World, a young girl hanging around the neck of her mother clung desperately to a stuffed Tigger doll. The mother had long black hair with bright silver eyes.

"The Creator will teach," the pigeon whispered in the abandoned room. "There will be more."

15

Turning Seventeen

Winthrop, Michigan
USA

Rumors of Winthrop's "anonymous sexual savior" had quickly unearthed a hidden congregation of dejected girls from every grade, every economic class, and every part of town, all of them eager for discreet release from anger, sorrow, and emptiness. Day after day, night after night, Brandon faithfully met the demand. For a while.

While those nights of "introduction and sharing" steadily converted Brandon from pariah to peer by the end of his sophomore year, the sheer number of incidents also transformed the sharp peak of excitement into the blur of tedium. Each new appointment, each new client, each new location became more predictable, more tiresome, and ultimately more sickening until by the close of eleventh grade, he no longer pursued partners.

However, they tirelessly pursued him.

One night, after Donald ventured off to who-knows-where-or-what, Brandon sat on the couch in the dark, reviewing life, inviting truth and insight.

One thing he knew for sure: Any of the pussy-jocks at school would love to have his sex life, but was that enough?

Yes, his contacts got him a job working for food and clothes money at O'Neill's Grocery. Yes, he had saved enough for a blue '97 Saturn that ran most of the time and looked presentable. And even on nights like this, his small bedroom provided a place to crash between "engagements." Better yet, its strong dead-bolt separated him from the booze-soaked tirades of his father.

Brandon laid back his head, examining the blank ceiling and accepting life's limitations. *"It's not good,"* he thought, *"but it's… it's acceptable."*

He sat up and rubbed his stiff neck. "But not really," he said.

His fingers stopped, tangled in the chain of Nancy's necklace. Slowly, he pulled it over his head and stroked the cross with his thumb.

He remembered that first night in the gravel pit—the euphoria of the moment, his trembling muscles, his lungs gulping for air, Nancy's hair as she nuzzled into his neck, the promise of love—

Clutching her necklace in his fist, he thought, *"There was no promise. I was just fourteen and stupid. Distraction is better."*

Gazing at the empty room, he recognized the lie.

"Okay. Maybe not better, but it's tolerable."

It's tolerable echoed in the hallways of his brain.

It's tolerable.

The phrase grew louder.

It's tolerable.

Stronger.

It's tolerable. It's tolerable. It's TOLERABLE!

"NO!" Enraged, Brandon slapped the leather couch cushion with open hands. He bolted upright and thrust his frustrated fists to the ceiling. Disillusionment slammed into his belly, dropping his thrashing body to the carpet. His roar reverberated down the hall as he lay motionless on the floor.

The doorbell jostled the room.

"What the—?"

Again, the chimes rang.

Brandon switched on a table light and stumbled to the door. Brushing back his hair, he turned on the porchlight. He recognized the short, black hair, the angular face. Toni Sharpe.

In ninth grade before his night with Nancy, Toni often ranked #1 on Brandon's Most Like to Fuck list, but since that football game, the two barely spoke three words.

Slowly, he opened the door.

"Toni?"

"No shit, Whistler. Let me in."

Brandon reached out and locked the screen door. "What do you want?"

Toni scowled and narrowed her eyes. "Is your dad home?"

"What?"

"Is your dad home?"

Brandon shifted his weight onto one foot. "You want my dad?"

"No, I don't want your dad. He's off chasing drunken pussy in Elysium or Grayson. I saw him drive off. Why do you think I'm here? Why does anybody come way the hell out here and ask you if your dad is home?"

Her words stunned him. "You mean you—"

"I want to come in, dipshit, just like the rest. Open the door."

Brandon leaned on the jamb, unsure what to do or say.

"Damn it, Whistler. I'm here to fuck. Come on. Let's go."

"*It's tolerable,*" his mind said.

"Hey! I'm getting old out here!"

"*Yes. Yes. It will be fine,*" Brandon tried to convince himself. "*It will be fine. It's tolerable.*"

He looked through the screen at the frustrated girl rattling the screen door. "Come on! Let me in!"

"*No. No, it's not tolerable. It won't be fine,*" he thought.

He reached back and touched the main door for reassurance. He couldn't do it. Not because it was Toni Sharpe, but because it was anybody.

He shook his head and began to shut the door.

"NO?" She slammed her fist against the door frame. "You're telling me no?"

Brandon sighed. "It doesn't work for me any more."

Veins on Toni's forehead bulged. Her face turned reddish gray in the porchlight. "Everybody but me? You'll fuck everybody but ME?"

The Dream Rescuer

"Well, yes, you, but that's not what I said. I said I'm done."

"You son of a bitch. I should cut off your—"

"My dick. I know. But being dickless wouldn't make much difference, would it?"

Toni stomped off the porch.

"You wait, Whistler. You wait!" she shouted. She slammed her car door, and gravel sprayed the driveway as she sped off, thrusting a middle finger out the window.

The red taillights wavered and bounced onto the main road, then disappeared into the darkness. The yard light flashed and flickered as a bird flew out of the empty barn, landing in the empty driveway.

"I don't have time for pigeons tonight. Night, Pete," he said, scowling.

He closed the front door and wandered back to the couch. Switching off the table lamp, he absorbed the silence.

His head pounded. His throat gagged, and he squeezed his head with both hands.

"She's you, you know," the bird said.

"Rejected and pissed. Yeah, I suppose she is."

He longed for the calm tenderness of his mother, the protection of the ideal father he would never know—

"Hurts, doesn't it?" the pigeon asked. "Losing a dream. Settling for less than perfection."

Brandon laughed. "Toni's not a dream."

"Not Toni. What you've lost. Excitement. Joy. Hope. Love. Especially love."

Brandon nodded and held his head in his hands. "It hurts a lot."

"It hurts because—" the bird left the sentence unfinished.

"Because what?" Brandon demanded.

"Do you want the whole truth or an easier answer?"

Brandon bit his lip and considered. "The whole truth."

"All right. To begin with, you're seventeen."

"What has that got to do with anything?"

"Seventeen is like riding a skateboard on a freeway. Reckless. Dangerous. Stupid. A sane person would get off the road and vanish into the ditch, hoping nobody notices he's there. However, at seventeen, a person doesn't

109

care about traffic. Childhood and puberty have already run over them like a truck."

"You sound like my mother."

The voice spoke reassuringly. "She loved you, you know. She still does."

The words echoed in the night across space and time.

Wiping his eyes with the back of his hand, Brandon whispered, "Yeah. Yeah, I know."

"Love is real. Love is forever," the bird continued.

Light quivered as truth hung in the air, waiting to be spoken. Brandon knew he didn't want to hear, but he needed to. He pulled up his legs and wrapped his arms around his knees. "Anything else?" he asked.

"Know what you are."

Gazing into the darkness, Brandon nodded and laid his head on his legs. "Shit," he mumbled. He saw all the girls he distracted. He saw the Toni he had rejected. He saw the red-headed covergirl he had never met. He saw himself.

He strained his mouth forming the words.

"So the whole truth is I'm a prick."

"But only if you want," the pigeon said as it flew into the silence of night.

16

Crossing Dingle

Fort Repentance, British Columbia
Canada

Jeannie loved her job at Literary License bookstore, the curiously pink landmark on bustling Dingle Avenue. She loved the books, the smell, the work, the people—all of it. She especially loved the responsibility and trust the storeowners had in a 17-year-old book nerd.

Fumbling with her keys, she locked the door, shook the latch to check its security, then turned to the street. Out on Dingle, traffic snarled and growled, jolted and dashed, sputtered and throbbed. She hoisted the book bag with all her father's latest requests, then turned to face the turbulent six lanes, the biggest obstacle on her daily trek home.

Nightly, the teeming rush hour traffic taunted and dared her, as well as any other foolhardy pedestrian, to cross. And every evening, Jeannie triumphed by simply walking to Newton Street at the end of the block, enduring the traffic light, then hustling to the other side. Once across, the hike was easy. Quiet, even.

This night, however, instead of doing its job of smoothly opening a free-flowing pathway to the opposite side, the signal mutinied against Jeannie, blinking erratically, if ever, and effectively demolishing her strategy.

Under an unsympathetic and disdainful corner light pole, Jeannie waited. And waited. And waited. Impatiently, she set down her bag and twisted her head with both hands until her neck cracked, relieving her tension.

The traffic signal for Dingle flashed yellow. Intent on beating the red light, excited vehicles roared and rocketed through the intersection.

When the last taillights cleared the crosswalk, the Newton walk light blinked assuringly. Jeannie adjusted her father's heavy book bag, quickly checked left and right for any speeding stragglers, then hurried forward into the street.

Halfway across the street, just when the white walker symbol transformed to a countdown of seconds, Jeannie's right leg crumpled. She gasped and dropped the book bag, doubling over in agony.

"God, no!"

12...11...10...

The traffic light flashed from green to amber.

6...5...4...

Car engines raced on her right.

"Oh, please, not now." She grasped for the elusive bag handles.

3...2...1...

The mocking Dingle light flashed green. Instantly, horns blared.

"Come on, lady! Move it!"

"I—I can't." Jeannie gasped, holding up a hand and balancing on one leg. "Just wait. I'm trying. I really am."

A semi-truck's air horn blasted.

Jeannie found the bag handles, struggled to straighten her good leg, and hopped across the final two lanes. Her pointless, whispered apologies melted into the din, totally unheard. Finally across the street, she bounced onto the curb, clutched the light pole, and leaned heavily against it.

The air around her darkened, and an angry man barked, "Hey! Come on! I gotta push the button."

Jeannie wheezed and hopped to the side. "Oh. Sorry. I'm really sorry."

The formless, faceless voice grunted, then disappeared into traffic as the signal changed. Once more, Jeannie clutched the pole, holding back the pain by gritting her teeth and clenching her eyes.

Someone tugged at her jacket. "Lady? Lady? Are you all right?"

Jeannie opened her eyes. A head of mussed hair and missing teeth stared up at her.

"I'll be fine. I just need a place to sit down."

"There's a bench over by the bus stop," the little girl offered.

Jeannie managed a smile and patted her shoulder. "Thank you."

"You need help?"

Jeannie thought for a moment. "Maybe—Can you carry my book bag? I think I can make it if I don't have to carry anything."

"Sure."

Tentatively, Jeannie let go of the pole, then bounced toward the bus stop, stopping occasionally to catch her breath. With a final hop and twist, she dropped onto the bench. Back at the light pole, the girl strained to lift the book bag. Unable to hoist the load above her ankles, she crouched and dragged it across the bustling sidewalk, abandoning it at Jeannie's feet.

"That's really heavy," she complained.

"Books for my mom and dad. They're writers."

The girl looked back and forth between Jeannie and the bag.

Jeannie sat up and rubbed her knee. "I'm Jeannie, by the way."

"Oh. I'm Ella. I'm eleven."

"*Ella*. That's a nice name."

"It means *all* in German. That's what my mom says."

"All?"

"Uh-huh. I'm all she ever wants to have."

Jeannie smiled. "Well, I'm sure—"

"Want to know why?"

"Why?"

"'Cause I'm a pain in the ass."

"Oh, well—"

"That's what she says, but I think it's because she hurt so bad when I was born. It hurts to have babies. Did you know that?"

"Well, yes, I've heard that."

"So don't ever have babies. Okay? I'm not going to."

"Well, I—" Jeannie winced.

Ella stepped toward her, then glanced up sharply at the traffic light. "Uh, I gotta go. Sorry."

"Go. Go. I'll be all right."

"You look like you hurt. Are you having a baby?"

"No. It's just my knee. I'll be fine. Go ahead."

Ella hurried toward the light pole. Waving a quick goodbye, the girl spun and scooted across the hectic street, her tiny body disappearing into the crowd on the opposite curb.

Jeannie sat a moment, catching her breath. Gathering her courage, she bent over and wrapped both arms around her throbbing leg.

"It's never hurt this bad," she moaned into her thighs.

Sobbing and choking, she sat up and leaned her head on the store window behind her. Tears distorted the street into melting, swimming globs and shapes. Frustrated, she closed her eyes.

"I hate this," she whimpered.

She shivered. It had been almost a year since her last Shimmering, the boy at Machu Picchu. She had nearly forgotten. "It's coming. Don't let it be this bad. No monsters. No killing like before. Please."

Bracing herself against the bench, she shook off her fear, gulped a lungful of air, and cautiously leaned forward to straighten her leg. Her thigh stretched. The muscles pounded incessantly, but tolerably.

"Just a little at a time," she said. "Slowly."

She pushed her knee down as she bent her ankle to raise her toes. The knee twinged. Each millimeter of movement cramped and jabbed. Every other body part told her to stop, yet she persisted.

Sidewalk traffic bustled around her—people, pets, young, old. Its judgmental glances stung her face.

"Only a few inches to go."

She bent further to put more pressure on her knee. The pain became a slow ache with brief spikes and spasms. Steadily, their intensity decreased until the joint popped into place and the pain vanished.

Jeannie sat back and exhaled. "Oh, God! Oh, God. Thank you!"

When she opened her eyes, the street before her, the buildings, and the rushing traffic brightened, quivered, shook violently, and disappeared.

Jeannie sat on a rock at the edge of a forest.

This was different than the other Shimmerings. The dreams always told someone else's story, not hers. She had never been a participant.

Through the green meadow before her, a river meandered from the mountains. Beyond the peaks, gray clouds rose like gray smoke, twisting and curling into a collage of snarling, ferocious creatures she had never seen. Sunlight off the mountaintop turned bulging eyes red and yellow. Ravenous mouths yawned open, baring sharp, dripping fangs. Grotesque faces shifted from reptile to mammal to human, yet none of them were real.

"What in the—"

A wet nose nudged her shoulder. "You know."

Jeannie jerked back and spun toward the voice.

A white bear—not a polar bear but a spirit bear, the animal of legend spoken of only in classes and rumors—stood next to her, its strong, round body relaxed, its omniscient face calming. The bear's presence neither threatened nor alarmed.

Throughout her other Shimmerings, Jeannie had learned to accept the obvious, no matter how preposterous. A talking bear was no different to her. She recognized the voice. The one that told her there would be more Shimmerings.

"You're a bear," she blurted. "I never knew. You're a bear."

"Now you do."

"A spirit bear."

The animal turned to her, dipped his head, and gazed up at her. The bear did not speak aloud. His voice spoke inside her. "Yes. Look to the clouds. Remember."

She scanned the range and the valley as the clouds' creatures rose, danced, and grabbed at the sky.

"I told you I didn't want more" she said. "You're not very helpful."

"What you want does not change what is. What do you see?"

"Monsters."

"Yes. You know their reality. Remember the names, where they have been."

"I don't—I—"

Jeannie studied the ever-changing shapes. "No. I do. Match—Matchi—"

The bear nodded. "Go on."

The word and its malevolent connotation dripped from her lips. "Matchi-auwishuk."

The bear nodded.

"They were in—Jefferson? Yeah. Jefferson. Where I was born."

"Yes."

"But they're not there anymore. They've moved. To—"

Jeannie stopped, jarred into silence.

"You know."

Jeannie paused, tilted her head. She shook her head. "I want to say Mount Elder—Mount Elder?"

"Close. You know. What else? Trust yourself."

Jeannie scrunched her face. "Its hard to trust yourself when you're talking to a bear."

"Close your eyes. Block the distraction. Remember Mount Elder. You were there."

Jeannie braced herself. The darkness clouded her memory. An image flashed in Jeannie's mind. She hesitated.

"You were there," the bear repeated.

"With Dad and my stepmom AJ."

"Yes. Who else?"

Jeannie's eyes jolted open and her jaw dropped. "You! Fishing in the lake. I saw you our first day there, but nobody believed me. 'There are no spirit bears around here,' they insisted."

She flailed her arms. "And you kept appearing and hiding. It was a game. One that I always lost."

The bear nodded.

"You were really a pain. You know that?"

Again, the bear nodded.

"You jerk!" She laughed.

The bear lowered himself to the ground and laid his head on his front paws.

"What happened the last day?" he asked.

Jeannie sat on the ground next to the bear. "The mist had just lifted and you let me see you across the lake."

"And—"

Jeannie savored the memory. "To the left, a bull moose waded in the shallows feeding on reeds. To the right, you drank. It was beautiful."

"Until?"

Her face darkened. "My dad and AJ came up and gazed across the lake, but they didn't see you or the moose or anything. They just looked at the mist."

The bear waited.

"I saw them once like that before, but I couldn't remember where or when. I still don't."

"What happened next?"

"AJ said, 'We need to go.' It was like she saw or knew something none of the rest of us could."

"Then what?"

"We left. Back to the city. Back to 'civilization.' No explanation or anything. We just went."

The spirit bear stared at her.

"Is that important?"she asked.

"Yes. Because now you know."

Jeannie thought and then lifted her face to the vanishing remnant of clouds. "The fog. The fog and the matchi-auwishuk go together. At least in Jefferson, they did."

Again, the spirit bear nodded.

"But I've never seen matchi-auwishuk. Have I?"

The bear looked at her intently. "Remember the Shimmerings."

"What about them?"

"What monsters did you see?"

"Monsters? I don't know. I—"

The spirit bear stared at her.

"The killer at Mount Elder? The guys in the Oaxaca cantina?"

The bear remained motionless.

"The killers are matchi-auwishuk?"

"There are more. You know this."

"Yeah, okay, but the last Shimmering I had. The one with the boy—Beetle. Is he matchi-auwish too?"

"You must ask."

"I *am* asking! Tell me."

"Not me."

Four clouds blew over the mountains. Two men. Two women.

The bear lifted its nose to the sky and said, "It is time. No more watching. No more Shimmerings. Time for action."

As the clouds faded, it took a second for the words to register.

"Wait!" Jeannie started. "No more Shimmerings? Really?"

"Ask and there will be no more."

The bear turned and lumbered away over the meadow toward the mountains. The light over the field shimmered, strengthened, and disappeared. The world went dark.

In a blink, Jeannie woke to the clamor of Dingle Avenue, sweat covering her forehead. Tentatively, she rose and tested her knee.

No twinges, no aching. It flexed easily.

She lifted her bag and followed Newton to Twelfth Avenue, the quiet lane that climbed to her house on the hill.

Once around the corner, away from the prying eyes of traffic, she began her covert exercise regime. She lowered the bag and rotated her arms to loosen her shoulders. Then, glancing around once more, she bent her knees and curled the bag eight times with each hand. When she finished, she stood straight and flexed her limbs again.

"The Shimmerings are over!" She felt strong, renewed. Confidently, she swung the bag over her shoulder. After adjusting the straps, she bounced to redistribute the weight in the bag.

The words of the Spirit Bear echoed in her mind. "Time for action."

Atop the hill, her tower rose above the houses and trees. "I probably don't want to know what that means."

At her parents' sidewalk, she turned to the mountains beyond the harbor. She remembered the clouds. "Matchi-auwishuk."

A speck rose from the trees below, black against the fading light of the sky. A single bird danced across the blue sky, drawing a picture against the celestial canvas. Dark lines dipped and swelled until a face emerged from the nothingness. Not a monster. A woman.

Someone Jeannie once knew. Gray eyes. Her own eyes. Black hair.

The bird veered from the portrait and flew closer to where Jeannie stood. It circled her once, twice, fluttered, and landed at her feet.

Its iridescent neck shining in the fading light, the bird gazed up at her and cocked its head.

Jeannie laughed. "Are you the same pigeon that landed on my windowsill?" she asked.

She caught herself and smiled at the sky. "First, I talk to a bear. Now a bird! That does it. I'm nuts."

The pigeon cooed, flapped its wings, rose, and landed calmly on Jeannie's head.

"What the—?" she sputtered, but before she could raise a hand to scare the bird away, she remembered. She remembered the spirit bear. She remembered her hometown of Jefferson, Minnesota. She remembered her parents—her father, AJ, and her birth mother. And for some reason a boy in Wisconsin.

She remembered more than she wanted to.

And less.

"I must ask," she told herself.

The pigeon cooed and flew off her head into the twilight. Jeannie watched until it disappeared, then she climbed the steps into her parents' house.

17

Changing Ways

Winthrop, Michigan
USA

Being a prick flustered Brandon. The dreams of joy, hope, and love disappeared the day his family left Madison for Winthrop. His role as Winthrop's carnal savior had not restored them. Instead, über-fucking not only failed to rekindle dreams, it also extinguished the excitement of sex.

That night Toni Sharpe drove away from his house, he adopted a simple code: No more! No more backstairs meetings. No more moonless drives to the gravel pit. No more cryptic notes stuffed into lockers. For the final weeks of the school year, celibacy reigned. The end of classes, not to mention vacation, brought sweet relief from the secret calls whenever his father drove away, the coded messages slipped into his textbooks, and the shortages of condoms.

No longer shackled by education or desire, he took extra hours at O'Neill's, stocking shelves, carrying bags, and delivering groceries to shut-ins. He missed the notoriety and exhilaration of his former life, but he refused to return.

"*Small chance of that,*" he thought.

After he had rejected her, Toni Sharpe spread lies of crabs and AIDS. Even those who disbelieved the rumors avoided him.

Which had its rewards.

Despite his outcast status with fellow students, working at O'Neill's enhanced his respectability with customers, co-workers, and his boss Andy. He greeted every customer he knew by name. If another clerk or cashier suffered from the flu, a root canal, or a monstrous hangover, he covered the hours. When blunt, crabby Andy pulled him aside to correct his method of sorting apples, Brandon nodded appreciatively, then thanked him for his faith and direction. New attitude and respect led to more responsibility, trust, and loyalty. Brandon almost learned to smile.

However, true reform—the elimination of his inner prickdom—proved difficult. Although life may have changed, his sentiments did not. He still had one more year of school, which disgusted him. Despite his restrained exterior, inside he ached for his dead mother and grandfather. Most of all, if he had the guts, he'd beat the shit out of his drunken asshole father and dump the body in Lake Superior.

One quiet Tuesday morning in late August, Brandon knelt in the cereal aisle stacking caseloads of Cheerios and Wheaties. As he reached behind himself for another box, a pair of neon sneakers stopped in front of him. When he wouldn't look up, the right toe tapped impatiently.

"Whatcha doin', stranger?"

The cheerful voice leapt happily through Brandon's brain.

Nancy Kirkman.

"Hey!"

"Brandon, you smiled!"

"Don't tell anybody. How are you?"

"I'm fine. Stand up and hug me, you."

"*She was taller before,*" he thought as he wrapped his arms around her.

He didn't care. Her embrace soothed and protected. The smell of morning in her hair lightened the stale air of the grocery store. Even in her arms, he missed her.

"How are you doing?" she asked, stepping back. "How are—you know—things?"

Brandon scowled. "Boring."

Nancy pinched his cheek. "Ah, the old Brandon. I missed that face. Boring?"

"I'm not doing that anymore."

"What do you mean? Are you sick?"

Brandon waved her off. "No. I'm fine. I'm just done. At least for awhile."

"School's starting in what? A week?"

"Yeah. It doesn't matter. I'll get through it. Only one more year."

Nancy examined his face. "You sure you're okay?"

"You mean physically?"

"Yeah."

"Yeah. I just—I dunno."

Nancy nodded. "I heard some good things about you, even off at college. Girls like you."

"Yeah? Great."

"What do you mean?"

"I don't know."

She read his expressionless face. "Yeah, you do. Basically, you've just been jacking off?"

Brandon drew a finger across the cereal shelf and nodded. "Yeah. That's it."

A shopping cart jolted to a stop beside them.

"Excuse me. Could you—?" a harried young woman asked. Inside the car, her baby flailed and screamed, its wails resounding throughout the store.

"Oh, I'm sorry," Brandon apologized, pulling Nancy aside to make room.

The mother retrieved her baby and bounced it on her hip to ease the crying. As the baby shrieked, the woman pushed out her lower lip and blew at a wayward hair that crossed her eyes. "No, that's okay," she said, kissing away the bouncing baby's squeals. "I just need some Cheerios. Can you grab me a box? One of the big ones?"

"Yeah, sure." Convinced that the faster he moved, the sooner the kid would shut up, Brandon snatched a box from the case and grandly presented it to her.

The woman grinned at him and moved the child to her other hip. "I don't really have any hands. Can you throw it in the cart?"

"Oh, yeah. Sorry."

She hesitated, then set her child into the carrier. "That's—That's great. Thanks."

"No sweat."

The two held each other's eyes until Nancy coughed and turned away.

Brandon stuffed his hands into his back pocket and shuffled his feet.

"Well, I—" The woman glanced between Brandon and her baby. "Excuse me. I have to go before she starts to cry again."

"Yeah," Brandon said. "Have a great day, okay?"

The woman smiled and waved shyly as she pushed her cart down the aisle.

When she rounded the corner, Nancy grabbed his arm and teased, "Who's she?"

"I don't know. I don't remember seeing her in the store before."

"But you have seen her around town, haven't you? And you saw a lot of her just now, right?"

"Cut it out," he whispered, lifting his head and keeping a sharp eye on the aisle where the woman disappeared.

"Oh, and she saw you, too. She likes you."

"Yeah, well." He returned to supplying the shelves.

Nancy fingered the oatmeal boxes on the shelf.

"What are you thinking?" Brandon asked.

"You still wearing my cross?"

Brandon reached under his collar and pulled out the necklace. He laid it over his white apron. "Yeah. Why?"

"Because I think it's time to remember how this all started—where you've been, where you are, and what comes next."

"Next? What do you mean next?"

"You once had grand expectations, right?

Brandon looked deeply into her inviting brown eyes. He loved her that night in the gravel pit. He still did.

"Yeah. Grand expectations. Yeah, I did."

"And most came true. Right?"

"Well, not the—Yeah. I guess. I don't know. I just don't care any more."

"Kinda like my business prof says. 'Sometime we outgrow our original skill set.' I get that. Maybe you've been doing girls so long it's time to try something else."

"I'm not doing guys!"

"That's not what I meant. Not that that's a bad thing," she said, touching his arm. "I have some college friends—I meant maybe you should start looking at grown women. You know. Ones with more experience and higher ambitions. Ones who are a little more—I don't know—adventurous?"

"Like who?"

"Like the lady with the kid. I know I've seen her before. I think at the gas station just before I came here. Her name Annie Douglas?"

"That sounds right, I guess. It doesn't matter. I can't fuck her."

"Why not?"

"She's married with at least one kid."

"Yeah? And where do you think she got that kid? The children's section of Walmart?"

"I don't know. She's out of my league."

"Why?"

"'Cause she's older."

"Brandon, I'm older. I've always been older. That never made any difference, did it?"

Brandon's shoulders slumped. "No, I guess not."

"So—?"

"Like I said. She's married."

"Danger, Brandon. Experience and danger. Listen, you can leave this one alone if you want, but I'm telling you. There are married women out there just hunting and hoping for someone to whip up the old crotch juices. You know?"

Brandon shook his head.

"I'm serious. You know that. Look at my mom."

Brandon turned away and sucked his upper lip between his teeth. For two years, nightmares of his father and Nancy's mother nauseated him. At other times, he visualized his mother and Sigurd Dorsett back in Madison. He refused to relate his own behavior to his parents', yet if libido were hereditary, he knew where the hunger came from.

His hands trembled. Being a prick hurt. He had to stop, and he had to stop completely.

Nancy stared up at him. "Well?" she asked.

Then again, not being a prick hurt as well. "I wouldn't know—know—" he started. He broke off his thought.

"Where to look?"

"Yeah. Yeah, I guess."

"I have an idea. What time do you get off work?"

"5:30. But—"

"I'll meet you out back." She reached up and kissed his cheek. "5:30. See you then." She grabbed a box of Rice Krispies and bounced down the aisle.

Brandon gazed at her firm ass as it turned the corner. He checked the time on the store clock.

10:00.

Seven and a half hours. *"I can do this,"* he thought, returning to the opened crate of Cheerios.

18

Sense and Outward Things

Fort Repentance, British Columbia
Canada

"Jeannie Jones!"

The gravelly voice shattered Jeannie's daydream. Across the street, the Stockleys' golden retriever leapt at the porch window, howling and pawing at the unseen intruder. The Flanagan girls playing hopscotch on the sidewalk wailed, flung their chalk, and scrambled for the safety of their house. Throughout the neighborhood, doors slammed. Curtains closed. Locks clicked. Terrified eyes peeked out kitchen door windows.

Jeannie stopped her climb, sighed, and shivered off images of monsters and devils. She knew the voice. Calmly, she steeled her nerves.

"Hi, Mrs. McNally. How are you today? I haven't seen you for a long time."

Scarlett McNally, a clattering pile of bones, bounced and sputtered, while her mousy nurse Maddie strained to push her wheelchair up Magnuson Hill toward Jeannie. Jabbing the air with a skeletal finger, the old woman screeched, "How am I? I'm 84 years old. I've got hemorrhoids the size of Quebec. My hair's falling out. And I haven't crapped in three days. Otherwise, I'm doing just fine."

Maddie leaned over Mrs. McNally to set the chair's brakes. The old woman furiously slapped her away. "Get off me, you spike-haired lesbo!"

"I was just trying to—"

"I know exactly what you were just trying. You were trying to cop a feel. Every day since my idiot son Andrew hired you. Now just hold the chair here—with both hands! You hear me?—until I'm done. Then you can take me home and escape to your basement dump."

Deflecting the attack on Maddie, Jeannie laid her hand on Mrs. McNally's shoulder. "You wanted me for something?"

"Huh?" Mrs. McNally blinked and turned to Jeannie. "Who are you?"

"Jeannie Jones? You called me. You wanted to tell me something?"

"I did? Oh, yes! I did! Jeannie Jones, I just wanted to tell you—I—uh— Oh, to hell with it. I forgot."

Jeannie breathed a sigh of relief and grinned at Maddie.

"Don't you smile, you red-headed—redheaded—Don't look at me that way! I know you think I'm crazy, but I'm not. I know you. You're a—a—a bastard. No, that's not the right word."

"A bitch?" Maddie offered helpfully.

"Yes. A bitch!" She paused and turned her ear toward her nurse. "How did you know that's the word I wanted?"

"You've been calling everybody that lately."

Jeannie snorted back her laugh, then turned to hide her face.

"Don't you laugh at me, Jeannie Jones! You know what you are! And you know what you did. You and your sister!"

"Um," Jeannie began tentatively, reaching for the old lady's hand. "Mrs. McNally, I don't have a sister."

Maddie groaned and desperately waved to warn Jeannie off the subject.

Mrs. McNally slapped Jeannie's hand away and croaked, "You what?"

Maddie's anguished eyes pleaded, "Please say you have a sister."

Confused, Jeannie hesitated. Then she remembered AJ's advice: "Mrs. McNally lives in an alternative reality. She doesn't mean to. She just does. It's the disease. When she gets that way, just—just follow her on the journey."

Jeannie slapped her forehead. "Oh, yes. My sister. Of course. You mean my sister—" She scrambled for a name, looking to Maddie for direction. Safely behind Mrs. McNally's back, Maddie shrugged regretfully.

"My sister—" Jeannie grasped for anything. "My sister—Beulah."

"Yes! Yes!" Mrs. McNally huffed. "That—that Beulah woman." She stopped and glared at Jeannie suspiciously. "Is that her name?"

"Yes. Remember? You gave her that nice silver necklace that had her name on it? She wears it everywhere. And people say, 'Oh, look. There goes Beulah Jones.'"

"That's her! Beu—B—What was that again?"

"Beulah."

"Right," Mrs. McNally said, leaning back in her chair.

Maddie relaxed, smiled, and joined the conversation. "You bought Beulah a necklace, Mrs. McNally? Why didn't you buy Jeannie one?"

"Her name's not Beulah. She'd look awfully stupid with someone else's name hanging around her neck."

"You're right. Maybe I'll ask my dad to get one with my name on it," Jeannie said.

"Your name's not Beulah!" Mrs. McNally spat. "You're always tryin' to get all the attention. All the time! You're just—just—"

"Incorrigible?" Maddie asked.

"That's it! Incorri—In—What was that again?"

"Incorrigible."

"Yes. In—What she said. That's what you are."

Maddie took a tissue from her pocket and dabbed at Mrs. McNally's mouth. "Here. You've got some dribble—"

"Stop it!" the old woman shrieked, batting Maddie's hand away. "You are always—always—I just want to—If I weren't confined to this damned wheelchair, I'd—I'd—I really would. My asshole is turning red just thinking about how mad I am at you. Take me home. Now!"

Jeannie stepped in to rescue Maddie from Mrs. McNally's rage. She touched the old lady's shoulder and leaned her face closer. "I'm really sorry I upset you. I am a really bad person. Please forgive me."

Mrs. McNally examined Jeannie's face as she struggled to recognize the young woman. "I don't forgive, especially after what you did. You hear me?"

Jeannie stepped back and dropped her chin to her chest. "You're right, Mrs. McNally. I shouldn't have done it. I'm sorry. I'll try to be better. I promise."

Mrs. McNally grunted and eyed Jeannie suspiciously. "Yes. Well, see that you do." Then, shaking a finger, she added, "But I'm watching you."

"I understand."

The matter settled, Mrs. McNally growled at Maddie, "Take me home. I have to eat some prunes."

"All right. Good-bye, Miss Jones," Maddie said timidly, mouthing the words "Thank you" as she turned the chair to descend the hill.

Jeannie smiled and nodded.

"Well, let's go! I'm not paying you to stand around picking your butt!"

Maddie shook her head and wheeled Mrs. McNally away.

Jeannie turned back toward her house. "There's not enough money in the world—"

She stopped to check the family mailbox and looked across the city to the mountains.

Matchi-auwishuk, she remembered.

The word the bear confirmed. The word that meant something once. Something about her mother. Her father. Something before the Shimmerings. Even before Canada.

Before she climbed the steps to her house, she looked after Mrs. McNally and Maddie slowly disappearing down the hill.

"*An alternate reality would be a blessing,*" she thought.

The wind shook the trees and blew Jeannie's long, red hair across her face. She pushed it back with her forearm and opened the door. Quietly, she slipped across the entry and bounded up the stairs to her room.

19

The Tormented Tormentor

Mount Komu ("The Entry")
British Columbia, Canada

On the cliff of Mount Komu, Sarah watched the clouds billow and swirl into dreamlike images of a world that no longer accepted her. Hands and faces, people and homes, altars and cathedrals, business and bustle. Civilization.

Beecher and Jeannie Jones, her earthly husband and daughter.

Sarah raised a hand to the gold chain on her throat. While alive, she had always thoroughly investigated her options before making her totally implausible selection.

She no longer had choices.

After she chose death and eternity with the Earth Man, decisions were no longer hers. From that point, alternatives faded.

In some ways, it was a relief. Time meant nothing here. Unlike life, in death the past never tormented because the clock never advanced to the future. Instead, the present quickly vanished into the haze of irrelevant memory. Anxiety, impatience, and aging failed to antagonize.

"I don't regret my decision," she said.

Above her, the cloudy remnants of her earthly life swelled, wavered, spiraled, and evaporated into mist.

"*I know,*" she thought. "*There may be more, but there may be less. Security is everything.*"

Since becoming queen, to maintain her position, Sarah had never encouraged nor attempted to thwart the Earth Man's violence and debauchery. To maintain peace, she never took sides in his Great War against good. Instead, to maintain her beauty and existence, she simply endured, no matter how soundly the Word defeated him in battle.

And yet, today she doubted. She squatted to pick up a stone at her side, holding it in one hand and examining it with the other.

She bit her lower lip. "*There is no security with him,*" she thought. "*He never wins.*"

Her neck burned beneath the chain.

"*But he always survives to fight another day in another place,*" the metal reminded her.

Sarah grimaced, nodded, and dropped the stone to her side. The chain was correct. That's why she never criticized. There was no point. "*Besides,*" she told herself, "*you belong to the Earth Man here. You are his to hold or dispose. It is only by his side that you exist. Apart from him, your body and all memory of you disappear.*"

As she thought before, she had no choices.

High above her, a wind cleared the sky, but below the surface of the mountain, the driving rhythm of the drums and dancing of the matchi-auwishuk vibrated the soles of her feet. She must go back to the cave and the Earth Man.

As Sarah made her way down the path to the opening in the mountainside, she saw a lone guard sitting on a boulder below her. She stopped short.

Of all the Earth Man's disciples, she abhorred the pishtaco the most. He had no loyalty. He butchered and defiled with egotistical abandon simply because he loved to slaughter.

Sarah pulled at her long, black hair with one hand and smoothed it with the other. "*He wants to destroy everybody!*" she thought.

Unaware of her presence above him, the pishtaco watched the path down the mountain, searching, waiting. Sarah's hand grazed her breast and her stomach fluttered. *"Everybody but me."*

That was why he was at the cave. He was waiting for her. That's why she couldn't get rid of him. He didn't want to kill her; he wanted to possess her.

In between glances down the path, the pishtaco sharpened his knife against a rock. Once. Twice. Then he blew away the loose dust from the blade and licked the sides clean.

Sarah's stomach tightened as the sharp edge sliced his tongue and he savored the blood. She leaned against the wall forcing down the bile inside her.

"No fear. No fear. I can destroy him any time I want," she told herself.

The pishtaco tossed the stone onto the ground and sheathed his knife. Carelessly ignoring the path above him, he explored the meadow below while a fly landed on his hat and searched for a weakness in the fabric.

Sarah recognized a deeper truth. The pishtaco and the Earth Man shared the same flaws.

"And to destroy him, I don't have to kill him. I just have to control him."

As she did the Earth Man. Yes, he had enslaved her with his chain of lust, but whenever she manipulated the Earth Man's passion, the world's tormentor became the tormented. The pishtaco would do the same.

"I wish I had learned that before he eliminated Frank," she thought.

The fly crawled fruitlessly across the hat and flew away defeated.

She smiled broadly, patting her chest. *"Desire and power,"* she thought. Their weaknesses. *"Desire and power."*

Calmly and confidently, she descended the rocky path toward the cave.

"Nice walk, Señora?" the pishtaco called.

As if the path skidded beneath her, Sarah caught herself on the rocky wall.

"Oh, it's you. I didn't expect to find anybody here."

The lie flowed more naturally than truth.

"Just watching out for El Jefe, *the boss.*" The pishtaco raised his curved knife, piercing his thumb and sucking the blood.

His ferocious eyes gleamed at her. "You didn't say whether you had a nice walk," he added.

She locked her jaw and narrowed her eyebrows. "Yes. Very nice. Thank you."

She walked steadily toward him and the cave entrance.

"I'm glad." The pishtaco sneered and slithered in front of her to block the opening. He bent low and cocked his head, daring her to say or do anything.

She fixed her silver eyes on him. "I'll mention your consideration to the Earth Man."

The pishtaco stood taller. The two locked gazes. Until the fly landed on the pishtaco's nose. He flinched.

Sarah smirked.

Desperate to camouflage his loss, the pishtaco waved away the fly and lowered his hat-brim. He stepped back, again sucking the blood from his cut.

Sarah brushed past him and strode deep into the cave, grinning into the darkness.

20

Climbing Mount Hebron

Winthrop, Michigan
USA

After locking the store's front door and punching his timecard, Brandon escaped out the back and found Nancy leaning on his Saturn.

"How did you know this was my car?"

"Something just spoke to me and said, 'Brandon Whistler's car.'"

"What?"

"Okay, it wasn't like a burning bush or something. It was the trunk."

"What are you talking about?"

"Go look."

Brandon walked to the back of the car and saw the words etched into thick dust. "Brandons a basturd."

"What the hell?"

Nancy stood next to him. "Well, judging from the handwriting and the rotten spelling, I'd say you had an unsatisfied customer."

Brandon thought, then scowled. "Toni Sharpe."

"That would be my guess. What did you do?"

Brandon shrugged. "I turned her down."

"Well, there you go. It doesn't matter. I told you I have an idea. Come on. Give me a ride."

The sun sparkled off her hair and eyes, melting Brandon's legs. *No* was not an option. "Where are we going?" he asked.

"Not far. Just the other side of town." She patted the trunk and crossed to the passenger side.

The whole town of Winthrop seemed to be eating their supper while Brandon weaved his Saturn through the quiet streets into the hollow on the north edge of town. "Here we are," Nancy said. "Pull into the church parking lot and stop at the far end. You can turn off the engine there."

Brandon did as he was told. The engine coughed and sputtered before finally dying.

"Now what?"

"This is it," she said, bubbling with pride.

"What?"

"My idea!"

Brandon scowled first at her, then the doors to Mount Hebron Church of the Rock. "You want me to go to church?"

"Yeah."

"You are nuts! I'll wear your cross, but I'm not going to church."

"Why not?"

"I don't—"

"Don't what?"

"I mean I don't even know if I believe in God. I don't even know if I want to."

"Ha!" Nancy slapped the dashboard. She gasped for air between bouts of laughter. Whenever she glanced at Brandon, she broke down again.

"What? What's so funny?"

"You—You think—I brought you here to meet God?" Her chin shifted and jerked as she fought back her giggles.

"Didn't you?"

Nancy held her breath and shook her head.

"You don't think I need saving?"

Nancy waved him off. "Hell, we all need saving, but you especially? That's between you and your conscience. Although from what I know of you, conscience doesn't affect you much."

Her words burned.

"I'm not that bad." He clutched the steering wheel.

Nancy patted his hand. "I'm not saying you're bad. You're trying to be good. I just don't think you give a rat's ass about God."

"Then why are we here?"

"Because," she said, gripping his hand for emphasis, "you want to meet women. Hot, dangerous, adventurous women."

"I did. I mean I do, but—"

Nancy pointed at the church with both hands.

"In church?"

"I'm telling you. You have a preference? I know you like blondes. How about brunettes? Oh! I know! Redheads! Didn't you say there was a centerfold—"

"Yeah. Shut up. That was a long time ago."

"Mount Hebron has whatever you want—ready, willing, and energetically able."

"How do you know?"

"This is where I was raised. Where do you think I learned?"

Brandon scrutinized her eyes for cracks in the story. "I don't believe you."

"I'm serious." She pulled out the Aphrodite medal that once belonged to Brandon's mother. "I swear every adult woman in that building is a charter member of this club."

He glanced from Nancy to the church. "Who—Where would I start?"

Nancy smirked. "Okay. So you remember our first time?"

"Of course, I remember. Wh—?"

"Can you carry a tune?"

"What?"

"Can you sing?"

Brandon raised his hands and shook his head. "Hang on a minute. I'm getting whiplash."

"Just answer my question. Can you sing?"

"A little. Why?"

Nancy pointed at the weekly events sign. "Choir practice. Tuesday, 7 p.m."

"Yeah? So?"

"Afterward."

"I don't get—"

"It's amazing how many people become interested in the 'music of geology' on Tuesday nights. There are almost as many cars in the gravel pit as there are rocks. And—And most of those cars just spent two hours here at the Mount Hebron parking lot."

"Kids?"

Nancy shook her head. "Oh, maybe a senior or two, but mostly frustrated men and women 'getting out of the house.' You know what I mean?"

Brandon examined the sign, then the door.

"What do you think?" Nancy asked.

"*Don't be a prick*," he thought.

"I don't know. It sounds risky," he said aloud.

"Well, sure it does. That's what makes it fun. It's kind of like diving off the high board. You stand on the platform looking at the water and it's terrifying. You can't breathe. You have to pee, but you just stand there with your knees knocking together. Finally, you just run off the board and let gravity do all the work. Before you can think, you're in the middle of the water, laughing and splashing and having a great time."

Nancy punched his arm.

"Redheads, Brandon. Or—Maybe—Maybe Annie Douglas. Huh? Huh?"

"Do you know if she even goes to church here?"

"Why do I care? You're the one who needs a woman. Come on, Brandon! Do some singing."

Brandon scratched his head, considering the idea. "I do like singing."

Nancy smiled. She waggled her eyebrows and playfully pecked his cheek. "And you're kind of good at it. Know what I mean?"

Shyly, Brandon dipped his head and played with the keys in the ignition.

"Off the board, boy. Now take me back to my car."

When Brandon leaned forward and switched on the engine, the bird and his mother who once encouraged his reformation flitted and faded into nothingness.

Cranking the wheel and stepping on the gas, Brandon sprayed loose gravel across the parking lot, then sped away from his memories.

Michael Frickstad

21

Illuminating the Darkness

Machu Picchu
Peru

Without complaint, Beetle struggled to his feet and looked to the empty valley. On the canvas of shadow, the air drew, colored, shaded, and defined the emerging picture. A face. A girl. Unfamiliar red hair that calmed and disturbed. Shining silver eyes that burned. A clouded face that thrilled and confused.

The Tourist.

Canadian, she had told him.

In the darkness, Beetle's thighs pulsated. He stared at the vision and massaged the birth stones of Viracocha.

She had asked more questions than he could ever answer, but he couldn't just walk away. It was his job to try. Not his job as tour guide, but as—as— what? Authority? Friend? Companion? Something. As puzzling as she was, Beetle knew he had to stay. The wind told him.

More than obligation, though, he *wanted* to be with her. He wanted to feel his breath catch when their eyes met. Although he did not always understand her words, he wanted them to tickle his ears. Accidentally or purposely, he wanted to feel the electric brush of her hand.

But beyond sharing the earthly sensation he felt, he wanted to proclaim all the wonders that the ruins had taught him. Translating the lessons to a spoken language she could understand, however, proved too difficult.

When the words would not form, when she could not understand his primitive spoken language nor his broken English, when she walked away in tears, he abandoned speech all together. Clutching her arm, he resorted to the communication of the earth, speaking through his touch.

Gripping her hand, caressing her cheek, pressing her lips with his fingers, he apologized. He flattered. He told her everything he couldn't before.

She smiled. She understood.

The rest of the afternoon, the two explored the ruins, climbing the various levels and strolling over the long plazas. The girl eagerly inquired about fashion and faith, legends and life, spirits and truth. At first, Beetle hesitated, but when the birth stones in his pocket warmed his thighs, he emptied the lessons of the ruins into her mind. While he was aware that the teachings were not his own, why the girl needed to hear them and why he was the one to tell her, Beetle did not know, but he trusted the stones and spoke silently.

The closer they came to the end of the Central Plaza, the more he realized she needed more than information. His words and thoughts were not enough. She needed direction. She needed truth. The stones—Viracocha himself—had more to tell than she could ask.

When the two reached the end wall, they turned, and Beetle placed the stones in the girl's palm, instantly releasing her curiosity, turning her questions from the history of the Machu Picchu to her essential nature now and forever. As they walked back holding each other's hand, Beetle allowed his mind to merge with the girl's and emptied the answers into her.

Then, the girl stumbled.

He had just finished the Peruvian legend of the pishtaco, the monster that kills and steals its victim's fat, when her feet collided and she immediately fell to the ground. When Beetle reached for her, she waved him off and gripped her right leg, examining her knee cap. She sighed in relief, then smiled. "I'm okay," she told Beetle. "Now tell me more about this pishtaco guy."

Her cold, bright eyes flashed an emotion Beetle couldn't define. An anger? A fear? Her shoulders retreated, so he softened the myth, portraying it as a parental object lesson to coerce children into good behavior.

The girl forced a laugh, but her crinkled brow and the flat air between breaths revealed she needed more truth. However, the stones silenced Beetle. It was time for her to leave. She would learn later, in another place, another time, with him or without him.

As the rest of the tourists gathered to return to the hotel, the girl spotted a couple—her mother and father—waved good-bye, and disappeared into the crowd, as if she had never been there.

All that was days, weeks, months ago, yet here was her face illuminating the Darkness of the Ancients. Carefully and quietly, Beetle turned from the valley and saw a tall, twisted tree stretching a hand through the fog like a friend. Hurrying across the plaza, he stood next to it, waiting, listening, hoping. The sturdy trunk drew his hands to its smooth bark. Its strength flowed through his fingers. His forehead leaned against the tree. "The Canadian girl," he asked. "Did she understand what was happening?"

"She heard. She will know. As will you."

"I already know much."

The leaves above him shuddered. "Tell me."

"I know the language of nature. I know the Andes, the rivers and lakes, the legends and the life, the sacred and the secular. I have weathered sun and storm."

"So who are you?"

The boy hesitated. "Who am I? I am—I am Beetle."

"For now. What is your origin?"

"I was born of the stones of Lake Titicaca. Viracocha, the Great Creator, breathed life into me."

Beetle brought his knees to his chest and laid his chin on them. The leaves above him shuddered again. "Lean back for one more lesson," the tree said.

"One more? I thought—"

"Patience. This is the beginning. Follow the path of Viracocha."

22

Closer Conspiracies

Mount Komu ("The Entry")
British Columbia, Canada

The pounding drums, stomping feet, and guttural chants at the end of the tunnel shook the cavernous path in front of Sarah. The flickering firelight and dancing shadows mesmerized her, luring her forward despite her reservations.

Control was necessary. She had nowhere else to go. Bracing herself, she rose to her full height, lifted her noble head, and strode into the throne room.

Drumsticks clattered to the ground. Dancers and drummers slunk to the side of the room, their furtive eyes glancing between their queen and lord. On his throne, the indolent Earth Man leaned back heavily, fingering the chin of a nymph-sized matchi-auwish. Sarah took a full breath, crossed the room, and eased into the throne next to him. She simply gazed forward into the room and waited for him to notice her.

Startled, the matchi-auwish covered her chin and pointed to Sarah. The Earth Man glanced back and snorted. Annoyed, he grimaced and dismissed the spirit. He sat forward. "You're back."

Sarah smoothed her dress, her face calm and illegible. "Yes. Thank you for noticing."

The Earth Man reached out, taking her chain and rubbing it between his fingers. Narrowing his eyes, he scrutinized her reaction. "Where were you?"

She looked down at her hands and picked at the nails. "Outside. At the cliff."

He lifted Sarah's chin and turned it toward him. He squeezed it and glowered. "You only go outside with me."

Just as she had expected.

"All right." Sarah returned to her nails, withholding righteous indignation.

The Earth Man hissed, "Are you even sorry?"

Sarah swung her head at him and held his glare. "I'm very sorry."

She did not say for what, nor did he reply. "I am back," she said. "That's what you wanted, isn't it?" Her eyes never wavered.

"Yes," the Earth Man finally grumbled, slouching back into his throne.

Glancing toward the still-gathered musicians and dancers, Sarah whispered, "Can you dismiss them? I don't want them to hear."

The Earth Man regarded her skeptically. Then standing, he clapped his meaty hands above his head. "I must speak privately with my queen."

"Sounds kinky," the pishtaco scoffed, leaning against the entrance. Calmly, he coiled his rope in ever-tightening circles.

"What did you say?" the Earth Man snarled.

The pishtaco glanced up. When the Earth Man's persistent scowl failed to soften, the pishtaco's rebellion withered. He tugged his beard and stepped back, gradually lowering his head.

"Leave."

The pishtaco attached the rope to his belt and rallied. He saluted elaborately. "Whatever you say, boss. You two have fun."

"Now!"

The pishtaco smirked as the Earth Man's subjects scurried past him, covering their heads. He waited patiently, then waved over his shoulder as he left the room.

The Earth Man glowered into the darkness, then gruffly strode before his queen. "Talk."

Sarah examined the ground. "I've done everything you've ever told me. Fucked you however and whenever you wanted. Followed you wherever you went. Wore your slave chain. I did it all. And now I'm not supposed to go outside without you?

"Never mind. I understand. I agreed to obey. It's part of the deal. What I don't understand is I come back and here you are with a matchi-auwish? Really? I mean am I important to you at all?'"

He glowered at her. "Remember who you're talking to."

"No, I get that. You are the king. You are who you are. I'm just confused. Do I—No. I mean, do you—Do you still want me?"

The Earth Man blinked and shook his head. "What?"

Sarah leaned forward and ran her fingers across her dress. "Don't get me wrong. I'm grateful. You—You rescued me back in Jefferson. And I needed it. I had left my husband and daughter. I had crushed my lover with a car. In the hospital, I floated between life and death. But you gave me another choice. If I left with you, you would restore me to beauty. Forever."

She sat forward, her arms resting on her thighs. "But before I could decide to leave life, I had only one question. I asked if you thought I could make you happy for eternity."

She raised her wet eyes to him. "And you assured me I could. Remember?"

The Earth Man's face blanked, but he nodded anyway.

Sarah rose and stood before him. "Today, as I sat at the edge of the cliff, watching the clouds brushing the mountaintops across the valley, I felt so— alone. You know? I asked myself—and now I'm asking you—do I make you happy?"

Standing, the Earth Man could not summon a response. Not a nod. Not a grunt. Nothing.

"Because the only reason I exist at all is to serve you. If you want me gone—If you want to obliterate me like the pishtaco did Frank—"

She brought a fist to her mouth. Her eyelids fluttered until tears formed in the corners of her eyes. "I mean if that's what you want—I owe you. I know that."

She laid her forehead on his chest. Her shoulders shook.

The Earth Man glanced around the empty room, then raised his thick hand and stroked her hair.

"What choices do I have?" she sniffed, raising her head. "I can't leave. I mean where would I go? Humanity ignores me, the matchi-auwishuk gurgle and stammer at the sight of me, and it's impossible for me to jump off the mountain to kill myself again. You know, I once had a vision that I could transcend this existence and start over, that I could go back to Jefferson and marry Beecher as if nothing had happened. Stupid idea."

The Earth Man's face twisted and his hands clutched his side. "Beecher? Beecher Jones?"

"Don't get mad. Beecher wasn't the point. Are—Are you still jealous of Beecher?"

The Earth Man flexed his hands and grunted.

Sarah lowered her head and collected her thoughts. "Don't be. Visions are just warped inventions of a sick mind. I know that, but—"

He eyed her warily. "What?"

"Jealousy is irrational, too. I mean Beecher and I exist in two different worlds. He's somewhere out there. I'm here. He's alive and I'm dead. Even if we saw each other again, nothing could ever happen. The only person—"

She hesitated, looking to the darkness past the entrance. The Earth Man jerked up his head.

"No. That's really crazy," she said.

The Earth Man grasped her arm. "What?" he demanded.

Sarah turned into him and laid her hands on his chest. "Darling, I have had impure thoughts, but not about Beecher Jones."

Her mouth contorted, stifling a smile. She whispered, "I'm sorry, but I just have to confess. I really—I mean really—I really want to fuck—the pishtaco."

She burst into laughter and swirled away, bent in laughter. Gasping for breath, she raised a hand and stammered, "The pish—The—Hah! I'm sorry. I'm sorry. The pishtaco. That loser."

"Loser?"

"No, No. I know he's your most vicious warrior. I'm sorry. It's just—"

""What?" he ordered.

"He's not what you think."

Sarah glanced at the entrance, then pulled the Earth Man's head close to hers. "He wants me."

"Wants you? What are you—?"

"Seriously! Okay, every time I return from outside like just now, he—well—he sees me—stops me—smiles and asks me how my walk was."

"So what?"

"I know. For you or me, that's just being polite. But a pishtaco being polite? Can you imagine? 'Excuse me, but would you mind if I cut you open and sucked out all your fat? It would make me ever so happy.' And smile? Pishtacos don't smile. Oh, they smirk and sneer, but never actually smile. I mean did he ever smile at you? But a guy who butchers people for fun, he asks a woman about her walk and smiles? Really?"

The Earth Man stroked his cheek. "No, no, no. Since he came to Canada, he's—"

"Right!" Sarah interrupted. "He's been ruthless. Sadistic. Bloodthirsty—Okay, more accurately, fat thirsty—That's what I mean. A smile is out of place."

Sarah regarded the Earth Man, then turned away and continued. "Okay, I'm blowing this all out of proportion. When you give him some gory task, he'll return to his brutal self. I'm sure."

Glaring into the distance, the Earth Man flexed his fingers.

Sarah grabbed his fists. "I know I seem ungrateful at times, but if I ever lost you—Don't do anything foolish. Pussy-whipped or not, the pishtaco is still dangerous."

"And Beecher Jones?"

"As I said, we exist in two different worlds. Nothing to worry about."

"And that vision. You said Beecher wasn't the point. What was?"

"I was lonely. I thought I was losing you. I just wanted the option to erase where I am now, eliminate any knowledge of it, and reset motherhood with my daughter Jeannie."

She looked up into his eyes. "Please. Don't be jealous. I only want you," she said, caressing his cheek.

The hardness in his eyes flickered. He clenched his jaw. "I won't be jealous," he said. "Go wherever you like whenever you like."

"Thanks," she breathed. She paused, waiting for hm to speak. "I only want you," she assured him.

The Earth Man's body tensed. "And I only want you," he said automatically.

"*They can't have you*," Sarah heard him think.

She pulled his cloak over her mouth to hide her smile. She had forgotten that Beecher still lived.

She closed her eyes and pulled the Earth Man's open hands over her breasts. Ignoring his probing fingers and grinding hips, she begged her vision of transcendence to come true.

The pishtaco sat on the cave floor outside the throne room. Whatever was being talked about in the throne room, he needed the orgasm of fat.

Or flesh.

He glanced back at the opening. He longed for what the Earth Man knew, what the weendigo Frank had known. He longed for Queen Sarah.

"Pishtaco!" the Earth Man bellowed from inside.

As the monster arose, Sarah emerged from inside. She smiled, her eyes sparking the pishtaco's lust.

"He wants to see you," she said as she squeezed past him and disappeared up the cave.

The pishtaco adjusted his hat, rose confidently, and stepped toward his sovereign's throne. "You called, boss?"

The Earth Man lowered his chin and glowered. "You're a real smart ass, you know that?"

"It's my most endearing quality."

The Earth Man flexed his fingers and narrowed his eyes. "We need to talk about that later," he said. "Right now, it's time."

"Time?"

"Your task."

The pishtaco licked his lips and sneered. "My task. I've been looking forward to it," he said. "Any special twist you want me to use?"

"Be creative. Enjoy yourself. Do your sadistic best."

"I won't let you down."

"Good. Oh, when you get back from the city?"

"Yes?"

"Don't say anything to anyone but me. None of the matchi-auwishuk, the musicians or dancers, and especially not Queen Sarah. Got it?"

Adjusting his lasso and knife, the pishtaco grinned widely and nodded. "Just you and me, boss. Just you and me."

"Well, what are you waiting for? Go. Go!"

The pishtaco glanced at the globular Earth Man. Although the fat enticed, he strode off to his task. *"Some day,"* the monster thought. *"Some day it will be your turn."*

The Earth Man heard.

He sneered and rubbed his hands together. *"I can hardly wait, fat sucker,"* he thought.

23

Evil in the Night

Fort Repentance, British Columbia
Canada

Amanda jolted upright and held her breath as she gazed into the silence.

All night long, the covers suffocated, thoughts fleeted, and memories gnawed. Just when sleep rescued her—

Gray light from the street corner squinted through the closed curtains, leering, threatening. Wiping the hair from her eyes, she scanned the bedroom for a movement, a sound.

With a trembling hand, Amanda fumbled for her husband's back. The soft lump grunted and turned over.

Around her, the entire room shivered at attention, waiting for the onslaught of—something. Something that shocked her awake. Something lurking in the darkness.

Amanda slid out of bed and smoothed her nightgown. She glanced back at Beecher, then skated across the hardwood floor to the window. When she slid the curtains open a sliver, she froze.

"*Fog,*" she thought, wrapping her arms around herself.

Silhouetted by the streetlamp, the parked cars hulked in the mist veiling the street.

She closed her eyes and fought back images of Jefferson: The constant fog. Beecher's house. The tree. Slime dripping from the mouth of Wayne Diego. The crunch and crackle of broken bones. The screams. The flash. Flame—

Amanda caught herself and pressed both her hands on the window frame. She craned her neck left and right to search the bushes and behind the parked cars.

Rising on her tiptoes, she saw nothing suspicious in either direction. *"Maybe that van down on the corner,"* she thought. *"No. That's the Flanagans'."*

Back among the tangled sheets, Beecher snorted and turned to his back. Amanda bit her lip and waited until his breathing settled into a light snore. Quietly, she pulled the curtain tight to prevent the light from awakening him.

She rubbed the chills from her forearms. *"What woke me? A sound? A smell? What was it? And where was it?"*

She saw nothing in the dark.

"In the hall?"

Haltingly, she ran a hand along the wall, edging her way to the door.

Pain crashed into her shin and crumpled her knees. Stifling a scream, she fell against the wall and sank to the floor, massaging her yelping leg. "Damn chair!" she moaned.

Beecher snorted. Amanda grimaced and held her breath until his rhythmic rattling resumed.

Once assured he was asleep, Amanda stumbled to her feet, leaning her head against the door. She listened for a sound beyond the pumping of her own heart.

Nothing.

She fumbled for the knob and cracked the door.

"You okay?" Beecher asked groggily behind her.

Amanda fell against the door.

"God, you scared me!" she whispered harshly.

"What's wrong?"

"I heard something. Or at least I think I did."

"What?" he asked, rising on an elbow.

"I don't know. Something."

She slowly opened the door and leaned her head out. Still no sound.

"Where are you going?" Beecher breathed.

"It's all right. Go back to sleep."

"No. Amanda, wait!"

"I'll be right back." She sidled out of the room and closed the door behind her.

Her stockinged feet made no sound as she limped down the hall. At the foot of the stairway, she peered into the darkness of the living room and looked for any movement beyond the open kitchen door.

All was still.

She glanced up the stairs. The nightlight in the upper bathroom glowed green and steady.

Amanda's nose twitched as she climbed toward the glow. With each step, the air trembled, first in her lungs, then in her ears. Expanding. Enveloping. She reached inside the bathroom and clicked on the light.

Empty.

She paused, then turned to the short hallway. The guest room door stood open, welcoming examination. However, the closed door that led to Jeannie's room both concealed and repelled.

"No. Not Jeannie." She shuddered.

She scuttled down the hall, one hand on the wall groping for a sign, a current, a warning. Outside the attic stairs, the door throbbed against her hand. As her body teetered, Amanda leaned her forehead forward and tapped lightly.

No answer.

Amanda rapped louder, slowly pushed open the door, and gently called up to the bedroom, "Jeannie?"

Still no answer.

Holding onto the railing, she padded up the steps to her stepdaughter's room. When her eyes adjusted to the darkness, she saw the empty bed. She shivered and steadied herself on the dresser.

"Jeannie?" she asked a little louder.

Above her, she heard a shuffle and sniffle. Amanda scurried across the room to the spiral staircase that led to Jeannie's tower.

"Jeannie, are you up there?"

"Yes," a soft voice quavered.

Amanda took three tentative steps up the stairs. "Are you all right?"

Jeannie hesitated. "No."

"Do you need help?"

The girl sniffed. "I don't know."

Amanda circled up the steps until her head emerged through the floor of the tower room. On the window seat, Jeannie sprawled on her side, gazing at the city lights blinking through the fog.

Amanda held the edge of the stairway, leaned her head on the floor, and watched the ghostly shape of the girl. "Do you want help?"

Jeannie sat up, sniffed and wiped the back of her hand across her glistening eyes.

"Yeah."

Amanda scrambled up the stairs and rushed to Jeannie's side, wrapping the weeping girl in her arms until the crying and quaking subsided into mere whimpering and shivers.

Sitting back, she pushed back Jeannie's hair and wiped the tears from her cheek. "Are you okay?"

Jeannie sniffed, grabbed a tissue, and feebly waved away Amanda's question.

"You're not okay."

Jeannie swallowed and shook her head.

"Another bad dream?"

Her lips clenched, Jeannie nodded.

When the girl broke down in tears again, Amanda hugged her tightly, rubbing her back and softly assuring her. "It will be okay. It will be fine."

Jeannie pulled back and adamantly shook her head. "No. No, it won't be fine. I wish it would, but it won't."

Amanda wiped the hair from her stepdaughter's face. "What's happening, Jeannie? You went months without nightmares."

"For months I didn't dream at all," Jeannie blubbered.

"And now three in a week?" Amanda took Jeannie's hand.

The girl nodded.

"What did you dream this time?"

Jeannie picked up her ragged, stuffed Tigger from the floor and hugged it with a child's arms.

Amanda's memory flashed a picture of a young Jeannie sitting on her bed in Minnesota, holding the same doll.

"I was five years old," Jeannie stammered. "It was night. There was noise outside, and—I—I ran to the window and out on the lawn was a huge—a huge—I don't know! A monster or something."

"Jeannie, monsters aren't real." Amanda wiped her mouth.

"This one was," Jeannie insisted. "And—it was growing and growing. And you—you were out on the lawn, screaming. And Daddy—Daddy was up in a tree. And you just kept screaming and the monster kept growing and Daddy was still up in that stupid tree."

Amanda held her breath and shuddered. "A tree?"

Jeannie nodded vigorously. "Yeah. And the—the whatever-it-was kept growing bigger and bigger. And then—Then it turned toward the house and started coming toward me. And it kept coming at the window with its huge wide-open jaw and its teeth bleeding this greasy, yellow gunk. I hid under my bed, but he kept coming and coming—I could hear it."

Jeannie choked and coughed.

Amanda hid her face. "Go on."

Jeannie shrugged helplessly. "There was a crash of light, and then—"

She looked out toward the city again.

"Then what?" Watching the mist-blurred lights, Amanda rubbed Jeannie's shoulder.

Jeannie shook her head. "I woke up."

Amanda hunched over and clutched her hair. She remembered. More than she wanted. More than she dared tell.

Jeannie stood, her frustrated arms churning the air. "I know what you're going to say. You're going to tell me again that it was just a dream, but it—"

Amanda grasped Jeannie's hand. "No. No, I wasn't going to say that. I was going to say—"

The words refused utterance. Although she could not speak, Amanda's eyes never wavered.

Jeannie's face widened.

"It was real! It actually happened! And you—You were there."

Amanda nodded. "I was there. But it happened a long time ago. You're safe. I promise."

"What—What was it?"

"What was what?"

"The thing. The monster."

Amanda sat on the window seat, hesitated, then started slowly. "Jeannie, I can't tell you, just like you can't tell me the rest of your story."

"*My* story? I don't have a—"

Amanda held up her hand. "Jeannie, you do. And it's okay."

Jeannie sat next to Amanda. "I don't. I promise."

Amanda shook her head and placed a hand over her stepdaughter's mouth. "How's your knee?"

Guiltily, Jeannie looked down and stroked Tigger's ratty head. She shifted and pulled the blanket around him.

"You've been secretive about it a long time, and that's okay. I'm not going to ask you to tell me until you want to, but there's more you're not saying. Right?"

Sheepishly, the girl nodded.

"You don't have to. Even though I really want to know."

She smiled and nudged Jeannie's leg. Jeannie grinned, but kept her silence.

"I want to tell you everything I know about that night. I think it would help you," Amanda continued, "but seriously, I'm not the person to explain all this. You need to talk to your father."

"He was there, too?"

Amanda nodded. "In the tree, just like you said."

"What was—What happened? Who else—?"

Amanda carefully took the Tigger doll from Jeannie's arms and stroked its head silently. She hid her eyes from Jeannie.

Jeannie's eyes darted from the doll to Amanda and back.

The question formed slowly in her mind. Finally, she whispered, "Did this have something to do with my real mom?"

Amanda rubbed her upper arm and looked at the floor. "You need to talk to your father."

Jeannie sat back. "I must ask."

Amanda nodded.

"I hear that a lot lately."

The two sat in silence for several minutes. Jeannie gently took back her Tigger and turned to the city lights outside. Amanda sat on the floor, quietly smoothing her night gown.

"AJ?" Jeannie said.

"Mm-hmm."

"Will you hold me?"

Amanda rose and sat behind Jeannie on the window seat. She wrapped her arms around the girl's waist and leaned her head upon Jeannie's shoulder.

Quietly, Jeannie said, "The monster was real."

She waited for Amanda's affirmation.

"Yes, but he's gone now."

Jeannie's eyes searched the shadows of the mountains beyond the city lights. Amanda watched the fog drifting past the cars on the street below.

"AJ?" the girl whispered.

"Mmm?"

"There are more monsters. I know what they are. I—I've seen them."

Amanda raised her eyes to the mountains and peered through the gloom to see what Jeannie saw. She sighed heavily and laid her head back on Jeannie's shoulder.

"You need to talk to your father," she said quietly.

Jeannie patted Amanda's hands and nodded.

Outside, a man stepped out from behind the Flanagans' van. A tall man with long boots. A bearded man wearing a wide-brimmed hat.

Ignoring the steepness of Magnuson Hill, he easily climbed the sidewalk toward the house with the tower jutting out of it. At the end of the path leading to the front door, he stopped. He lifted his hat and examined the front of the house, his green eyes glowing in the foggy night. Pushing back his long hair, he smiled.

Confidently, he pointed at the house, replaced his hat and strolled deeper into the encompassing fog.

24

Michigan Reborn

Winthrop, Michigan
USA

Mount Hebron Church of the Rock in Winthrop defied church convention, rejecting affiliation with any established denomination, yet adhering to "fundamental Christian principles." In other words, The Rules. However, scandal and immorality continued to plague the members, whether young or old.

A contagion they heartily embraced.

While other fundamentalists relished every least transgression as an excuse for judgment, Mount Hebron considered their own moral slips as pathways to glory. Reformation was Rule #1, repeated ad nauseam.

It was also the church's main selling point.

Year after year, their billboard on H19 on the north edge of town blared the phrase "Michigan REBORN!" touting hundreds of annual conversions.

Winthrop's Gentiles—the Lutherans, Catholics, and Methodists—noted that Hebron's figures consisted of well-intentioned, repentant-but-weak mortals who regularly stumbled, fell, and reconverted.

Whatever that detail meant to others, to Brandon Whistler it signaled opportunity, a burgeoning market for someone with his abilities. This Palace of Pretenders with its pews upon pews of relapsed housewives and divorcees enticed him and assured him of success.

"*Catch them on the way down. Catch them on the way up,*" he thought.

To wheedle his way into church life, he learned The Rules and governing rituals—the manners, catch phrases, responses, confession to Pastor Goodwin for sins like cursing and smoking—all culminating in baptism at Topper Lake. When the congregation's fall schedule began, he joined the choir, Sunday school, and even volunteered to attend an outreach convention in Traverse City as a youth delegate.

Not once did he mention his hatred for his father. Not once did he mention his deal with the manager of the liquor store and the chief of police. Not once did he mention his role as sexual savior.

Nor did anybody ask.

Just as Nancy predicted.

The plan, which she and Brandon named *Expanded Horizons*, succeeded immediately. By Thanksgiving, half the sopranos and altos in the choir, Brandon's Sunday school teacher, and the Council President's wife had utilized his services. Secretly. Eagerly. Gratefully.

Although whispered kitchen gossip proclaimed his prowess as a lover, nobody spoke up as accuser or whistle-blower. No one risked casting the first stone.

"The prick is back." Brandon sneered with pride.

He knew no one would talk. They were secret, not stupid. The women in the grocery aisles whispered together and dipped their heads whenever he looked their way. Their spouses on the street glanced furtively at him and quickly detoured into the nearest stores.

Arrogantly, he swaggered past with his chest expanded and shoulders pulled back, challenging anybody to say anything.

The past three years, the whole high school knew what he did with its girls. Now, all Mount Hebron knew what he did with their women. Nobody breathed a word. Their hidden truths hovered and bullied them into tight-lipped submission.

Besides, every woman, despite her age or marital status, yearned for her opportunity. To reap the harvest of his wife's contrition, every man avidly preserved the peace in his household. The whole church, determined and lustful, blindly accepted the professed innocence of a high school boy, even though they knew his guilt.

And their own.

As Nancy predicted, Brandon's presence added welcome vitality, adventure, energy, and thrill to the congregation's marriages. Not to mention furthering their knowledge of geology gleaned from the bottom of Oakley's gravel pit.

The unspoken wish, both feared and desired, was that Brandon would save them from themselves, that he would see the light and save his soul by giving up his profession. Or leave town. Or both.

Brandon chuckled at the idea. He wasn't giving up anything or going anywhere. As Nancy had told him to do, he had leapt off the high board and let gravity do its work. She was right; he was in the middle of the water, having a great time, fucking at least three generations of Winthrop women.

Although Mount Hebron secretly targeted him for redemption, their attention both flattered and intoxicated him. Instead of deterring him, each feeble-conversion-attempt-turned-copulation maintained his fidelity to infidelity. And he enjoyed it.

"*Brandon Reborn*," he thought.

25

Lost

Fort Repentance, British Columbia
Canada

Beecher Jones leaned back in his office chair and massaged his forehead between his thumb and forefinger. The blinking cursor on his computer screen mocked him mercilessly.

He scrolled back over the previous paragraph, the previous page, the previous chapter. "My god!" he said, slapping the desk and throwing up his hands.

Leaning close to the screen, he read and reread. Despite his facial contortions, the words still melted into mush.

He pushed himself back and rose from his chair. Reaching his hands out to both sides, he first twisted left, then right, before stretching for his toes. When his spine cracked, he paced the room, shaking his arms and bouncing on his heels. Staring at the ceiling, he recited the multiplication table in his best Donald Duck voice. Channeling John Wayne, he listed all the countries he could remember alphabetically. He tried translating the Gettysburg address to Spanglish. Anything to jar loose the evasive story.

His new book had begun easily, but now the plot simply confused and numbed. The characters written to soar sputtered and splatted into a wasteland of triviality.

He glanced up at the flickering computer screen that dared him to write something significant. "Shut up," he growled.

He decided to take a five-minute break and scrolled the control panel to the *Sleep* command. When his finger slipped, the computer dutifully shifted into *Shut Down* mode.

"Argh!" Beecher punched at the keyboard as each open program flipped past and the screen went blank.

A quiet rhythmic tap on the door disrupted the storm.

Beecher sat back, locked in a death stare at the blank screen. "Come in, Amanda."

His wife peeked her head around the door. "You busy?"

"I wish."

Amanda hugged him from behind and kissed him on top of the head. "Tough day already?"

"Nothing's working. I might as well be typing Swahili polar bear recipes."

Amanda hugged him tighter. "Ooh! I love Swahili recipes. But instead of polar bear again, can we sample penguin pilau this time instead? I love penguin pilau."

He smiled and patted the arms around his chest. "What's up?"

Amanda sat on the desk in front of the computer and picked at the corner of the desk. "Jeannie."

"What's going on?"

Grabbing the desk with both hands, she began, "Remember how after we got married, she came home from school, excited about—well, everything? Words bubbled out of her mouth faster than she could think of them. Her eyes were all googly and her hair all frizzed out. She'd gush for hours about the color of the sunset on the mountains. And then she got your telescope, and she'd spend all night in her tower looking for constellations."

"Yeah?"

"When was the last time she gushed about anything?"

Beecher thought a second, then shook his head. "I don't remember."

"Her soccer accident."

Beecher considered a moment. "The Langley bitch."

"That's when it started. Four years ago. I don't know why, but it did. And now—Every night, she comes home and goes straight to her room. Except she—"

"Except?"

"Did you ever notice? Sometimes she'll run up the stairs one at a time, then come back down to get something in the kitchen and run back two at a time. Some days she'll do that three or four times before closing her door. And the whole time, not a word. Barely an acknowledgement that she knows we're here.

"And then there's supper—She always used to talk at supper. Remember?"

"Maybe she just doesn't have anything to say."

"She's a teenager, Beecher. She has lots to say. She just doesn't know how to say it."

"Amanda, she's seventeen. She's probably in love."

"No."

"She could be."

Amanda shook her head. "She's always told me everything. Not now."

Beecher pulled back. "Everything? She never told me a word."

"Of course not. You're her father."

"Yeah, and you're her mother."

"Stepmother."

"What does that matter?"

Amanda paused for a moment. "I'm detached just enough that she can talk to me about boyfriends and girl stuff."

"Girl stuff?"

Amanda cleared her throat and tilted her head. "The stuff that guys don't want to acknowledge happens to girls."

Beecher removed his glasses and scratched his head. "Oooooh. Oh, yeah. Thanks for taking care of that, by the way."

Amanda smiled. "You're welcome."

She leaned over, kissed Beecher and sat on his lap.

"Maybe that's what—"

"No."

"And not boys?"

Amanda shook her head. "It's the nightmares. She's remembering."

"Remembering what?"

Amanda held Beecher's hands around her waist and patted them. "What we hoped she never would. What we hid from her all this time. Jefferson. You. Me. Art Benson. Sarah. Wayne Diego. That whole thing outside your house."

Beecher flinched.

"She had the nightmares before, but they stopped for awhile after you taught her 'to see forever' with the telescope. Remember?"

Beecher leaned his head into her neck.

"They came back when we got home from Peru," she said.

"I hated that country," Beecher joked.

Amanda slapped the hands encircling her waist. "Beecher, she says there are more monsters. You need to talk to her. Not me. You. Her father. The Storyteller."

"But she also needs the Flame—You—"

Amanda shook her head. "Later. After she learns who she is and what happened to her."

She squeezed Beecher's hands. "And to her mother."

He sighed heavily. "What am I going to tell her?"

"Whatever she asks."

He nodded, then asked, "Where is she?"

"In her tower."

Beecher patted Amanda's belly. "Okay. Let me up."

She rose and helped Beecher to his feet. She grabbed his shirt and pulled him down to kiss his lips.

"You're a good man, Beecher Jones."

"Yeah. Yeah. I bet you say that to all the guys."

"Only the ones I marry." Amanda grinned.

Beecher turned to open the door, but her hand on his shoulder stopped him.

"Like us, she's not alone," Amanda said. "The Word always works in threes."

Beecher's upper lip twitched. He swallowed visions of Jefferson—the Earth Man and his fog tormenting Jefferson, Sarah lying in the hospital, the weendigo devouring Einar Nordhaus, the Battle of Grave Swamp—

Amanda was right. In her and Beecher's time, the Sacred Trinity—Art Benson as the Herald, Beecher as the Storyteller, and Amanda as the Flame—all united to overcome the evil of the fog.

"*Jeannie's not alone. She has her own trinity, one to save the world,*" he thought.

Beecher sighed and closed the door behind him.

26

Zit Swish

Winthrop, Michigan
USA

Outside the little one-bedroom cabin in Alderson's Woods, quarter-sized snowflakes settled lightly on the trees and ground. Inside, Brandon fell to the side of the bed, limp and exhausted. He lay on his back, his breath labored and deep.

A disheveled head of gray-streaked brunette hair lay on his chest. A damp tongue flicked and pressed a nipple. He gasped as an insistent yet gentle hand reached to his drained and limp penis.

Brandon wrapped his arms around the naked body atop him. "Maggie! Three times. Three fucking times!"

"Mmmm," said Maggie MacArthur, the Mount Hebron choir director. "Or three times fucking. What's wrong with four?"

She stretched up and began nibbling the boy's earlobe.

Brandon turned to the side and let her continue her titillation. At fifty-five, Maggie still had an athletic body:

Smooth. Mostly.

Firm. Mostly.

Electric. Definitely.

Still, she was a grandmother whose weathered wrinkles framed her eyes and mouth. A grandmother widowed when a whore fucked her lawyer husband to death on a business trip to Kalamazoo. A grandmother determined to make up for lost opportunities.

Brandon gasped as her tongue tickled him below his jaw.

"You're not answering my question," she said. "What's wrong with four?"

"Nothing. Four times is great. I'm all for four times, but let me catch my breath."

Maggie raised herself on her elbow. "Are you okay?"

Brandon turned to her and smiled. "Yeah."

He pushed her breasts together and sucked both nipples at the same time.

Maggie gasped, laying back her head and pushing her chest toward him.

"You breathe fine," she groaned.

"But not enough yet. Let me rest a second. Okay?"

Maggie smiled and snuggled into Brandon's heat. "Okay, fine."

Brandon smoothed Maggie's hair and gazed up at the ceiling. "What time is it?"

"Late."

"We have church in the morning."

"No big deal. Except—"

She broke off and sat up, examining Brandon's necklace.

"What's this?"

"Huh? It's just a necklace."

"Have you always worn this?"

"Yeah. Why?"

"Where'd you get it?"

In the darkness above them, Brandon imagined Nancy Kirkman's face, the dashboard lights of a parked Honda Civic, his hands pushing the cross aside, her bare tits, the empty biology lab, her unclasping the necklace and handing it to him.

"I don't know," he stammered. "A friend, I guess."

"You guess?"

Brandon shrugged.

"A girl. Right?"

"I suppose so—"

Maggie dipped her head, wagging her finger at him and shaking her head.

"Yeah. Okay. A girl. So what?"

Maggie stifled a laugh with her fist. "Do you know what this is?"

"It's a cross."

Patting Brandon's bare chest, Maggie kissed his forehead. "Yes. Yes, it is. It's the cross Mount Hebron presents its eighth-grade girls after they complete chastity class. We call it the Purity Promise."

"Purity Promise?"

"Every girl who pledges to remain celibate until her wedding day receives this. She is to wear it close to her heart to remind her of her promise should she ever be—you know—tempted."

"'Every girl.' That explains—" Brandon bit his lip, holding back his own laugh. Maggie smiled and shoved against his chest.

"I assume you tempted the young lady." She reached between his legs.

"Well—she was the one doing the tempting, but—yeah."

"You are a bad man, Brandon Whistler." She buried her head into his neck, then lay in his arms, kneading his penis. Suddenly, she sat up and laughed.

"Oh! This is perfect."

"What now?"

"Do you know what tomorrow is at church?"

"No—"

"Zit-Swish Sunday."

Brandon looked up at her. "What's that?"

"It's actually called Intern Sunday, but—"

"Intern Sunday?"

"Yes. Every two years, Mount Hebron hosts an intern from the University of the Rock in Bellamy."

"Bellamy, Wisconsin? Is that legal?"

Maggie playfully slapped Brandon's shoulder. "Yes, it's legal."

"What do they do?"

"They teach the chastity class! That's what's so funny. They protect the Winthrop youth from themselves by arming them against the lustful attacks of Satan and his minions."

"Youth like me?"

Maggie looked down at Brandon. "Yes, and minions like me. I think I'll keep you for myself."

While she rubbed his cock, Brandon leaned his head back and felt himself growing in her hand. He closed his eyes and envisioned his first night at Oakley's gravel pit with Nancy.

"How many will be there?" he asked quietly.

"Interns? Just one."

"Boy or girl?"

"Doesn't matter. Whoever it is will be a zealous creep intent on 'saving the youth of America'."

"Mmmm."

Brandon slowly ran his hand up Maggie's thigh. She opened her legs, welcoming his probing fingers.

"Do you think they really want to stop—?"

"I think—" Maggie gasped as Brandon's fingers slid inside her. "No. I think they're here as an excuse for never having fucked."

"Why do you call it Zit-Swish Sunday?"

"You'll see when Pastor Goodwin introduces the new one. If it's a girl, it will be a squat, pimply-faced co-ed wrapped in a XXXL URock hoodie proclaiming the blessings of chastity and sobriety to the potentially wayward and salacious Winthrop hussies."

"The zit," Brandon suggested as he pressed and examined.

Maggie sighed as Brandon became harder and harder. She clenched her eyes and rocked her hips against his hand. "Yes."

"And the swish?"

Between her shortened breaths, she explained, "A boy—thin, lanky guitar player with a—seventh-hand eBay guitar."

She gulped and sat up straighter.

"Mmm—black dress pants and button-down white shirt. Oh, my god, Brandon—" She straddled his legs and pulled his member toward her crotch.

Brandon sneered, pulled his hand back. "And?"

Maggie licked her fingers and stroked him. "They—um—they spout every—every condemnatory verse in the Bible at the football jocks."

She leaned over and kissed his chest. "'No sex,' they say. 'No defiling the innocent'."

"So?"

"The swishes want the jocks for themselves."

"Swishes as in gay?"

"Yes," she moaned, guiding his hand.

"How long are they here?"

"Ten—t-ten weeks."

"So I better do this before I'm saved again. Right?"

Maggie tipped back her head, exhaled through her nose and nodded. She raised her hips and guided his penis inside her. He raised his mouth to her nipples and pulled her chest closer.

The snow falling outside the window danced through the darkness as the writhing bodies inside groaned in unison.

The cabin fell silent.

27

What Does and Does Not Matter

Beecher stopped at the head of the stairway. A thin light fringed the door frame of the steps to Jeannie's room.

He rapped on the door and peeked in. Except for literary and scientific posters, a few textbooks, and Jeannie's jacket hanging on its wall hook, the stairway was empty.

"Hello?" he called.

"Up here," Jeannie answered, high up in her tower.

As a former teacher, Beecher recognized the significance of Jeannie's words. More than simple access to her sanctuary, they signaled an intimacy coupled with confidentiality.

He reached her room, then threaded his way between her bed, bookcases, computer desk, and dresser to the circular staircase leading to the tower itself. Slowly and carefully, he climbed the thin steps, cautious of the unforeseen sensibilities of a teenager. Before his head rose through the floor, Jeannie said, "Hi, Daddy."

"Hey, baby. What are you doing?"

Jeannie sat against the wall, her elbow on the window ledge, her head in her hand. "Just looking at the city."

Beecher kissed the top of her head. "And the mountains?"

Jeannie nodded. "Yeah."

They both gazed at the strength and majesty of the Rockies that rose beyond the city.

"You like mountains a lot, don't you?"

Jeannie nodded. "Almost as much as stars."

"Which are your favorite? The Andes? Alps? Himalayas?"

Jeannie shook her head. "These."

Beecher nodded, his hands on Jeannie's shoulders. Neither spoke as clouds descended over the peaks.

Jeannie broke the silence. "Did you want something?"

The disappearing mountains distracted him. He could not speak.

"Daddy?"

"Yeah, sorry. AJ is concerned so she sent me here. She's worried something is wrong."

Jeannie crossed her arms on the ledge and laid her head on them.

"So she was right. Something is wrong. Is it a boy?"

"No, Daddy." She swallowed.

"You sure? I bet AJ five bucks it was a boy." He sat on the window seat next to her.

Jeannie smiled. "I'm sure."

"So—?"

Jeannie touched the window as she gazed at the vanishing mountains. Unable to face her father, she looked down at her hands. "Wait here a minute."

She sank down the staircase and came back carrying Tigger. She handed the doll to Beecher. "You remember him?"

"Tigger? Sure. Your mom and I bought him for you at DisneyWorld."

She squeezed Beecher's hand and looked into his eyes. "Tell me about Mom."

Beecher took a deep breath and swallowed. "That's what AJ thought."

He rubbed the back of his neck and leaned over his knees. "What did you want to know?"

"Whatever it is you're afraid to tell me."

He laughed. "God, you're smart."

"I take after my father."

Beecher rose and circled the room, one hand on his hip and the other kneading his neck. When he came back, he stood over her and lifted her chin. "You have your mother's eyes."

"Thanks." Jeannie wrapped her arms around Tigger and squeezed the doll's nose as she searched for the right question. She started, but stopped. Her tight lips held back the words. She took a deep breath. "What happened to Mom?"

Beecher had rehearsed this scene hundreds of times in his head, still her words startled him. Unsure what to do, he sat next to her on the window seat. "Je—Jeannie, you—you know. She died."

"I know she died, but you never told me how."

"Yes, I did." He rubbed his sweaty hands on his thighs. "She died in a car accident."

"I know that's what you said, but—" Her cheeks blushed the same color as her hair.

Beecher examined his hands in his lap. "Yeah. Okay."

He searched the transparent dome above them for help.

"First, there are things I don't want to remember or even think about. Things I can't fully explain. If what I tell you is not enough, I'm sorry. I don't know what else to say."

"Tell me what you can."

Beecher wiped his hands on his thighs again and bounced his knees. "First of all, your mom died from a car crash. I never made that up."

"But?"

"But—it wasn't an accident."

"Okay." Jeannie clutched the edge of the window seat.

Beecher cleared his throat. "In Jefferson where you were born, there was a man. A very bad man. His name was Frank Thorstad. And he did something very bad to your mom."

"What?"

Beecher choked. "That's one of the things I don't want to remember. Anyway—Anyway, your mother drove our car to his house and—and she crushed him between the car and a tree. She killed him, and—later, she died from her injuries."

"Injuries?"

Beecher's voice broke. "Her face crashed through the windshield. The glass—shredded the skin. The impact crushed her cheekbones and jaw. She lived much longer than anybody expected, but she never had a chance. Not really."

Jeannie clutched her Tigger to her stomach and gazed at the floor. "This Frank—" She hesitated. "Did he deserve to die?"

Beecher's hands shook as he clutched his head, struggling to crush the memories clattering through his brain. Jeannie's warmth next to him awaited his answer. Violently, he shook his head to fling away the thoughts. Still, he saw Sarah's red, contorted face spitting at him.

He heard her rage, her words, her confession slicing into his brain: "We fucked like animals, and you know what? I loved it."

Again and again, the words rumbled and churned in Beecher's gut: "You want to know something else? I'd do it again."

He squeezed the seat cushion to force back the emptiness of Sarah closing the front door and driving to her death. His nostrils flared and traces of her perfume once again stung his nose. He leaned over, his head between his knees.

He forced himself to speak. "It really doesn't matter what I think, Jeannie."

He stood and grabbed the back of his head, tears welling in his eyes.

"Did she hurt you, Daddy?"

Beecher shook his head. "As I said, it doesn't matter."

"Yes, it does. Did Mommy hurt you?"

Beecher swirled and grasped Jeannie's shoulders. "No, it doesn't! It doesn't, you hear me? It's over!"

Jeannie shrank in his grip. "Daddy! You're hurting me!"

Immediately, Beecher threw up his hands and sprang away from her, his arms clutched around his chest. In his daughter's fear-filled eyes, her innocence, and her faithfulness, he saw the Sarah he had always cherished, but never known.

He dropped to the floor and lowered his head to the rug. He could not move. He could not speak.

Tentatively, Jeannie knelt beside her father and rubbed his back. "Daddy?"

Beecher remained unmoving, silent.

"It's okay, Daddy. I won't ask any more questions. Okay?"

He sat back on his feet and reached out a single hand. Jeannie ducked under his arm and disappeared into his embrace.

Beecher kissed the top of her head. "The most important thing is we lost her."

He wiped Jeannie's wet cheek. "The most important thing."

Jeannie rose and sat on the window seat, looking out to the mountains.

"And we have AJ," Beecher added. "That's a good thing. Besides you, she's the best thing that ever happened to me."

"I love AJ."

"Good. Good." Beecher removed his glasses and rubbed the nob on his nose. "Jeannie, all this happened twelve years ago. Why do you want to know now?"

"Peru."

"Peru?"

"There was this boy in Peru. At Machu Picchu. His name was Beetle. He was a worker there. A guide. I liked him because he was more like me than anybody else we met. He was another kid. So while you and AJ and the rest of the adults gobbled up all that stuff about building the city, the agriculture, and the climate, I—Honestly, Daddy, I didn't care how the granite fit together, the layout of the ruins, all that archeology crap."

"So, what did Beetle tell you?"

"All sorts of stuff. What people do. What they believe. What kids like us do for fun. The weird food."

"My stomach is still grumbling."

"This will make it worse. Have you ever heard of a pishtaco?"

"Yeah, I get them all the time at Ramon's Mexican."

Jeannie bumped into Beecher's shoulder. "Not *fish* taco. *Pish*taco."

"What's that?"

"A legend. Kind of like—like the boogie man you and AJ used to scare me with. Beetle said the pishtaco kills people, then carves them up and sucks out all their fat."

"So a pishtaco is a fat sucker? And?"

"Beetle said they're still around."

"Fat suckers?"

"Yeah. Just a couple of years ago, the cops picked up some guys who killed people, sucked the fat out of them, and tried to sell it to some medical lab in the States."

Beecher held his chin and tapped his teeth. "That's what a guy named Beetle said?"

"Yeah! Anyway, as I thought about this monster's name, another name kept interrupting my thoughts. I had never heard it before that day, but I knew it."

Beecher wiped the sweat from his forehead.

"Wynn? Wayne? Something like that."

Beecher flinched. "Wayne Diego?"

"That's it! Do you know him?" Jeannie grabbed his arm.

Beecher gently removed her hand and walked away silently.

"Daddy, are you all right?"

A shiver crawled up Beecher's back and shook his shoulders. He turned to Jeannie in a daze, his breath short and erratic.

Jeannie's eyes widened. "Daddy, you're scared!"

Beecher pursed his lips.

"Is that Wayne Diego person part of it?"

Beecher pulled at his collar and turned to the window. The clouds covered the mountains.

"Did he—?"

"No! Don't think of him. Not Wayne Diego. Not Frank Thorstad. None of it!"

Jeannie outlined the design on the seat pad with her finger. The spirit bear spoke inside her.

"Daddy? I don't want to scare you any more, but what is a matchi-auwishuk?"

Beecher's face shuddered and paled. He clenched his shaking hands until he regained calm. Carefully, he chose his words.

"Are. The word *matchi-auwishuk* is plural. They are bad. They are evil incarnate."

He crossed the room to the telescope. Carefully, he stroked the barrel.

"Jeannie, the night I gave this to you, when you panned across the moon to its edge, what did you learn?"

"When I fell on my butt? I learned Everywhere is really big."

Beecher smiled. "Right. Everywhere is really big. And the matchi-auwishuk are almost as big. Wayne Diego, Frank Thorstad, and your pishtaco are all part of them. They work with someone called the Earth Man and fight the Word however they can."

"Daddy, you said Frank Thorstad was dead."

"Yes,"

"He still exists even though he's dead?"

"As far as I know. Yes."

Jeannie rose and circled the room, gazing into the darkness beyond the dome.

"So my mother still—"

Beecher stared at the floor. "Yes."

He jammed his hands into his pockets and shifted his weight. "Jeannie, what happened with your mom and Frank and Wayne Diego and—all of it—I always tried to protect you from that. I was wrong."

The stiffness in Beecher's body relaxed, and he yielded to the Storyteller he always was. He pronounced the truth.

"Whenever your brain spits up words or names like *pishtaco*, *matchi-auwishuk*, *Frank Thorstad*, *Wayne Diego*, or the *Earth Man*, there's no reason to fear. No matter what anybody says or does, no matter who lives or dies, no matter what monsters gather against the universe, not even your fat-sucking pishtaco, the Word always wins. The Word wins.

"You will have many more questions, many more answers that will terrify you, but you are loved. Not just by people you know—AJ, me, or even your mother—but by the Word. You are loved stronger and wider and longer than a thousand universes. Nothing and no one can take that away from you, no matter what they do to you or me or anybody you love."

Jeannie examined her father's face. "My mother—"

Beecher hung his head. "When your mother died, she chose forever with the Earth Man. That's why she still exists."

Breathing deeply, Jeannie gazed blankly across the room.

"You still look confused," he said.

Jeannie looked to the dome. "My mother still exists. With all the bad. She exists."

"She's stuck," Beecher said. "Yes, it was a choice she made, but if she knew you, I don't think she'd do it again. You were so little. She was so confused. Now she's stuck, but—"

"She still loves, doesn't she?"

Beecher nodded. "I'm sure she does."

With one arm hugging Tigger to her chest, Jeannie reached out and took her father's hand. Beecher kissed her fingers. "Daddy? I'm—I have more questions I need to ask. Not now, but—I need to."

Beecher watched her turn away to gaze at the mountains to the North.

"*Of course, you do,*" he thought. He disappeared down the stairs.

At the office door, Beecher shifted his weight from foot to foot and bit his lip.

Amanda looked steadily at her husband. "She knows, doesn't she?"

"She does now. Not all, but she's learning—and remembering."

Amanda rose and took Beecher in her arms.

"What if I lose her too?" he asked, sniffling into her shoulder.

"She'll do what she has to do. No matter what, you still have me. You will always have me."

"What are we going to do?"

Amanda held her husband tightly. "Whatever we have to. But—"

Beecher stepped back and caressed her face. "But what?"

"What we have to do is not up to us."

Downhill from the Jones house, the last few stragglers exited Hammond Park for the evening. Mothers gathered up their children. Runners veered off the paths across the grass toward the gate. Basketball games dwindled with last shots flung at chain-netted hoops. Outside the park walls, streetlights popped on, adding a greenish tint to the vestiges of golden light fading to gray.

One person remained. A lanky man sitting under a pine tree.

Unconcerned by the darkening sky, he unsheathed the knife hanging on his belt and fondled the skin-wrapped hilt. Enamored of his own workmanship, he raised the weapon above him to study the sleek, bowed blade he had perfected out of self-mined, self-forged, self-sharpened steel.

An irritating chatter distracted him.

Across the park, a gray squirrel hopped and skittered across the open field toward the pine tree, searching for food. It dug and combed through the blades of grass, so focused that the danger ahead eluded it. Despite the man's menacing smile and his threatening knife, the squirrel worked blindly toward him, twitching its nose, separating smells.

With his knife still held above him, the man scrutinized the heedless squirrel. He twisted the blade to inspect its keen edge.

"It will do."

Before the squirrel could even lift its head, the man lunged, slicing through the air and hacking the animal in two. Before a drop of blood spilled from the torso, the man impaled its upper half and lifted it above his mouth, allowing the life to drain onto his tongue.

After he licked the last dash from his lips, he flicked both halves of the carcass away from him with the tip of his knife, then wiped the blood from the cutting edge, stroking each side across the grass in front of him. Satisfied he had erased the last trace, he stood and sheathed his weapon. He attached his rope to his other hip, adjusted his hat, and zipped his jacket. Up the Magnuson Hill, lights brightened the windows of the Joneses' tower.

The tall man's green eyes narrowed hungrily. He wiped his mouth.

A white Park Patrol car, its blue, flashing grill lights piercing the darkening running path, inched through the park announcing, "Hammond Park will be closing in ten minutes. Please exit at this time."

The tall man tipped his hat to the inhuman pre-recorded voice and strode across the grass toward Twelfth Avenue. The Park Patrol ignored him as he hopped the fence and climbed the hill.

28

Skye Light

Winthrop, Michigan
USA

Usually, Mount Hebron greeted its interns with a curiosity focused on its own redemption, then celebrated their departure with relief and relapse. It was not prepared for Skye Jeffers.

Unlike her female predecessors, Skye was no zit. The woman Pastor Goodwin introduced had a clear, angular face, a long neck, and athletic curves that shivered the abdomen of every man, while terrifying every woman in the congregation. Her short, auburn hair pulled across her forehead framed her honest smile.

Standing at the front of the sanctuary in her white pullover sweater and Navy blue pants, she held her hands behind her back as the pastor praised her academic achievements and his hope for her mission's success. When she thanked the congregation for the opportunity to serve Mount Hebron, her rich, soothing voice and quiet modesty both invited and intimidated with an unspoken maturity and sexual energy that defied description.

After the service, Brandon stood at the back of the sanctuary, watching. Like the men paralyzed in their fantasies, the "arrogant prick" wilted into an impotent worm. He jammed his hands into his pockets and leaned against the last pew, frustrated and tense. She reminded him of the pin-up of long ago, but younger, stronger, more enticing.

"It's the hair," he thought.

In the choir loft, Maggie MacArthur gathered the stack of choir folders and skirted the sanctuary between the pews and wall. At the back of the room, she playfully bumped Brandon's shoulder.

"Oh, hi," he mumbled.

"Help me with these?"

"Huh? Oh, yeah. Sure. What do you—"

Maggie smiled at him. "Brandon, I just wanted to see if you're still talking to me."

Brandon grabbed the pew in front of him, gazing once more at the floor. "Yeah. I mean, why not? I—uh—"

Maggie set the folders on the pew and glanced forward at the crowd circling Skye Jeffers. "It's okay. I get it."

"Get what?"

"Brandon, it's okay. I'm an old lady. My grandkids are nearly as old as you. I know that. I have no illusions. We had a night—"

"A couple of nights."

Maggie tilted her head. "A couple of nights. But I know you—You want this girl."

Brandon reached down and picked up a folder. He opened it, pointing at the music inside as if asking her a question. "It was fun," he said softly.

Maggie leaned against him, peering intently at the music. "Yes. Yes, it was. But you can do better than me. You can have any girl you want."

Brandon glanced at the crowd surrounding Skye. He rubbed the Purity Promise cross beneath his shirt and shook his head.

"No." He closed the folder and laid it back onto the stack. "I can have any girl who wants me."

He stood straight and wrapped his arms around himself. "It's not the same."

"It's something." Maggie examined the distraught face, then picked up the stack of folders.

Brandon glanced once more to the front of the church as Pastor Goodwin shooed the last women away from Skye. Brandon shook his head, left the room, found his winter jacket, and fled into the January cold.

Throughout the next two months, the bulk of Skye's internship, Brandon craved a word, a look, a touch. In this one person, he saw the divinity of womankind—the Exalted Idol, the Devouring Mistress, the Reassuring Mother, the Sovereign Deity—all he had desired in Nancy Kirkman.

However, he knew a simple word from his mouth would disintegrate her.

If she disappeared, he himself would crumble to dust and blow away. He must earn her, shield her, and possess her. To acquire the Winthrop women and girls had only demanded stamina and passion, but to obtain Skye Jeffers, to receive even a glance, would require commitment, determination, and, most of all, patience as he clung tenaciously to a belief in the possible.

So he waited.

Through hours of youth group meetings, hours of worship services, hours of Bible study, he waited.

And waited.

And ignored the other women in church, in school, in town.

Skye's essence produced celibacy far more effectively than URock's mission statement or Pastor Goodwin's sermons or Mount Hebron's chastity classes or any Purity Promise. He could not let his hunger discourage him.

So he waited.

For two and a half moths, he waited.

He waited until Skye was no longer available.

On the first Sunday in March, an unusually warm morning with snow melting off the Mount Hebron roof, Pastor Goodwin delivered a powerful message on I Corinthians 13, "The Love Chapter." After the offering, he halted the service, his face serious and stern.

"I have an announcement to make. This is quite serious, so please listen carefully. As you know, we have been hosting URock interns for the past two decades, silently hoping that we would find somebody to take over the youth ministry permanently. Two weeks ago, the Council and I decided that Skye Jeffers would be that person. However, as of today, Skye will no longer be serving Mount Hebron as youth minister, either as intern or permanently."

The congregation's collective gasp nearly sucked the air from the room.

In the top row of the choir loft, Brandon clasped the pew in front of him and stretched his neck, scanning the church. The entire congregation sat in stunned silence. Skye sat in the front row of the congregation, her head hanging low, her hands lying limply on her lap.

"*She couldn't have done anything wrong,*" Brandon thought. "*She—*"

"*Of course! She* has *to leave,*" he rationalized from his pew. "*What's here for her in Winthrop?*"

He himself would graduate from high school and be gone in just a few weeks. He still had not finalized his plans for the next year, but now he could follow Skye, and—

"Please stand up, Skye," Pastor Goodwin continued.

Dipping her head to the side and twisting her fingers, she complied.

"While we will miss you in this capacity—You've done a marvelous job, Skye. Hasn't she done a marvelous job, Church?"

The congregation clapped enthusiastically, yet cut their applause short when Pastor Goodwin held up his hand. "But—"

His face turned stern and glared at the quiet young woman. A black pall of suspicion floated over the quiet room.

Brandon held his breath. Sniffles and stifled sobs pierced the silence. Furtive, guilty eyes ping-ponged between him and Skye, accusing him of defiling the innocent.

"As I said," Pastor Goodwin continued, "although we will miss her in the capacity of youth director, we must rejoice that she has been offered another position, one more suited to her talents and personality, one that she has graciously accepted because the Lord has called her. It is her duty to consent to His will."

A sigh eased the tension in the room. Brandon wiped his sweaty palms on his pants leg and pushed down on his shaking thighs. He glanced at Skye's motionless form standing at the front pew. While hushed bedlam raged around her, she stood calmly looking at the hands at her waist.

"And doing your duty for the Lord makes you happy. Doesn't it, Skye?"

Skye quietly nodded.

"Do you want to tell the congregation what your new post is?" Pastor Goodwin grabbed a wireless microphone and left his pulpit to stand in front of Skye.

She nodded. The pastor offered her his hand, inviting her to stand beside him. She slid from the front pew and stood next to him, still wringing her hands. She could not speak.

"Go ahead," the pastor said softly, handing her the mic.

Looking to the ceiling for guidance, Skye brushed the hair from her face, took a deep breath and sighed.

"I—I—uh—I really like what I do here at Mount Hebron, but my new job requires my full attention, that is if I want to do good work. And I really want to do good work for the Lord."

She glanced at Pastor Goodwin.

Brandon sat straight in his pew. Her head bowed, he could not see her face, but he recognized a lightness in her shoulders.

Skye put her fist to her mouth and inhaled deeply. She held her breath until she regained her composure.

"So—effective immediately, I am resigning my job as youth worker here at Mount Hebron—" She swallowed, then looked directly at the congregation.

"—to make the necessary preparation for my new role as—" She waved her hand in front of her and lowered her head. She sniffed.

"—my new role as—"

Pastor Goodwin put an arm around her shoulder. "Go ahead, Skye. We all love you. It's okay."

"My new role as—"

Suddenly, her head snapped up. Her face beamed and she shouted, "Wife of Pastor Edwin Goodwin!"

Silent gloom burst into joyous bedlam. Quiet tears became raucous laughter. A clamor of "Praise the Lord!" and "Alleluia" shook the walls. The choir pushed their way from their loft to congratulate the happy couple. Skye flung her arms around Pastor Goodwin and kissed him on the mouth to even more uproar.

Nobody noticed Brandon slipping out the sanctuary door.

29

Look to the Sea

Pacific Coast
Peru

Two days after his final lesson at Machu Picchu, two days of fasting and fighting his way down the mountains and through the jungle, Beetle stood at the edge of the Pacific Ocean, the Stones of Viracocha in his hands.

The ground spoke through his bare feet. "You have done well. You are ready to begin."

"Begin what?" Beetle asked.

"To follow and find."

"Follow and find what?"

"Follow your path. Find your patience."

"There is no path. There is no ground. Where do I start?"

"Through sickness and trial, you have survived. You have learned without teachers. You speak without words. Life is no longer a solid path of dirt. Let go of limitations. What you knew is no longer necessary. Look to the sea."

The morning sun peeked over the mountains behind the boy, illuminating the ocean ahead. Near the shore, a trail of thick foam atop the water led far out to sea. Beetle followed its route with his eyes.

"I have heard of you," he shouted to the path.

"Yes," it said.

"Viracocha. Foam of the Sea."

"Yes."

"I do not understand where I am going or what to do when I'm there. I hear no leading. The stones are silent."

"They need not speak. Simply look at them and watch."

Beetle raised his hand and examined the stones. The Canadian girl's face gazed back at him.

"Do you see?"

"Yes. I think so." Beetle's stomach pulled him toward the sea foam.

"You are ready," the waves said. "Be where you must. Come."

He trusted the voice.

With the mountains and Machu Picchu behind him, the Pacific in front of him, Beetle nodded and laid the stones on the shore. After shedding his hat and clothes, he picked up the stones and tossed them one by one into the ocean.

As he mounted the path, his chest fluttered. The foam not only held his weight, but warmed his feet, inviting him forward. Shaking off the tension, Beetle pushed back his shoulders, took a deep breath, and disappeared into the distance.

30

Seeking Liberation

Mount Komu ("The Entry")
British Columbia, Canada

Climbing toward the exit from the cave, Sarah smirked in the fading firelight. When the Earth Man first spoke of the pishtaco, he had raved how the creature solidified their mission against good and the Word, emphasizing the monster's revolting and savage past.

His praises only lasted until Sarah sowed the seeds of doubt.

After she set the Earth Man's jealousy against the pishtaco's lechery, her captor's once triumphant smile hardened to an icy glare. His boisterous praise degenerated into seething. At times, his gluttonous, flexing jaw threatened to devour the pishtaco whole.

Just as she planned.

And the pishtaco fell right into her trap. Although he could not come within ten feet of Sarah without incurring his master's wrath, he still stalked her every move, following her everywhere.

Suddenly, the monster burst from a dark corner. "Headed somewhere?"

Sarah jerked back. "Oh, my god! You scared me. Why do you do that?"

Steadying herself against a wall, she reassumed her royal demeanor and rose to her full height. "I'm going outside," she replied curtly.

Her glare ordered him to move aside.

Instead, he crossed his arms and leaned back. "Does the Earth Man know that?"

"Yes! You could go ask him if you don't believe me. Of course, he's not in a good mood right now, but you knew that."

The pishtaco bristled, his sneer turning to a scowl. He wiped his hands on his shirt and allowed her to pass.

As she stepped past him, she smirked. "If you really want to know where I'm going, you can always come with me."

The pishtaco stepped back to examine Sarah's long body and gray eyes. He pushed at the stirring in his loins, then licked his lips. "All right. Where?"

"Outside." She turned and climbed the tunnel toward the opening to the outside world.

Sarah emerged from the cave and slipped into bright sunlight. The pishtaco crept around the immense stones, then stood next to her. Spreading her arms, she raised her face to the cloudless sky. "Can you feel that?"

He propped himself against the rock and pulled down his hat brim obscuring his pale face. "What?"

"The sun. Warmth." She drew her hands over her face and opened her collar. Her long fingers exposed her neck and cleavage beneath the Earth Man's chain. She tauntingly ran her nails over her glistening skin.

The pishtaco gulped and looked away.

"I'm just curious. I mean, can you feel temperature since you're not really human."

The pishtaco furrowed his eyebrows. Excited spit slid over his chin to his lifting chest. Sarah turned so the sun glinted off her black hair, her fingers, her neck, her chain. She smiled to herself as the desire to ravage clutched at his throat.

"You died a long time ago," he snarled at her. "Does heat mean anything to *you?*"

Sarah leaned back against another boulder. "Not as much as when I was alive. I don't know that it needs to. Still, whenever I come out of the earth, whether out of a mountain, a swamp, or a desert, I always relax and bathe in it whether the feeling is real or not. Habit, I guess."

The pishtaco grunted.

Sarah pointed down the mountain. "Anyway, I thought I'd cross the meadow and sit by the creek for awhile. What do you think?"

The pishtaco looked down the mountain past the strewn rocks to the meadow. Across the field of waving grass and wildflowers, a creek flowed out of a dense grove of trees.

His hand flinched. His fingers searched for the knife's hilt.

"Are you all right?"

The pishtaco licked his lips again. Through short breaths, he murmured, "Fine. Yes. Fine."

"Want to check out that grove?"

The pishtaco grasped her shoulder. "No!"

Patiently, Sarah turned, removing his hand from her shoulder. "What's wrong?"

His mouth disappeared into his beard as he stared past her to the grove. Slowly, he shook his head.

Sarah regarded him quizzically, then agreed. "Okay. The creek all right?"

The pishtaco nodded.

When they reached the stream, she sat on the bank and lowered her feet into it. She smoothed her dress over her legs and leaned back on her hands. The pishtaco squatted next to her and picked up a blade of grass, pretending to examine it as he glanced from her chest to the grove.

Suddenly, he shot up and shielded his eyes.

"Bird," he said, pointing over the treetops.

A fluttering silhouette swooped up, down, circling nearer Sarah and the pishtaco.

"I like birds," Sarah said. "You don't see many this high in the mountains. I wonder what it is."

"Not good," the pishtaco muttered.

The beast's vulnerability prickled the air. Sarah loved it.

"A bird? You're afraid of birds?"

"Not good," he repeated, backing away from the creek.

"What do you mean?"

Before the pishtaco could answer, the bird plunged between the two, driving them to the ground. When Sarah raised her head, the bird flapped and fluttered to the grass next to her.

She sat up and grinned. She nudged the pishtaco with her elbow and pointed to the bird. "It's a pigeon. A white pigeon. You can't be afraid of a pigeon."

"Not good," he growled.

"What do you mean not good? It walks. It flies. It coos."

She raised a hand to the bird, which slowly, one faulty step at a time, advanced toward her, its eyes trained on her unshaken calm.

"No." The pishtaco slowly slid his knife from its sheath.

Unconcerned, the pigeon bobbed its head and stepped onto Sarah's hand.

"Just ignore him," she told the bird, leaning her mouth toward its beak.

The bird blinked twice at her.

"He doesn't know," it said.

Before Sarah could think, a brilliant light streaked past her eyes, and the pigeon's head vanished. Its lifeless body toppled from her hand to the grass.

She shrieked, recoiling to the ground. The pishtaco towered above her, grimacing and wiping his knife on his pants.

"What—? What did you do?" Sarah screamed.

The beast sneered at her, holding the two pieces of the pigeon in front of Sarah's face, one in each hand.

"I did *this*!" he barked at Sarah. Then at the headless bird, he bellowed, "You will not stop me! No matter what you do, it will be done!"

He tossed the pieces into the creek and glared at the quivering woman. "It will be done," he said, stomping across the meadow toward Mount Komu.

Gasping for breath, her arms swirling through the water, Sarah sloshed into the water to retrieve the heart and head segments. "No! No! Where are they?"

Sunlight glinted off sodden feathers, and Sarah dove at the bird remains. Grasping the head and body from the current, she shook with nervous laughter, held them aloft, and sloshed to the bank. She stumbled up to level ground, water and weeds dripping from her nose. Hopeless and panicked, she jammed the two segments together.

"This can't be! How could he—? The bird talked to me. I swear it talked." Fearfully, she touched the body, then the head.

No life stirred.

She pushed the head back onto the neck and held them together. "You have to live! What did you mean 'he doesn't know'? Come back! Come back!"

Holding the pieces to her chest, she rocked and babbled until her hands glowed—red, gold, yellow. Light exploded from her. Terrorized by flame, she flung herself into the creek, the current pulling her deeper and deeper as the water hissed. Amidst her gulping and splashing, the sky burned.

Helpless and resigned, she pulled the bird to her chest, lay back, and waited for the end.

Sarah awoke to a gentle rocking, her head bobbing easily above the shallow stream. She opened her eyes slowly, squinting at the bright sun above the meadow. When she sat up, her buttocks sank softly and safely to the creek bottom.

Slowly, she surveyed the world around her. Ahead, water meandered down the mountain. To her right, the rocky top of Mount Komu rose toward the sky. Behind her, the stream trickled out of the mountain glade.

On her left, the pigeon, a thin dark line encircling its otherwise clean white neck, stood on the bank watching her.

"Thank you," it said without sound.

"You speak," Sarah said, wiping back her hair.

The pigeon nodded.

"And you spoke to me before, when the pishtaco—just before he—"

"Yes."

"You said 'he doesn't know'."

The pigeon bobbed its head. "He does not know who you are or what you are or why you are here."

"The pishtaco?"

"Him, too."

"You mean the Earth Man."

"It is difficult for him to know you before you do."

"But I know who I am. I'm his queen. A third of the Unholy Trinity."

"You were. Once you were less. You will be more."

"More? I'm chained to a monster," she said pulling her necklace from her dress. "What could I possibly be that I'm not now?"

"Now is not the time. For the moment, return to the cave and the Earth Man."

"And the pishtaco? He said, 'It will be done.' What did he mean?"

"Let go of his words and his actions. As you've seen, you need not defeat the pishtaco. There is no game to win or lose. You will be who you are with no triumph, no fear."

The pigeon cocked its head, flapped its wings, and flew away. Sarah leaned back in the stream and followed its flight high above her. First, it circled over the crest of the mountain, then swooped down over the meadow and above the creek. Finally, it approached the dark grove of trees behind her, where a white bear awaited its return. The pigeon landed on the bear's head, and the two watched her a moment before vanishing into the shadow.

Sarah sat quietly in the current, closed her eyes, and breathed. She dipped her hands into the water and bathed her face. Holding her palms to her nose, she smelled the flame that healed the bird, the water that cleansed her of the pishtaco's hate, and the essence of life still within her.

31

What Is Essential

Mount Elder
British Columbia, Canada

The spirit bear stood in the stream that ran from the mountain spring above him. Shimmering images swam through the water flowing between his legs, jumbling, tumbling, and flickering in the sparkling light. Just who the people were, where they were going, or what they meant bewildered him. He slapped at them, trying to block them with his paws, but catching them proved impossible. Before he could even focus on one, the faces bounced around, under, and through his feet.

It was futile. For each one he attacked, another twenty flowed past.

He could take no more. Leaping to his hind legs, he flailed and roared at the sky, then splashed out of the stream. Water sprayed around him as he shook his heavy white body. Snuffling, he growled and hacked at the dry ground. Then, he lay in the grass, resting his head on his paws.

Although the air was clear above the thinning trees, malevolence drifted on the breeze. *"The battle is near,"* he thought.

"Yes," a voice said.

The pigeon materialized out of nothing and waddled onto the bear's immense paw. "The Trinity is needed," it said. "The time is near."

"I have not found them. I have never heard those names before: the Sacrifice, the Original Thought, and the Dream Rescuer. Who are they? How am I to know them?"

"Remember Jeannie Jones, her dreams, her Shimmerings."

"Jeannie Jones? I've known her since before she was born. She knows the Trinity? Is she one of them?"

"Look to the faces in the stream."

Counselor lumbered back to the water. Below the surface, the faces sharpened in the brightening water.

Faces from Jeannie's Shimmerings: the cantina owner in Mexico, the peasant boy from Peru, the Radcliffes in Canada, the monsters, Counselor himself.

Faces of Jeannie's family: her father Beecher, her stepmother Amanda, her mother Sarah.

A boy. Clawing, clutching bodies. Shadowy figures, living and dead.

A tour guide walking out onto the ocean.

The images shuddered in his belly, buckling his knees and shaking his massive shoulders.

A thousand questions jarred against his skull. He couldn't breathe. He couldn't see. He collapsed to the shore, thrashing helplessly, stretching for the pigeon.

"What?" the bird asked, landing near Counselor's head.

"I—I can't do it. Even if I found them, I wouldn't know what to say. I no longer hear the words of the ancients. I don't have spells, visions to teach me. It's impossible. How am I to think? *What* am I to think?"

The pigeon dipped its head to its chest. "Be still. Thought only distracts and disguises. All misery—anger, sorrow, stress, frustration—is created by activity of the mind. You have done this before. Stop chasing ideas and inventions. There is no need to think. It is enough to know."

Counselor shook his head. He knew more than he wished. More than Jeannie. More than Sarah, her mother, the Earth Man's woman. More than any of the faces.

He knew the virtue and corruption that threatened them.

"The battle is beginning and I'm not even human. What am I to do?"

"Gather the Trinity and guide them."

"Gather who? How? Guide them where?"

The pigeon shook its head. "Follow me to where all is known, all is told."

"All?"

"All that is good. All that is needed. Follow me."

"Where?"

"To find the Source."

The bird flapped its wings twice and disappeared into the light beyond.

The great white bear closed his heart's eyes to hold the pigeon's words until they seeped through his fur and his skin, sank into his veins, and rushed through his body into his soul and mind. Counselor rose to his back paws and studied the opening beyond the tree line.

The Battle was beginning. The Trinity—whoever they were—needed his Guidance. To do that, he needed to know more than some. He needed to know all.

He lowered himself to all fours and plodded upstream to find the Source. At the tree line, the water next to him gurgled. "Watch me!" it said.

Counselor stopped, turned, and watched the stream dance and flow down the mountain, through the trees, across the valley, to the ocean. Extending to the sky, the distant waves reflected the peace and warmth of the sun.

"No matter how violent the beginning, no matter how chaotic the journey," he thought, *"the destination is calm."*

He would learn what he could, share what he must. He would return.

32

Behind Everything

Fort Repentance, British Columbia
Canada

Fever State, Christine Cummings' new thriller, burst onto the book market stronger than anybody in NewYork, Toronto, or Vancouver ever anticipated. Only one book chain in North America predicted the blockbuster. Literary License. In particular, the Fort Repentance branch.

All day long, the staff sorted and repacked orders from the Penticton and Kelowna branches, losing track of time. The crowds swarmed and phones jangled until 9:00 p.m. when Tonya McMahon, the manager, announced loudly, "Sorry, folks. That was the last *Fever State*."

The customers groaned and melted out the doorway.

Hurriedly, Tonya locked the door and pulled the blinds. "Let's get out of here. Another shipment is coming in at eight o'clock. Be here early, folks. Jeannie, you need a ride?"

Jeannie pulled on her jacket and grabbed her parents' copies of *Fever State*. "No, that's okay. I like the exercise."

"You sure? Could get wet."

"A little water isn't going to kill me. I'm fine. See you in the morning."

The two slipped out the back door and split from each other into the night.

As soon as Jeannie crossed Dingle, traffic dwindled and the streetlights quietly led her through the heavy air up the hill toward her house. Thunder rumbled out west past the harbor.

"It *is* going to rain. Damn it." She wrapped the plastic bag tightly around her parents' books and jogged the last two blocks.

Just as she turned to the house, a jagged bolt of lightning crackled into the rod above her tower. An earth-rattling crash shook the sidewalk, driving Jeannie to her knees.

As the first tentative drops of rain splattered her face, she scrambled toward the shelter of the house, but skidded to a stop at the porch. She could not move.

The porchlight was dark, as were the windows.

"That's not right."

Huge raindrops drenched her hair and jacket as she searched for an explanation.

Afraid of each step, she climbed the stairs, pulled open the screen, then reached to unlock the main door.

The knob fell off in her hand, and the door fell away from her. Thunder rumbled up from the harbor. Softly, she pushed the door farther open.

"Dad? AJ?"

Silence and stillness answered from inside. Jeannie flicked on the lights.

Ahead, the splintered office door dangled from twisted hinges. Shattered picture frames and glass shards paved a trail down the hallway to the kitchen. Jeannie' dry tongue caught in her throat. She coughed and set her bag on the floor.

"Dad?" she called.

Her shoulders shivered as she pulled off her wet jacket and hung it over the bannister. Slowly, she felt her way along the wall, shoving aside debris with her feet.

"AJ?"

Cautiously, she pushed open the dented door and turned on the kitchen light.

Fragments of the table and chairs protruded from the walls, stabbed into the sheetrock. The empty cupboards yawned clumsily, their doors torn from their hinges. The fine powder of smashed dishes covered the floor.

Across the room, two decapitated bodies, their feet lashed together, hung upside down over the refrigerator.

Jeannie's stomach lurched into her throat, gagging and choking her. Nausea drove her sliding and retching across the tile to the twin sinks.

Blank eyes stared up at her from two lifeless heads.

Her father.

Amanda.

Jeannie fell to the floor, pulling her head and knees to her chest. Her body convulsed.

She could not vomit. She could not breathe. She could not see. All was devastation. The room. The bodies. The heads.

Abruptly, Jeannie raised her head and scanned the kitchen, the walls, the cupboards, the floor.

"Something is missing," she thought.

Clutching her mouth with one hand, she forced herself to look at the bodies hanging from the refrigerator, the clothes, the floor beneath them, the stainless steel door.

"It's not—It's not right," she said aloud.

Slowly, she rose and walked toward the bodies. Careful to avoid touching anything, she clasped her hands behind her back and investigated the rope.

Not hemp. Not synthetic. Yet she knew it.

Taking a deep breath, she forced herself to the sink and the heads. Crossing her arms about her body, she examined the space from the refrigerator to the sink and back. Despite the vicious attack and the beheading, there was no blood anywhere. Two clear vials stood on the counter.

Jeannie's right knee twinged, but she stood erect. "Fat," she said rubbing her leg. "A pishtaco."

Suddenly, she remembered the names that frightened her father—Wayne Diego, Frank Thorstad, the matchi-auwishuk, the Earth Man—and realized that death and mayhem not only plagued her Shimmering dreams. They now infested her reality. *"Evil is never over,"* she thought.

Yet she heard her father's words: "No matter what, the Word wins…. Love is stronger and wider and longer."

The sirens had stopped hours ago, but the yellow, red, and blue flashing lights still sliced through the drizzle. Out on the street, a crowd of neighbors gathered, attracted to the lights like flittering moths. A coatless Jeannie sat on the front steps, cold rain dripping from her nose and hair.

Inside the broken door, the chaos of officialdom buzzed—police, medical examiners, drivers, photographers, reporters. Voices rose and overlapped. Heels clomped through the hallways, up the stairs, in and out of the kitchen. Tense, impatient workers elbowed past each other. Cameras clicked and whirred.

At the end of the sidewalk, a single, timid voice rose above the sound of rain and grumbling.

"Miss Jones? Jeannie? It's me. Maddie? Mrs. McNally's nurse?"

A small woman broke through the crowd and waved shyly. Jeannie, her face blank, acknowledged her with a lifted chin.

The officer stepped aside and allowed Maddie to pass. As other police and medical technicians shuffled past them, Maddie sat next to Jeannie and touched her shoulder. "Miss Jones? What's going on?"

Jeannie shivered in the cold and hugged herself. She shook her head. "I—I can't—"

She swayed forward. Maddie caught and embraced her.

"It's okay. It's okay." She rubbed Jeannie's shaking back.

Daniel White, Fort Repentance's chief major crimes investigator, emerged from the house.

He gently patted Jeannie's shoulder. "Miss Jones, we need to take your parents out now. You don't want to be here. Is there somewhere else—"

Maddie gasped. "Jeannie, your parents—?"

Jeannie's contorted face and quivering lips explained without words.

"They're dead? What? How—What—"

White held up a hand. "Miss Jones?"

Jeannie raised her head and wiped her nose. "Yeah. I'd love to be somewhere else. Only, I don't have—"

Teardrops and rain flooded her face.

Maddie took both of Jeannie's hands. "Yes, you do have a place. You come home with me. Is that okay, Officer?"

Jeannie shook her head. "No, Mrs. McNally would—"

"Mrs. McNally won't even remember who you are. She'll think you're a new plant or something."

Inspector White interrupted. "Where would you take her? We still need to talk—"

"Just down the street. Third house on the left."

"Okay. I'm sending Officer Sallis with you. I'll be there as quickly as I can."

Maddie helped Jeannie off the step. When the two plus Officer Sallis entered Scarlet McNally's house down the street, medical examiners wheeled the first gurney to the curb.

In the darkness of Mrs McNally's sparsely furnished guest room, Jeannie dreamt, but she did not sleep. She hid her face in her pillow and fell to her side reliving all the violence she'd seen.

Her Shimmerings—the Oaxaca cantina, the Radcliffes.

Her nightmares—Wayne Diego, the matchi-auwishuk, the Earth Man.

Her life—her mother, her father, AJ.

The tour guide Beetle's story of the pishtaco.

Then, asleep in a strange bed, she confronted a new vision—a cold, enraged boy fleeing through woods and towns, checking behind him, pressing forward into the unknown.

The same slaughter and fury from her dreams and reality drove him away toward the unexplainable.

She repeated her father's words: *You are loved. Stronger and longer and wider than a thousand universes.*

The words were more than for herself. They were for all she had known or would ever know.

The unexpected warmth of the spirit bear inhabited her blanket and enclosed her. Instinctively, she curled up and nestled in its tender presence.

"I did ask," she said, pulling the blanket over her and turning to her other side. "I still have more questions though."

A loud rapping, metal on wood, startled her.

"Jones?" a gravelly voice rattled.

Rap-rap-rap!

"Jones, are you in there?"

Rap-rap!

"Jones! I don't think she's in there. JONES! I'm leaving."

"No. No. I'm here. Just a second."

Frantically, Jeannie rolled off the bed and snatched a tissue from the bedside table. She roughly blew her nose, then wiped the tears from her face. Shakily, she flattened her frazzled hair and opened the door.

A steel-tipped cane whooshed past her face.

"Oh, my! Mrs. McNally!" She pulled the door close to her and peeked from behind it.

"I came to see you," Mrs. McNally barked from her wheelchair, flailing her cane.

Turning on Maddie, she said, "All right, bitch-face. Push me in. Then get lost. I want to talk to Jones alone."

Maddie stepped forward. "Oh, Mrs. McNally, I don't know if Jeannie—"

"Shut up and get out!" Mrs. McNally glanced at Jeannie.

In that glimpse, Jeannie felt a presence and security beyond the sputtering, crazed old woman. She held up her hand.

"It's okay, Maddie. We'll be fine." She stepped around the chair and pushed Mrs. McNally into the room, positioning the wheelchair next to the bed. Warily, Maddie watched the room as Jeannie closed the door.

Jeannie sat on the bed opposite Mrs. McNally, her hands in her lap. "You wanted to see me?"

Mrs. McNally growled and contorted her face. "It's about your sister."

"My sister? Mrs. McNally, I don't have a sister."

"Your sister Beulah!"

"Honestly, ma'am. I don't have a sister. I—"

Mrs. McNally narrowed her eyes and grunted.

Jeannie sat up, remembering AJ's advice: "Just go with her on the journey."

"Oh, yes. Yes. Beulah. What about her?" Jeannie raised her hands and gnawed on her knuckles.

Mrs. McNally dipped her head and looked up into Jeannie's eyes. Her icy scowl thawed as she placed the cane across the chair's arms and raised both hands to Jeannie. "First of all, come here."

Jeannie's mouth quivered. "I—I—What?"

Mrs. McNally summoned with both hands. "Come on. I'm an old lady. I can't hold these up forever."

Jeannie rose, then leaned over the old woman.

Mrs. McNally patted Jeannie's dampening cheeks. "I know you don't have a sister. I've always known you don't have a sister."

Jeannie sniffed and nodded. Mrs. McNally drew the sobbing girl into her lap.

"It's all right, honey. Crying is all right. You go ahead." The old woman petted Jeannie's hair until the tears subsided.

When Jeannie calmed, Mr. McNally handed her a tissue and ordered her to blow her nose. "It helps to get the snot out," she said.

Jeannie laughed, did as she was told, and sat back on the bed. Gently, she took the woman's wrinkled, papery hands in front of her and kissed them. "Thank you."

"That's why I'm here."

Jeannie examined the kind face in front of her. "You know more than we think you do, don't you?"

Mrs. McNally shrugged. "Look, young lady. There aren't many moments when my brain works. My body either. So sometimes I just kind of rent them out to whoever can use them best."

The old woman's eyes twitched and sparkled.

"Like now. You're not Mrs. McNally, are you?"

"That's not what I'm here to tell you."

Jeannie scooted farther back on the mattress. "What then?"

"You are not wrong to feel as you do right now. Somebody just wrecked your whole life. You're on your own. You're terrified."

Jeannie hugged herself and nodded.

"Except you're *not* alone."

"It sure feels alone," Jeannie said.

Ancient hands shook Jeannie's legs. "Listen. I have more money than Nova Scotia, so you don't have to worry about school or a place to live or anything. You will finish high school. You will go to college. You will be whoever and whatever you need to be. Not only that, you're going to be *where* you need to be."

Jeannie watched the bed's surface. "I'm sorry."

"For what, Jeannie?"

"I never got to ask my dad or AJ all the questions I had. Too many facts. Too little time."

"Still you know."

"I know what?"

"Where the answers lie."

"I really don't know."

Mrs. McNally slapped the bed in front of her. "Jones! You don't have dreams for nothing."

"Dreams?" Jeannie's head jerked up. "You know about my dreams?"

"Of course!"

"How? How do you know?"

"I know everything."

Jeannie slid to the edge of the bad and grasped the frail hands in front of her. "The only creature I know who knows everything is—"

Jeannie gazed at the woman's timeless face. The person or whatever it was behind those eyes said, "You were told to ask questions. You did, but you will always have questions. Questions about many things. None are wrong. Ask them all."

The voice was so familiar.

The woman caressed her cheek. "For now, stay here. You cannot change what is or what was, only what is to be. Learn what you can. When it's time to learn more, you will know where to go, what to do, why, and whom to ask."

Jeannie ran a hand through her hair.

The woman peered up at her. "You don't know *why* this makes sense because Mrs. McNally is a crazy, old bat?"

Jeannie laughed. "Right."

"She'll be back in a moment."

The woman leaned back in her chair and bellowed, "Maddie! I've had enough. Get me the hell out of here!"

Her face tightened as Maddie opened the door. Officer Sallis stood behind them, watching carefully. Mrs. McNally shook a warning finger at Jeannie. "And you. You! I'm only gonna say this once. If you ever get in trouble, there's only one thing you can do. And you better do it. You hear me? One thing!"

"What's that?"

"Listen to the bear!" Mrs. McNally proclaimed. "All right, whore-spawn. Let's go. I got a salmon at home that's spoiling in the fridge. Call the kids and tell them we're coming."

Maddie forced a smile and pushed Mrs. McNally and her chair away.

"Come on, copper," the old lady called to the detective. "The girl needs rest. You can talk in the morning."

Jeannie's eyes pled for Sallis's cooperation. He twisted his face, nodded, then followed Mrs. McNally and Maddie down the hall.

Jeannie closed the door and shut off the lights. In bed, she pulled the covers over her face and nuzzled into the pillow.

"Thanks, bear."

As the house quieted, she slept.

33

Heave in Unholy Time

Winthrop, Michigan
USA

Choir practice was a hopeless jumble of congratulations and good wishes to Skye on her engagement.

Since her announcement, Brandon lived in denial. "She can't love Goodwin. He's a—He's just a hack preacher."

In his accustomed perch at the far right corner of the choir loft, Brandon pretended to study the bass line of Sunday's special music. The other men waited patiently for the women to take their spots for rehearsal to begin. Skye bubbled and gushed as the women fawned over her ring.

Inwardly, he fumed. Outwardly, he rose and skirted between wall and pew, joining the congratulatory line. Unlike the sopranos and altos who surrounded Skye with warm hugs, Brandon simply offered his hand. When she took it, everything he felt welled inside his stomach and coursed out through his fingers. Skye smiled awkwardly and slowly withdrew.

Brandon's shoulders cramped. He lowered his head and climbed back to the basses. He caught Maggie's fleeting glance as she clapped her hands and opened her director's folder.

"All right, everybody. Let's do this quickly so we can go downstairs for coffee and treats."

"Yeah! Treats!" Andy O'Neill bellowed, slapping Brandon's knee. The rest of the choir laughed and opened their music while Brandon's belly knotted.

After a cursory run through Sunday's music, everybody clambered downstairs to the basement dining room for the reception. A long, hand-printed banner over the kitchen window read "Congratulations, Edwin and Skye!" The counter was packed with pink-and-blue frosted white cupcakes, plain beige sugar cookies, and dishes of butter mints and peanuts. Clear glasses of watery lemonade and stacks of empty, green Mount Hebron cups surrounded the giant coffee maker.

"Skye, where's Edwin?" the organist called.

"Oh, he was called to the hospital in Houghton a few hours ago. He should be here anytime. If not, I get his cupcake!"

The crowd laughed, claiming their own cupcakes, brownies, and coconut bars, defying gravity and the laws of motions by piling multiple layers of treats on their single-ply paper plates.

As the food dwindled, Brandon flattened himself against the beige concrete walls to blend in, but emboldened women thwarted his vain camouflage efforts. Congratulating him on his upcoming graduation, they hugged him good night and held their bodies against him. Three slipped notes into his pants pockets with their names and phone numbers. Others whispered "Call me" into his ear as they discreetly rubbed his crotch with their thighs.

Finally, Skye announced loudly, "We have to go, people! I need to lock up and repel the pagan Lutherans."

"Edwin hasn't made it yet."

"Like I said," Skye answered, "the cupcake is mine."

People laughed and filtered toward the exit. Hoping for one last look, one last word with Skye, Brandon leaned against the wall near the door.

The last woman out of the dining room, Maggie MacArthur, stopped and leaned to Brandon. "She's not what you think."

"What do you mean?"

Maggie clenched her mouth and shook her head. "She's—Her necklace—She's taken."

Brandon looked down at Maggie, then glanced at Skye as she walked back to the kitchen to shut off the lights.

"The cabin's empty tonight," Maggie said, then disappeared up the stairs and out the front door.

The basement light vanished around him. Brandon grabbed the railing and trudged up the steps.

"Brandon, can you wait a minute?"

Skye looked up from the bottom of the stairs.

For just a moment, he lost his bitterness and fear. Then, catching himself, he assumed his scowl, shrugged, and muttered, "Yeah, sure."

Skye smiled and climbed past him. "Let's go sit in here."

She opened the sanctuary door, left the lights off except for the electric candle behind the golden cross on the altar, and led him down to the middle pews.

Sliding toward the center, she patted the seat next to her. "Please. Sit."

Brandon sat and leaned forward on the pew in front of him. "Yeah?"

Under Skye's examining eyes, his shoulders flinched. He diverted his eyes to the altar cross. "What?" he grumbled.

Skye cocked her head. "Are you mad at me?"

Brandon said nothing. He looked down at the floor between his arms. "*It doesn't matter*," he thought. "*She's as good as gone.*"

"What did I do?"

"Nothing," Brandon sat back and examining his fingernails.

"Nothing," she repeated. "Well, something's biting your ass."

He snapped his head toward her.

Skye smiled. "Okay! That got your attention. Now tell me what it is."

Brandon grimaced and worked his lips between his teeth. Conflicting images flowed through his mind:

The red-headed women he had never seen and always wanted—the pin-up, the faceless vision.

All the women he used. The ones who used him.

The ones he discarded. The ones who discarded him.

The people who left him—his grandfather, his mother, Nancy Kirkman.

The only one left to him—his drunken asshole father.

His righteous rival—Edwin Goodwin.

His moral ideal—Skye.

All flickered in a single tear emerging from the corner of his right eye. Skye wiped it away with her thumb. "Brandon, are you in love with me?"

He sat still a moment, then shrugged.

Skye sat back, placed her elbow on the pew, avoiding Brandon's face at her side and the altar at the front of the room.

"Nancy warned me of this."

"Nancy?"

"Nancy Kirkman."

"You know Nancy Kirkman?"

Skye nodded. "I've known her a long time. Plus, we both go to URock."

"In Bellamy? But how—"

"Brandon, it's a small campus in a small town. I know everybody there. And when she found out I was going to her home church for my internship, she—she told me all about the town, the church, the people. You."

"What did she tell you?"

She looked hard at him. "Everything."

"You mean—"

"Everything, Brandon. High school. Your parents. Your 'role.' Her Purity Promise necklace. Why you first came to Mount Hebron. Everything."

He wiped his mouth. "Do you—"

"Do I what?"

"Do you have a Purity Promise cross?"

Skye closed her mouth. "I did. Once upon a time. Not anymore."

She pulled a necklace from under her sweater and laid the pendant on her chest. "Nancy gave me this instead before I came here. She thought it would be appropriate."

Brandon sat up. "Aphrodite," he said.

"You know it," she said.

"Nancy gave you that? It's—It's my mother's."

Skye nodded to herself. "That explains a lot. You know what it means."

"It means she—you. You?" Brandon turned to her, waiting an explanation.

Skye raised her eyebrow. "Yes, me. See? No matter what you've done, I'm in no position to judge. Do you understand?"

Brandon nodded. "You know—?"

"About your women here? Yes." Skye shifted in the pew. "Did you know Maggie MacArthur's probably your greatest fan. Not mine, but—We had a long talk to straighten out some things when I first got here."

The room chilled. Brandon rubbed the goose bumps from his arms. "Straighten out things?" he asked.

"Actually, I needed her to forgive me."

"Forgive you? For what?"

Skye tilted her head and steadily watched his face. "For her husband."

Brandon's lips tightened against his teeth. "Her husband?"

Skye held his eyes until the truth crushed him.

"You were his—his—"

"His whore. You can say it."

"And he—"

"Died inside me. Yes."

"Shit." Brandon's chest tightened as the Skye of his carefully constructed dream world dismantled into her reality.

"Exactly," Skye said, taking his hand. "But the story has a good ending. It got me off the streets. I ran away to Bellamy, found God, started at URock. I'm a new person. Mostly."

"Mostly?"

Skye waved off his question. "Before practice tonight, Maggie and I had a talk about you."

Brandon leaned forward on the pew ahead, then rested his chin on his folded hands. His stomach tightened against his belt.

Skye rubbed his back. "She told me what you said. That you couldn't have any girl you wanted; you could only have the ones who wanted you."

Brandon laid his cheek on his hands, her gentleness reminding him of Nancy's that first night.

"Nancy said you've always been looking for that someone. From what Maggie and most of the choir ladies say, you've been looking pretty hard."

Brandon dipped his eyes to the floor. Skye leaned forward and laid a hand on his arm.

"I understand. And I'm flattered that you think that's me."

Brandon waited for her to continue. She didn't. "But?" he asked into his arms.

"No *buts*. I'm flattered."

Brandon sat back and examined the back of his hands. "Thanks."

The electric candle light glowed behind the cross. The sound of their thoughts vanished into the silence.

Finally, Brandon ventured, "Now what?"

Skye looked off to the wall. "You go off wherever you need to go and I marry Edwin."

Brandon grimaced. He couldn't breathe. He couldn't think. "Okay," he whispered.

Neither moved.

"Except—" she said.

He slid down and laid his head on the back of the pew. "Except?"

She turned and raised herself over him. "Except this." She slipped a hand between his legs and kissed him firmly on the mouth.

The electric candle flickered.

Brandon woke in the darkness under a pew. Skye lay on top of him, her legs entwined with his, her soft breath on his neck. For the first time in months, he smiled. A happy smile. A satisfied smile. A smile of dreams fulfilled.

"Skye, are you in here?" Pastor Goodwin called.

Before Brandon breathed, Skye slapped her hand over his mouth.

"Skye?"

The overhead lights flashed on. Footsteps started moving down the aisle.

"Edwin? Is that you?" Skye called.

Panic tore through Brandon's body. Skye pulled his face against her shoulder.

"Of course, it's me. Where are you?"

"Are you alone?"

The footsteps stopped. "Yeah. Where are——"

"Then turn the overheads off."

Brandon squirmed farther under the bench and down her body to hide.

"Why?" Edwin asked.

"Just do it, please."

Edwin paused. "O...kay."

The footsteps shuffled back to the door. The light above vanished. Skye rolled out from under the bench.

"Now what?" Edwin asked into the sudden darkness.

Skye peeked over the pew back. "Okay. Come down the aisle a little."

"What's going on?"

Brandon shivered nervously under the pew. Violently, he shook his head at Skye.

"Just do it, please," Skye called to her fiancé. "You'll like it. I promise."

"How far?"

"I'll tell you when to stop."

"You can see me? I can't see a thing!"

"Edwin!"

"Okay. Okay."

Edwin tentatively found his way down the aisle. Brandon felt the pastor's weight on the floorboards as he approached.

Five rows back.

Four.

Three.

"Okay. That's enough," Skye said.

Brandon's heart thumped against his chest.

"Now what?" Edwin asked.

Skye rose and slid out of the pew.

"Now this."

Brandon heard the kiss that minutes ago had been his. He pulled his arms close to himself and pressed his chin hard against his chest.

"Skye, you're—you're—"

"Yes, Edwin. I'm naked."

"This is—This is wrong. We can't—I mean—"

"Yes, we can. Come with me."

Brandon shook his head as four feet walked past to the front of the church.

"What—?" Edwin stammered.

Brandon peered under the pews ahead into the dimness of the altar candle.

"Edwin, we don't have to wait for a ceremony. Right here, right now, I give myself to you. Now and forever."

Again, Brandon heard the kiss. He saw the couple's feet. Edwin's shoes tottered for balance as Skye's toes stretched upward and her bare legs leaned into him. Brandon's gut cramped and twisted.

"Seriously?" Edwin whispered.

"Seriously."

Another kiss.

"Thank you," the pastor said.

Brandon licked his mouth and savored the taste of Skye that lingered. He pulled his knees tight against his belly.

There was a rustle, the sound of Edwin's falling clothes. Then silence, turned to breathing. Heavy, loud breathing.

Brandon clenched his eyes, struggling to disregard the bodies that simultaneously fought against and into each other. Frantically, he searched his memory for Skye's hidden face. His whole body shuddered.

Suddenly, Edwin groaned once, twice. Skye whimpered. Louder. Louder. A quick moment of silence. Two tense gasps echoed off the bottom of the altar. Off the ceiling. The windows. The pews.

Edwin fell to the side.

All the girls Brandon had in high school flashed on the pew above him, faster and faster: Nancy Kirkman. Denise Rentz. Kristin Zolnowski. Carol Ellison. Rachel McDonald.

Mound Hebron women climbing naked over gravel piles. Customers from O'Neill's sneaking down into the store's basement to hide behind crates of paper towels.

Aphrodite. Adonis. His mother. Sigurd Dorsett and his wife Lacy. His father. Gracie Manning and her husband Sean. Faceless women and men he would never see.

His mother's gravestone. Three sodden Legion Club sluts lying over his drunken, unconscious father in a once sacred bed.

A younger Skye Jeffers lying under a strange man, gasping and crying for help. Maggie MacArthur smiling as Skye pushed the man to the side and screamed. A gratified Maggie leaning back and laughing uproariously as the man slipped out of Skye. Desperately, the girl wrapping herself in the hotel bedspread.

And now a nameless, faceless redhead—sturdy and muscular—exploding into a room, controlling his visions, his desires, his life.

Reflexively, Brandon opened his eyes just as Skye's free hand dropped to the floor below the altar and reached toward Brandon's pew. She turned her head and saw him shivering under the benches.

His future demolished, he mouthed, "Why?"

She stared at him and mouthed, "I love you."

The words meant nothing. Nancy Kirkman's Purity Promise burned into his chest.

Skye turned her head back toward the ceiling and draped her arm over Edwin. Both her hands smoothed the pastor's back and hips.

Maggie MacArthur's face glared down from the bottom of the bench.

Slowly, silently, Brandon turned over, rose, and grasped the back of the pew in front of him. Holding his breath, he scrutinized the drowsing couple. His eyes narrowed as he wiped his mouth with the back of his hand.

He pulled Nancy Kirkman's Purity Promise away from his chest and rubbed it between a thumb and forefinger. It singed his hand and tortured his brain.

Taking a deep breath, Brandon focused his mind on the images of the past and future. With his eyes shut against reality, he obliterated everything in one massive mental explosion. He reopened his eyes.

Skye and Edwin lay exhausted in the flickering light.

Brandon's temples throbbed. His fingers flexed. He jaw clenched.

He had to run. Run until his pounding heart exploded. Run until Brandon Whistler was no longer a memory. Run until the earth vanished.

Edwin coughed and groaned. Skye turned to her side, her auburn hair blazing in the candle light.

Brandon swallowed and snarled. "They must be erased," he said, leaping over the pews.

The words and voice of Tom Petty blared through the tinny phone speakers jarring Nancy Kirkman awake:

"Runnin' down a dream
That never would come to me..."

Entangled by sheets and bare legs, she fumbled for the ringtone on the bedside table, the floor, and under her pillow, but found nothing.

The body wrapped around her rolled over and yanked away the sheets, dumping Nancy to the floor. Petty kept singing:

"Workin' on a mystery, goin' wherever it leads,
Runnin down a dream"

Her bare skin stuck to the tile floor. "What the fu—?" she grumbled crawling back to the bed. A rattle diverted her attention. Amid the assorted dust bunnies and crusty socks under the frame, the phone vibrated deeper toward the wall.

"Come here, you little shit," she ordered as she twisted and squeezed after the unknown caller. With a desperate fling of her right arm, she snagged the phone, then crawled out and onto the uncovered mattress.

Using her butt to shove the lifeless body aside, she thought, *I have to get a different ringtone. I'm not old enough for Tom Petty."*

Punching the *Accept* button, she answered dully, "Hullo?"

"Nancy?"

"Yuh?"

The person next to her jumbled up the sheet and pulled it into his stomach. Nancy's head pounded. *"Where am I?"* she thought.

"Nancy, this is Maggie MacArthur, choir director at Mount Hebron in Winthrop."

"Maggie MacArthur? What—?"

The body grunted and turned to the wall, pulling a pillow over its head.

"Our youth intern Skye Jeffers said you were friends at URock. Is that right?"

"URock. School. That's where."

Her free hand touched the body's thigh. *"Oh, shit!"*

Nancy sat straighter and brushed her hair behind her ear. "Skye. Yeah. We're friends. Why?

"I'm afraid I have some bad news."

Wrapping an arm across her naked breast, Nancy glanced at the body behind her and bent over her knees. "O...kay."

"How to say this? Okay. This morning, Rolf Darby—Do you know Rolf?"

"The custodian. Sure."

"Anyway, Rolf went by the church and he—uh—Rolf went into the sanctuary and found—he found the corpses of Pastor Edwin and Skye lying on the altar."

Her shoulders sagging, Nancy rose and leaned against the wall. "What—What happened?"

"They were—The sheriff says they were beaten to death, probably with the missing altar cross."

Nancy sank to the floor, gazing at the naked back, arms, and legs wrapped around the crumpled sheet on her bed. Words and questions would not form on her lips.

"Nancy, are you there?"

The body grunted and pushed closer to the wall.

"Nancy?"

"Yes," she whispered behind a quivering fist. Next to the door, a wrapped bundle barely disguised the glinting object inside.

"Nancy, do you know where Brandon Whistler is?"

"Brandon Whistler?"

"I know you were good friends…"

"He told you that?"

"He didn't have to. One night when we were…together…I found a Purity Promise around his neck that had the initials NK on it."

Nancy closed her eyes and rested her head on the wall.

"That was yours, wasn't it?" Maggie asked.

"I—I don't know. Probably. Yeah—"

Nancy rose and stood over the bed. The body slept fitfully. She licked her lower lip, then opened the bundle. Inside she found a golden cross and Brandon's mother's Aphrodite necklace.

The one Brandon had given Nancy.

The one Nancy had given Skye.

"Nancy, his dad's reported him missing. The police are looking everywhere for him. If he had anything to do with Edwin and Skye, he needs to disappear. Like forever."

"And if he's innocent?" Nancy asked, holding the necklace aloft.

"Is he?" Maggie replied.

Nancy could not bring herself to answer. Instead, she hung up the phone, then hid it with the necklace in her dresser.

Watching the body on the bed, she whispered, *"Brandon, what did you do?"*

As the body burrowed between the mattress and wall, Nancy remembered the unsung words from the Tom Petty ringtone:

"I rolled on as the sky grew dark
I put the pedal down to make some time
There's something good waitin' down this road
I'm pickin' up whatever's mine....
I'm runnin' down a dream

Taking a robe from her closet, she wrapped it tightly around herself before sitting on the bed, wiping the boy's hair back, and gently shaking him awake.

Nobody ever found Brandon Whistler. Over lovers and time, even Nancy's memory of him faded. No more fantasies, expectations, or distractions. Like his wish upon a star at eight years old, like his dream of love, like his belief in truth, he disappeared without a thought.

34

Up to the Foundation

Mount Elder
British Columbia, Canada

Not quite morning but beyond the night, a regal, gray-purple sky guided Counselor over the low hills near the inlet north of Hartley Bay.

He had learned. He had returned. Now he must collect the Trinity and share.

"Travel by foot is easier for a bear than for a human," he thought.

Experience had taught him that. Through his existence, he had done both. Although he had grumbled and resisted since his latest arrival on earth, he now appreciated the efficiency of four legs and massive body. Brush and terrain deferred to his presence, opening a simple path through the woods and heights. Progress was effortless.

At the top of the last rise, he surveyed the length of the inlet out to the bay itself. The violet reds of morning broke over the hills behind him, revealing the low mist that floated over the surface of the water.

Counselor rose onto his hind legs, pawing and sniffing the air.

"This is the place. The Peruvian will be here soon," the bear thought lowering himself to all four feet.

In all his earthly human incarnations, Counselor had never heard the stories of the southern spirits, never encountered the wisdom nor the perversions of Incas and Aztecs, never heard how the Word spoke to and through stone and the flesh of the Hidden People. This would be different.

Counselor wove his way down through the forest and fog to the water's edge. Balancing his heavy body on the rocks protruding through the surface, he stepped onto the inlet cautiously, reverently, barely disturbing the flat surface.

Dipping his tongue into the water, he tasted the sacredness of the moment. "It is time."

The world stopped.

Flocks of birds plunged into the trees and perched devoutly among the branches. Above them, the wind held its breath in anticipation. The dark green forest and the hard, gray rocks eagerly awaited the turning of the world.

A single bird, a white pigeon, fluttered out of the trees as the sun broke over the mountains. The light cascaded down the slopes, creating a smooth pathway down the heights, across the water and tunneling under the morning fog.

Counselor lifted his snout, sniffed the air once more, and followed the path with his eyes. Far off, a human figure walked across the glassy water into the canopy of mist.

A boy. In body, almost a man, but still a boy. Naive, curious, fragile.

As still as forever, the bear waited for him to emerge from the tunnel.

The morning light exploded around the boy, dispelling the fog and revealing the spirit bear waiting on the shore. The boy hesitated, then, seeing nobody else around them, he advanced on the unfamiliar animal. When he reached Counselor, he stopped, his quizzical face reflecting off the still water below him. He spoke without words. "Who are you?"

"I am who I must be," Counselor answered.

"The Creator?"

"No."

"I seek Viracocha the Creator."

Counselor shook his head gently. "No. You seek the One Whom All Seek. The one known by many names. You say Viracocha. Others say the

Transformer, Yahweh, Allah, or the Tao. Multitudes of names spoken of one omnipotent, omniscient, acclaimed being."

"*Many* names?"

The bear nodded. "Many names. One Word."

"But you're not the One."

"No."

The boy's shoulders sagged.

"You are disappointed. Why?"

"Because you are not Viracocha."

"Are you?"

Confused, the boy shook his head. "No, I'm just Beetle."

"Not *just*. You are Beetle, son of Tutu, brother of Sisa. You are Chaupi, he who is the middle of everything. Sent here to find a new name, a new existence. Follow me."

The bear hopped across the rocks to the shore, then tromped toward the forest.

"Where are we going?"

"To the mountains."

"I just came from mountains."

"Different mountains. Those where you began and those you see now are but the Roof of the Earth. Those we will find are the Foundation of Heaven."

The boy scratched his head. "A foundation composed of mountains. I don't—"

"Why did you leave Peru?"

"How did you know I came from Peru?"

"I have been taught much so I can teach you. Why did you leave Peru?"

"I don't know."

"You do. You told me. You seek the One Whom All Seek. The one you call Viracocha. You seek the Word."

"Well, yes, but—"

"Ah, yes. The *but*. That is good. You understand."

"I understand what?"

"That there is a *but* before finding the Word. A *because*. The reason you left your teacher."

"I had no teacher."

"You did. You had your mountain, your ruins. Why did you leave Peru and come here?"

The boy shifted his weight to one foot. His memories clattered and clunked: Machu Picchu, the conversation with the tree and ground, Viracocha, the face in the night—

"The Canadian girl?"

Counselor regarded the boy's innocence.

"Your mission."

The boy's face brightened, then fell.

"There is no shame in incomprehension. Only in willful ignorance."

The boy turned away. "What then is my mission?"

"Follow me to the mountains and beyond. We will find your purpose and reach your ultimate goal, the One Whom All Seek."

Reluctantly, the man-boy strained up the hill, glancing back at the water he had just crossed.

Counselor sensed his hesitation. "Yes. The water was simpler. However, it was but a preparation. Come."

Beetle scrambled to Counselor's side.

"The lesson of the tree," the bear said. "What was it?"

Beetle examined the ground. At first, he only saw stones, dirt, and stray leaves. Then, the locks of his mind broke open. The Word spoke to him and he heard.

"Patience," Beetle said.

"Yes. Come," Counselor replied leading the man to the Foundation of Heaven.

Michael Frickstad

PART THREE

DIRECTION AND DELIVERANCE

35

Beyond Opposites

Beaver Flat Lodge
British Columbia, Canada

The tires crunched as Jeannie pulled her Jeep into the Beaver Flat Lodge graveled parking lot. Dawn had not yet broken over the eastern range, but moonlight bathed the world in a silver glow. Ghostly shadows of passing clouds gamboled across the lot and over the mountains beyond. The silhouette of the main building with its faux-Alpine peaks and crannies sprawled across the sky, a bewitched prisoner held captive by the heartless and brutal pines. Along the wooded ridge, a string of duplex cabins snaked beneath the trees lurking in the dark. Below the main lodge, the flat, black waters of Beaver Flat Lake mirrored the moon and stars above them like a second sky.

Jeannie turned off the engine and collected herself.

"This is it," she thought. Nine years of physical training to rehabilitate her knee and protect her body from the dangers and rigors of mountain life. Eight years since the Tower Shimmering. Seven years of world travel, school, and research. Six years of asking the spirit bear questions and collecting the answers.

Five years since her parents' murder.

Jeannie sighed and stared at the moon above the lake.

"No fear," she told herself. *"The whole story, Daddy. You and AJ promised to tell me. I'm ready to hear."*

She broke her gaze and turned on the Jeep's interior lights. Stretching her neck and turning from side to side, she checked her face in the rearview mirror. *"Not sure Mrs. McNally would have approved the pony, but I like it."*

Besides, the interview coach who Mrs. McNally had hired for Jeannie said a ponytail made her look approachable, yet in control. She also complimented Jeannie's bright eyes and long, low brows because they diverted attention from her freckled nose and cheeks.

"Freckles are an imperfection," the coach had said.

However, the British Columbia provincial recruiter never noticed. He barely gave Jeannie a chance to say yes before he sent her to the lodge. He praised her confidence, knowledge, and experience. He never mentioned her freckles. With a smile and a handshake, she got the job. It was almost as if it had been created just for her.

Still, the night before leaving Fort Repentance, the future had driven Jeannie to the shelter of her bed, complaining of being lost. Speaking an unbidden truth, Mrs. McNally cackled, "Well, you ain't gonna find yourself in bed. Get your sorry butt up!"

When Jeannie rose, the old lady softened and took her hands. "I'm going to tell you something that's not just from an old lady in a wheel chair. You understand?"

Jeannie examined Mrs. McNally's face as the old woman dabbed the tears from Jeannie's cheek with the bedspread. She recognized the eyes. "The spirit bear?" she asked.

"For one. And your father, your stepmother. And a crazy old lady in a wheel chair. Okay?"

Bracing herself, Jeannie sat taller and nodded.

"You remember all the Shimmerings? All your trips? You remember all the people and monsters you saw? They all led you to this point for one reason."

"To find my mother?"

"That's part of it, yes."

When a confused Jeannie regarded her, Mrs. McNally said, "You need to find your mother. All right. Let's go with that for now. To find your mother—and do anything else in life—is a simple two-step process: know what you want; get what you want."

"It's not really that easy," Jeannie thought.

Yes, her excursions with her father and stepmother had convinced her she wanted to be a mountain guide, but their deaths complicated her goal with the desire for revenge.

And yes, her Shimmerings and answered questions had showed her where to be: Beaver Flat Lake. Close to Mount Elder. Close to the Word. Close to finding her mother, the Earth Man and the Whole Story. When the recruiter Mr. Okerlund granted her the job, she even knew she was close to getting what she wanted.

However, close was not there. Even if she had completed the first step—knowing—getting was going to be a lot more difficult. This she would have to do all on her own.

No parents. No school. No Mrs. McNally.

There was something her father had said, but she couldn't quite remember the whole thing.

"It doesn't matter. I got this," she thought. *"No fear, Jeannie. Move on."*

Alone in the darkness, she tapped her index fingers on the steering wheel to refocus.

Was she dressed right? Dress-casual clothes worked great at the interview, but she had no idea what the lodge manager expected for orientation. She had never met or even spoken to the man. Consequently, before she left Penticton, she had made eight different choices before settling on a navy blue sweater vest over a red, gray, and white plaid flannel shirt, khaki slacks, and low-top hiking boots.

"Too casual? Not casual enough?" She glanced in the rearview mirror and pressed her palms on the ceiling above her.

The physical tension strengthened her upper body and concentrated the energy in her shoulders as she repeated the mantra "Breathe. Press. Relax. Breathe. Press. Relax."

Jeannie lowered her hands and gripped the wheel. The spark of energy tingled in her fingers. Her clenched chin trembled as the air whistled through her nostrils.

"It's all fine. It's all good. Just one more stage in the process."

She released the wheel and shook her hands vigorously. Once her fingers loosened, she leaned her head back against the seat.

The drive to the lodge had erased the memories and dreams that propelled her—her father and stepmother's corpses, matchi-auwishuk and weendigoes, the Oaxaca and Radcliffe murders, the South American pishtaco—

No, she was close to something else. More than horror and death. More than her dead mother. Something in the the unspoken words of Beetle, the Peruvian guide. Something about the Wisconsin boy from her Shimmerings.

Shaking off the cobwebs of early morning, she repeated her slogan, "No fear." She leaned forward and examined the hulk of the lodge.

A lamp blinked on in a corner balcony room. Jeannie shivered. She picked up her portfolio and opened the car door.

"Here we go," she mumbled, hoping for one more direction from the spirit bear.

None came.

Bryce Welch stood in the glow from the desk lamp, rubbing his eyes with both hands. "Five o'-fucking-clock! That's not even morning. It's the middle of the God-damn night."

He leaned on the desktop and groaned. Lowering his head toward his desk and raising his back, he punched his chest and shook the room with a belch.

"No more pepperoni after midnight," he muttered.

He pulled a small, round mirror from his desk and examined his face.

"Oh, God."

In disgust, he lifted his Beaver Creek t-shirt and vigorously wiped at the sleep encrusting his eyes. Then, he checked the mirror once more. Licking his hand, he brushed and picked at his spiked hair, then smoothed his goatee.

Satisfied with his look, he pressed his lips and puckered twenty times, scrunched his forehead, and hyper-smiled until a fart rattled the room.

"Ah. Good one." He jiggled a leg and stuffed the mirror back into his desk.

He sat in his chair and slapped his face.

Outside in the parking lot, a car door slammed.

Welch closed his eyes and rested his head in the palms of his hands. Faint footsteps climbed the steps to the deck and crossed the wooden balcony to the lodge's entrance. Down the hall, the door creaked open, then shut roughly.

"*I really have to oil that fucking thing,*" he thought. He picked up the manilla folder and took out the new guide's application and résumé.

"J. Jones," he read aloud. "That doesn't tell me shit."

Welch crossed his arms and glared at the folder. He had told the provincial office the kind of person the job needed: a six-foot male. Couple hundred pounds. Someone to pacify the city tourists who thought every squirrel rustling in the bushes was a grizzly starved for urban meat. Someone who intimidated and calmed people at the same time. Unfortunately, other than input, he had no authority in the hire.

He picked up a small rubber ball from the desk and bounced it off the floor next to him.

"*It'd be great if they hired somebody up for a little prospecting. There's gold in these mountains. I just have to get it out of the ground.*"

Harley and Kai, the groundskeepers Welch hired, were perfect for what he needed: adequate workers and dumb as squirrels. Pliable enough to learn to use explosives.

"*It'd just be nice if either of 'em knew the difference between moose turds and moss.*"

Welch stroked the thin, gold strand around his neck.

A light tap on the door startled him. Welch bowed his head over a pile of file folders. "Come in."

Jeannie opened the door and stood in the frame. "Mr. Welch?"

"*Shit,*" Welch thought, closing his eyes. "*A woman.*"

He raised his head and glanced at her.

"*I hate redheads. Especially freckled ones.*"

He stood, wiped his hands on his rumpled jeans, and offered one to her.

"Call me Bryce," he said brusquely. "You are——?"

Ignoring his hand, she narrowed her eyes.

"What?" Welch said, smoothing back his hair.

"Nothing," she said. "You just look familiar. I'm sorry."

She pointed to her personnel file on top of the heap in front of him. "I'm Jones. Jeannie Jones."

"Oh, yeah. Sorry." He twisted his neck and sighed.

"I totally understand. It's still early."

"Mm-hmm. Have a seat." Welch pointed to the chair in front of his desk.

Glancing at the room, Jeannie set her portfolio on her lap, and pulled out a folder.

"So, you need a drink or something? Coffee? Water? Whiskey?"

Jeannie squirmed. "Uh, no. I'm fine."

"Suit yourself."

Welch sat back in his chair and bounced the rubber ball at his side. "Evidently, you impressed Okerlund back in Victoria."

"Well—"

"So how'd you do it? I'm guessing the hair."

Jeannie looked up. "Excuse me?"

"Never been much for redheads myself, but you do have great eyes. Nah, that can't be it. Okie would never see your eyes. He's just a prick lookin' for big—"

Welch's eyes fixed on Jeannie's chest. "Well, you got those too. So how'd you impress him?"

Jeannie glared at Welch until he raised his eyes to hers. "I told him where I had worked before."

Welch raised his gaze. "Vancouver? Winnipeg? Vegas?"

Jeannie took a deep breath and focused on his thin, pointed eyebrows. "As it says on my résumé, the Alps, the Andes, the Himalayas—"

Raising her application and pretending to read it, he nodded. "Pretty impressive. Anything around here?"

"I was raised in BC, spent summers and winters around Alta Lake."

"No, I meant around Beaver Flat. Alta's just a glorified suburb of Vancouver."

Jeannie nodded slowly. "Yes. Above Kelowna. Glacier National Park. Field—"

"Couldn't have spent much time in any one of them. What are you? Eighteen?"

Jeannie bit her cheeks. "Twenty-three."

Welch tilted back his chair. He bounced the ball at his side again. "Really?"

"Is there a problem?"

Welch leaned forward and threw the résumé on the desk. "No. No. I was just thinking."

He sat back and stroked his goatee as he inspected her.

Jeannie shivered.

"How long do you think it will take you to learn the park?"

"I've been here before, so maybe a week or so. At least to learn the basics."

Welch chuckled. "Right."

Jeannie glared at him. "You don't believe me?"

"Lady, I've been here for four years and I still couldn't tell you where Gospel Trail is."

Jeannie straightened and set her jaw. "Across the parking lot."

"What?"

She pointed out the window. "There's a sign."

Welch turned his chair to the window and peered into the darkness. The lighted welcome sign pointed travelers to the lodge, Beaver Flat Lake, cabins, campgrounds—and Gospel Trail.

He swiveled his chair to face Jeannie. Scowling, he bounced his ball three times at his side.

Jeannie covered her mouth and concealed a smile. "If you'd like to explore more of what's here, maybe I could help you."

Slowly, he examined Jeannie, training his eyes on her chest. "Explore? Yeah. I could...explore."

Jeannie glowered at him.

Welch held up his hand. "I'm just giving you shit. Look. I get it. You're a mountain lover, the wild air and all that naturalist crap, but hot as you are, I'm not going out there with you or anybody else. Too much bad shit has happened."

"What do you mean?"

"Grizzly bears, mountain lions, crazy-assed butchers."

"Butchers?"

"Yeah, butchers. Ever heard of the Mount Elder Murd—Shit. I wasn't supposed to say anything."

Raising her hand to stop him, Jeannie said, "I know about the Mount Elder Murders. I researched them in college. That was a long time ago."

226

"Not that long. People are still spooked. *I'm* still spooked. If I go anywhere in these mountains, it's with someone who knows his way around."

Jeannie's stomach gurgled and she brought the back of her hand to her mouth. "Or *her* way."

Welch grinned and nodded. "Or her way. Okay."

"Look, Mr. Welch. I'm aware of the dangers. I've prepared, but I'm not stupid. I thought I would begin by exploring within a mile or two of the lodge here. See what's on all the postcards and in all the guidebooks. Then, as I become more accustomed, I could take off weekends and find other destinations. Places few tourists, guides, or even locals ever get to see."

Welch shook his head. "Look. You work here; you're my responsibility. If you think I'm going to let you—"

Jeannie held up her hand. "Please. I know. I know. I'm short. I look weak. Even frail."

Welch sniffed. "All gingers are frail."

Jeannie lowered her head and sucked her lower lip between her teeth. "Mr. Welch—"

"Bryce."

She fixed her gaze on him. "Mr. Welch, I know I'm not what you expected, but you know you can't fire me, right? Whether I have red hair or not. At least not before I've even started? I swear I can take care of myself or anybody I'm entrusted with."

Bryce raised his eyes.

"I *can!*"

"Look, we need someone who can—"

"Would you like me to prove it to you?"

He snorted and sat back, hand behind his head and his feet propped up on his desk. "Prove away."

Jeannie stood and walked to the door.

"This ought to be good."

"Stay there," she ordered as she closed the door behind her.

"What the hell? Jones, you—?"

Before he could finish his question, Jeannie's head crashed through the door. She shoved and ripped her way through the center panels, then tore the remains from the hinges. Swinging the frame against the door jamb, she broke off the doorknob and dropped it onto the desk in front of the gaping Bryce. It clattered and rolled off the edge to the floor.

She licked her fingers and wiped the small trickle of blood from her forehead. First looking at her hand, Jeannie raised her head to Welch and narrowed her gaze. "Just so you know I'm not frail," she said.

Welch sucked in his mouth and wet his lips. "Yeah… Okay."

Jeannie picked the knob from the floor and placed it on top of her résumé.

Welch gulped, then stammered, "Um—I—I—uh—"

"Yes?"

"I'm going to have to charge you for the door."

Jeannie nodded. "I expected that. Do I have a room?"

Welch gulped and nodded. "Downstairs."

He opened Jeannie's file folder and peeled back the tape from her room key. He stood and held it to her. "Number 5."

She took the key, stepped over the mess at her feet, and walked toward the doorway.

"Jones!"

Jeannie turned back. "Yes?"

Welch tried to ignore the pants tightening around his crotch. "You need a hand?"

"No, thanks."

She turned to leave, then stopped. "Oh, and Mr. Welch?"

His breath short and irregular, he mumbled, "Yes?"

Jeannie nodded toward his bulging pants. "Good luck with that."

She disappeared down the hall into the vanishing moonlight.

Welch picked up the doorknob, sat behind the desk, and watched out the window as Jeannie crossed the parking lot and grabbed her bags from the Jeep. Embarrassed, he turned back to the mirror on his desk and examined his eyes, his chin, the Adonis tattoo on the side of his neck.

The gold cross hung around his neck warmed his skin.

He leaned back his head and pulled the necklace from under his shirt, rubbing its cross between the fingers of one hand. Memories of dark cars, empty cabins, and church basements flooded his mind. He closed his eyes and rubbed the doorknob against his crotch.

Minutes later, his body straightened, convulsed, and fell back against the chair. The doorknob rolled out of his hand and came to rest next to the forgotten rubber ball.

36

Ever Desiring, Ever Desireless

Beaver Flat Lodge
British Columbia, Canada

Three weeks later, Jeannie stood at the entrance to Gospel Trail and waved to the last bus exiting the parking lot.

"Five days," she thought. "Five different groups of lodgers. Five day-long trips around Beaver Flat Lake on the flat, dull trail that only offers different views of the same thing—the lake and the mountains above it. Not once did we follow bear tracks or explore the slopes. Nothing off the path."

"Next week," she thought, as the final green and yellow motor coach disappeared into the trees and headed east toward Calgary.

She had served her probationary period: two weeks of exploring the popular highlights, then five days of Welch-approved guiding across terrain less challenging than a Fort Repentance sidewalk. But after today, Gospel Trail would be relegated to the day campers passing through on their way to Vancouver. The rest of the park belonged to Jeannie and the week-long lodgers.

Welch called from the balcony as she approached. "Hey, Beautiful. First full week with people finally over. Everybody off all right?"

Jeannie cringed and stuck her hands in her back pockets. "They all smiled and waved. I guess that's all right."

Welch leaned over the railing as Jeannie approached the employees' entrance below. "Kitchen help and the grounds folks are going into town for supper and a movie. Wanna go with them?"

Jeannie shaded her eyes from the sun reflecting off the windows behind him. "No, I'm hot and sweaty. I'm going to take a shower, read for a while, and enjoy the quiet."

The glare of the sun hid his face, but she felt him looking down her shirt. "Need help?" he asked.

She cringed and flexed her shoulders. "No thanks. I can handle it."

Inside the lodge basement, her skin crawled as she found her key. Outside her room, she glanced back to the outside door.

Nothing.

She slid the key into the lock, then leaned back to check the stairway down the hall. The one that led upstairs toward Welch's office.

Nothing there either.

Not knowing whether to be relieved or insulted, she sighed, quickly unlocked the door, and disappeared inside.

Jeannie leaned against the wall and let the shower stream the shampoo from her hair. Gulping the moist air, she leaned her head back as the water ran from her chin to her throat, her throat to her collarbone, over her chest and down her flat stomach. With her washcloth, she wiped the sweat from her skin, scoured her legs and toes, and cleaned the pores of her speckled cheeks. To flush the sluggishness from her mind, she lowered her face into the current.

Cleansed of physical and emotional grime, she stood in the still-swirling steam of the stall, toweling her limbs and body while plotting the next week's tours.

"*Not too far at first,*" she thought. "*Don't want Bryce shutting things down before I really get started.*"

She stepped from the shower, steadying herself on the stall door while she bent and flung her hair back and forth. Harder. Faster. Retrieving the towel, she rubbed her scalp, then stepped in front of the mirror to pull a brush through the snarls. Unable to see herself through the mist, she opened the bathroom door to let in cooler air, but no matter how long she waited, the mirror remained cloudy.

"Gah!" she yelled, swiping the glass with her wet towel, only obscuring her image even more. She threw up her hands, slapped the towel on the counter, and stepped into her room for a new set of clothes.

As she pulled open a dresser drawer, a voice behind her said, "Nice ass." Jeannie whirled.

Bryce Welch lay on her bed, smirking at her. Naked.

With nowhere to hide what had already been seen, she leaned against the dresser. "Did you want something?"

He raised his eyebrows and smiled.

She shook her head. "Of course, you do."

Pulling back her shoulders, she cupped her breasts. "These?"

"That would be a start." Welch rose from the bed.

He stood over her, a gold cross lying on his bare chest at the same level as her face. Unintimidated, she gazed up at his scraggly goatee and the tattoo on his neck. She felt his penis rise and brush her stomach. "What did you have in mind?" she asked.

"Surprise me."

Jeannie lightly touched the cross, then rested her palm on his chest. She glanced up at his face, breathed long and warm between her thumb and forefinger, then lightly licked his skin.

Welch shuddered. Awkwardly, he reached around her for the dresser to regain his balance.

"Like that?" she asked.

"Yeah. Yeah, that's great." He clutched the dresser top.

She lowered her hand to his stomach and repeated the breath and flicking tongue. Again, he wobbled.

"Do whatever you want," he whispered.

"Really?"

"Absolutely."

She licked two fingers. Deliberately, she touched the tip of his penis and trailed her fingers down the shaft.

His knees buckled and his stomach shook uncontrollably. He moaned.

"Whatever I want. Right?"

"Yes. God, yes."

232

"You're sure?"

Welch adjusted his stance in anticipation. "Do it."

Jeannie set her feet and pounded her fist into his scrotum.

Welch collapsed into Jeannie, his hands fumbling at the dresser behind her. His throat snapped and gagged. He couldn't breathe. He couldn't cough.

With one arm wrapped around Welch's waist, Jeannie drove a shoulder into his stomach as her free hand clutched his testicles and shoved them deep into his groin.

In one move, she straightened her legs and lifted his helpless body. Unconcerned by the *thunk* of his head against the dresser, she carried him into the hallway and slammed him into the concrete wall.

Still gasping for air, Welch sank to the floor, his hands tucked between his thighs. He lay on his side in a puddle of drool, grasping at the air as Jeannie flung his clothes at him. "Fifteen minutes! Your office," she ordered.

She slammed the door and locked it behind her.

With a single knock, Jeannie burst into Welch's office, her face and hair flaming. Welch curled deeper into his desk chair, his arms wrapped around his stomach.

"All right. Let's get this straight, MISTER Welch. I don't care what you do or say. I am not quitting this job and I am not fucking you."

When Welch moaned and pushed the chair away, Jeannie yanked it back to her.

"There's a reason I'm here at Beaver Flat and you're not it. You and me? That does not exist."

Welch opened his mouth, but Jeannie grabbed his jaw and shut it.

"I don't want to hear it. You listen to me. Now I'm not going to say anything to anybody in Victoria about this and neither are you. I'll work my five days a week. I'll show the tourists things they never knew existed. They'll all be happy. They will tell their friends. They'll keep coming back again and again. The provincial office will be ecstatic."

Sitting on the desk in front of him, she leaned close to his face. "Five days of work here a week. That's what I signed up for. We'll be colleagues. We'll be civil. You'll smile. I'll smile. We'll be professional and act like nothing ever happened. But—"

"But?" Welch croaked.

"The other two days are mine. Don't even think of looking for me. I'll go where I want, do what I want, and I'll be back here, ready to go on Monday morning."

Welch blinked and crossed his legs. "What are you planning—"

Catching her words, she threw up a hand and gazed at the floor. Breathing deliberately, she said, "It's none of your business, but I have things to see. Things to discover. The whole park. The lakes, the glaciers, the mountains, the sky, plants, animals."

"By yourself?"

"You still think I can't handle—?"

"No. No. It's just—" He coughed into his fist. "If you go out like that, I'm legally responsible if anything happens—"

Jeannie regarded him, then lowered her eyes to think. She scratched her chin, then hopped down from the desk. "Right. Right."

While Jeannie crossed to the window to peer at the mountains, Welch reached inside his desk for his rubber ball and bounced it against his teeth.

Jeannie tapped on the window. "Okay. Here's an idea. How about I take a walkie-talkie with me on weekends and I check in once a day?"

Nervously, Welch pounded the ball on the back of his neck.

"How about three times? Once when you get up, once when you stop for lunch, and once before dark. Nothing detailed. Just where you are, where you're going."

Jeannie returned to Welch's desk. With a single finger, she rubbed the edge and countered, "Where I am. I won't know where I'm going."

Welch coughed and held his stomach. "Fine."

Jeannie bounced a hand on his desk. "You still hurt?"

"God, yes. Even my nose hairs ache."

"Good. I guess we're done here." She turned to leave.

"Uh—About downstairs—" Welch said, rising tentatively from his chair.

"You're sorry?"

"No. Well, yes, but—I wanted to ask—Am I—I mean—Are you—Are you a lesbian?"

"Is that what you thought when I touched your dick?"

Welch flushed. "No. I—You seemed—I mean how did you do that? How did you learn—"

"I read. A lot."

"Just read?"

"That's enough."

"But—"

"Enough to realize sex doesn't matter."

"Doesn't matter? Have you ever—?" Welch shivered under Jeannie's glare and crossed his arms.

"No, and I don't really want to."

"But orgasms are—"

"Oh, I know about orgasms and the wonders of my anatomy. I just don't need to have sex."

Welch glanced at her crotch, then quickly looked away. "So you're—handy."

"Exactly. I don't need another person—male, female, or whatever—to mess up my life. I don't need the—the—"

Welch's face turned darker. "Distraction?"

"Right. And I don't need a label like straight, gay, or bi to define me."

"How about waffle?"

"Just stop. It's not going to happen. I've got more important things to do with my life than you."

Welch readjusted his arms protectively. "Okay. Five days on, two days off. Check in three times on off days. And I won't—I won't try anything ever. If I did, you'd chew off my balls and feed them to a grizzly."

Jeannie smiled in spite of herself. "At least."

Welch nodded. "Got it."

Jeannie hesitated at the door and examined Welch as he gazed out his window. *What is that symbol on his neck?* she wondered. As she flipped back her hair, she decided, *Just a tattoo. Worthless decoration.*

Welch coughed, then yelped in pain.

Jeannie laughed to herself. *Not everything's worthless,* she thought. *The goatee isn't so bad. And his dick—Well—*

She hesitated, then closed the door behind her.

37

Sacred Universe

Beaver Flat Lake Provincial Park
British Columbia, Canada

After a springtime of work and tolerating the awkward moments around Welch, Jeannie loved her job.

During the week, she steered people over the mountains, through the forest, and across streams. On special occasions, she showed them the glaciers and fields to the north. From the rocks above the tree line to the deepest, grassy valleys teeming with wildflowers, she revealed a reality few visitors even read about.

Throughout weekends, she climbed and roamed by herself, controlled only by her inclinations. Armed with awareness and skill, she struck out to find what she wanted to see and do what she wanted to do. For direction, she depended on whim, not logic or prudence.

Following the directions she once received from the spirit bear, she asked what she needed to ask—questions about her father and stepmother, about the Word and the Earth Man, about her mother. When the universe answered, she barely thought of Bryce Welch.

It wasn't that she hated him. She didn't hate him. She hated thinking about him. Weekends were her time to unplug from the world of work and connect to the power of the universe. Besides, if she were going to think of anybody, it would be—

Nobody. She didn't need anybody.

She needed the night when she could see light in the darkness.

Saturday nights particularly electrified her. Whether above the tree line atop a peak or alongside a river flowing through a valley meadow, she lay on her back with her arms beneath her head, staring into the darkness above.

First, the placid moon twirled and danced, a glimmering ballroom of shadows gliding across its white-faced plains. Across the sky, stars and planets twinkled, vanished, re-sparked, and multiplied in the ever-opening depths of space, spinning and bounding through the universe. Aquarius the Water Bearer, Lyra the Harp, Sagittarius the Archer, Cygnus the Swan, and, most importantly, the Great Bear—constellations in the shapes of animals and gods—cavorted across the darkness. Without fail, the spectacle overwhelmed her.

In speechless awe, Jeannie closed her eyes and breathed in the energy of the universe. Her senses intensified and transformed her every pore, every follicle, every breath into eyes, ears, nose, and tongue. Imagination overcame reality. Strength overcame weakness. Dreams overcame terror.

Beetle.

Beneath her, she felt the earth rotate and bear her toward the peace, truth, and reality essential to the universe. In silence, she heard the voice of the spirit bear encourage and direct her.

Beetle.

The hard images of her Shimmerings, her parents' murder, and the underworld of the Earth Man melted and floated into nothing.

When she awoke on Sunday mornings refreshed and energized by holy communion with the cosmos, she rose and hiked back toward the lodge. At the end of the day, she always found herself on Aster Point across the lake from the main building. While the sun settled behind the mountains, she made camp on the shore and reviewed the lessons of the weekend.

All except the unexplainable one.

Why she kept thinking of Beetle and Bryce Welch.

Calmed by the rippling water and the breeze, she looked to the sky for diversion. She smiled at the Great Bear. As her father taught her, she found the Pointer Stars, and followed them to the constancy of Polaris, the North Star, the solid direction of the Word.

Wrapped in her sleeping bag next to Beaver Flat Lake, Jeannie woke to wisps of frost tickling her nose. To escape the cold, she snuggled deeper into the nylon and rubbed away the tingle.

"It's July. I should be sweating," she complained. "And why is it still dark?"

She checked her watch in the moonlight.

4:30.

"That's why," she groaned, plunging her head deeper into the bag's inner coziness.

"If I can just get an hour more of sleep—It has to get warmer."

The outside world would not let sleep happen. While the mosquito of consciousness whined in her ear, every minuscule rock needled and dug into her ribs. Every bird screeched like a siren. She thrashed. She groaned. Finally, she yanked off the bag and glowered over the water.

"What?" she yelled.

The morning peace answered. The brightening sky lifted its face above the mist lying over the lake. Through the fog, icy feathers skated lazily across the calm water, waving and smiling. On the shore, frost melted into beads of pearl hanging from the blades of grass.

Jeannie sighed and nodded. "Good morning to you, too."

Again, she rubbed her wrinkled nose, then leaned back on her hands. Arching her body toward the sky, she inhaled life. With each breath, oxygen sped through her veins and muscles, invigorating her senses.

Atop the crag at the end of Aster Point, she munched a quick breakfast of trail mix and a couple swigs of water, while above her the clouds and birds chased each other across the sky. Across the water, moose waded in the reflection of the snow patterns on the mountaintops.

"Definitely worth waking up for," she thought. She sat, leaned over her legs, and focused her energy. Defying her morning aches, she held her extension until her back muscles released, allowing her to lay her chest flat on her knees.

While she ignored the walkie-talkie at her side, she could not ignore her obligation of calling in. Her shoulders shuddered. Welch was probably sitting back in his chair waiting for her call while he scratched his crotch. Raising the handset to her ear, she forced herself to press the call button.

"Bryce, you there?"

"Yeah, beautiful. Go ahead."

Jeannie winced at the memory of him lying naked on her bed. She gagged and forced her words. "I'm about three miles out. It will be at least an hour and a half before I get back to base."

"Okay. No worries. Nobody's gonna show up until noon, anyway. Then they got all that first-day bullshit to do—get their stuff, eat, get the briefing. Hey, none of the staff is here yet. You wanna—?"

He didn't have to finish his question. Jeannie knew what he wanted. Her face twitched as her vision of him sharpened. His pointy, black beard. The symbolic tattoo on his neck. His rising penis.

"I don't know," she said. "How are your balls doing?"

Jeannie felt the silence deflate his cock. She smiled as she pressed the talk button. "Bryce, are you there?"

"Get back when you can," the radio crackled.

Jeannie laughed and stuffed the walkie-talkie into her backpack. Before rising, she closed her eyes, listening for one last message from the world. The clear, glacial-green water invited her to bathe away Welch's grime before returning to the lodge.

"Right," she said. "The tendersheep don't need a grungy, old hag leading them through the woods."

At the forest edge, she undressed, neatly folded her clothes, and stacked them under a tree with her pack before returning to the lake. After first scanning the shore for prying eyes, she dipped her toes into the water.

"Gah!" she yelped.

Chills erupted over her arms and legs. However, she knew the deeper she walked, the sooner her skin would adjust to the temperature. Rubbing her skin, she pressed on, one step at a time, through the biting air as the soothing water engulfed her legs and climbed above her knees, her thighs, her waist. Pulling back her hair, she relaxed, lowered herself into the warmth, and then leaned forward to swim to the end of the point.

At the base of the crag, she dove straight into the depths, pulling and kicking herself to the bottom. There, she righted herself, bent her knees, and drove her body like an arrow to the surface. When her head broke the stillness of the lake, she gulped the crisp, pure air and sprayed all frustration from her drenched, sweeping hair.

Above her, pinks and purples streaked the morning sky. Jeannie smiled and flipped onto her back while above her, a bird circled the lake like a blessing. "Thank you," she whispered, emptying herself of all noise and distraction. Her hands touched the crag.

Startled back to responsibility, she thought, *"Morning can't last forever. Better get back."*

On an outcropping, she wiped away two days of wilderness from her face, arms, legs, and body, then scrambled up the rock. In the distance stood the clear bulk of the main lodge with the line of duplexes disappearing into the woods behind it. Standing naked and proud, she stretched her arms and shouted at the windows, "Can you see me, Bryce? Huh? Can you see me? I DON'T CARE! You can't have any of it!"

With the encroaching world of work and worry erased, Jeannie sat and hugged her knees to her chin. As she floated on a wave of serenity, an airy caress—the breeze from the far-off wings of the blessing bird—grazed her cheek. She lay on her back, shielding her eyes from the brightening sky with her forearm.

Until the slap! The splash!

Jeannie flipped to her stomach, her hands flat on the rock, her eyes jerking across the lake's surface. Ever-widening circles rippled the tranquility.

Tense seconds passed into minutes as the surface smoothed under a fluttering mass of morning flies.

"Ah! Breakfast on the lake," she said, relaxing and pulling her legs under her. "Fish, one. Flies, nothing."

The calm crashed. A lake trout sprang high into the air—writhing, gasping, snapping at the swirling flies—then splashed back to the water below.

Jeannie's heart froze. Before she could breathe, another trout leapt. And another. And another.

Soon the water boiled and churned with swarming, flopping fish. Jeannie dropped flat to the rock, her fingers grasping at the stone.

"Some—Something is wrong! Very wrong!"

Her frantic body wriggled toward the shore, but a violent crack and the trembling crag slammed her into a ball, her head ducked under her arms. As she peeked across the heaving lake, a billowing cloud of rock and snow erased the side of Stovetop Ridge.

Jeannie gasped. *"A landslide? How—?"*

Again, the earth lurched beneath her. The water blackened, whitecaps surging and breaking across the surface.

"Earthquake!"

On shore, stampeding bears, mule deer, squirrels, moose, and coyotes crashed, climbed, and clawed through the forest up the mountain.

Again, an explosion shook the earth.

Words jumbled and jangled in Jeannie's brain. *"Quake—No! Thun—What—?"*

Above her, the air vibrated with geese and jays and eagles. The lake boiled with panic-stricken fish leaping and splashing toward the shore. Beneath her, the rock shifted and shuddered, eluding her futile grasp.

Nothing had prepared her for this—not her physical training, her education, her experience. Even though they always protected her from storms, vicious animals, and even Bryce Welch, she had never faced a crumbling world.

The last remnants of the stampede disappeared up the mountain. "I remember!" Jeannie exclaimed. "Follow the animals. I know that!"

She struggled to her feet, but a gasp and groan from the mayhem of the lake froze her steps. After a moment's hesitation, she rejected her instincts and rushed to the rock's edge. From the tumbling waves rose a head of long, black hair.

"Wha—? Who—?"

Transfixed, Jeannie gaped as a man—tall and bronzed—reached for footing on the rock.

At his touch, the crag settled. Jeannie's legs wobbled while he inched up the rock, the water and fish calming behind him. At the top, he staggered as if unsure where he was, who he was, or why he was.

As he wiped the water from his face and hair, Jeannie waited for his eyes to meet hers. Their mutual nakedness neither intimidated nor excited her, so when his quizzical face recognized her presence, she straightened and invited his scrutiny.

He tilted his head and examined her face.

"*I won't run away,*" she thought.

The stranger swallowed, then one halting step after another, moved toward her. The closer he came, the more the chaos around them dissolved. The fish settled into calm waters. The birds flitted into the trees. The land animals peeped from the rocks and trees.

Soon, the man and woman stood face to face in the morning sun, studying each other. With an awkward hand, the man reached toward Jeannie's face, but stopped. "*It's all right. You can touch me. I won't break,*" she thought.

He bit his lower lip and cleared his throat. His dark eyes spoke to Jeannie without words. The unintelligible message confused her. Something about mountains, oceans.

She squinted. "*He's not from here, but—*"

"I know you," she said aloud.

The man nodded and wiped his dripping hair.

"From where?"

"Long ago."

His lips had not moved. He made no audible sound, yet she heard him clearly.

"How—? Did you just tell me 'long ago'?"

The man nodded.

Jeannie shook the haze from her brain. "Of course, you did."

The man smiled.

"*This should prove interesting,*" she told herself.

"Come," he answered, walking toward the woods.

Still cautious of a shaking earth, Jeannie followed him to where she had left her clothes and pack.

Little remained of the pile she had left so neat and organized, just shreds of her clothing and sleeping bag. However, her walkie-talkie lay undamaged on the moss at the bottom of a tree.

"What? I had—? Where did all my clothes, my pack go?"

A circle of animals emerged from the trees surrounding them.

"You no longer need them."

Jeannie recognized the voice. The spirit bear.

She smiled as the reassuring presence stepped from the circle.

"You're not just a dream," she said. "You're more than a voice from the Shimmerings or the Big Dipper."

"I have always been real," the bear said. "We've just been in other places."

"Or bodies," Jeannie said, remembering the old woman in Mrs. McNally's guest room.

The spirit bear nodded. A cool breeze blew over Jeannie's naked body.

"What did you do with my clothes?"

"I did nothing. The panic destroyed them. They are sorry."

"They?"

"The animals."

Jeannie scanned the circle and felt each creature's guilt. As a congregation, they lowered their heads, repentant of destroying what they hadn't known was there.

When Jeannie nodded her forgiveness, the animals rose.

"What do we do now?" she asked.

The man picked up her walkie-talkie, raised his head and sniffed the air. High above the mountain, a bird circled. Nodding, the stranger squatted, peering through the brush above them. Encouraged, he smiled and stood. "Come," he said aloud.

Instead of answering the man, Jeannie spoke to the spirit bear. "I can't go anywhere dressed—or undressed like this. How would I explain you? Or this man? Bryce will—"

The bear stopped her. "Not to the lodge. Come with us."

"Where—?"

"Your mother is near."

"Mother? What—?"

Jeannie remembered the Shimmerings. Mount Elder. The murder. Matchi-auwishuk. The Earth Man.

Of course, her mother was nearby. That's why Jeannie took this job. The demands of work and that bastard Bryce Welch had distracted her from her goals.

The animals gathered around the bear and the naked man and faced her. The circling bird fluttered and landed in front of them all.

"And you're all here to help me?" she asked.

243

"We all share the same mission," Counselor said. "To cleanse and preserve the world of dreams."

"All?"

"Even the most unlikely," the bear told her.

The animals nodded their agreement. Innocence and confidence beamed from the man's face. The bird flapped its wings, circled twice and flew high overhead.

Jeannie understood.

"All right. Lead on," she said, taking one last look across the lake to the lodge before the man, bear, and animals guided her up the mountain.

38

Glitter

Beaver Flat Lake
British Columbia, Canada

Back in his office, Welch propped his feet on his desk. Glancing at the clock over the fireplace, he smiled and bounced his rubber ball at his side.

"Hour and a half," he thought. "Harley and Kai should be calling in soon."

Outside his window, the serene lake reflected the forest and sky. The sun parted the clouds, revealing patches of blue and the mountain tops. Dust from the morning explosions settled in the distance. A flock of birds circled above the mountains. "Probably buzzards looking for bodies."

Welch's base radio crackled.

"Hey, Boss. Kai here."

Welch dropped his feet and picked up the microphone behind him. "Go ahead, Kai."

"All done on this end."

"Sounds like you guys did a good job." Welch grinned and stroked his goatee. Veiling his elation with concern, he reached into his bottom desk drawer for a quick shot of whiskey. "You okay?"

"Hell, yeah. No sweat. I've had more trouble farting in church."

"Great. Hey! About supper tonight. Gonna be taters in the kettle?" *Gold nuggets for harvesting.*

"Hell of a mess up there, but there's a lot just laying on the ground, I'm telling you. Seen them myself. They may be pre-mashed, but you don't mind, do you?"

"Hell no. Long as we all get some, I'm fine. I'm kind of hungry. *Greedy.* You?"

"Famished."

"And Harley?"

"He's always hungry."

"No. I mean how'd things go for him?"

"Same thing for him. Says the spuds is just laying there like pussy in a whore house waiting for the taking. On my way to meet him now."

"Okay. Come on in. I'll pay you and get you some wings." *A helicopter out of here.*

"Roger. Taters and wings. Love it. Out."

"Roger. Out." Welch set the microphone back next to the base unit on the ledge behind him.

"The moron belongs in a movie," he muttered, bouncing his ball against the floor and waiting for the next call.

He explored the room for something to do in the meantime. Finally, he opened the side drawer of his desk, reached deep inside, and pulled out a dirty rock. Lying in the hollow of his palm, its dense weight calmed his disposition. His face radiated a peculiar reverence.

"Spud," he said. His smirk broadened as he turned the rock over in his hands and examined each hollow and bulge.

To strip off the stone's grime, he sipped water from a bottle, drooled onto the heaviest end, and massaged the rock with probing fingers and kneading palms. When the thin coat of mud dried, he polished the stone with his shirt until every ridge and crevice gleamed. Then he held it up to catch the dusty light drifting through his window.

Welch kissed the smoothness of the rock. He touched the surface with his tongue, letting the metallic taste linger and seep into his mouth. Then he snapped his lips shut and pressed them together to prevent the flavor from escaping. Bringing the rock to his nose, he breathed deeply, letting his mind drown in the flooding odor only lovers detect.

Reaching inside his shirt, he withdrew the golden cross suspended from a thin chain around his neck. Like the rock, he kissed the medal. Reverent of the memories it evoked, he pulled the necklace over his head and laid it next to the rock. Then again propping his feet on his desk, he closed his eyes, recalling hidden rooms and dark cars.

Schools. Houses. Churches.

Girls. Women.

Nancy Kirkman. Maggie MacArthur. Skye Jeffers. Jeannie Jones.

He touched his Adonis tattoo, reached between his legs and gasped at his own touch.

"*Jones*," he thought. "*If she ever—I could—*"

The golden glow from his desk enveloped him as his cheeks and shoulders tensed. His erratic breathing stopped and his whole body stiffened. His arched body shook once—twice—then fell back into the seat. His head fell to the side. Absently, he nodded, spent and satisfied.

As the radio console on the shelf smugly mocked him, Welch twisted his mouth and shifted in his chair.

Only a month ago, Noah Aldridge, Beaver Flat's chief ranger and incompetent numbnuts since the Ice Age, had declared a park-wide emergency because some North Dakota idiots dumped their RV garbage into an outdoor latrine. In call after call to the provincial capital, he demanded Victoria establish roadblocks at every exit and road between Beaver Flat and the Alberta border.

"You'd think he'd be a little quicker calling when half of two mountains disappear."

Welch grabbed a pencil from the plastic Canucks Hockey souvenir cup on his desk. Minutes ticked by on the fireplace clock. He drummed the eraser on the desk blotter.

Taking a tissue, he wiped at the dampness of his pants.

"Come on, you old bastard."

Still no call.

The minute hand on the fireplace clock clicked one…slow…minute after another. Welch jammed his pencil back into the cup, bounced his ball at his side, and waited.

"Damn it! Come on!"

He spun his chair to the wall and varied the bounce pattern, tossing the ball at the floor so it caromed off the wall back to his hand. He practiced the move so he barely glanced at the ball as it returned. The fireplace clock chimed 8:00. Welch checked his own watch in frustration, then stood at the widow and dribbled the ball.

"*Jones is out there somewhere,*" he thought.

He squinted and watched for movement on Gospel Trail that surrounded the lake.

"*She said she was coming in. She can't be that far away.*"

He saw nothing. He felt guilt and fear for the first time since he escaped Mount Hebron.

"*She's a tough little bitch. She'll be fine.*" Besides, what could he do?

"*She's not a bitch. She*—" He could call her and tell her to hurry back.

The rubber ball banged off the floor and slapped back into his hand.

"Don't be stupid, Welch!" he ordered himself, pounding the ball against his head. "Remember the timeline!"

Of course, he couldn't call Jones. Before he could tell her about the crisis, Noah had to inform him there was a crisis.

The radio crackled on the shelf. "Beaver Flat Lodge, Park Warden here."

"Here we go." Welch smirked. "This is almost too easy."

Welch crossed to the bathroom and tossed the tissue into the toilet. He grabbed the microphone and held it for a moment.

A second more and he depressed the call button. "Yeah, go ahead, Noah."

"I'm afraid you got a problem, Bryce, my boy."

"Problem?" Welch asked, his voice seeking a trace of innocence.

"Ee-yuh. You feel that big rumble out there a couple hours ago?"

"Yeah, didn't think much of it. We get them little tremors from rock slides all the time. This something different?" He turned his chair to the radio and sat.

"No rock slide this time. Two of the mountains completely fell apart. Total landslide."

"Rock slide. Landslide. What's the difference? Like I said, we hear them all the time."

"Well, you're right. Usually there's just a chunk off a cliff out in the wilderness somewhere. This time there were two. Almost like a bomb hit 'em. Stovetop Ridge on the east side of the park—well, that's the worst. It's just a pile of rubble. Mahlen Peak on the west side isn't much better."

"Wow!" Welch said, opening his pants and dabbing at his shorts.

"Yeah," Noah replied. "Anyhow, before everything all settled down, rocks and mud and trees blocked off the road to the lodge."

Welch laughed. "Come on, Noah. Minor inconvenience at the most. There's always the back way."

"No, there's not. That's the problem, eh? The Stovetop collapse took out the main road from the east and Mahlen took out the back road to the west."

Welch snapped the rubber band on his wrist to add a touch of pain to his voice. "You mean—?" he said, awkwardly raising the inflection to sound concerned.

"There's nobody coming in or out of there for awhile. At least by road. You're trapped there, Bryce."

"Trapped? Shit! Let me sit down a minute," he said, rambling to the window to view the remains of Stovetop Ridge.

He then returned to the desk, picked up the rock and kissed it again before injecting worry into his words. "Oh my god, Noah! The tours! The buses were supposed to be here today. You don't think—"

"Don't worry. Already checked on them. Got delayed over in Banff. Never even got close. Already on their way back to Calgary, eh?"

"Good. Good," Welch said, taking his jacket from its hook, zipping it, and pulling the hem as low over his hips as possible. He paused as if to contemplate the severity of Noah's assessment of the road situation.

"Shit! Listen, Noah. I have to call you back. I got some people out there in the woods I gotta get ahold of, make sure they're okay. You know? Then if I can get them back here, can you send a chopper to get us out?"

"How many you got?"

"Couple of grounds keepers and a tour guide."

"Cook? Waiters?"

"Nah. They weren't scheduled until one, two o'clock. They should all be fine."

"So grounds keepers, guide…and you," Noah said. "Four?"

Welch rolled his eyes.

"That's right."

"Should work. Give me a chance to make some arrangements. Where are they?"

"The two guys left early this morning. Weren't going too far. Talked to the guide earlier. Said she was out on the other side of the lake and was coming back. She should be here any second now."

"She? You mean Jeannie Jones?"

"You know Jones?"

"Bryce, everybody knows Jeannie Jones. That ginger could lift a Buick with one hand. You don't have to worry about her. Besides, she knows her way around. She's seen more of this park than you and me put together. And I've been here forty years!"

Welch recalled Jeannie's head breaking through his door, the punch to his groin, her slamming him into the wall. Noah was right. He didn't have to worry about her.

But he did.

More than he wanted. More than he should. He had gold to collect.

"Yeah," Welch said. "You're right. You're right. She'll be fine." He breathed on the rock and further polished it with the end of his sleeve.

"Okay," Noah said. "Make it as quick as you can. We need to have the choppers as long as we can to check out the damage."

"Will do."

The high-pitched whine of Harley and Kai's four-wheelers and the rattle of spraying gravel in the parking lot interrupted him.

"Oh. Here come the guys. Back in a bit."

He hid the rock and necklace in the open desk drawer, then switched the radio to Jeannie's channel.

"Jones, this is Welch. Come in."

No answer

"Jones, this is Welch. You there?"

He watched the inscrutable face of the base radio and listened for an answer. The dials stared silently back at him.

"What the—? Come on!" He cranked the volume knob.

Harley and Kai burst through the door.

"All set, boss," Harley bellowed. "Want to go check out what we done?"

The necklace and rock in his desk glowed at him from the drawer.

He blinked. "Uh—Yeah," he stammered, standing and pulling the jacket low over his hips. He glanced at the silent radio. "Yeah, show me what you got."

He quickly locked his desk, pulled on his lodge cap, and ushered the two out the door.

Behind them, the radio remained silent.

39

The Dawn of Life

Mount Elder
British Columbia, Canada

After hours of zig-zagging through the woods, Jeannie marveled how she had climbed two-thirds of the mountain naked with little physical discomfort. The ground at this altitude usually consisted of sharp, fang-like rocks and dead, clutching branches. Here, the higher she walked, the more the earth softened to a spongy, softly-massaging carpet under her bare feet. A benevolent and sensitive air warmed and cooled itself to meet her body's needs.

Jeannie timidly glanced at the man also climbing easily beside her. She knew him somehow from "long ago," he said, but what she remembered wasn't something from a distant past. It was something about him here. Not the hair or the eyes or his muscular body. It was how he talked to her, how he spoke without words.

His eyes caught hers. "Hi," his smile said.

Blushing, Jeannie stopped short and looked back at where they had climbed. Narrowing her eyes, she crossed her arms tightly across her chest and tucked her chin against her throat. The man drew to her side and sighed loudly to halt the animals. When Counselor turned, the man tilted his head toward the woman. The bear realized her restraint, then waddled back down the trail to her. "Yes?"

Embarrassed, she pushed her hair back. "Okay. Where are we going? And why?"

The spirit bear nodded up the mountain. "When we reach the lone fir up there, you will see where. When we arrive, you will know why."

She sensed the bear knew all about the man and the answer to her million more questions: "Who is he?" "Why is he here?" "What aren't you telling me?" Examining the bear's eyes, though, she saw no dissemblance; she detected only sincerity and truth. "Okay," she said, accepting his guidance and letting him lead up the mountain.

Minutes later, the entourage broke from the woods at the fir tree, but instead of the stark rockiness they had expected to find above the tree line, they found a lush grassland divided by a lazy creek drifting through it.

Jeannie stepped forward and asked the sky, "What is this? We're too high—"

The bear stood beside her, his stolid face waiting. Finally, the weight of his patience turned her face toward him.

"This is not what you know," his massive, silent figure said. His ursine eyes reassured her. "Come," he said, leading Jeannie, the man, and the animals toward the stream.

"Wait," Jeannie said. "That mountain across the meadow. Is that—?"

"Mount Komu. *The Entry.*"

"That's what I thought. What does that mean? Entry to what?"

The bear and man exchanged looks. The bear gently came to Jeannie's side. "When you are ready. We must first follow the water to its source."

She squinted at the glittering ripples and traced the water flow through the meadow to a dense grove of trees.

"In that grove? It looks different. Almost—I don't know—almost— weightless. What is it?"

"The Latin name is 'Vitae Primordia'—The Dawn of Life. It is also called the Foundation of Heaven."

Jeannie looked back down the path they had climbed and across the meadow to Mount Komu. She took a deep breath, exhaled, and examined the path at her feet. A white bird flew over the group and disappeared into the trees. The bear gently nudged her elbow with his nose.

"Please. Sit beside the water."

As Jeannie hung her feet in the stream and the bear lay next to her on the bank, the stranger sat further off. Minutes passed without words.

Jeannie leaned forward to scrutinize the bear's eyes. "What is it you want to tell me?"

The bear's thoughts spoke clearly.

"In the world of dreams, you are a unique person, Jeannie Jones. Special. Chosen. Led. Your past led you to Canada. Your present has led you here to the Dawn of Life."

"And my future?"

"Your future will lead you to Mount Komu. There you will join the latest trinity."

"The trinity my father spoke of?"

"The trinity chosen by the Word, yes, but not for the same purpose."

"Who are the other two?"

"At Mount Komu, you will find who you seek. And who seeks you."

Jeannie sat back, staring into the rich blue sky. "Will I find my mother?"

The bear rested his chin on the ground. "When it's time. From here, you will find who you need when you need. Even those you don't want."

"Bryce Welch?"

The bear did not move.

"You won't tell me?"

"Neither your past nor your future is negotiable. Live in the now."

Jeannie looked across the bear to the stranger exploring a blade of grass. "This man? Who is he? He says I know him, but I don't remember."

"Who do you want him to be?"

She called to the stranger. "Do you have a name?"

Intent on his blade of grass, the man answered, "Not the one I need."

"Give him one," the bear said.

"Really?"

The stranger laid his blade of grass at his side.

"I can help," Jeannie assured the man.

The man paused for permission from the bear. Counselor nodded.

"Come. Kneel in front of me," she urged.

Again, the bear approved. The man crossed to Jeannie and knelt. Carefully, Jeannie studied the man's face. "Do you trust me?" she asked.

The man checked the bear's expression, then nodded.

"*Do I trust myself?*" she thought.

She reached out and touched his smooth face. "*If Bryce Welch were more like this man*—"

Her elbow tightened and trembled as she pushed back the man's long hair and ran her thumb across his eyebrows. As her mind detached from her hand, she watched her fingers move behind his ears down his jawline to his chin.

He smiled when she closed his mouth.

Jeannie swallowed, then licked her lower lip "I think you look like—Ethan."

"Ethan. Hebrew for 'solid, enduring'," the bear said.

Again, she traced the man's jawline. "*Definitely not Bryce. Maybe*—"

She blinked and removed her hand. "Yes. Yes. Ethan."

"Ethan," the man said. He nodded.

She dipped her head. "I'm Jean."

"Or Jeannie. I know," he said silently.

"How do you do that? Talk without words?"

The bear walked to the entrance and said, "Inside the glade, all your questions will be answered. The only way to understand is to enter and see."

"Enter? I thought Mount Komu—"

"Was the Entry. It is. First, you must learn what is valuable and what is unnecessary. The glade is the teacher. When you know the lessons of the Source, you will cross the meadow."

"How long will that take?"

"Time is irrelevant. Now is forever."

"*Forever*," Jeannie thought, remembering the blackness of space and her dead mother.

The animals waiting at the entrance all rose in anticipation as she looked upstream into the glade. Silently, they urged her to lead them into the unknown forest. She took a deep breath and exhaled.

Confused, yet confident, she reached out her hand to Ethan. "Okay. Let's go."

Ethan hesitated.

"Take her hand," the bear urged. "Enter together."

Examining Ethan's questioning eyes, Jeannie thought of somebody—something. She did know him, as—

The man reached for her, and together they followed the spirit bear, leading the animals toward the glade.

At the entrance, Ethan set Jeannie's radio on a rock outside.

"Won't we need that?" she asked.

"It won't work inside," the bear said.

Jeannie paused and looked across the meadow at Mount Komu. An angry, gray cloud descended over it.

She looked down at the hand in hers. "Okay," she said. "Let's go."

The air shivered as the humans and animals disappeared into darkness.

40

The Gate Hidden in Dreams

Mount Komu ("The Entry")
British Columbia, Canada

The whop-whop-whop inside the chopper hardened Welch's jaw. Jones said she was near the top of Mount Komu, waiting by a stream on the edge of a meadow. How could that be? Nothing grew on Mount Komu save the occasional wildflower.

"Are you sure she said *north* of Beaver Flat Lake?" Charley the pilot yelled over the engines.

"Yes! By Mount Komu! Keep flying. It's gotta be soon."

Welch jerked at his goatee and searched the mountainside below. Since the explosions, the park investigators had overrun the park and his office. They kept asking questions. Too many questions.

"You sure you heard right?" Charley yelled through the rotor noise. "Let's go back and check the park map."

"*I can't go back*," Welch thought. "*They're waiting for me.*"

At the lodge, whenever Welch's eyes twitched at a new provincial chopper landing in the parking lot to bring new investigators, Harley and

Kai pulled him into the men's room, extorting a larger share of the groceries.

"Fuckers been watching too many tv shows. No way they're that smart."

Whether they were or not, he had no choice but to give in. They knew too much. At the least, destruction of the mountains meant prison.

He bit his fist. Thank God Jones had called. If she hadn't, that could have meant a charge of murder. Now, he just had to find her.

"Just a few more—Holy shit!" he shouted at Charley. He leaned forward in his seat and pointed straight ahead.

Charley craned his head. "What?"

"Up there! Between those two mountaintops."

"It's just—"

"It's a meadow, like she said. Fly up there."

"That's ridic—"

"Shut up and fly this thing."

Charley's unspoken obscenities rebounded off the glass cabin as the chopper flew through the pass. On the other side, his eyes widened.

He sat forward himself and shouted over the rotor. "I've never seen anything like that. A meadow this high?"

"Me neither. Now there's supposed to be a stream," Welch shouted.

"There! Down the middle. And a woods farther upstream. Up there."

Suddenly, Charley punched Welch's arm. "I see her!"

"Where? I don't—"

"Right up there. Whoa! She must be really anxious to see you. She's got no clothes!"

"What?!" Welch leaned forward. Jeannie's dark red hair and light skin stood out against the green of the meadow. He sat back and scratched his head.

"What do you want me to do?" Charley asked.

"Set it down and let me out. I'll see what's going on."

"You want me to fly around front and make sure it's her?"

"It's her! Who else would it be? Just land this fucker."

Welch left Charley with the helicopter and approached the naked woman, careful of spooking her. "Jones, is that you?"

She kept her back to him as she examined the rock next to her. "It's me," she answered.

"I'm glad you're alive. I was worried."

She twisted her head. "Worried?"

"Yeah, when I didn't hear from… Yeah, worried."

Jeannie began to turn back, but caught herself. She glanced at him once more and said, "Thank you. I'm alive."

"What are you doing here?"

"Waiting for you. I need you to do me a favor. Tell your pilot to go back to the lodge and get me some clothes."

"I can get you a blanket and you can—"

"No. You and I need to stay here."

"Me? What for?"

"I'll explain later. Oh, and tell him to bring back a set of clothes for you, too."

"Clothes for you and me? You sure?"

"Yes. It's important. You'll see."

"Okay." Welch shook his head.

Back at the chopper, after Welch convinced Charley it was best not to argue with a naked redhead, the pilot dutifully took off, hovering a moment over the unperturbed Jeannie. When she smiled and waved, exposing her naked breasts, the whole helicopter fluttered, steadied, then flew off toward Beaver Flat Lodge.

Once the thudding chopper blades disappeared, the breeze whispered through the grass. Welch swallowed, then walked up behind Jeannie. She did not move.

Watching her smooth shoulders rise and lower with each slow breath, he rubbed the Adonis symbol on his neck. The memory of his gold necklace and the altar cross he had stolen warmed his throat and chest. His fingers flinched forward to touch her, but he quickly hid them in his armpits. He cleared his throat and asked, "Now what?"

Jeannie looked over her shoulder. "Take off your clothes."

Welch flinched and stepped back, stunned. Jeannie held a steady gaze on him. With one hand, he adjusted his pants and with the other he pulled on his neck. "I never—I never thought I'd hear you say that."

"Don't get excited." She nodded at his crotch. "Oops! Too late. Sorry. Anyhow, we're going for a walk. When we get where we're going, you'll understand."

"Of course, it's too late," Welch thought. Her hair framed her silver eyes and lay seductively over her freckled shoulders. Just as he had dreamed countless times in his countless erotic fantasies—those in the woods, in the lodge, in the kitchen.

He closed his eyes and again pulled at his pants.

He remembered her wet, glistening body fresh from the shower. Her touch. Her breath.

His eyes snapped open as he recalled her slamming him against the wall. Her words spat at him in his office: *"I am not quitting this job and I am not fucking you."*

His body shook as his genitals battled against both fear and arousal. His body chilled as Jeannie smiled and raised her eyebrows.

"Well?" she said.

Words failed him. He pulled off his shirt. When he finished undressing, he folded his clothes and laid them on the rock next to Jeannie's walkie talkie. "What now?"

Jeannie giggled at his erection. "You really have a problem with that, don't you? Never mind. Follow me."

Futilely attempting to hide his arousal, Welch awkwardly padded sideways across the grass to where the stream emerged from the woods.

"We're going to walk between these two trees," she told him. "It will be intense at first, almost overwhelming, but nothing bad can happen to you. I promise. Anytime you're scared, just tell me and we'll leave. Okay?"

Welch avoided looking at the freckles between her breasts and gazed at the truth of her eyes. "Nothing scares me," he said.

"Okay," Jeannie answered, smiling. "I'm going in first. No matter what you see, all you have to do is walk between the two trees."

He bit his lip and flexed his fingers. "Yeah. Fine."

Jeannie patted Welch's arm and stepped through the gate. The ground shook and around her the air rippled. In a second, she was gone.

"What the—?"

From the other side, Welch heard, "Walk through the gate. That's all you need to do."

The trickle of the water in the stream repeated the instruction. "Walk through the gate. Walk through the gate."

He closed his eyes, inhaled deeply, held his breath, and stepped forward. He reached out and felt warmth travel from his fingers up his arms and across his whole body.

On the other side, Jeannie took his hand and led him forward. "You're here."

41

Still Water

The Dawn of Life

Welch opened his eyes. A new world drifted and swayed around him.

Below his feet, the forest floor, a velvet purple carpet, rose and fell, massaging his cramped arches. Above, the sun-less heavens blushed red. Long, yellow arms streaked the sky and welcomed him to the glade.

Ahead, the light animated the air with a calm busyness. Plump trees and bushes hovered above the ground, their branches beckoning Welch farther into the garden. Clumps of multi-colored and multi-shaped fruits and berries dangled from them. The clear golden stream emerged from deep in the shadows, its current tranquil and steady.

Jeannie led him forward, but he stopped short, sniffing and searching the air. "What's that smell?" he asked.

"Smell? What do you mean?"

"I don't know. I've never smelled it before."

"Is it like flowers? Food? A kitchen?"

"No, not a thing. More of a—I don't know."

"More like a quality?"

"Yeah. Like—"

Jeannie smiled. Her eyes sparkled in the dim light. "Peace? Happiness? Calm?"

Welch knew that didn't make sense. He searched for something familiar, but the only thing familiar was Jeannie. "Something like that. Yeah."

"It's probably all of those. Plus joy, wisdom, love. And so much more."

Welch gripped tightly to Jeannie's hand. "What is this place?"

"It's called the Dawn of Life. It's a place of learning."

"Learning what?"

Jeannie's mouth tightened as she squeezed his hand. "Come. We need to walk."

Her touch sucked the breath from his lungs. Catching himself, Welch searched her face for clarification. Her brilliant eyes shivered his stomach as her freckled skin shimmered and faded.

He gasped and refused to move. "Not until you tell me why."

Jeannie crossed her arms and looked at the ground. She took a deep breath. "Because you're safe here."

"Safe from what?"

Her words measured and purposeful, she raised her eyes to his. "You know there's nowhere to hide out there, right? They know."

Welch blanched. "Who—?"

"Noah. The Mounties. Everybody you don't want to knows about the bombs and gold."

"What are you—?"

Jeannie held up a hand. She wrinkled her nose and nodded. "Please follow me. You'll see."

His stomach trembled again. "Okay," he muttered.

Side by side the two walked silently upstream. The trees and bushes pulled aside, and orange-furred squirrels skittered ahead of them. As they walked, Welch searched the sky, pivoting and reaching out his arms.

"It's all right to wonder," Jeannie assured him, "but know that right now, you're just seeing the obvious—the colors, the trees, and the light. There is so much more to learn."

"Like what?"

Covering his eyes with her hand, she said, "Listen carefully."

In the blind silence, Welch felt the warmth of her breath on his chest.

"Do you hear it?"

Taking her free hand for security, he asked, "Hear what?"

"The music."

"Music? I don't hear—"

"Shhh. Close your eyes and lie on the ground."

When she released his face, Welch followed her to the earth, lying on his belly and allowing Jeannie to turn his ear to the ground. He felt her silky weight against his back and legs. As her gentle hand stroked his shoulders, his muscles and thoughts relaxed. Rather than exciting, her touch soothed.

"Hear that?" Jeannie asked.

He could hear no sound, but—

With her lips close to his ear, she whispered, "It's not really a sound. It's more like—"

"A thrum. I hear it," Welch answered. He reached his hands forward and gently rubbed the ground near his face.

Jeannie's fingers stroked his hair. "It's different for everybody," she said.

Welch lay flat and spread his arms and legs. "It comes from inside me."

He breathed slowly and allowed the music to fill him.

"Welcome to the new reality. Here you'll see more, hear more, know more than you ever imagined."

"More than floating trees and silent music?"

Jeannie laughed and sat up. "They're just the beginning."

"What else?"

"Well, for example, malleable time."

Welch turned to his side. "Malleable time?"

Jeannie hugged her knees to her chest. "Time that's different for everybody and everywhere. A time where the past and the future are all now. For example, a few hours ago, I called you at Beaver Flat to come get me. Right?"

"Yeah?"

"Well, while you were out there calling your pilot and getting the helicopter, I lived a lifetime here."

Welch twisted his face. "You've aged well."

Jeannie shrugged. "Our bodies mean nothing. There is no young or old here. We all just are."

"You are so full of—"

He broke off. He gazed at her hands, then examined his own. Light shone through her palms. "*Something's wrong with her skin,*" he thought.

"Other people have lived longer and more often than I," she said.

Welch straightened. "These other people. Are they here now?"

Avoiding his eyes, Jeannie nodded.

Welch scowled and flexed his fingers. Her hair covered the bare shoulders he had so longed to see. "Okay," he said. "Let's get to the important stuff. What's the deal with being naked?"

Jeannie laughed. "Ah. The real Bryce Welch. It's not to frustrate you. I promise. It's just that nothing made by machines—clothes, jewelry, tools—can exist here. The place provides all a person needs."

"The other people are naked, too?"

"One is, but—" Jeannie giggled. "Not—No, I guess you could call that person naked too."

"You mean fucking's okay here? Great! So I have a chance. Let's start."

"Bryce, I told you before. Sex doesn't matter."

Nancy Kirkman. Winthrop High School girls. Skye Jeffers. Welch shook away the memories. "Oh, believe me. It matters," he said.

Jeannie changed the subject and pointed ahead of them. "Just beyond that tree on the hill—the one actually rooted to the ground—is the source of this stream. It's what I need to show you. Come."

Atop the hill, a makeshift bench provided an uncluttered view of both a pond and the darkening forest beyond. Jeannie called over the water. "Ethan? Are you here?"

Welch scowled and sank to the bench. "Ethan. A guy. Shit."

"Just watch the water."

Leaning forward on his knees, Welch studied Jeannie's ethereal face, shoulders, body. "*She's wrong. Sex matters.*"

He turned to the glassy stillness of the pond and waited. Two minutes. Three minutes. Nothing changed.

Suddenly, two hands broke the stillness of the water and a bronzed man rose from the depths, wading toward the shore. In his face, light shone in him and through him.

Bewildered, Welch sat straight and looked at Jeannie. In her face, he saw the same illumination. He glanced down at his opaque hands, then snapped up his head. "You're translucent! You're both translucent."

Still dripping with water, the calm man stood before the bench and reached out his hand. "Bryce?"

Welch gulped as he watched his own hand extend to the stranger.

"I'm Ethan," the stranger said. Then turning to Jeannie, he asked, "Right?"

"You're not sure what your name is?" Welch asked.

Jeannie explained, "In the world we just came from, humans arrive as infants and their parents designate their names. Ethan came here as an adult and got to approve his. I suggested Ethan. He liked it, but he's still not used to it."

Ethan placed a hand on Jeannie's shoulder. "Are you sure he's ready for this place?"

"It will be fine. You'll see."

Neither had spoken a word.

"H—How the—?" Welch stammered. "What's going on?"

Lowering Ethan's hand, Jeannie said, "It may be too soon for telepathy."

Ethan nodded.

Welch fumed as their touch lingered on each other.

Turning to Welch, Jeannie explained, "It's another difference. I know this is all coming quickly, but you'll get used to it."

A sharp jolt thrust Welch flailing through the air. With a thud, he landed, sprawling on the soft grass yards away. Desperately, he clawed his way to his feet. He crouched with raised fists ready to charge his attacker.

Until he saw the spirit bear looking at him.

"Bryce, this is the friend who brought Ethan and me here," Jeannie explained.

"He's a fucking bear!"

"Thank you for noticing," the animal said.

"You can talk?"

"Well, not really, but you can hear."

"We don't use our voices here," Jeannie added. "It's easier in the long run, believe me."

"But he's a bear!"

"In this lifetime," the animal said. "I've been human. I've been spirit. I've been other. Through them all, I've been alive. That is enough."

"Do you have a name like this Ethan prick?"

"I have had many names. They are no longer relevant. Today, I direct the lessons of the Dawn of Life. You may call me Counselor."

"Okay, Counselor. Why am I here?"

"To learn from the Source."

"The pond," Jeannie explained.

"What is with the fucking pond?" Welch yelled.

"Please. Watch," Counselor said.

Welch glanced from the bear to Ethan to Jeannie. Patient and placid, the three waited for his decision.

Welch bit his lip and took a seat. Jeannie and Counselor sat on either side of him, as Ethan stood behind them. Jeannie explained, "The still water of the Source is like a giant screen revealing life as it is, was, and will be, without distraction or distortion. It is open, serene, unwavering."

Welch glanced at Jeannie's gentle hand on his. Her touch calmed his breathing.

When Ethan laid his hands on Jeannie's shoulders, the sky darkened. Below them, the watery display revealed a cave cut into a rocky mountainside. Deep inside the blackness, a beam of light searched the inner walls.

Frozen to the bench, Welch glanced between the water and the hands on Jeannie's shoulders. He wiped his upper lip and crossed his arms in front of him.

The picture followed the beam scanning the cave floor. In a wavering circle of light, a hand reached down to pick up a rock.

Instantly, the point of view shifted outdoors. From the cave, a large man ducked into the sunlight, the shadow from a protective helmet hiding his face.

Welch's breath shortened as the man took off his headgear and held up the rock in his hand. The sun revealed his tiny pointed beard.

"Fuck! What is this?" Welch hissed through clenched teeth. "How does it know—"

The picture went black. Jeannie's grip on Welch's arm silenced him.

When the picture reappeared, the man—Welch himself—sat in his office, cleaning the rock of grime and dirt. A golden shine brightened his hungry eyes and the Adonis tattoo on the side of his neck.

When the picture vanished and reappeared, a silent Welch talked into an unresponsive radio's microphone. Abruptly, two men barged into his office.

On the bench, Jeannie turned to the fuming Welch. To calm him, she said, "It's Harley and Kai. They look different in the water."

"I know who they are. I'm leaving."

"Where will you go?" Ethan asked.

"Out!" The furious Welch started toward the head of the stream.

Jeannie interrupted. "If Charley finds you and not me—"

Welch nearly fell over his own feet. He was caught.

If Charley found Welch at the gate with no clothes and no Jones, he'd assume worst. Anybody would.

"There's more in the Source," Counselor said.

Welch slunk back to the bench.

The new picture revealed a new office where Harley and Kai sat before an older man wearing a park uniform.

"Again with Harley and Kai? What are they—?"

Jeannie explained. "That's Noah Aldridge's office. They're telling him about the gold and the dynamite, how the three of you were going to sift through the rubble and find enough nuggets to make you rich. You really don't know much about gold mining, do you?"

Welch squirmed. "I'm gonna kill those bastards."

"Killing solves nothing," Counselor said. "Stay."

"Are you dreaming?" Welch scoffed.

Counselor nodded pensively. "Dreaming. Yes. Dreams are good. You believe in dreams."

The bear leaned his heavy body against Welch. "Dreams breathed the earth into existence."

Welch snorted. "Dreams are shit. I've had lots of them."

"Many, yes, but only one you would chase across the universe, only one that could erase the painful images."

Welch puffed his cheeks, forcing down memories of uneaten birthday cake, a darkened closet, an empty bed, a gold cross on an altar in flickering light, the river between northern Michigan and Ontario.

"If you mean money—"

"Not money. Not gold. Nothing you can hold in your hand. Escape," Counselor said.

"Escape?"

"You've chased it your whole life."

Welch glowered at Counselor, only to confront the gray eyes of Jeannie Jones. In them, he recognized the spirit bear's truth.

All the girls and women of Winthrop, Michigan—Toni Sharpe, Maggie MacArthur, even Nancy Kirkman and Skye Jeffers—had only been what they said they were: diversions and distractions. All along, Jeannie Jones had been his dream, the light in his darkness that beamed and beckoned.

"Counselor is right," Jeannie said aloud. "Stay."

Welch would have agreed right then, but Ethan placed his hand on Jeannie's shoulder. The act was so simple, so innocent, yet so intimate that it choked the air from Welch. He swallowed the hard truth: Like every other dream he had chased and lost, his goal of reaching Jeannie Jones had failed, crushed by a translucent man, a white bear, and a strange new world.

Welch glared at the hand resting on Jeannie's unflinching shoulder. *"This is where she belongs. I don't,"* he thought.

But where could he go? He had no sanctuary from the law outside in Beaver Flat, no solace here in the Dawn of Life. He crossed his arms and hunched his shoulders.

With her face fixed on Welch's, Jeannie lifted away Ethan's hand. She mouthed a single word. "Stay."

Welch's bulging eyes reddened. He wiped his crinkled forehead.

"Fuck it," he muttered. He shook his head and stomped downstream.

Jeannie, Counselor, and Ethan watched silently as he disappeared through the floating trees toward the gate.

42

The Great Escape Paradox

The Dawn of Life

Welch leaned against the gate, staring at his neatly folded clothes on the rock outside. Jeannie's walkie talkie lay tantalizingly close to them. He scratched his head and considered his next move.

Counselor approached and stood placidly at his side, watching the mountain meadow. "They'll be waiting, you know."

The bear spoke truth. Harley and Kai, Noah Aldridge, the Mounties, the cops back in Michigan—they were all outside, looking for him.

Welch smoothed a nervous hand over his head. He couldn't go back to Beaver Flat, and he couldn't survive in the woods. He didn't know how. Flying away was impossible. Yes, when the chopper returned, he could kill Charley and steal the machine—that would be easy—but he could barely drive a golf cart, let alone fly a helicopter.

"I'm not going to jail," he muttered.

Counselor nodded. "What are you going to do?"

Welch pulled at the back of his neck and gazed at the golden stream. "I—I don't—I don't know. What can I do?"

The bear nodded. "You've wondered this before. When you were eight, your parents packed up your house in Wisconsin and moved you to Winthrop, Michigan. You found out later it had something to do with a man named Sigurd Dorsett."

Welch trembled. "How did you know that?"

"I know much," the bear said silently. He lay next to Welch, his head on his paws. "Place your hand on me and close your eyes."

"Why?"

"To know what I know."

Welch sank his hand into Counselor's body fur. His hand tingled as the past appeared in his mind—his grandfather's gravestone, an empty baseball glove, his mother's empty room, her Aphrodite pendant, his father's liquor bottle dripping onto the living room carpet, Nancy Kirkman's golden Purity Promise cross lying on her naked breast.

When he finally opened his eyes to the glade, the floating trees rolled away over the purple hills to the dark red sky.

"There is more," Counselor said. "Your role in the town and church. Skye Jeffers and Edwin Goodwin. Your flight from the States. Your journey across the prairie carrying a stolen cross. I know."

Welch picked at the bark of the tree next to him. "Does Jones? I never wanted her to know. I wanted—"

Counselor stood. "I know. You wanted to be her dream. Unfortunately, like you, she has her own hopes, her own goals, her own purposes."

"Does she know about me?" Welch asked.

"Not yet."

"So she will."

Counselor nodded.

Outside, clouds spilled over the mountain across the meadow. Snow flitted through the air, skimming across the rocks before nestling into the welcoming blanket of the grass.

Inside the glade, the Music grew. The ground hummed. The air sang. The trees danced.

"You're the Counselor. So counsel me. What do I do?"

The bear raised his head. "You still have choices. You can settle for the who, what, where, and when of life outside the glade—out amongst the clouds, the rocks, the snow. Or you can stay here and find the why and how of forever."

"Both choices suck."

"Maybe. But all your options here will give you what you need, what you and your parents always sought."

"Which is?"

"I told you before. Escape."

Welch leaned back against a gate tree and watched the red sky.

A minute passed before the bear spoke. "This place is called the Dawn of Life. What does that mean to you?"

The frustrated man looked at his clothes atop the rock. "It means I'm walking around buck naked on a Canadian mountaintop."

"Why do you think you're in Canada?"

"Well—I don't know," Welch growled. "I came up here in a helicopter from Beaver Flat, and—Oh, look out there! There's my clothes right where I left them in British Fucking Columbia!"

Counselor licked his paws with lengthening strokes of his tongue. "You are correct. *That's* British Columbia, but when you entered the gate, you made a decision to leave the earth you knew—the temporal, the concrete— for the spiritual and abstract."

"I didn't know that then. Besides—*Spiritual* and *abstract*? This place seems real to me."

"The words do not mean imaginary. Nor do *temporal* and *concrete* mean reality. All four exist simultaneously, but only together do they constitute truth. That's why you feel stalled."

"Because I can't recognize truth? Thanks."

"Because you are frightened."

"I'm not afraid of nothing."

"You are."

"Oh, yeah? Of what?"

"Of the Source. Of what it taught you about yourself and others. What it all means. I understand. But know this: nobody out *there*—in Canada—is coming to look for you *here*—in the Dawn of Life. The Mounties? The state of Michigan? They can't harm you. They are ruled by Natural Law, which is weak and fallible. The Dawn of Life is governed by Unnatural Law, which is far stronger than fear or rationality."

Welch watched the snow gently falling on the meadow and his clothes. Counselor rose and rubbed his shoulder against the bewildered man.

"A paradox, isn't it?"

"I don't remember what that is," Welch said.

"A senseless contradiction that is nevertheless true. A proposition where the idiotic is the most logical."

Welch laughed. "That's it!"

"It has a name. The Great Escape Paradox. It's nothing new for you. Your whole life you've faced and resisted it, but you're making progress. By coming to the Dawn of Life, you've completed the first step in its promise." The bear nodded at the meadow filling with snow. "The decision to stay or leave is the second step."

"I have no idea what to do."

"The Dawn of Life is trying to help."

"It's doing a pretty piss-poor job."

Counselor glanced up at Welch. "You just don't notice all it's doing to remove whatever sidetracks you."

"Like what?"

"Out there, on that mountaintop in British Columbia, it's snowing. It's cloudy and cold. Here——"

"I know!" Welch said. "I escaped Canada. I get that."

Counselor stared at Welch's tight, red face. He began carefully. "But in this place—the Dawn of Life—are you cold?"

"No."

"Are you dry?"

Welch rubbed his arms and his face sarcastically. "Yeah, I seem to be. So what?"

"No cold. No snow. The skies—different colors, but—are there any clouds here?"

Welch craned his neck to check the sky above the glade. "No."

"Are you hungry?" Counselor stood stoically facing out the gate. The silence laughed.

Welch spun, searching the floating forest behind him. "Did you hear— Am I hungry? No!"

"When was the last time you ate?"

The leaves overhead and grass shook with gaiety. Welch peered deeply into the glade. The forest brightened and the stream sparkled.

"I don't know," Welch sputtered. "Sometime this morning before the explosions."

"Have you been thirsty?"

"I haven't thought about it. I've been busy running after Jones."

Laughter swelled among the dancing trees.

"All right! Who's out there?" Welch shouted.

"Ignore what you hear. Listen to me," Counselor said. "Have you been thirsty?"

"I'm not cold. I'm not hungry. I'm not thirsty. So what?"

"Are you horny?" a voice asked. Jeannie peeked around a bush and smiled.

"What the—Jones?"

"An important question," Counselor nodded.

"Am I horny? I—There's been too much to think about—"

"Hmm," Jeannie said. "You're not cold. You're not hungry. You're not thirsty. And you're standing in the woods with a naked woman you've wanted to screw ever since she crashed her head through your office door—a woman who touched your dick and grabbed your balls—and you feel nothing?"

Welch sputtered and stammered, but Jeannie placed three fingers over his mouth. "Do you want to know why things are different?" she asked.

Welch nodded.

"Because *here*—" She swept her hand across the interior of the grove with its golden water and undulating purple ground.

"—is not *there*," she said, pointing at the snowy meadow outside. "Unlike the Canadian Rockies, the Dawn of Life provides everything you need when you need it."

"Tell him what he really wants to know," Counselor said.

"Ah, that. Why you're not dying to have sex. Look down."

Welch stepped back, warily watching Jeannie. Then, cautiously, he glanced at his groin. Like a male doll, Welch's body renounced sex. No hair. No scrotum. No genitals of any kind. Only flat, even skin.

Instantly, his head snapped up. Guttural spits and groans bubbled out of his mouth, then exploded into a wail that shook the velvety ground beneath them.

"Oh, God! No!" Gasping for air, Welch fell to his knees. "It's gone! It's gone."

Jeannie assured him, her hand on his quivering shoulder. "Like I told you, sex doesn't matter."

Welch curled into a fetal position. "Jones, what did you do?"

"I didn't do anything. It's the glade. The Dawn of Life. Here, there is no hunger. No thirst. No distraction. See?" she declared, spreading her arms wide, revealing her own neutered body.

"But outside, you—you were—"

"Normal? Whole? Yes. Out there, our bodies acquire their earthly essentials as needed. Here, procreation is not necessary; therefore, neither is sexuality."

"But you—and that Ethan—I didn't—"

"Notice? I know. Yes, Ethan's the same as you. We've all changed. Hold up your hand and look at the sky."

Muted light shone through his skin.

"No, no, no!" Welch rocked his knees from side to side. "I want out. I want normal!"

Counselor stood over him. "You are normal. There is nothing to be afraid of. As I said, you've completed the first step to the Great Escape Paradox."

"WHAT THE FUCK IS THE GREAT ESCAPE PARADOX?" Welch howled, his arms stretched between his legs.

"Ah!" Counselor nodded. "To escape from yourself, you must escape to yourself. That is why you are here. That is why you exist."

As Welch stared at the bear, his jaw chomping aimlessly at the air. Words failed to form in his brain or on his tongue.

"We'll leave you here," Counselor said. "If you decide to return outside, to the concrete and temporal, you may walk back through the gate. If you seek the abstract and spiritual as well, you'll find us at the pond."

Welch could not answer.

"Come," Counselor told Jeannie.

The two turned, followed the golden river toward its source, and disappeared behind the floating forest. Bathed in red light, Welch regarded the mountain meadow beyond the gate.

The snow had stopped. Welch's clothes and Jeannie's walkie-talkie awaited him on the rock.

43

The Source

The Dawn of Life

No matter how many times he decided and walked away, Welch always returned to the gate.

"*One last time*," he thought.

He leaned back against one of the gate trees. Outside, Mount Komu loomed, a hulking sentry guarding the mountain range. To his side, the sparkling, golden stream gurgled from the forest, clearing as it passed into the open meadow and reflecting a now clear, blue sky.

Welch felt the energy rippling between both trees, a signal of change. If he followed the stream outside, he could be back at the lodge within the hour.

"And be arrested within minutes. If I stay here—"

Kneeling on the ground, he ran his palms over the calming softness of the velvety grass. He sat back on his ankles, examining the clean, even skin between his thighs.

"*But I want it back. That can only happen out there.*"

His chin quivered uncontrollably as he felt his Adonis tattoo.

Outside, a flitting shadow darted across the ground, grabbing his attention. Welch squinted into the brilliant light above. Swooping and fluttering, a bird sailed and lurched across the sky to Mount Komu's summit, then swooped down the slope to the meadow. When it reached the stream, it veered to follow the current toward the gate.

The bird didn't soar. It flapped and fluttered, pounding its way closer to the glade, then abruptly bounced to a landing upon the rock next to Welch's clothes. Its iridescent neck sparkled in the light.

"Another fuckin' pigeon? You better not shit on my clothes," Welch called through the opening.

The pigeon inspected the rock, the clothes, and the walkie-talkie. Its head snapped up, its eyes fixed on the entrance.

Welch flailed his arms. "Get out of here, you stinking rat. You don't belong here."

The pigeon ruffled its wings, then lifted from the rock to circle the meadow once more. Flapping its wings hard against the thin atmosphere, it flew up the side of Mount Komu, then at the summit, swerved violently, hurtling toward the gate. Welch's eyes widened, his jaw dropped, as the pigeon's beak careened toward his forehead. Welch gasped as the bird grew, the wind pounding its tiny neck feathers.

With both arms clutched around his head, Welch collapsed to the ground and shriveled into a ball behind a gate tree, cowering and braced for the crash of light, the shattered air, the thundering earth.

They never came.

Confused by silence, he opened one eye. The pigeon stood before him, its head tilted.

Two translucent human feet stepped next to the bird.

"What the—" Welch looked up into the face of Ethan.

"I'm not your rival," Ethan said.

"My what?" Welch asked, rising to his feet.

"Your rival. Jeannie Jones belongs to nobody. Me. You. Counselor. Nobody."

"You think I'm jealous of you? You're just a—"

Ethan held up a hand. "The Source knows. I'm sent to tell you. Jeannie is not a prize to be won. She is who she is and will be what she must. As will you and I. We all have our own purposes for being here and now, our own purposes beyond place and time. That's what we are here to discover."

"It is, huh?"

"You didn't know that when you came?"

"I had no idea this place existed."

"Ah. That explains your reaction to the pond. But even after seeing the Source, you still don't know what to do?" Ethan asked.

Welch shook his head. "You mean whether to stay here or go back to the lodge? No."

"I see. Now I understand why I am here. You still have more to learn. Come with me."

The pigeon flapped its wings and landed on Ethan's head. Welch laughed and sneered.

"Is the pigeon coming?"

Ethan held Welch's arm and answered, "He's taking us."

The bird spread its wings wide and flapped them once. The air flashed, snapped, and smothered all sound and movement.

When the glade blinked back into focus, Welch found himself with Ethan on the rock bench at the edge of the pond. There was no sign of Jeannie or Counselor. "The Source?" he asked.

"Yes."

"Is this going to be another video?"

"In a moment. For now, listen and watch."

The Music throbbed in Welch's feet and ears. Deeper in the woods, trees and bushes jumped and danced, summoning a menagerie of beaver, squirrels, mountain goats, and others into a line that led from the hill to the water's edge.

The pigeon landed before the leaders, a cow and bull moose. When they signaled their readiness, the bird nodded its head and stepped aside as the line of animals waded into the pond.

Weaving and singing, the trees joined the chorus inside Welch's brain, first as a soft single note, then an expanding harmonic crescendo. The rocks, the grass, and the air added the rhythm.

As the animals gathered in the center of the pond, the water glowed, brighter and brighter. The assembly formed a circle that rotated and swelled with the symphony. At the climax, the earth pounded, the light and water flashed, the Music broke. In the hush, the circle bobbed once, twice, and on the third bounce, all the animals sank beneath the surface, never to reappear.

The pigeon strutted alone on the shoreline.

"What—" stammered Welch.

Ethan pointed to the pond. "In this place, the Source, you've seen your past and present. But there is more to it than information. Other skills, other realities. Much is effortless to understand, to perform. Much is difficult and painful."

"Such as why the animals just drowned themselves?"

The pigeon landed on Ethan's shoulder. The two gazed steadily at Welch.

"There are truths you must recognize before you can decide your future, whether to return to what you know or to accept an unknown reality," Ethan said. "Truths of this world and the last. Watch the water."

Welch ran his hand over his hair.

The smooth surface transformed into its yellow canvas, unfolding scenes as the pigeon skimmed the surface: A large, two-story house in a small town. A man peering at a computer, writing. A steely-eyed woman sitting behind the wheel of a parked car. A small red-headed girl asleep in bed, hugging a stuffed doll. A physically-deformed man staring at the house through a thick, unyielding fog.

Welch leaned forward. "What—? Who—?"

"Just watch."

A swamp aglow with sprits, monsters, violence, terror, and blood. A bandaged face with a ventilator hose protruding from it. The writer defying a ravenous demon. A blonde woman holding a ball of fire. An island rising out of the swamp, then crashing back into the muck.

The pond's surface glazed over, calm and lifeless, leaving Welch to digest what he had just seen. He wiped his mouth.

When the picture reappeared, the new scene startled him. Fort Repentance. The city built around an ocean harbor. The mountains soaring over it. Even the peculiar house on a hill with an odd tower rising from its roof. He had never seen the city personally, but somehow he knew it.

A young woman appeared, walking toward the eccentric house.

Before she unlocked the door and turned the doorknob, she pushed her hair back away from her eyes. The sun radiated her thick, red hair. Her silver eyes reflected off the door window.

"Jones," Welch said. "What is she doing? Why am I watching this?"

"Your purpose."

"My purpose?"

"Jeannie Jones is why you are here. You need to know who she is and why she came to the Dawn of Life. There is much to see. When you know, your decision will be easier."

Welch settled himself onto the bench. Images rippled across the liquid screen—Jeannie, her childhood, the death of her father and Amanda.

Welch saw her dreams and Shimmerings. All of them—the murders in Oaxaca and on Mount Elder, the Earth Man and his queen, Counselor.

And he saw himself.

He stood and held up his hand. "Okay. I don't—Please, make it stop."

He shifted his weight between both feet and wiped his mouth with his forearm.

"Do I need to know *all*?"

Ethan nodded. "Eventually. If you want, you can learn like the animals."

"The animals are gone."

"The animals learned. They made their decision. Yours is bigger. There is more you must know."

Welch worked his lower lip between his teeth. "How long will it take?"

The pigeon spread his wings and hovered over Welch.

"Follow the bird," Ethan said.

The bird circled the rock, then flew out over the pond.

"I—I'm not following him out there!"

The bird swooped around the pool, then hovered over it, waiting.

"If you want to learn the fastest way, follow," Ethan said.

Cautiously, Welch descended to the shore. At the water's edge, he tested the surface with a toe, then slid his foot outward.

The water supported him.

Carefully, he turned sideways and shimmied across the pond.

"Hey! The water's holding me!" he shouted.

He stomped one foot on it, then jumped and landed hard with both feet. "It's solid," he cried.

Tap-dancing across the water, he laughed up at the pigeon.

"This is cool. What do I do now?"

"Let go," Ethan called.

Before the words could form in Welch's mind, the rigid surface liquified and he splashed into the water face first.

Sputtering and fuming, he rose from the pond, shaking his fists at the man on the shore. "You fucker! If I ever—"

He stopped, lowered his hands, and gazed into their emptiness. He raised his head and scanned the ripples spreading away from him. As he wiped the water from his face, he closed his eyes. In his darkness, he saw. He heard. He understood. His eyes snapped open. The pigeon drifted down and perched on his shoulder.

"I—I—" Welch gasped. "I know about Jones. I—"

"She is who she is," Ethan told him. "And will be who she must."

Welch examined Ethan's innocent face. He hesitated. "Right, and I know why she's here. Her mother. The woman in the hospital bed—"

Suddenly, he gazed at Ethan. "And you—You! I know!"

"You know some, but not all."

"No, but I—I want to," Welch said, amazed by his vision and curiosity.

"You may know as much as you need."

"How?"

"Go deeper."

Welch glanced at the water around him, then set his jaw. "That's—That's where the animals are, isn't it? They didn't drown. They went to learn even more—To learn everything."

"Everything they need."

As Welch nodded and considered his options, the bird spread its wings and flew off, sweeping high above the Source.

Taking a deep breath, Welch raised his hands over his head, then dove into the depths. As he disappeared, his feet sliding silently beneath the surface, the bird landed on Ethan's shoulder. The two sat on the stone bench and waited.

When Welch never rose from the water, Ethan smiled at the bird. "He knows," he said. The pigeon nodded and spread his wings over the man. The two disappeared into the shadows.

44

Bird Watching

The Dawn of Life

Jeannie and Counselor walked slowly upstream through the glade toward the Source. Jeannie's mind swirled with questions she dared not ask. If Counselor heard, he did not respond.

Ahead, the stone bench sat above the still pond. "What do you think Bryce is going to do?" Jeannie asked.

The calmness of the water along with the pigeon materializing on the rock revealed the truth. "He's already done it," Counselor said.

Reluctantly, Jeannie followed the bear toward the bench. As she approached the stone, the pigeon fluttered away and landed on the opposite shore.

Counselor laid himself next to the rock and motioned for Jeannie to sit. "There is something you must see."

Across the pond, the pigeon lifted from the ground and sailed low across the water. The surface darkened.

The pond slowly revealed the image of a young boy riding in a car. Rain pelted the window. The child's face revealed both fear and anger.

"I—I've seen him," Jeannie said softly.

Counselor nodded.

"In my nightmares?"

"And you in his."

Jeannie sat forward. Piece by piece, the boy's story revealed itself. His move to Michigan. His grandfather's death. His mother's suicide. His father's drunken attack on his boss.

"I never knew any of this," Jeannie said.

"No, but it happened."

The boy grew. His face changed from childish innocence to teenage insolence, from wonder to wrath.

Jeannie caught her breath. "It's—Bryce Welch. Bryce is the boy from my nightmares?"

The bear nodded, still focused on the water.

The images turned dark. Naked bodies writhing, wrestling in parked cars, darkened rooms, and hideaways.

Jeannie squirmed. Hugging one arm across her chest, she tilted her head and frowned at the pond. The sheer number of partners overwhelmed her. And intrigued her.

She hated him. She had always hated him. And wanted him.

When Bryce or Brandon—or whatever his name—switched from Winthrop High girls to Mount Hebron churchwomen, Jeannie lowered her head behind a hand.

She remembered finding him as a naked adult on her bed with his Adonis tattoo. As much as she despised his lewd comments, lecherous looks, and his uncontrollable, bulging pants, she had relished his quivering body as she licked his chest, the gasp as she touched his penis, and his words "*Do whatever you want.*"

She detested her desire. And her violent reaction.

"You must see," Counselor said.

Jeannie breathed deeply and raised her eyes.

On the surface of the water, the image turned to the interior of a church. Jeannie grimaced as once more Welch's naked body struggled against yet another woman, this time under a pew. Jeannie gagged as the woman rose from the benches and took another man in front of the altar.

Light flashed across the water as a snarling Welch rose from his hiding spot and leapt over the pews.

Jeannie pulled her knees to her chest as blood splashed on the church walls. Over and over, the crazed animal drove a heavy, gold cross into the skulls of the sleeping couple.

Unable to breathe, unable to run, Jeannie retched and cringed when Welch reached into the carnage and hefted the bodies onto the altar. Livid and lost, he wiped his blood-soaked forearm across his mouth and slammed the electric candle to the floor.

The picture blinked, revealing a fully dressed Welch sitting on the steps beneath the altar, his fury spent and his head in his hands.

Jeannie's jaw trembled and she wiped her eyes.

Welch rose and held the cross at waist level, examining the scratched and scarred surface with a tender stroke of a single finger. Then he stormed out the door, disappearing into the night.

The pigeon streaked across the pond and the screen went blank.

Jeannie shuddered. "Gold. Lust and gold. They control him."

Counselor nodded. "This is who he is."

She looked blankly at the pond. Visions of her parents' death melded with Welch's savagery. "I—I wanted—Not this. I never wanted this."

Jeannie bit her lip. "I should have known. I hate him."

"Does it help to hate?"

"Does it *help*? I don't care! He's a monster."

When she saw the spirit bear's calm face, she looked down at her hands flexing into fists.

The spirit bear examined Jeannie. "There is more you need to see. Throughout your life, you loved your father's wife Amanda, but you missed your mother."

Jeannie nodded sheepishly.

"You knew she existed in forever, but when your father told you how, that she had chosen to become the Earth Man's queen rather than to return to life with you and your father, you vowed to reach beyond the barrier of death and bring her back."

"Rescue her," Jeannie said, biting her lower lip and looking away from both the bear and the pond.

"*Rescue* was the right thing to say. You were young. You were angry, but didn't know the dangers. The Word who once protected your father tried to warn you. That's why you had the Shimmerings and nightmares. To learn of weendigoes and pishtacos, of matchi-auwishuk, and the evil of the Earth Man. Despite the warnings, despite what your mother had done to you, your father, and Frank Thorstad, you still loved her. You accepted the risk. You persisted. You forgave."

Jeannie shuffled her feet. "I was stupid."

"No. You knew mercy. You wanted to save her from herself."

Jeannie considered Counselor's words carefully, then nodded.

"But that ended when the pishtaco killed your father and Amanda. You knew he was from the Earth Man. You knew your mother had chosen the Earth Man over your father. In an instant, compassion disappeared, replaced by vengeance."

Jeannie lowered her head and examined her hands.

The spirit bear nudged her thigh. "Look to the Source."

Jeannie watched as the pond lightened. Two faces looked back. Her mother Sarah and Bryce Welch.

Counselor examined Jeannie's face. "They are who they are. Hate does not change them. It only changes you. Do you understand?"

Jeannie glanced from one to the other. Setting her jaw, she brushed back her hair. "I am who I am," she said.

Disappointed, the bear turned slowly from her.

"Yes. Yes, you are. Go to your mother. She is near."

"Where?"

The surface of the Source glowed again. Jeannie clutched her chest and sat straight at the image. Out and beyond the gate, out in the old reality, Mount Komu.

Before she could speak, a calming hand touched her shoulder.

"Who—?"

Jeannie stomach lightened at Ethan's soft eyes and relaxed cheeks. The image of Bryce Welch vanished from her mind.

Ethan took her hands and squeezed them. "You must go there, to Mount Komu."

Her breath shortened as she examined his eyes. She had known him. She forgot to ask how. "To the Entry?"

"Yes," Ethan replied. "Into the mountain. You must escape yourself by escaping to yourself."

286

Jeannie blinked, suddenly feeling her hand in his. "Why—Why are you here?"

Counselor pushed between them and stood next to Ethan. "Go now. It is time," he told her. "Follow the bird."

Jeannie looked from the bear to Ethan. The two nodded. She breathed deeply and followed the pigeon to the gate between realities.

45

Dawn into Dusk

Mount Komu ("The Entry")
British Columbia, Canada

Jeannie laid a hand on the boulder outside the gate and caught her breath. Images of obliterated mountains and shattered innocence twinkled in drops of melting ice. Still, except for a thin layer of frost that covered the grass above the creek bed, all was as she and Welch had left it. His folded clothes still lay atop the rock. His boots stood below, awaiting their owner's return.

Chills shivered her clouded arms. "*Where did he go?*" she wondered as she rubbed away the cold.

Somewhere, somehow, he disappeared from the Dawn of Life with no word of his destination or motive.

Her eyes swept the meadow, following the creek slowly twisting down the mountainside. Her stomach churned and she stared at her palms. In one, she saw the savage murder, the blood, the greed; in the other, the pointless lust and sex that nevertheless enticed. She wiped away the memories against the boulder and sat against it.

"*He is who he is. Worse than I thought, but more—I don't care. He's gone. I don't have time to worry about him. I have work to do.*"

Raising her face, Jeannie let the sun bathe her cheeks. "Ethan—"

She rubbed a hand across her arm, her chest, her thighs. Blood flowed through her regenerated veins and arteries. Her face glowed as her flesh thickened.

She glanced back at the gate and recalled his eyes, his long hair, his soft voice. The light shifted on the stony Mount Komu.

"*Back to my purpose. Ethan said use the Entry.*"

Absently, she explored her body for signs of femininity, and remembered her sexuality would only return as needed.

"*I guess I don't need it.*"

Her hand brushed the folded shirt on the rock next to her. Its fleecy softness warmed her hand, so she slipped her arms into the sleeves and buttoned the shirt around her. It fit as if it were her own, as did the jeans, socks and boots.

She smiled at the sky.

As the blood pulsed through her fingers, she raised herself onto the rock and slid her hands under her thighs. The rejuvenated skin sensed a familiar pulsing from under the rock. Jeannie narrowed her eyes.

"It's like the Music—more primitive, magnetic but less appealing," she said.

Unlike the thrum of the glade that enveloped like the air, this beating rose from inside the earth, an erratic, sinister vibration quivering against her legs and feet. Fascinated, she watched the shaking hem of her jeans as the rhythm rumbled through her bones. Unable to identify the rawness, she pushed her hands harder against the rock to find the cadence amidst the aberrations and stammers. Rather than the comfort of the familiar, a dark, alien invitation drew her to the unexpected.

She straightened her back and nodded at the broken rock ahead. "You must go there," Ethan had said. "To Mount Komu."

Hopping off the rock, she scrambled up the mountain in exploring mode, relying on her training and instinct to propel her forward.

Halfway up the mountainside, the air crackled and chafed. Stopping to catch her breath, Jeannie searched the path ahead, her senses tingling, alive. Dryness stung her eyes.

"*Smoke,*" she thought.

The slap of metal on stone caromed off the mountain wall, followed by a long rasping scrape. Again. And again. Sometimes punctuating, other times clashing with the rhythm of the ground.

Abruptly, the slap-scrape stopped, almost annoyed. Jeannie froze and held her breath.

"I'm not going to hurt you," a voice called. "Even though I want to."

Jeannie's cheek twitched. She knew the voice, the accent. Cautiously, she peeked around a boulder. A man with a curved knife tipped his hat and raised his wicked, green eyes.

The horrors of the Oaxaca Shimmering, the Peruvian fat-sucking legend, and her parents' headless bodies lashed and hung together over the refrigerator flashed before her.

"Pishtaco," she said.

He sneered and licked the air.

Her gray eyes narrowed. "Thank you for cleaning up my parents' blood that night. That was a nice touch."

He flipped the rock to the ground. "You're welcome. Did you notice the vials of fat?"

"That's how I knew it was you," Jeannie said.

"Good. Mission accomplished. Shall we go?" he said, pointing his knife at a break in the mountain wall.

"And if I say no?"

The pishtaco shook his head and sheathed his blade. Unruffled, he scrutinized Jeannie's face. "You have your mother's eyes."

"So I'm told."

The pishtaco sneered and gestured toward the opening.

Under Jeannie's feet, the rhythm vibrated. Smoke wafted from inside, beckoning her.

Smiling, she picked up the pishtaco's sharpening stone and weighed it in her hand. She playfully tossed the rock above her head, caught it, and in one motion, crushed it to dust against the mountain wall.

"I'm ready," she said. "Lead on."

The pishtaco twisted his shoulders and forced a smile. "Ladies first."

Following the drumbeat and smoke, the two disappeared into the Entry.

The rhythm echoed and trembled as the gold-streaked cave turned darker, rockier, and more precarious. Still, the incessant thumping led them up, down, and around corners until ahead, light gamboled and played across the tunnel wall.

Jeannie stopped the pishtaco's arm. "Is that fire?"

"What do you think?"

Jeannie glowered. "I *think* I'd like to see you fly off a cliff."

The pishtaco smirked and nodded her forward into the rhythmic chaos.

Around a central fire, leaping, whirling creatures stomped their feet to pounding mallets hammering a cadence that entangled spirit, air, and consciousness into insensibility. At the height of their rapture, a shriek drove the assembly to the floor scrambling for the walls.

All except the rotund man with the flushed, blubbering cheeks who crouched beside the fire. Like the pishtaco, Jeannie had never met him, but she knew him.

The Earth Man.

She and the pishtaco stepped into the room. Arrogantly, the man rose and turned to them.

"You came," he said.

Jeannie tipped her head to the pishtaco. "Like I had a choice."

"Good job," the Earth Man told the monster. "You can leave now."

"But—"

The Earth Man's glare forced the creature into the crowded darkness.

Quietly, the ruler drew stick figures in the ashes. A man. A woman. A child.

As if pulled into the room by the gold chain around her neck, a dark-haired, silver-eyed woman entered, her dress faded and tattered. Weariness supported the wooden crown on her head.

"Cinderella Castle. A crying, little girl wrapped around a woman's neck, a stuffed Tigger clutched between them. Mickey Mouse and Goofy. DisneyWorld." Jeannie remembered.

"This who you're looking for?" the Earth Man asked. "Your mother? Not quite what you remember, is she? How about you, Sarah? This the little girl you remember?"

Sarah raised her chin and forced a smile. "You've grown," she told her daughter. Her skin reddened under her chain.

Jeannie nodded. "And you—you—"

"Got older? Not really. I've been this age since I died. I'll always be this age." Sarah crossed her arms and stretched her neck. Her lips grimaced.

"You look tired," Jeannie said.

"Yes. Who knew death could be so exhausting?"

In the flickering flames, Jeannie saw the Source; the Dawn of Life; the heavy, white body of Counselor; Ethan rising from Beaver Flat Lake; Bryce Welch huddling by the gate.

"Maybe you should try something else," she said, bitterly.

Sarah winced and tugged at her necklace.

The Earth Man smiled. "Good burn, kid. If she still existed in your world, maybe she could. But she's in mine. Different place. Different rules."

Sarah absently removed her crown and turned it in her hands. "I assume your father explained about my injuries in the car crash. Why I'm here."

Jeannie nodded sullenly.

Glancing at the Earth Man, Sarah said, "He told you I'm not here by force?"

Again, her daughter nodded.

"He's right. I'm not," she said, loosening the chain around her neck. "Not really. I chose this. This is where I belong."

Rubbing the hem of her shirt, Jeannie narrowed her eyes and gritted, "There are other alternatives."

"There were," Sarah said.

Jeannie glared at the Earth Man, then corrected her mother. "There *are*."

Sarah watched her daughter closely. "Name one."

"A place unlike anything you've ever known. A place with no time. A place unhampered by the restrictions of life. I just came from one."

Sarah glanced at the Earth Man. He glowered at her and shook his head. Her neck reddened.

"Tell her," Counselor whispered inside Jeannie's brain.

Startled by the voice, Jeannie raised her hand to her mouth. Her eyes watered. "Mom, help me understand. You had me. You had Dad—"

"Your father?" Sarah's silver eyes pierced the flickering light. "YOUR FATHER? Your father is the reason I chose this!"

"You don't know what that did to him. He—He—"

"Don't you dare tell me how he loved me. You don't know what it was like. You were five!"

"I'm not talking about then. I'm talking about what he remembered just before he—when he—"

Jeannie saw the blankness in her mother's face. She glanced at the Earth Man and the darkness where the pishtaco hid. Her jaw dropped and she returned to Sarah. "You—You had nothing to do with it. You don't know, do you?"

"Know what?"

Jeannie glanced at the Earth Man. His smug sneer confirmed her suspicion. "You didn't tell her?"

"Jeannie?" Sarah asked.

"My father is dead." Jeannie glared at the Earth Man. She looked about the room at the crowd awkwardly avoiding her eyes. "I'm sorry. I thought you knew. I just—I'm sorry. I was wrong."

She walked away holding her stomach.

"Tell her," Counselor whispered again.

"You need to leave here," Jeannie murmured to Sarah.

"Give it up," the Earth Man said. "Your mother's—"

Sarah raised her hand and turned on the Earth Man. "Wait! You knew Beecher died and didn't tell me? My god! What is your prob—"

Her eyes snapped wide. She realized the whole truth. "He didn't just die. You killed him!"

"I didn't kill anybody."

"No, I forgot. You don't kill. You don't have to. That's why you hired the pishtaco. You had the pishtaco kill Beecher Jones?"

The Earth Man pulled at his beard.

"Why? Why would you do that?" Sarah demanded.

A rumble grew in the Earth Man's chest. "Your dream," he snarled.

"Dream? What dream?"

"Replaying life. Finding Beecher, marrying him, having a new Jeannie, being a real mother—"

"That wasn't real!" Sarah exploded. "I made it up to make you jealous."

"You—You lied?" the Earth Man thundered.

"You killed Beecher Jones?"

The room trembled.

"Someday," Counselor spoke into Jeannie's consciousness. *"Someday there will be a great awakening when you—and she—know this existence is a dream to be rescued. Today can be that day. Help her."*

Jeannie's whisper broke the quiet. "Mom? Come away with me."

"It's all right, dear one," Sarah said. "As ridiculous as the Earth Man and I are, this is where I belong."

She lowered her head and turned away.

"Mom, you can just—"

Sarah wrapped her fingers around her chain. She coughed and strained as her neck burned. "No, Jeannie. Even if I wanted—"

The Earth Man stood over Jeannie. "Get out, bitch," he said.

As he reached toward Jeannie, Sarah yelled, "No! Leave her alone."

Stepping between them, she took Jeannie's shoulders. Bearing deep into her daughter's cold, steel eyes with her own, she asked, "You all right?"

Suddenly, she saw. She heard.

Wheeling on her husband, she demanded, "Jeannie's right, isn't she? I have options. Even now."

The Earth Man's cheeks puffed and reddened. He seized her chain and yanked her to him.

"You are mine!" he growled into her face. "Now. Always. Remember?"

He jerked the chain and Sarah squealed helplessly.

"REMEMBER! I'm not going to—"

Without warning, he broke off and shoved Sarah away. He considered his hands, then raised his head to Jeannie. His brain clicked. His eyes blinked. He stepped back to study her, then raised a finger.

"What?" Sarah asked.

The Earth Man waved her off.

"What are you thinking?" she insisted.

Looking first at Jeannie, then Sarah, the Earth Man said, "You're right. You do have options. Go."

Sarah's jaw dropped. "Are you kidding?"

"No. Leave. Go wherever you want."

"Really?" Jeannie stepped between them.

"Absolutely." Turning to Sarah, he said, "Here. Let me take your chain."

After removing the necklace, he pecked Sarah's cheek. "You go find whatever you need. Thanks for the memories."

Warily, Jeannie took her mother's arm. "Come on. Let's go."

"Oh, no, no, no," he said, clutching Jeannie's shoulder. "Your mother goes, not you."

"What?"

"Things have been kind of boring around here. You should perk things up quite nicely."

"No!" Sarah shrieked.

Snatching his wife by the hair, the Earth Man hurled her to the ground. With his arm wrapped around Jeannie, he pulled her face to his. "Your mother gets this other world you speak of. I get a new piece of ass. Everybody wins."

Sarah grasped for her daughter. "I'll stay. I'll stay!"

Ignoring his wife, the Earth Man smiled and trailed his finger down Jeannie's face to her neck, her collar bone, her chest. Slowly, the finger made a figure eight around her breasts. He flicked his tongue on her earlobe and whispered, "Come on. Set her free."

Jeannie pushed off and stumbled to the wall. She listened for Counselor, but could not hear.

Slowly, resolutely, she lay prone on the cave floor, placed both palms next to her head, and listened with her whole body.

The Earth Man and her mother waited.

46

Confrontation

Mount Komu ("The Entry")
British Columbia, Canada

Counselor spoke the Word to Jeannie through the earth:
"Let go! Move beyond Mount Komu. It doesn't exist and never did."
Jeannie's breath calmed as she rubbed both hands across the ground, absorbing the words. "What do you want me to do?" she asked.
"Discard your fear. The past is a dim reflection of what can never be. The future has never heard of your present. Enter the place of neither being nor non-being. Shine with the original brightness of the Word."
Jeannie patted the floor and raised her head. Above her, her mother stood chewing her knuckles. The Earth Man scowled, awaiting an answer.
"Remember your Trinity. The Dream Rescuer, the Sacrifice, the Original Thought. The time is now."
Slowly, Jeannie rose to her hands and knees.
"Well?" the Earth Man snapped.
Sarah, her eyes clenched, whispered to herself, "Don't do it. Don't do it."
Shouts and struggles crashed the quiet, scattering the matchi-auwishuk from the door. The pishtaco burst into the room, flinging a battered, naked

man at his king's feet. Tossing aside his hat, the monster straddled his victim and pulled his knife. "He wanted to see you about the girl," he snarled through his thick beard. "I can take care of him right now if you want."

Weakly, the prisoner raised his head. His matted hair and bloodied face could not disguise his contemptuous sneer.

Jeannie grabbed her mouth.

"You know him?" the Earth Man asked her.

"She knows me," Bryce Welch gurgled through bloody lips.

While Welch disgusted her, Jeannie detested the pishtaco. "Get off him!" she ordered, hoisting the monster by the hair and tossing him aside. Then, reaching for Welch, she asked, "Bryce, what are you doing here? I never—"

Clutching Jeannie's strong arm, Welch struggled to his feet and leaned against her for support.

"You never thought you'd ever have to see me again? Surprise." Welch coughed and wobbled to the side.

"Really, I can kill him right now," the pishtaco offered. "I'll even make it entertaining."

The Earth Man shook off the suggestion and examined Welch's defiant glare and naked body. He smiled. "A eunuch?"

"Not by choice," Welch said.

"So who castrated you? Your father? Your mother? Your priest? They did a pretty thorough job."

Welch glimpsed at Jeannie. "It's a long story," he explained.

"I'm sure it's disgusting. Somebody get him a robe."

The pishtaco persisted. "Really, boss, I've developed a new method of dissection. It's—"

"Not now!"

A matchi-auwish scurried into the room and draped a robe over Welch's shoulders.

Jeannie interrupted. "Bryce, where have you—?"

Welch held up a hand, coughed harshly, then adjusted the robe. He straightened as much as possible before croaking to the Earth Man, "Let me see if I have this right. You'll only let Jones's mother go if the daughter stays in her place. Is that it?"

The words staggered the Earth Man. "How did you know—"

Ignoring the question, Welch turned to Jeannie, fixed his eyes on hers, and took a long breath. "Do it," he said.

"Bryce, I'm not going to do anything you—"

Welch held her shoulders. "Remember the words," he said with no sound. "*Shine with the original brightness of the Word*. Do it."

The voice was not Welch's. It was Counselor's.

Jeannie glanced around the room. No one else had heard. As she searched Welch's face, the message pulsated in his pupils. "There is no reason to worry. There is no such thing as life or death."

Jeannie stretched her tingling fingers. "You're not really Bryce Welch, are you?"

Welch never blinked. "I *am* Bryce Welch."

Truth spoke to her. "And more?" she asked.

"Yes."

"What do I do?" she asked in silence.

"Exist! Exist in the Dream."

"What dream—"

Welch nodded and tightened his grip on her shoulders.

Jeannie's eyes widened. She knew. "Your tattoo. It's gone. You've been to—"

Welch maintained his stare as he lowered his head. "Not just the tattoo. Adonis is gone. I learned as you said, sex doesn't matter. And never did."

With a quick grin, she turned to the Earth Man. "Yes," she nodded. "Yes, I—I was wrong. I'll stay. Let my mother go."

Sarah's scream shook the room. Before she could reach her daughter, the pishtaco intercepted her, clinging the thrashing woman to his chest. His laughing eyes danced as he cupped her breasts. Her knuckles white with rage, Jeannie dragged the monster to the ground, crushing its throat while air hissed from its nose. Still, it clenched Sarah to its chest.

The Earth Man thrust Jeannie aside and grasped the monster's head. An electric zap jolted through his hands, and the pishtaco collapsed to the floor. The Earth Man stood over the shuddering body. "I'll deal with you later," he snapped.

Jeannie raised her mother to her feet, hugged her protectively, and glanced at Welch. He closed his eyes and nodded weakly. She took Sarah's shoulders and said, "Mom, I'm going to stay here. You go with Bryce."

"No! I won't!"

"Well, you're not staying here," the Earth Man barked. "Go! Good luck."

Then taking the wobbling Bryce Welch's hand, he said, "Hey, cockless. I don't know who you are, but thanks. The bitch is all yours."

The shaky pishtaco rose to its feet. "You're all right," the Earth Man told it. "Get these two out of here."

Dusting himself off, the pishtaco checked his knife and croaked, "The easy way or the fun way?"

"I don't give a shit. Just save the robe."

The pishtaco forced a sneer, then pushed Sarah and Welch into the darkness.

The Earth Man lifted Jeannie's chin. "You and I need to get acquainted, don't you think?"

With a quick glance after Welch and her mother, Jeannie took the Earth Man's arm and patted his groin. "Absolutely."

47

Other Lives Unknown

Mount Komu ("The Entry")
British Columbia, Canada

Sarah and Welch stumbled from the cave into the light. Behind them, the pishtaco extended his knife and stepped forward "Now—"

In one swift movement, Welch sprang to life, snatching the knife from the pishtaco and jamming the blade into the boulder. With a cracking ring, the blade snapped off and spun through the air.

Welch handed the pishtaco the weapon's hilt. "See ya," he said, grabbing Sarah's arm.

"No! Stop! How— Where—Where are you going?"

"Away, just like the Earth Man wanted," Welch called back, climbing the path up the mountain.

"Wai—"

"Sorry. Can't talk. Gotta run. Have a nice day."

Bryce hoisted Sarah over his shoulder and, leaping and dodging over the rocks, hauled her up the mountain.

The bewildered pishtaco fingered the hilt in his hand, while down the path, the fractured blade glinted in the sunshine.

Beyond the grassy meadow below, the glade stood thick, strong, and foreboding. A white bird flew out of the trees to the cave entrance and led Sarah and Welch up Mount Komu.

The pishtaco's cheek quivered. He could not follow. He twisted the hilt in his hand and scowled. A low growl built in his stomach, gripped his throat, then exploded as he flung the remains of his knife after the bird.

Furiously, he turned back to the cave.

"I think he's gone," Sarah said. "You don't have to carry me."

Welch bent and lowered her to the ground. "Good. No offense, but I was getting tired."

Sarah flexed her knees and stretched her arms above her. "I never thought we'd get out of the cave. I thought you were almost dead."

Welch laughed. "Well, you're *all* dead."

The bird fluttered above, urging them forward.

"Come," Welch said. "We must keep moving."

"You know where we're going?" Sarah panted as they climbed ever higher.

"Someplace you know," he replied, his eyes on the summit.

"What about Jeannie?"

Bryce smiled back at her. "You'll see. Come on."

Deep in the cave, the Earth Man escorted Jeannie into his personal sanctuary.

"Here we go."

Jeannie brazenly stepped past him and examined the empty room. She circled the room, checking the stone walls for dust. Back at the door, she glanced at the Earth Man and nodded.

"You like it?" he asked.

"Not quite what I expected of royal chambers, but I guess it will do."

The Earth Man glared at her.

"No. Seriously. It's fine. I just expected—I don't know—furniture or something. It's secluded and all, but it could use something."

"Like what?" he challenged.

Jeannie held the Earth Man's robe and leaned into him. Her knuckles pressed against his chest. "Well," she drawled, "like a bigger bed."

The Earth Man lifted her face and gazed into her eyes. "You really are your mother's daughter," he said.

He briefly left the room and returned with Sarah's chain. "I want you to have this," he said.

"Gold," she said, sitting on the bed. "The walls are full of it. You don't need this to keep me here."

"What do you mean?" he asked.

Looking askance, she patted the bed. "I know I'm like my mother, but you don't need a chain to keep me by your side. I'm here because I want to be." She smiled seductively and slowly slid a hand between her legs.

The Earth Man stepped back and slipped off his robe. "Let's go."

Jeannie stopped him. "Slower. We've got time."

"We've also got now," he said, stepping out of his trousers.

"Yes, but this is our first time. Let's make it special." She picked up his robe and trousers, then handed them to him. "Put these back on with your shirt and I'll show you."

He held his clothes in both hands and looked into Jeannie's gray eyes. The same eyes Sarah used to captivate him.

"It will be worth it. I promise," she said.

In his rush to stumble back into his trousers, the Earth Man toppled headlong onto the small bed, caromed off, and flopped to the floor on his back. Jeannie picked up his clothes and stood over him.

"Calm down, big boy. I'll wait for you."

She dropped his pants on him and bit her lip as he struggled to force his flabby legs into them. As he stood, wriggling and grappling to pull them over his bulging belly, Jeannie felt the vibration in the air as Welch and her mother clambered across the mountain above them. *"Just a few more minutes,"* she thought.

"Okay. Now what?" the Earth Man wheezed as he tugged at the last button.

"Let me start." Loosening his robe, she stroked one hand over his immense, shirted chest. Her other hand fumbled under the tails, then massaged his bare skin.

"Which one do you like better?" she whispered in his ear.

"I like them both, but——"

"But?"

He covered the hand under his shirt.

"The right hand's better for you. Okay," she said. "Lie down on the floor."

Lying on his back, he breathed heavily as she straddled him. Unable to speak, he gasped as her right hand reached under his shirt and wandered over his stomach, his chest, all the way to his shoulder bone.

She kissed his neck, then grasped his free hand and drew it to her own chest. "Do you like this better," she asked drawing it over her flannel shirt. "Or this better?" She lifted her shirt and pulled his hand under it.

The Earth Man stopped. Something was wrong.

"Which one?" she asked.

"Underneath."

She smiled down at him. "So you like skin."

The Earth Man breathed heavily and nodded.

"That's what I expected. Let's try this."

She sat back on his hips and raised his shirt. He twisted, turned, and bent until she had pulled it over his head. She traced her fingers across her own shirted chest, then asked, "Would you unbutton mine?"

He grunted and reached up, groping roughly at her buttons. He finished the last one, but before he could thrust open the shirt, she stopped him. "Slower," she whispered.

Her knees on the hard floor felt Welch and Sarah's footsteps above.

She leaned forward and closed his eyes with two fingers. "Wait," she said. Then, opening her shirt, she laid her bare chest on his.

"You can take it off now," she whispered.

The Earth Man reached around her and pulled the shirt off one arm at a time.

"Hold me," Jeannie sighed into his chest. The two lay motionless on the floor, synchronizing their breathing.

"Do you like this?" Jeannie asked.

"It's okay," the Earth Man admitted, grudgingly.

Jeannie reached down between his legs. "You seem to like it a lot."

"I think I'm ready now!"

Jeannie laughed.

"You've done this a lot, haven't you?" he gasped.

"No. You're my first."

"I don't believe——"

"Shhh. I told you I want this to be special."

"Right. Right. Okay."

Slowly, she kissed the flabby skin beneath her as she listened to the footsteps slow down on the mountain above. She patted the Earth Man's chest and asked, "Are you sure you're ready?"

He laughed. "Yes, I'm ready."

"I mean really ready?"

"I'm ready. Get naked, woman." He scrunched her buttocks in his huge hands.

"All right, but just so you know, expect the unexpected."

"What does that mean?"

She rolled over, faced away from him, stood and lowered her jeans. The Earth Man untied his belt.

"You might want to wait a second," Jeannie said.

"For what?"

"Well——" Jeannie timidly turned to him, revealing her sexless body.

"What the——?" he sat up.

"You see, you might have this problem."

"Me? You're the one who—who——"

"Who what?"

"You got no nipples, no cunt, nothing."

"That's true. You see your problem?"

"What's my problem?"

"You traded my mother for somebody who not only doesn't want to fuck you, but *can't*."

"But how? What?"

"Oh, I'm just learning that myself. You see, that special place I told you about? There, incarnate beings don't need food or sex or speech or any one of a thousand things."

"This is not what I agreed to!"

Jeannie shrugged. "Sorry about that."

"No. No! The deal is off. Get out of here. Pishtaco!"

The pishtaco, who had been waiting outside the entrance, stepped into the opening.

Pulling a blanket around himself, the Earth Man demanded, "Where's my wife? Did you kill her?"

"No. She and the man took off at the top of the cave."

The blanket slipped from the Earth Man's fingers. "Took off? Where?"

"I don't know. Up the mountain, I guess."

The Earth Man flung the blanket to the floor. "What the fuck? I told you to kill them."

"No, you told me to get rid of them. They're gone."

The Earth Man's jowls wobbled and bounced. "Well, find them! Take the Mexican baykok, the weendigoes— Hell, take all the damned matchi-auwishuk."

The pishtaco shrugged and turned to leave. Abruptly, he stopped and leered at Jeannie. "Say, boss, when we get back, if you're done with the daughter there—"

"Find them!"

"All right," the pishtaco said, backing through the curtain.

"What could he want with me?" Jeannie asked.

"He wants to carve you into little pieces. It's what he does best."

"Well, he can try," Jeannie said, lifting the massive stone throne and placing it in front of the fire. "So we wait?"

The Earth Man stepped back, amazed. "We wait."

She crawled onto the throne and crossed her legs, sulking. "I hate waiting."

48

A Leap Beyond

Mount Komu ("The Entry")
British Columbia, Canada

At the summit of Mount Komu where solid stone broke into airy nothing, Welch and Sarah stood at the cliff's edge.

Welch looked across the ridges in the distance. The colors of the sky and mountains deepened. Vibrant blues and yellows. Rich, dark reds and purples. Spatters of white and green among the grays and black.

"It's beautiful, isn't it?" he said.

Sarah saw only the crumbled rock beneath her. She had contemplated her life and death here many times, sometimes with hope, sometimes with regret, mostly with apathy and frustration. "If you like cliffs and rocks, I suppose. Why did you bring me here?"

The white bird landed on the ground and paced the rim of the cliff.

Welch nodded, then gazed far away. He weighed his words. "You know this place."

"Yes."

Welch lowered his eyes to the base of their mountain. "After all you've seen with the Earth Man—deserts, swamps, forests, oceans—you have a limited view of mountains?"

Sarah's silver eyes fixed on the strange man. "Because they're just cliffs and rocks."

"Below us, yes, but look out there, beyond the near at hand, beyond the horizon."

Sarah shook her head. "I gave up dreaming when I was alive," she said. Bending, she picked up a disc-shaped stone. "Mostly, I just come up here and throw stones off the cliff."

Welch nodded. "When you throw them, what do you see? What do you hear?"

"What's to see?" She flung the stone away with a wide, side-arm toss. "They fly out. They drop. They bounce around the rocks below. They disappear."

"Wishful thinking?" Welch asked.

"What do you mean?"

"Do you want to fly away, escape somewhere into oblivion, away from now?"

"And crash into the rocks below? No, but thank you for the offer."

Welch's earnestness halted her cynicism. She regarded him carefully. Like a mother, she licked her thumb and rubbed at the dried blood on his face. He never flinched. He simply closed his eyes as she wiped away the past— her own as well as his.

"You're a very observant young man."

Looking far off the cliff, Welch thought a moment. "In the Dawn of Life, there is a pond called the Source, which teaches everything about the past and the future."

"The Dawn of Life. One of the places Jeannie spoke of?"

Welch nodded. "I learned much there. Things I had forgotten and never knew about myself; things about Jeannie, her father, her stepmother, the Earth Man; you; why Jeannie needed to stay with the Earth Man; why you need to be here on this cliff."

"To erase myself?"

Welch crossed his arms and gazed at his feet. "No. To escape yourself."

Sarah recalled her decision to live with the Earth Man, her avoided motherhood, the tedium of existence. Welch heard.

"Escape would be a good thing," she said.

"The Great Escape Paradox says, 'To escape *from* yourself, you must escape *to* yourself.' We all have a lot to escape from."

"Including you?"

"Including me."

"Do I want to know?"

Welch looked out at the mountains beyond the rubble below. He shook his head. "No, but it's why I'm up here with you."

Sarah laughed. "You want me to jump off a cliff?"

Welch kicked at the ground. "About that," he said, turning to her. "I want us both to."

Sarah coughed. "Wait. You want me to jump off this mountain with you and die? Again?"

Reaching down, he took her hands. "No, not to die, but I do want you to jump off the cliff."

She drew back her hands. "Did this pond at the Dawn of Life tell you that?"

Welch breathed hard, then looked over the cliff again. "It's the right choice," he said.

He sniffed the wind. "They're coming, you know. The Earth Man. The pishtaco. The matchi-auwishuk. Jeannie."

"Here? Why?"

"Because the Earth Man can't have Jeannie the way he wanted. He wants you back. And he doesn't trust the pishtaco to return you."

"So to avoid a fate worse than death, I am to choose a second death? I don't like that option."

"That's not the option I'm offering."

"Aha!" the Earth Man bellowed behind them.

Welch and Sarah swung around. At the head of a throng of matchi-auwishuk armed with rocks and clubs, their flabby ruler dragged Jeannie up the mountain by her auburn hair.

"It seems your daughter and her friend there cheated me out of a wife and a cunt," the Earth Man cried, waving his free hand.

"I don't understand," Sarah said.

"That bloody eunuch there took you, my eternal whore, and left me with your daughter who's barely human, let alone female. They conned me and I will not be conned. I came to reclaim you."

"I had nothing to do with that."

"I don't care. Get your ass over here."

"What's the pishtaco doing here?" Sarah asked.

"Ha! He's the one who told me you came this way. For his service, he gets the leftovers."

The pishtaco peeked from behind the Earth Man's bulk and tipped his hat.

"Well, that's friendly," Sarah said.

Welch leaned to Sarah's ear and whispered. She raised her eyebrows. Welch nodded.

"Hey, you bastard!" the Earth Man roared. "Get away from her and shut the fuck up. You're not doing this again."

Welch stepped forward. "No, no, no. I'm sorry. I was just telling her this is all my fault. Don't take it out on her and Jeannie. You want to hurt someone? Hurt me."

Jeannie broke from the crowd. "Bryce, don't—"

Sarah rushed to Jeannie and took her face in both hands. Heavy tears welled in her eyes. "Jeannie, are you all right?"

"I'm—fine."

Sarah engulfed her daughter in her arms and buried the young woman's head in her neck. Then, pushing back Jeannie's thick, red hair, Sarah kissed her forehead, her cheek, her ear.

Jeannie's eyes flashed opened, and she pulled Sarah's face even closer to her ear, intent on the sound of her mother's kisses.

"How touching," the Earth Man jeered. "You'll have time for this when we get back to the cave. Come on. Let's go."

An unspoken voice explained the rest to both women.

Still wrapped in each other's arms, Jeannie and Sarah turned to Welch. "Just like casting stones?" Sarah asked.

Welch nodded. "To life."

"Now?"

Welch set his jaw and nodded. "Now."

Sarah and Jeannie locked eyes, clutched each other's hands, and bolted toward the cliff.

"What the—? Quick! After them!" the Earth Man shouted.

Before spirits and beasts could reach the fleeing women, the two sprang over the edge and disappeared into the air below.

"I'll get them, Boss." The pishtaco lunged from the crowd. Driven by his energy, the matchi-auwishuk followed, forgetting the mountain's edge.

"No!" the Earth Man wailed as they screamed and flailed through the emptiness before crashing into the rocks beneath them.

In the silence that followed, Welch joined the Earth Man and wrapped an arm around his shoulder. "I guess it's just us, Dad."

His red cheeks bulging in rage, the Earth Man hoisted Welch by the neck and flung him away. Like a rubber ball, the human's body bounced off the ground and plummeted over the ledge, his "Thank you!" fading into the depths.

Lightning blazed through the sky once—twice—three times—and drove Earth Man to his knees. Thunder exploded and convulsed the ground beneath him. Grasping at the shifting stone, he dragged himself to the cliff as Welch's body vanished into nothing.

49

Learning to Be

Crossroads

After a brief moment of fear and falling, darkness enfolded Jeannie and Sarah in warmth and strength. A shocking, breathtaking moment exchanged for a place of nothing. And everything.

In the endless night, Sarah held her daughter's hand. "Where are we? Are we dead?"

"I don't know. I don't think so." Jeannie clutched her mother's hand to her stomach. "We're still talking. We're still hearing. I feel your hand."

"You're not dead," an unspoken voice answered.

Jeannie reached out a hand and felt the heavy presence of the spirit bear. "Counselor, it's you."

"Counselor?" Sarah asked. "Who's Counselor?"

The bear's white body emerged from the emptiness. Sarah stammered, "You're—You're a bear."

"I did not mean to frighten you," he told her. "Don't ever be frightened again."

"And you can talk!"

"Yes."

"Without—Without——"

"Without words. Yes."

"Where are we?" Sarah asked.

"The place you wanted."

The silence around them gave way to the thrum of disembodied voices—A chorus. Hundreds. Thousands. A multitude.

"I—I can hear, but I can't see them. Who are they? Where are they?" Sarah asked.

"They are here and they are nowhere. They are everybody and nobody. Without bodies, they need neither space nor time. They need no food nor light. On an eternal plane, they live without need or intention. They live simply to be. They are the Music."

"What are we doing here?" Jeannie asked Counselor.

"Discovering possibilities. Your mother once opted to stay with the Earth Man. You decided to rescue her. You both chose to leave that existence and come here. Now—"

"Another choice?" Sarah asked.

"Don't worry. It is not complicated nor are the consequences as dire. You simply elect to stay in this known or in another place. An unknown."

Sarah held up her hand and shook her head. "That's enough. I already know what I want. I've seen enough of 'other'—life as mother and wife, existence with the Earth Man. If 'an unknown' means something like that, I pick this 'known'."

The spirit bear nodded slowly. He nudged Jeannie's side. "Your mother is wise. You must also make a choice."

"I want to know more before—"

Counselor shook his great head. "Your choices are not the same as hers."

"Not the same?"

"Remember the Trinity?"

"The Dream Rescuer, the Sacrifice, and the Original Thought?"

"Yes."

"What about them?"

"To discover your new choices, you must recognize who is which."

"I already know."

Counselor waited silently. Jeannie continued.

"You are the Original Thought. You have been here longest and led us. As much as I hate him, Bryce Welch was the Sacrifice. He stayed with the Earth Man while Mom and I jumped. The Dream Rescuer—Well, that's me. I freed Mom from the Earth Man."

Counselor sat back. Jeannie hesitated.

"Isn't that right?" she asked.

The bear sat motionless. "Right or wrong is not up to you. What is true?"

"That has to be true," Jeannie said.

Sarah laughed. "Mr. Bear, can we have bodies?"

She and Jeannie materialized in front of the white bear, their silver eyes shining from smooth faces and their unclothed bodies glorifying the Music. Sarah turned to her daughter. "I may not know much," she said, "but if I learned anything since I died, it's what you want is not necessarily what is."

"What do you mean?"

Sarah took Jeannie's hands. "Freeing me from the Earth Man—whose dream was that? Yours?"

"Well, kind of, but mostly I guess it was yours."

"Right. So if you were the Dream Rescuer, how did you get me out of that cave to the cliff? When did you tell me to jump into oblivion?"

Jeannie shook her head. "I don't—What are you saying?"

Sarah took Jeannie's hands. "Baby, you weren't the Dream Rescuer. The Dream Rescuer was Bryce Welch. You were the Sacrifice to get me out of the cave."

Jeannie eyes widened. "Oh, no. No, Mom. Not Bryce. You don't know him. Wherever he went, he lied, he stole, he even murdered. At Beaver Lake, he destroyed mountains. In Michigan, he destroyed women. Who knows what else? Before he could ever rescue, he had to atone. He had to sacrifice."

"He did! He didn't have to, but he did. He sacrificed much. Did you know that long before he met you, he was in love with you?"

"He told you that?"

"Mothers know these things. And you loved him."

"No, I—"

Counselor interrupted. "That whole life is over. Bryce is not who you thought he was. Nor is he who you wanted him to be."

Jeannie waved her hands in frustration. "But he—I—"

The bear nudged Jeannie. "That life is over. Bryce Welch is now who, what, when, and where the Word needs him to be."

Jeanie curled her lips, digesting the truth. "How?"

"In the Dawn of Life, he drowned all he was. He dove deep into the Source and washed away the boy Brandon Whistler, as well as the evil that pitched him into the wilderness. He washed away the man Bryce Welch who demolished and corrupted the weak. He learned the central truth of where time and life begins. And afterward, he fulfilled your mother's dream and spared you from the destroyer of dreams."

"Destroyer? Who's the Destroyer?"

"Not who. What. Vengeance. Before it could ruin you, Bryce convinced you and your mother to leap beyond the world, while the pishtaco and the matchi-auwishuk crashed into the rocks below Mount Komu—demolished, obliterated, forgotten."

Jeannie protested, "He—I—I mean—I lived better than he did. I'm good. I've always been good. Tell me I'm good." She broke down and hugged the spirit bear tightly.

"Yes, you are good. You are beautiful," Counselor said. "Better than you'll ever know."

"How did Bryce Welch become so important?" Jeannie's face contorted and tears fell down her cheek. Counselor gently licked them away.

"It's called grace."

"What did he do to deserve it?"

"Nothing. That's what grace is. You don't have to deserve it. You just have to accept it. Bryce did."

"Am I nothing because I hate him?"

"You have come far since the Dawn of Life," he said. "Like Bryce, you learned much there. But forget that. Let your new existence begin. Let hate go. All of it. Accept who you were meant to be."

"So Bryce is the Dream Rescuer. Am I at least the Sacrifice?"

Counselor shook his large white head. "No."

"What the—" Jeannie jerked away from the bear. "Who is?"

"Your mother."

"Me?" Sarah asked. "I haven't sacrificed anything."

"Yet," Counselor said steadily.

The word weighed heavy over Jeannie and Sarah. Jeannie looked from her mother to the bear. Her face contorted. "No Rescuer, no Sacrifice. Am I anything?"

"Yes." The spirit bear nodded.

The Original Thought," Jeannie said.

"Yes."

She threw up her arms and turned away. "I don't have any idea what that is."

"You hear it in the turning of the earth. You see it in the depth of the sky. It lives within you. It is far older and more significant than any human endeavor. Far greater than the Sacrifice or the Dream Rescuer. It is to embody the Word when it says:

"*In me, there are no rivals.*

"*No male and female,*

"*No self and other,*

"*No good and bad,*

"*No life and death.*

"*The world is unity.*

"*Simply One.*"

Counselor leaned against her. She wiped at her eyes and said, "I still don't understand."

"The Original Thought is that you leave everything behind to become one with the Word."

Sarah's shoulders shook and she brought a fist to her mouth.

"So—no more earth," Jeannie said.

"No more earth," the spirit bear said. "No more good and evil. No more Trinity."

"No more Trinity? What?"

"In the Original Thought, three become one. You and another person join with the Word to become a brand-new being living one life."

Turning away, Sarah looked to the darkness and the voices.

"And the world we came from? The world where we are now?" Jeannie asked.

"You will not remember them."

"Will they still exist?"

Counselor nodded. "Until all become one. In the meantime, they will seek—and find—their own Dream Rescuer."

"Their own Bryce Welch."

"Yes. And it will be fine."

Behind the others, Sarah shook her head.

"And the other person I am to join—?" Jeannie asked.

"You knew him when he rose from the waters of Beaver Flat Lake. You knew him when he led you to the gate of the Dawn of Life."

"Ethan?"

Counselor nodded.

"I thought I knew him before. Did I?"

"Yes. In Peru. Machu Picchu."

"Wait! Ethan is—Beetle?"

"And the other half of the Original Thought to join with the Word, solid and enduring in One Life."

"*Solid and enduring.* That's what *Ethan* means."

"Yes."

"And you?" Jeannie asked Counselor. "Will I see you again?"

"When all become one, you will be me."

Sarah burst forward, her feet and hands clutching for answers and space. "No, Jeannie, I just found you. The dream, remember? Your dream. My dream!"

Crumbling at Jeannie's side, Sarah hugged her daughter's legs. Jeannie embraced her mother and wiped her mother's cheeks. "All will be one, Mom. You, me, Dad, Amanda, Counselor. All of us with the Word itself. One. Do you see?"

The mother's jaw trembled. "All I see is that you are leaving me."

Jeannie held Sarah tightly as she sobbed herself dry.

Carefully, Counselor approached Sarah and nudged her. Shakily, she rose and held Jeannie at arm's length. She caressed her daughter's face and forced a smile.

"It's the ultimate choice, right?" Her voice caught as she turned to the bear. "It's the one we all get to make one day, right?"

Counselor nodded.

From the emptiness, Ethan emerged. When Jeannie recognized him, she smiled. He hesitated, then took her hand. Calmed by his touch, she stroked his arm. "I didn't know where we met before," she said.

"I never forgot," he answered.

Jeannie pushed back Ethan's hair. She asked Counselor, "So we just—?"

"Go. If you want."

Jeannie looked at Ethan, the bear, and then her mother. Sarah smiled through her tears and nodded. Ethan and Jeannie stepped into nothingness.

Left alone with the spirit bear, Sarah said, "The Original Thought."

The bear nodded.

"And me?"

"The Sacrifice." The bear turned. "If you will, you may follow me."

"Where?"

"To find the voices."

Sarah bent and kissed the bear's forehead. Then, like Ethan and Jeannie before them, the universe enveloped the two.

The Land of Great Silence

"And me?"

"What have you learned?"

"People don't belong. They become."

"Yes. What else?"

"I learned the words spoken long ago to the masters, words to be taught, words to be lived."

"Say them."

"Unhinge dreams from reality. Do not interfere nor stand apart.

"To rescue the dream and perfect the world, perfect your heart.

"Leave the gold hidden in the mountains and be rich.

"Discard all interest in wealth or fame that swallow the eternal You.

"Live momentarily and extravagantly.

"Overcome failure by disregarding success.

"Live upright by ignoring the world's rights and wrongs. To live otherwise is to die and to die is to live.

"Know that all beings, all objects, all thought, life and death, illusion and truth, dream and reality, spring from a single source, one body, one Word."

An invisible smile creased the firmament.

"You learned them well."

"So what do I do until the Great Unity?"

"Until then, dreams still exist. Good and bad. They perplex. They stifle. They warp. There are more to rescue and more worlds to save. You know this."

"Yes."

"As you said, 'words to be taught, words to be lived'."

The stars and worlds waited.

"Where shall we begin?"

"Where would you like?"

"Forever."

Polaris and the Music rang.

* * *